# THE
# DREAMTHIEF'S
# DAUGHTER

# MICHAEL MOORCOCK

# THE DREAMTHIEF'S DAUGHTER

## A TALE OF THE ALBINO

ASPECT®

WARNER BOOKS

A Time Warner Company

Aspect® name and logo are registered trademarks of Warner Books, Inc.

Warner Books, Inc., 1271 Avenue of the Americas, New York, NY 10020

Visit our Web site at www.twbookmark.com

A Time Warner Company

Printed in the United States of America
First Printing: April 2001
10 9 8 7 6 5 4 3 2 1

Library of Congress Cataloging-in-Publication Data

Moorcock, Michael.
    The dreamthief's daughter : a tale of the albino / Michael Moorcock.
        p. cm.
    ISBN 0-446-52618-5
        I. Title

    PR6063.O59 D74 2001
    823'.914—dc21                                          00-043836

Book design by H. Roberts Design

For my god-daughter, Oona von B
And for Berry and Co.

# Author's Note

On May 10, 1941, a few months after Britain had unexpectedly won the crucial Battle of Britain and at last stopped the Nazi expansion, Rudolf Hess, Hitler's deputy and his oldest remaining friend within the Nazi hierarchy, flew to Scotland on his own initiative. He had crucial information for Churchill, he said. Arrested, he was interrogated by MI5, British military intelligence. What he told MI5 was immediately suppressed. Certain files have since disappeared. Some existing files have still not been made public. Hitler attacked the Soviet Union on June 24, 1941. Many believe that Hess was appalled by Hitler's decision and was trying to make a final bargain with Churchill. Churchill never permitted a meeting with Hess, who died in mysterious circumstances in 1987.

# BOOK ONE

*Sleep, and I'll steal your silver;*
*Dream, and I'll steal your soul.*

—WHELDRAKE, "The Knight of the Balance"

## CHAPTER ONE

# Stolen Dreams

y name is Ulric, Graf von Bek, and I am the last of my earthly line. An unhealthy child, cursed with the family disease of albinism, I was born and raised in Bek, Saxony, in the early years of the century. I was trained to rule our province wisely and justly, to preserve the status quo, in the best traditions of the Lutheran Church.

My mother died giving birth to me. My father perished in a ghastly fire, when our old tower was partially destroyed. My brothers were all far older than I, and engaged mostly in military diplomacy abroad, so the estate, it was thought, would be my responsibility. It was not expected that I would wish to expose, any longer than necessary, my strange, ruby eyes to the light of common day. I accepted this sentence of virtual imprisonment as my due. It had been suffered by many ancestors before me. There were terrible tales of what had become of twin albino children born to my great-grandmother.

Any unease I had in this role was soon subdued as, in my questioning years, I made friends with the local Catholic priest and became an obsessive fencer. I would discuss theology with Fra. Cornelius in the morning and practice my swordplay every afternoon. All my bafflement and frustrations were translated into learning that subtle and dangerous art. Not the sort of silly swash-buckling boy-braggadocio nonsense affected by the nouveaux riches and ennobled bürgermeisters who perform half-invented rituals of ludicrous manliness at Heidelberg.

No real lover of the sword would subject the instrument to such vulgar, clattering nonsense. With precious few affectations, I hope, I became a true swordsman, an expert in the art of the duel to the death. For in the end, existentialist that I am, entropy alone is the only enemy worth challenging, to conquer entropy is to reach a compromise with death, always the ultimate victor in our conflicts.

There's something to be said for dedicating one's life to an impossible cause. Perhaps an easier decision for a solitary albino aristocrat full of the idealism of previous centuries, disliked by his contemporaries and a discomfort to his tenants. One given to reading and brooding. But not unaware, never unaware, that out-side the old, thick walls of Bek, in my rich and complex Germany, the world was beginning to march to simplistic tunes, numbing the race mind so that it would deceive itself into making war again. Into destroying itself again.

Instinctively, still a teenager, and after an inspiring school trip to the Nile Valley and other great sites of our civilization, I plunged deeply into archaic studies.

Old Bek grew all around me. A towered manor house to which rooms and buildings had been added over the centuries, she emerged like a tree from the lush grounds and thickly wood-ed hills of Bek, surrounded by the cedars, poplars and cypresses my crusader forebears had brought from the Holy Land, by the Saxon oaks into which my earlier ancestors had bound their souls, so that they and the world were rooted in the same earth. Those ancestors had first fought against Charlemagne and then fought with him. They had sent two sons to Roncesvalles. They had been Irish pirates. They had served King Ethelred of England.

My tutor was old von Asch, black, shrunken and gnarled, whom my brothers called The Walnut, whose family had been smiths and swordsmen since the time their first ancestor struck the bronze weapon. He loved me. I was a vessel for his experience. I was willing to learn anything, try any trick to improve my skills. Whatever he demanded, I would eventually rise to meet that expectation. I was, he said, the living record of his family wisdom.

But von Asch's wisdom was nothing sensational. Indeed, his advice was subtle and appealed, as perhaps he knew, to my aestheticism, my love of the complex and the symbolic. Rather than impose his ideas on me, he planted them like seeds. They would grow if the conditions were right. This was the secret of his teaching. He somehow made you realize that you were doing it yourself, that the situation demanded certain responses and what he helped you to do was trust your intuition and use it.

Of course, there was his notion of the sword's song.

"You have to listen for the song," he said. "Every great individual sword has her own song. Once you find that song and hear it clearly, then you can fight with it, for the song is the very essence of the sword. The sword was not forged to decorate walls or be a lifted signal of victory and dominance, but to cut flesh, bone and sinew, and kill. She is not an extension of your manhood, nor an expression of your selfhood. She is an instrument of death. At her best, she kills in justice. If this notion is objectionable to you, my son—and I do not suggest for an instant that you apply it, simply that you acknowledge its truth—then you should put away the sword forever. Fighting with swords is a refined art, but it is an art best enjoyed when also a matter of life and death."

To fight for the ultimate—against oblivion—seemed to me exactly the noble destiny the Raven Sword, our ancestral blade, deserved. Few down the centuries had shown much interest in this queerly wrought old longsword inscribed with mysterious runic verses. It was even considered something of an embarrassment. We had a few mad ancestors who had perhaps not been exemplary in their tormented curiosity and had put the sword to strange uses. There was a report in the Mirenburg press only in the last century. Some madman posing as a legendary creature called "Crimson Eyes" had run amok with a blade, killing at least thirty people before disappearing. For a while the von Beks had been suspected. The story of our albinism was well known there. But no person was ever brought to justice. He featured dramatically in the street literature of the day, like Jack the Ripper, Fantomas and Springheeled Jack.

Part of our vulgar and bloody past. We tended to want to forget the sword and its legends. But there were few in the empty, abandoned and lost rooms at Bek, which had no family to fill them any longer, who could remember. Only a few retainers too old for war or the city. And, of course, books.

When it was time for me to handle that sword whenever I wished, von Asch taught me her main songs—for this blade was a special blade.

There were extraordinary resonances to the steel, however you turned it. A vibrancy which seemed feral. Like a perfect musical instrument. She moved to those songs. She seemed to guide me. He showed me how to coax from her, by subtle strokes and movements of my fingers and wrists, her songs of hatred and contempt, sweet songs of yearning bloodlust, melancholy memories of battles fought, determined revenge. But no love songs. Swords, said von Asch, rarely had hearts. And it is unwise to rely on their loyalty.

This particular weapon, which we called Ravenbrand, was a big longsword of black iron with a slender, unusual leaf-shaped blade. Our family legend said that it was forged by Friar Corvo, the Venetian armorer, who wrote the famous treatise on the subject. But there is a tale that Corvo—the Raven Smith, as Browning called him—only found the sword, or at least the blade itself, and wrought nothing but the hilt.

Some said it was Satan's own blade. Others said it was the Devil Himself. The Browning poem describes how Corvo gave his soul to bring the sword to life again. One day I would go with our Ravenbrand to Venice and discover for myself what truth there might be to the story. Von Asch went off and never came back. He was searching for a certain kind of metal which he thought might be found on the Isle of Morn.

Then it was August 1914 and for the first months of that war I longed to be old enough to join it. As the realities were reported by the returning veterans—young men hardly older than myself—I began to wonder how such a war could ever be ended.

My brothers died of disease or were blown apart in some nameless pit. Soon I had no other living relative but my ancient grandfather, who lived in sheltered luxury on the outskirts of Mirenburg in Waldenstein and would look at me from huge, pale, disappointed grey eyes which saw the end of everything he had worked for. After a while he would wave me away. Eventually he refused to have me at his bedside.

I was inducted in 1918. I joined my father's old infantry regiment and, with the rank of lieutenant, was sent immediately to the Western front. The war lasted just long enough to demonstrate what cruel folly it was. We could rarely speak of what we'd witnessed.

Sometimes it seemed a million voices called out to us from no-man's-land, pleading only for a release from pain. *Help me, help me, help me.* English. French. German. Russian. And the voices of a dozen disparate empires. Which screamed at the sight of their own exposed organs and ruined limbs. Which implored God to take away their pain. To bless them with death. Voices which could soon be ours.

They did not leave me when I slept. They turned and twisted in millions, screaming and wailing for release throughout my constant dreams. At night I left one horror to inhabit another. There seemed little difference between them.

What was worse, my dreams did not confine themselves to the current conflict but embraced every war Man had instigated.

Vividly, and no doubt thanks to my intense reading, I began to witness huge battles. Some of them I recognized from history. Most, however, were merely the repetition, with different costumes, of the obscenity I witnessed twenty-four hours a day from the trenches.

Towards the end, one or two of the dreams had something else in common. A beautiful white hare who ran through the warring men, apparently unnoticed and unharmed. Once she turned and looked back at me and her ruby-colored eyes were my own. I felt I should follow her. But gradually the nightmares faded. Real life proved hard enough, perhaps.

We, who were technically the instigators of the war and subject to the victor's view of history, were humiliated by the Treaty of Versailles in which the Europeans squabbled with ruthless greed over the spoils, disgusted President Woodrow Wilson and stripped Germany of everything, including machinery with which to rebuild. The result, of course, was that as usual the common people were forced to pay far too high a price for the follies of exiled nobles. We live, die, know sickness and health, comfort and discomfort, because of the egos of a few stupid men.

To be fair, some of those nobles, such as myself, elected to stay and work for the restoration of the German Federation, though I had no liking for the swaggering aggression of the defeated Prussians, who had thought themselves unbeatable. These proud nationalists were the ones who supplied the rhetoric which, by 1920, was fueling what would be the Nazi and Bolshevik movements, admittedly towards rather different ends. Germany defeated, impoverished, shamed.

The Serbian Black Hand had fallen upon our world and blighted it almost beyond recognition. All that Bismarck had built up in us, a sense of unity and mission, had been diverted to serve the ambitions of a few greedy businessmen, industrialists, gunmakers and their royal allies, a sour echo which many of those, in Berlin for instance, chose to ignore, or turn into an art of bitter realism giving us the likes of Brecht and Weill. The sardonic, popular rhythms of *The Threepenny Opera* were the musical accompaniment to the story of our ruin.

Germany remained on the verge of civil war, between right and left. Between the communist fighters and the nationalist Freikorps. Civil war was the greatest danger we feared. We saw what it had done to Russia.

There is no faster way of plunging a country into chaos than to make panicky decisions aimed at averting that chaos. Germany was recovering. Many thinking people believed that if the other great powers had supported Germany then, we should have no Adolf Hitler. Creatures like Hitler emerge frequently because of a vacuum. They are conjured whole from yearning nothingness by our own negativity, by our Faustian appetites and dark greed.

Our family and its fortunes had been greatly reduced by the War. My friend the priest had become a missionary in the former German colony of Rwanda. I became a rather sorry, solitary individual. I was frequently advised to sell Bek. Bustling black marketeers and rising fascists would offer to buy my ancestral seat from me. They thought they could buy the authority of place in the same way they had bought their grand houses and large motorcars.

In some ways, by having to manage my estates rather more desperately than in the past, I learned a little of the uncertainty and horror facing the average German who saw his country on the brink of total ruin.

It was easy to blame the victors. True, their tax on us was punitive, unjust, inhumane and foolish; it was the poison which the Nazis in Munich and other parts of Bavaria began to use to their own advantage.

Even as their popular support began to slide, the Nazi Party was able to take control of almost all the power in Germany. A power they had originally claimed for the Jews. But recently, unlike the Jews, they actually did control the media. On the radio, in the newspapers and magazines and movies, they began to tell the people whom they should love and whom they should hate.

How do you kill a million or so of your neighbors?

Well, first you say they are Unlike. They are Not Us. Not human. Only like us on the surface. Pretending to be us. Evil underneath in spite of all common experience. Then you compare them to unclean animals and you accuse them of plotting against you. And very soon you have the necessary madness in place to produce a holocaust.

This is by no means a new phenomenon, of course. The American Puritans characterized everyone who disagreed with them as evil and godless and probably witches. Andrew Jackson helped start an imaginary war which he then pretended to win in order to steal the treaty lands of Indian nations. The British and Americans went into China to save the country from the opium they had originally sold it. The Turks had to characterize Armenians as godless monsters in order to begin their appalling slaughter of the Christians. But in my time, save for the embarrassments of Martin Luther's fulminations against Jewry, such talk was strange to me in Bek and I could not believe that ultimately a civilized nation would tolerate it.

Frightened nations, however, will accept too easily the threat of civil war and the promise of the man who says he will avert it. Hitler averted civil war because he had no need of it. His opposition was delivered into his hands by the ballot boxes of a country which, at that time, had one of the best democratic constitutions in the world, superior in many ways to the American.

Hitler's opponents were already in his power, thanks to the authority of the State he had seized. We could all see this, those of us who were horrified, but it was impossible to convince anyone. So many German people so badly needed stability they were willing to cleave to the Nazis. And it was easier to forget a Jewish neighbor's disappearance than it was the concerns of your own relatives.

And so ordinary people were led into complicity in that evil, through deed or word or that awful silence, to become part of it, to defend against their own consciences, to hate themselves as well as others, to choose a strutting self-esteem over self-respect, and so devalue themselves as citizens.

In this way a modern dictatorship makes us rule ourselves on its behalf. We learn to gloss our self-disgust with cheap rhetoric, sentimental talk, claims of good will, protestations of innocence, of victimhood. And those of us who refuse are ultimately killed.

For all my determination to pursue the cause of peace, I still maintained my swordsmanship. It had become much more than a mere *pasatiempo*. It remained something of a cause, I suppose, a method of controlling what little there was still in my own control. The skills needed to wield the Raven Blade were highly specialized, for while my sword was balanced so perfectly I could easily spin it in one hand, it was of heavy, flexible steel and had a life of its own. It seemed to flow through my hands, even as I practiced.

The blade was impossible to sharpen with ordinary stone. Von Asch had given me a special grindstone, which appeared to be imbedded with pieces of diamond. Not that the blade ever needed much sharpening.

Freudians, who were busily interpreting our chaos in those days, would have known what to think of my tendency to bond with my blade and my unwillingness to be separated from it. Yet I felt I drew power from the weapon. Not the kind of brute, predatory power the Nazis so loved, but a permanent sustenance.

I carried the sword with me whenever I traveled, which was rarely. A local maker had fashioned a long gun case, into which Ravenbrand fitted discreetly, so that to the casual eye, with the case over my shoulder, I looked like some bucolic landsman prepared for a day's shooting or even fishing.

I had it in my mind that whatever happened to Bek, the sword and I would survive. Whatever the symbolic meaning of the sword was, I cannot tell you, save that it had been handled by my family for at least a thousand years, that it was said to have been forged for Wotan, had turned the tide at Roncesvalles, leading the monstrous horses of Carolinian chivalry against the invading Berber, had defended the Danish royal line at Hastings and served the Saxon cause in exile in Byzantium and beyond.

I suppose I was also superstitious, if not completely crazy, because I sensed there was a bond between myself and the sword. Something more than tradition or romance.

Meanwhile the quality of civil life continued to decline in Germany.

Even the town of Bek with her dreaming gables, twisted old roofs and chimneys, green-glazed windows, weekly markets and ancient customs, was not immune to the twentieth-century jackboot.

In the years before 1933, a small division of self-titled

Freikorps, made up mostly of unemployed ex-soldiers commanded by NCOs who had given themselves the rank of captain or higher, paraded occasionally through the streets. They were not based in Bek, where I refused to allow any such goings-on, but in a neighboring city. They had too many rivals in the city to contend with, I suspect, and felt more important showing their strength to a town of old people and children, which had lost most of its men.

These private armies controlled parts of Germany and were constantly in conflict with rivals, with communist groups and politicians who sought to curb their power, warning that civil war was inevitable if the Freikorps were not brought under control. Of course, this is what the Nazis offered to do—to control the very forces they were using to sow the seeds of further uncertainty about the future of our poor, humiliated Germany.

I share the view that if the allies had been more generous and not attempted to suck the last marrow from our bones, Hitler and the Freikorps would have had nothing to complain of. But our situation was manifestly unjust and in such a climate even the most moderate of burghers can somehow find himself condoning the actions of people he would have condemned out of hand before the War.

Thus, in 1933, fearing Russian-style civil conflict worse than tyranny, many of us voted for a "strong man," in the hope it would bring us stability.

Sadly, of course, like most "strong men," Hitler was merely a political construct, no more the man of iron his followers declared him to be than any other of his wretched, ranting psychopathic type.

There were a thousand Hitlers in the streets of Germany, a thousand dispossessed, twitching, feckless neurotics, eaten up with jealousy and frustrated hatred. But Hitler worked hard at his gift for cheap political oratory, drew power from the worst elements of the mob, and spoke in the grossest emotional terms of our betrayal not, as some perceived it, by the greed of our leaders and the rapacity of our conquerors, but by a mysterious, almost supernatural, force they called "International Jewry."

Normally such blatant nonsense would have gathered together

only the marginal and less intelligent members of society, but as financial crisis followed crisis, Hitler and his followers had persuaded more and more ordinary Germans and business leaders that fascism was the only way to salvation.

Look at Mussolini in Italy. He had saved his nation, regenerated it, made people fear it again. He had masculinized Italy, they said. Made it virile as Germany could be made virile again. It is how they think, these people. *Guns and boots, flags and prongs / Blacks and whites. Rights and wrongs . . .* As Wheldrake put it in one of those angry doggerel pieces he wrote just before his death in 1927.

Simple pursuits. Simple answers. Simple truths.

Intellect, learning and moral decency were mocked and attacked as though they were mortal enemies. Men asserted their own vulnerable masculinity by insisting, as they so often do, that women stay at home and have babies. For all their worship of these earth goddesses, women were actually treated with sentimental contempt. Women were kept from all real power.

We are slow to learn. Neither the English, French nor American experiments in social order by imposition came to any good, and the communist and fascist experiments, equally puritanical in their rhetoric, demonstrated the same fact—that ordinary human beings are far more complex than simple truth and simple truth is fine for argument and clarification, but it is not an instrument for government, which must represent complexity if it is to succeed. It was no surprise to many that juvenile delinquency reached epidemic proportions in Germany by 1940, although the Nazis, of course, could not admit the problem which was not supposed to exist in the world they had created.

By 1933, in spite of so many of us knowing what the Nazis were like, they had taken control of parliament. Our constitution was no more than a piece of paper, burning amongst great, inspired books, by Mann, Heine, Brecht, Zweig and Remarque, which the Nazis heaped in blazing pyres at crossroads and in town squares. An act they termed "cultural cleansing." It was the triumph of ignorance and bigotry.

Boots, blackjacks and whips became the instruments of political policy. We could not resist because we could not believe what
had happened. We had relied upon our democratic institutions.
We were in a state of national denial. The realities, however, were
soon demonstrated to us.

It was intolerable for any who valued the old humane virtues
of German life, but our protests were silenced in the most brutal-
ly efficient ways. Soon there were only a few of us who continued
to resist.

As the Nazi grip tightened, fewer and fewer of us spoke out,
or even grumbled. The storm troopers were everywhere. They
would arrest people on an arbitrary basis "just to give them a taste
of what they'll get if they step out of line." Several journalists I
knew, who had no political affiliations, were locked up for
months, released, then locked up again. Not only would they not
speak when they were released, they were terrified of speech.

Nazi policy was to cow the protesting classes. They succeeded
fairly well, with the compliance of the church and the army, but
they did not entirely extinguish opposition. I, for instance, determined to join the White Rose Society, swore to destroy Hitler and
work against his interests in every way.

I advertised my sympathies as best I could and was eventually
telephoned by a young woman. She gave her name as "Gertie"
and told me that she would be in touch as soon as it was safe. I
believed they were probably checking my credentials, making sure
I was not a spy or a potential traitor.

Twice in the streets of Bek I was pointed out as an unclean
creature, some kind of leper. I was lucky to get home without
being harmed. After that, I went out as little as possible, usually
after dark. Frequently accompanied by my sword. Stupid as it
sounds, for the storm troopers were armed with guns, the sword
gave me a sense of purpose, a kind of courage, a peculiar security.

Not long after the second incident, when I had been spat at
by brownshirt boys, who had also attacked my old manservant
Reiter as an aristocrat's lackey, those bizarre, terrifying dreams
began again. With even greater intensity. Wagnerian, almost.

Thick with armor and heavy warhorses, bloody banners, butchering steel and blaring trumpets. All the potent, misplaced romance of conflict. The kind of imagery which powered the very movement I was sworn to fight.

Slowly the dreams took shape and in them I was again plagued by voices in languages I could not understand, full of a litany of unlikely, tongue-twisting names. It seemed to me I was listening to a long list of those who had already died violent deaths since the beginning of time—and those who were yet to die.

The resumption of my nightmares caused me considerable distress and alarmed my old servants who spoke of fetching the doctor or getting me to Berlin to see a specialist.

Yet before I could decide what action to take, the white hare appeared again. She ran swiftly over corpses, between the legs of metal-covered men, under the guns and lances of a thousand conflicting nations and religions. I could not tell if she wished me to follow her. This time she did not look back. I longed for her to turn, to show me her eyes again, to determine if she was, in fact, a version of myself—a self freed at last from that eternal struggle. It was as if she signaled the ending of the horror. I needed to know what she symbolized. I tried to call out, but I was dumb. Then I was deaf. Then blind.

And suddenly the dreams were gone. I would wake in the morning with that strange feeling of rapidly fading memory, of a vanishing reality, as a powerful dream disappears, leaving only the sense of having experienced it. A sense, in my case, of confusion and deep, deep dread. All I could remember was the vision of a white hare racing across a field of butchered flesh. Not a particularly pleasant feeling, but offering a relief from that nightly conflict.

Not only my nightmares had been stolen, but also my ordinary, waking dreams, my dreams of a lifetime of quiet study and benign action. Such a monkish life was the best someone of my appearance could hope for in those days which were merely an uneasy pause in the conflict we began by calling the Great War to end wars. Now we think of it as an entire century of war, where one dreadful conflict followed another, half of them justified as holy wars, or moral wars, or wars to help distressed minorities, but almost all of which were actually inspired by the basest of emotions, the most short-term of goals, the cruelest greed and that appalling self-righteousness which no doubt the Christian Crusaders had when they brought blood and terror to Jerusalem in the name of God and human justice.

So many quiet dreams like mine were stolen in that century. So many noble men and women, honest souls, were rewarded only with agony and obscene death.

Soon, thanks to compliance of the church, we were privileged to see in Bek's streets pictures of Adolf Hitler, Chancellor of Germany, dressed in silver, shining armor and mounted on a white horse, carrying the banner of Christ and the Holy Grail, recalling all the legendary saviors of our people.

These bigoted philistines despised Christianity and had made the swastika the symbol of modern Germany, but they were not above corrupting our noblest idealism and historical imagery to further their evil.

It is a mark, I think, of the political scoundrel, one who speaks most of the people's rights and hopes and uses the most sentimental language to blame all others but his own constituents for the problems of the world. Always a "foreign threat," fear of "the stranger." "Secret intruders, illegal aliens . . ."

I still hear those voices in modern Germany and France and America and all the countries we once thought of as far too civilized to allow such horror within their own borders.

After many years I still fear, I suppose, a recurrence of that terrible dream into which I finally plunged. A dream far more real than any reality I had known, a dream without end. A dream of eternity. An experience of the complexity of our multiverse in all its vast, limitless variety, with all its potential for evil and its capacity for good.

Perhaps the only dream that was not stolen from me.

# CHAPTER TWO

# Uninvited Relatives

I was still waiting for another call from "Gertie" when in the early months of 1934 I had an unexpected and rather alarming visitor to Bek.

My people are related through marriage and other kinships to the traditional rulers of Mirenburg, the capital of Waldenstein, which the Nazis, and later the Soviets, would annex. Although predominantly of Slavic stock, the principality has for hundreds of years been culturally linked to Germany through language and common concerns. It was my family's practice to spend the Season in Mirenburg at least. Some members, such as my rather unwholesome Uncle Rudy, disgraced in Germany, chose to live there almost permanently.

The rulers of Mirenburg had not survived the tenor of the century. They, too, had known civil war, most of it instigated by foreign interests who had always sought to control Waldenstein. The Badehoff-Krasny family had been restored to power, but more as clients of Austria than as independent rulers. They had married into the von Mincts, one of the great Mirenburg dynasties.

Hungary, of course, also possessed an interest in the tiny country. The current Prince of Waldenstein was my cousin

Gaynor, whose mother had been one of the most beautiful women in Buda-Pest and was still reckoned a powerful political mind. I knew and admired my aunt. In middle years she was an impressive woman, maintaining her adopted country with all the skills of a Bismarck.

She was ailing now. The rise of fascism had shocked and exhausted her. Mussolini's successes were an abomination to her, and Hitler was inconceivably shallow and vicious in his political rhetoric, his ambitions and claims. But, as she said when last I saw her, Germany's soul had been stolen already. Hitler was merely addressing the corpse of German democracy. He had killed nothing. He had grown out of the grave, she said. Grown out of that corpse like an epidemic which had rapidly infected the entire country.

"And where is Germany's soul?" I asked. "Who stole it?"

"It's safe enough, I think." She had winked at me, crediting me with more wit than I possessed. And that was all she had said on the subject.

Prince Gaynor Paul St. Odhran Badehoff-Krasny von Minct lacked his mother's calm intelligence but had all her wonderful Hungarian beauty and a charm which often disarmed his political opponents. At one time he had shared his mother's politics, but it seemed he had followed the road of many frustrated idealists in those days and saw fascism as the strong force that would revitalize an exhausted Europe and ease the pain of all those who still suffered the war's consequences.

Gaynor was no racialist. Waldenstein was traditionally philo-Semitic (though not so tolerant of her Gypsies) and his fascism, at least as he presented it to me, looked more to Mussolini than to Hitler. I still found the ideas either foolish or unpalatable, a mélange of kulak bigotry, certainly not in any serious philosophical or political tradition, for all their seduction of thinkers like Heidegger and their incorporation of a few misunderstood Nietzschean slogans.

It shocked me, however, to see him arrive in an official black Mercedes, festooned with swastikas, wearing the uniform of a captain in the "elite" SS, now superior to Rohm's SA, the original rough and ready Freikorps fighters who had become an embarrassment to Hitler. There was still a considerable amount of snow. It would not be until the summer that Ernst Rohm and all Hitler's other Nazi rivals and embarrassments were murdered in the so-called Night of the Long Knives. Rohm's great enemy, now rising rapidly in the Party, was the colorless little prude Heinrich Himmler, the boss of the SS, with his prissy pinz nez, an ex–chicken farmer, whose power would soon be second to Hitler's.

My manservant Reiter disdainfully opened the door for them and took my cousin's card. He announced, in high sarcasm, the honor of the arrival of Captain Paul von Minct. Before they were taken below stairs by a determined Reiter, Gaynor was addressed as Captain von Minct both by his driver and by the skull-faced Prussian, Sergeant Klosterheim, whose eyes glittered from within the deep caverns of their sockets.

Gaynor looked splendid and sinister in the black and silver uniform with its red and black swastika insignia. He was, as usual, completely engaging and amusing, making some self-deprecating murmur about his uniform even as he followed the servants up the stairs. I invited him, as soon as he was in his rooms and refreshed, to join me on the terrace before dinner. His driver and the secretary, Klosterheim, would take their supper in the servants' hall. Klosterheim had seemed to resent this a little, but then accepted it with the air of a man who had been insulted too many times for this to matter. I was glad he wasn't eating with us. His sickly, gray skin and almost fleshless head gave him the appearance of a dead man.

It was a relatively warm evening and the moon was already rising as the sun set, turning the surrounding landscape to glittering white and bloody shadow. This would probably be our last snow. I almost regretted its passing.

As I lit a cigarette, I saw a movement in the copse to my left and suddenly, from the bushes, darted a large white hare. She ran into a stain of scarlet sunlight then hesitated, looked to left and right and loped forward a few paces. She was an identical animal to the one I had seen in my dreams. I almost called to her. Instinctively I held my peace. Either the Nazis would think me mad, or they would be suspicious of me. Yet I wanted to reach out to the hare and reassure her that she was in no danger from me. I felt as a father might feel to a child.

Then the white hare had made her decision and was moving again. I watched her run, a faint powdering of snow rising like mist around her feet as she sped rapidly towards the darkness of the oaks on the far side. I heard a sound from the house and turned. When I looked back, the hare had vanished.

Gaynor came down in perfect evening dress and accepted a cigarette from my case. We agreed that the sun setting over the old oaks and cypresses, the soft, snowy roofs and leaning chimneys of Bek did the soul good. We said little while, as true romantics, we savored a view Goethe would have turned into a cause. I mentioned to him that I had seen a snow hare, running across the far meadow. His response was odd.

He shrugged. "Oh, she'll be no bother to us," he said.

When it was twilight and growing a little chilly, we continued to sit outside under the moon exchanging superficial questions and answers about obscure relatives and common acquaintances. He mentioned a name. I said that to my astonishment he had joined the Nazi Party. Why would someone of that sort do such a thing? And I let the question hang.

He laughed.

"Oh, no, cousin. Never fear! I didn't volunteer. I'm only a nominal Nazi, an honorary captain in the SS. It makes them feel respectable. And it's a useful uniform for traveling in Germany these days. After a visit I made a few weeks ago to Berlin, they offered me the rank. I accepted it. They assured me that I would not be called up in time of war! I had a visit, a letter. You know how they cultivate people like ourselves. Why, Mussolini even made the king a fascist! It helps convince old fogies like you that the Nazis are no longer a bunch of uneducated, unemployed, unthinking butchers."

I told him that I remained a skeptic. All I saw were the same

thugs with the spending power of a looted state willing to pay anything to cultivate those people whose association with their Party
would give it authority in the wider world.

"Precisely," he said. "But we can use these thugs for our own
ends, can't we? To improve the world? They know in their bones
that they have no real moral position or political programs. They
know how to seize and hold power, but not much else. They need
people like us, cousin. And the more people like us join them, the
more they will become like us."

I told him that in my experience most people seemed to
become like them. He said that it was because there were not yet
enough of "us" running things. I suggested that this was dangerous logic. I had heard of no individuals corrupting power, but I
had seen many individuals corrupted by it. He found this amusing. He said that it depended what you meant by power. And how
you used that power when it was yours. To attack and slander tax-
paying citizens because of their race and religion, I said. Power to
do that? Of course not, he said. The Jewish Question was a nonsense. We all knew that. The poor old Jews were always the scape-
goats. They'd survive this bit of political theater. Nobody ever
came to serious harm doing a few physical exercises in a well-
ordered open air environment. Hadn't I seen the film of those
camps? They had every luxury. He had the grace to change the
conversation as we went into dinner.

We spent the meal discussing the Nazi reorganization of the
legal system and what it meant for lawyers trained in a very different tradition. At that time we had not seen the ruin which fascism brought to all who professed it and still talked about the
"good" and "bad" aspects of the system. It would be a year or two
before ordinary people came to understand the fundamental evil
which had settled on our nation. Gaynor's views were common.
We had grown used to anti-Jewish rhetoric and understood it to
have no meaning beyond gathering a few right-wing votes. Many
of our Jewish friends refused to take it seriously, so why should we?
We all failed to understand how the Nazis had made that rhetoric
their reality.

Although the Nazis had developed concentration camps from the moment they came to power and used exactly the same methods at the beginning of their rule as they would at the end, we had no experience of such appalling cruelty and horror, and in our desire to avert the foulness of the trenches, we had created a worse foulness from our unthinking appetites and fears. Even when we received credible stories of Nazi brutality we thought them to be isolated cases. Even the Jews scarcely understood what was happening, and they were the chief objects of that brutality.

That is how we take for granted the fundamental social bargain of our democracy, whose deep, historic freedoms were won for us by our ancestors, step by noble step, through the centuries, the bones and sinews of our common compact. When those structures are forgotten or destroyed, we know no other way to think.

So familiar had their democratic freedoms and rights become to those citizens that they constantly asked "What have I done?" to brutes who had overturned the rule of law and replaced it with violence and raging hatred, with loathing and unwholesome sexuality. These were not policemen but torturers, thieves, rapists and murderers who had been given power by our own lack of moral courage and self-respect. And now they controlled us all! We have nothing to fear, the great FDR would tell us, but fear itself. Fear won in this case.

Although not of a superstitious disposition, I felt that real evil had fallen upon our world. Ironically, the century had started with the common belief that war and injustice were rapidly being eradicated. Had our complacency encouraged attack? It was as if some demonic force had been attracted by the stink of the Boer War's carnage, by Leopold's Congo, by the Armenian genocide, by the Great War, by the millions of corpses which filled the ditches, gutters and trenches of the world from Paris to Peking. Greedily feasting, the force grew strong enough to begin preying upon the living.

After dinner it was a bit chilly for the terrace, so we smoked our cigars by the fire in the study and enjoyed our brandy and soda and the familiarity of old-fashioned, civilized comforts. I realized that my cousin had not come for a vacation. Some sort of business brought him to Bek, and I wondered when he would raise the issue.

He had spent the past week in Berlin and was full of gossip about Hitler's new hierarchy. Göring was a great snob and liked to cultivate the aristocracy. So Prince Gaynor—whom the Germans preferred to call by the name of Paul von Minct—was the personal guest of the *Reichsmarschall* which, he said, was a great deal better than being Hitler's personal guest. Hitler, he assured me, was the most boring little man on the face of the planet. All he liked to do was drone on and on about his half-baked ideas while a flunky played the same Franz Lehár records over and over again. An evening with Hitler, he said, was like the longest evening you could imagine with your prissy maiden aunt. It was hard to believe his old friends, who said he used to keep them in fits of laughter with his impressions and jokes. Goebbels was too withdrawn to be good company and confined himself to sly remarks about the other Nazis, but Göring was great fun and had a genuine love of art which his colleagues only pretended. He was making it his business to rescue threatened paintings from the Nazi censor. In fact his house in Berlin had become a haven, a repository for all kinds of art, including ancient German folk objects and weaponry.

Although that ironic, slightly mocking tone never left him, I was not convinced that Gaynor was merely playing along with the Nazis in order to keep Waldenstein free from their direct influence. He said he accepted the realpolitik of the situation, but hoped that it would suit the new German masters to let his little country remain at least superficially independent. Yet I sensed more than this. I sensed his attraction to the whole perverse slew of corrupted romanticism. He was drawn by the enormous power he saw Hitler and Co. now wielding. I had the feeling that he did not want to share in that power; he wanted to take it all for himself. Perhaps he intended to set himself up as the new Prince of the Greater Germany? He joked that he had as much Jewish and Slavic blood as he had Aryan, but it seemed the Nazis turned a blind eye to some of one's ancestors if one was useful enough to them.

And it was clear that "Captain von Minct" was currently useful enough to the Nazis for them to equip him with a staff car, a
driver and a secretary. And from his manner, it was obvious he
was here on some connected business. I could only believe my
eyes and use my intelligence. Had Gaynor been sent here to
recruit me, too?

Or perhaps, I wondered, he had been sent to kill me. Then
logic told me that he'd have many better means of doing that than
inviting himself to dinner. The one thing the Nazis were uncon-
cerned about was the murder of their opponents. They hardly
needed to be clandestine about it.

I needed fresh air. I suggested we stroll onto the terrace. The
moonlight was dramatic.

Abruptly, he proposed that his secretary, Lieutenant
Klosterheim, join us. "He's a little touchy about being treated as an
outsider and he's rather well-connected, I understand, to Goebbels's
wife's people. An old mountain family. One of those which refused
all honors and maintained their landsman status as a matter of pride.
The family had some kind of fortress in the Harz Mountains for a
thousand years. They call themselves yeomen-mountaineers, but my
guess is they kept themselves through banditry during most of their
history. He also has other relatives in the Church."

I no longer much cared. Gaynor's company had begun to irri-
tate me and it was growing harder for me to remember that he was
my guest. Klosterheim might relieve the atmosphere.

This fantasy was dispelled the moment the cadaverous,
monkish figure in his tight SS uniform came out onto the terrace,
his cap under his arm, his breath steaming with a whiteness which
seemed colder than the surrounding air. I apologized for my rude-
ness and invited him to drink. He waved a pocket *Mein Kampf* at
me and said he had plenty to engage him in his room. He carried
the air of a fanatic and reminded me in many ways of his neurotic
Führer. Gaynor seemed almost deferential to him.

Klosterheim agreed to take a small glass of Benedictine. As I
handed him his drink he spoke to Gaynor over my shoulder.
"Have you made the proposition yet, Captain von Minct?"

Gaynor laughed. A little strained. I turned to ask him a question and he raised his hand. "A small matter, cousin, which can be discussed at any time. Lieutenant Klosterheim is very direct and efficient, but he sometimes lacks the subtler graces."

"We are not very gentlemanly at Klosterheim," said the lieutenant severely. "We have no time to cultivate fine manners, for life is hard and constantly threatened. We've defended your borders since time began. All we have are our ancient traditions. Our craggy fortresses. Our pride and our privacy."

I suggested that modern tourism might consequently be welcomed by his family and bring them some relief. Some ease, at last. A busload of Bavarians round the old place and one could put one's feet up for a week. I'd do the same, only all I had was a glorified farmhouse. I don't know what encouraged such levity in me. Perhaps it was a response to his unremitting sobriety. Something unpleasant glinted from his eye sockets and then dulled again.

"Perhaps so," he said. "Yes. It would give us the easy life, eh?" He consumed his Benedictine and made an awkward attempt at grace. "But Captain von Minct came here, I believe, to ease one of your burdens, Herr Count?"

"I have none that need easing," I said.

"Of responsibility. Of stewardship." Gaynor was now cultivating a rather over-hearty manner. Klosterheim had no trouble sounding threatening but Gaynor wanted my approval as well as whatever it was he had come for.

"You know I place little value on our remaining heirlooms," I said, "except where they pertain to personal, family matters. Is there something you want?"

"You remember the old sword you used to play with before you went to the War? Black with age? Must have rusted through eventually. Rather like von Asch himself, your tutor. What did you do with that old sword in the end? Give it away? Sell it? Or did you place a more sentimental value on it?"

"Presumably, cousin, you speak of the sword Ravenbrand."

"Just so, cousin. Ravenbrand. I had forgotten you christened it with a nickname."

"It has never had a different name. It is as old as our family. It has all sorts of legendary nonsense attached to it, of course, but no evidence. Just the usual stories we invent to make generations of farmers seem more interesting. Ghosts and old treasure. No antiquarian or genuine historian would give credence to those legends. They are as familiar as they are unlikely." I became a little alarmed. Surely he had not come here to loot us of our oldest treasures, our responsibilities, our heritage? "But it has little commercial value, I understand. Uncle Rudy tried to sell it once. Took it all the way to Mirenburg to get it valued. He was very disappointed."

"It is more valuable as a pair. When matched to its twin," said Klosterheim, almost humorously. His mouth twisted in a peculiar rictus. Perhaps a smile. "Its counterweight."

I had begun to suspect that Klosterheim was not, as they say in Vienna, the full pfennig. His remarks seemed to bear only the barest connection to the conversation, as if his mind was operating on some other, colder plane altogether. It was easier to ignore him than ask him for explanations. How on earth could a sword be a "counterweight"? He was probably one of those mystical Nazis. It's an odd phenomenon I've noticed more than once, that fascination with the numinous and the supernatural and a preference for extremist right-wing politics. I have never been able to understand it, but many of the Nazis, including Hitler and Hess, were immersed in such stuff. As rational, no doubt, as their racialism. Dark abstractions which, when applied to real life, produce the most banal evils.

"Don't minimize your family's achievements, either." Gaynor recalled our ancient victories. "You've given Germany some famous soldiers."

"And rogues. And radicals."

"And some who were all three," said Gaynor, still hearty as a highwayman on the scaffold. All face.

"Your namesake, for instance," murmured Klosterheim. Even the act of speaking seemed to add a chill to the night air.

"Eh?"

Klosterheim's voice seemed to echo in his mouth. "He who sought and found—the Grail. Who gave your family its antique motto."

I shrugged at this and suggested we return inside. There was a fire going in the hearth and I had an unlikely frisson of nostalgia as I remembered the great family Christmases we had enjoyed, as only Saxons can enjoy their Yuletide festival, when my father and mother and brothers were all alive and friends came from Castle Auchy in Scotland and Mirenburg and France and America, together with more distant relatives, to enjoy that unchallenged fantasy of comfort and good will. War had destroyed all that. And now I stood by blackened oak and slate watching the smoke rise from out of a guttering, unhappy fire and did my best to remember my manners as I entertained the two gentlemen in black and silver who had come, I was now certain, to take away my sword.

"Do you the devil's work." Klosterheim read the coat of arms which was imbedded above the hearth. I thought the thing was vulgar and would have removed it if it had not entailed ripping down the entire wall. A piece of Gothic nonsense, with its almost alchemical motifs and its dark admonishment which, according to my reading, had once meant something rather different than it seemed. "Do you still follow that motto, Herr Count?"

"There are more stories attached to the motto than to the sword. Unfortunately, as you know, our family curse of albinism was not always tolerated and some generations came to see it as a matter of shame, destroying much that had been recorded where it pertained to albinos like myself or, I suspect, anything which seemed a little strange to the kind of mentality which believes burning books to be burning unpalatable truths. Something we seem prone to, in Germany. So little record remains of any sense. But I understand the motto to be ironic in some way."

"Perhaps." Klosterheim looked capable of carrying only the heaviest of ironies. "But you lost the goblet, I understand. The Grail."

"My dear Herr Lieutenant, there isn't an old family in Germany that doesn't have at least one Grail legend attached to it and usually some cup or other which is supposed to represent the Grail. The same is true in England. Arthur had more Camelots than Mussolini has titles. They're all nineteenth-century inventions. Part of the Gothic revival. The Romantic movement. A nation reinventing herself. You must know of half-a-dozen such family legends. Wolfram von Eschenbach claimed it was granite. Few can be traced much past 1750. I can imagine, too, that with your recruitment of Wagner to the Nazi cause, your Leader has need of such symbols, but if we did have an old goblet it has long since gone from here."

"I agree these associations are ridiculous." Gaynor took himself closer to the fire. "But my father remembers your grandfather showing him a golden bowl that had the properties of glass and metals combined. Warm to the touch, he said, and vibrant."

"If there is such a family secret, cousin, then it has not been passed on to me. My grandfather died soon after the armistice. I was never in his confidence."

Klosterheim frowned, clearly unsure if he should believe me. Gaynor was openly incredulous. "You of all the von Beks would know of such things. Your father died because of his studies. You've read everything in the library. Von Asch passed what he knew on to you. Why, you yourself, cousin, are almost part of the museum. No doubt a better prospect than the circus."

"Very true," I said. I glanced at the hideous old "huntsman's clock" over the mantel and asked him if he would excuse me. It was time I turned in.

Gaynor began to try to charm his way out of what he now understood to be an insult, but his remark about me was no more offensive than most of his and Klosterheim's conversation. There was a certain coarseness about him I hadn't noticed in the past. No doubt he had the scent of his new pack on him. It was how he intended to survive.

"But we still have business," said Klosterheim.

Gaynor turned towards the fire.

"Business? You're here on business?" I pretended to be surprised.

Gaynor said quietly, not turning to look at me, "Berlin made a decision. About these special German relics."

"Berlin? Do you mean Hitler and Co.?"

"They are fascinated by such things, cousin."

"They are symbols of our old German power," said Klosterheim brusquely. "They represent what so many German aristocrats have lost—the vital blood of a brave and warlike people."

"And why would you want to take my sword from me?"

"For safekeeping, cousin." Gaynor stepped forward before Klosterheim could reply. "So that it's not stolen by Bolsheviks, for instance. Or otherwise harmed. A state treasure, as I'm sure you will agree. Your name will be credited of course, in any exhibition. And there would be some financial recompense, I'm sure."

"I know nothing of the so-called Grail. But what would happen if I refused to give up the sword?"

"It would make you, of course, an enemy of the state." Gaynor had the decency to glance down at his well-polished boots. "And therefore an enemy of the Nazi Party and all it stands for."

"An enemy of the Nazi Party?" I spoke thoughtfully. "Only a fool would antagonize Hitler and expect to survive, eh?"

"Very true, cousin."

"Well," I said, as I left the room, "the Beks have rarely been fools. I'd better sleep on the problem."

"I'm sure your dreams will be inspired," said Gaynor rather cryptically.

But Klosterheim was more direct. "We have put sentimentality behind us in modern Germany and are making our own traditions, Herr Count. That sword is no more yours than it is mine. The sword is Germany's, a symbol of our ancient power and valor. Of our blood. You cannot betray your blood."

I looked at the inbred mountaineer and the Slavic Aryan before me. I looked at my own bone-white hand, the pale nails and faintly darker veins. "Our blood? My blood. Who invented the myth of blood?"

"Myths are simply old truths disguised as stories," said Klosterheim. "That is the secret of Wagner's success."

"It can't be his music. Swords, bowls and tormented souls. Did you say the sword was one of a pair? Does the owner of the sister sword seek to own the set?"

Gaynor spoke from behind Klosterheim.

"The other sword, cousin, when last heard of, was in Jerusalem."

I suppose I could not help smiling as I made my way to bed, yet that sense of foreboding soon returned and by the time I put my head on my pillow I was already wondering how I could save my sword and myself from Hitler. Then, in a strange hypnagogic moment between waking and sleeping, I heard a voice say: "Naturally I accept paradox. Paradox is the stuff of the multiverse. The essence of humanity. We are sustained by paradox." It sounded like my own voice. Yet it carried an authority, a confidence and a power I had never known.

I thought at first someone was in the room, but then I had fallen back into slumber and found my nostrils suddenly filled with a remarkable stink. It was pungent, almost tangible, but not unpleasant. Acrid, dry. The smell of snakes, perhaps? Or lizards? Massive lizards. Creatures which flew as a squadron under the control of mortals and rained fiery venom down upon their enemies. An enemy that was not bound by any rules save to win at all costs, by whatever it chose to do and be.

Deep blue patterns like gigantic butterfly wings. It was a dream of flying, but unlike any I had heard of. I was seated in a great black saddle which appeared to have been carved from a single piece of ebony yet which fitted my body perfectly and from which radiated a kind of membrane blending with the living creature. I leaned forward to place my hand on a scaly skin that was hot to the touch, suggesting an alien metabolism, and something reared up in front of me, all rustle and clatter and jingling of harness, casting a vast shadow. The monstrous head of what I first took to be a dinosaur and then realized was a dragon, absolutely dwarfing me, its mouth carrying a bit of intricately decorated gold whose tasseled decorations were as long as my body and which threatened to sweep against me when the head turned and a vast, glowing yellow eye regarded me with an intelligence that was inconceivably ancient, drawing on experience of worlds which had never known mankind. And yet, was I foolish to read affection there?

Emerald green. The subtle language of color and gesture.

*Flamefang.*

Was it my voice which spoke that name?

That vibrant stink filled my lungs. There was a hint of smoke wreathing the beast's huge nostrils and something like acid boiled between its long teeth. This beast's metabolism was extraordinary. Even as I dreamed I recalled stories of spontaneous combustion and would not have been surprised if my steed had suddenly burst into flames beneath the saddle. There was a sensual movement of huge bones and muscles and sinews, of scraping scales, a booming rush as the dragon's wings beat against gravity and all the laws of common sense and then, with another thrust which thrilled my whole body, we were airborne. The world fell away. It seemed so natural to fly. Another thrust and we had reached the clouds. It felt strangely familiar to be riding on the back of a monster, yet guiding her with all the gentle fluid ease of a Viennese riding master. A gentle touch above the ear with the staff, a fingertip movement of the reins.

While my left hand held the traditional dragon goad, the other gripped Ravenbrand, pulsing with a horrible darkness and perpetually running with blood, the runes in her blade glowing a brilliant scarlet. And I heard that voice again. My own voice.

*Arioch! Arioch! Blood and souls for my Lord Arioch!*

Such barbaric splendor, such splendid savagery, such ancient, sophisticated knowledge. But all offering a vocabulary of image, word and idea utterly alien to the Enlightenment humanist that was Ulric von Bek. Here were ideals of courage and battle prowess which whispered in my ear like enticing obscenities, thoroughly at odds with my training and traditions. Cruel, unthinkable ideas taken for granted. Here was a power greater than any modern human being could ever know. The power to transform reality.

The power of sorcery in a war fought without machines, yet more terrifying, more all-encompassing than the Great War which had recently passed.

*Arioch! Arioch!*

I could not know who Arioch was, but something in my bones conjured a strong sense of subtle, alluring evil, an evil so sophisticated it could even believe itself to be virtuous. This was some of the scent I had smelled on Gaynor and Klosterheim, but nothing like the wholesome beast stink of my dragon, her massive, sinuous multicolored wings beating a leisurely course across the sky. Her scales clashed faintly and her spiky crests folded back against her spine. My modern eye marveled at these natural aerodynamics which enabled such a creature to exist. Her heat was almost uncomfortable and every so often a droplet of venom would form on her lips and flash to earth, burning stone, trees, even setting water ablaze for a short while. What strange twist of fate had made us allies? Allies we were. Bonded in the same way that ordinary men are bonded to ordinary animals, almost telepathic, a deep empathetic heartbeat that made our blood one, our souls' fates united. When at the dawn of time had we come together to form this complementary union?

Now man and beast climbed higher and higher into the chilly upper air, steam wafting from the dragon's head and body, her tail and wings growing faintly sluggish as we reached our maximum altitude and looked down on a world laid out like a map. I felt an indescribable mixture of horror and ecstasy. This was how I imagined the dreams of opium or hashish eaters. Without end. Without meaning. A burning world. A martial world. A world which could have been my own, my twentieth-century world, but which I knew was not. Armies and flags. Armies and flags. And in their wake, the piled corpses of innocents. In the name of whom the flags are raised and the armies sent to war. To fight to the death to defend the virtues of the dead.

Now, as the clouds parted completely, I saw that the sky was filled with dragons. A great squadron of flying reptiles whose wings were at least thirty feet across and whose riders were dwarfed. A squadron that waited lazily, adrift in the atmosphere, for me to lead it.

In sudden terror I woke up. And looked directly into the cold eyes of Lieutenant Klosterheim.

"My apologies, Count von Bek, but we have urgent business in Berlin and must leave within the hour. I thought you might have something to tell us."

Confused by my dream and furious at Klosterheim's graceless intrusion, I told him I would see him downstairs shortly.

In the breakfast room, where one of my old servants was blearily doing his best to attend to my guests, I found them munching ham and bread and calling for eggs and coffee.

Gaynor waved his cup at me as I came in. "My dear fellow. How kind of you to join us. We received word from Berlin that we must return immediately. I'm so sorry to be a bad guest."

I wondered how he had received such news. A private radio, perhaps, in the car?

"Well," I said, "we shall just have to be content with our dull tranquillity."

I knew what I was doing. I saw a contradiction in Klosterheim's eye. He was almost smiling as he glanced down at the table.

"What about the sword, cousin?" Gaynor impatiently directed the servant to unshell his eggs. "Have you decided to give it up to the care of the State?"

"I don't believe it has much value to the State," I said, "whereas it has great sentimental value to me."

Gaynor scowled and rose up in his chair. "Dear cousin, I am not speaking for myself, but if Berlin were to hear your words— you would not have a home, let alone a sword to keep it in!"

"Well," I said, "I'm one of those old-fashioned Germans. I believe that duty and honor come before personal comfort. Hitler, after all, is an Austrian and of that happy-go-lucky, tolerant nature, which thinks less of such things, I'm sure."

Gaynor was not slow to understand my irony. He seemed to relish it. But Klosterheim was angry again, I could tell.

"Could we perhaps see the sword, cousin?" Gaynor said. "Just to verify that it is the one Berlin seeks. It could be that it's the wrong blade altogether!"

I was in no mood to put myself or the sword in jeopardy. Fantastic as it seemed, I believed both my cousin and his lieutenant to be capable of hitting me over the head and stealing the sword if I showed it to them.

"I'll be delighted to show it to you," I said. "As soon as it comes back from Mirenburg, where I left it with a relative of von Asch's, to be cleaned and restored."

"Von Asch? In Mirenburg?" Klosterheim sounded alarmed.

"A relative," I said. "In Baudissingaten. Do you know the man?"

"Von Asch disappeared, did he not?" Gaynor interrupted.

"Yes. In the early days of the War. He wanted to visit a certain Irish island, where he expected to find metal of special properties for a sword he wished to make, but I suspect he was too old for the journey. We never heard from him again."

"And he told you nothing about the sword?"

"A few legends, cousin. But I scarcely remember them. They didn't seem remarkable."

"And he mentioned nothing of a sister sword?"

"Absolutely nothing. I doubt if ours is the blade you seek."

"I'm beginning to suspect that you're right. I'll do my best to put your point of view to Berlin, but it will be difficult to present it in a sympathetic light."

"They have called on the spirit of Old Germany," I said. "They'd be wise to respect that spirit and not coarsen its meaning to suit their own brutal agendas."

"And perhaps we would be wise to report such treacherous remarks before we are somehow contaminated by them ourselves." Klosterheim's strange, cold eyes flared like ice in sudden firelight.

Gaynor tried to make light of this threat. "I would remind you, cousin, that the Führer will look very positively on someone who bestows such a gift to the nation." He seemed a little too emphatic, revealing his desperation. He cleared his throat. "Any preconceptions that you, like so many of your class, are a traitor to the New Germany will be dispelled."

He was almost unconsciously speaking the language of deceit and obfuscation. The kind of double-talk which always signals a dearth of moral and intellectual content. He was already, whatever he had said to me, a Nazi.

I went with them to the outside door and stood on the steps as their driver brought the Mercedes around. It was still dark, with a sliver of moon on a pale horizon. I watched the black and chrome car move slowly away down the drive towards those ancient gates, each topped by a time-worn sculpture. Firedrakes. They reminded me of my dream.

They reminded me that my dream had been considerably less terrifying than my present reality.

I wondered when I would be receiving my next Nazi guests and whether they would be as easily refused as Gaynor and Klosterheim.

# CHAPTER THREE

## Visiting Strangers

hat same evening I received a telephone call from the mysterious "Gertie." She suggested that around sunset I go down to the river which marked the northern edge of our land. There someone would contact me. There was a snap in the air. I was perfectly happy to stroll down through that lovely rolling parkland to the little bridge which connected, via a wicket gate, with a public path which had once been the main road to the town of Bek. The ruts were hardened into miniature mountain ranges. Few used the path. Now one rarely saw anything but an occasional pair of lovers or an old man walking his dog.

Just on that point of dusk between night and day, when a faint shivering mist had begun to rise from the river, I saw a tall figure appear on the bridge and wait patiently at the gate for me to unlock it. I moved forward quickly, apologetically. Somehow I had not seen the man approach. I opened the gate, welcoming him onto my land. He stepped swiftly through, closely followed by a slighter figure, who I thought at first must be a bodyguard, since it carried a longbow and a quiver of arrows.

"Are you Gertie's friends?" I asked the prearranged question.

"We know her very well," answered the archer. A woman's voice, low and commanding. Her face hooded against the evening chill, she stepped forward out of the tall man's shadow and took my hand. A strong, soft, dry handshake. The cloth of her cloak and the tunic beneath had a strange shimmering quality and the shades were unfamiliar. I wondered if this were some sort of stage costume. She might have been a German demigoddess in one of those interminable folk plays the Nazis encouraged everywhere. I invited them up to the house, but the man declined. His head lift-ed from within a darkness it seemed to carry as a kind of aura. He was gaunt, relatively young, and his blind eyes were glaring emer-alds, as if he stared past me into a future so monstrous, so cruel and so agonizing that he sought any distraction from its constant presence.

I believe your house has already been microphoned," he said. "Even if it has not been, it's always wise to behave as if the Nazis could be listening. We'll stay out here for a while and then, when our business is done, perhaps go into the house for some refreshment?"

"You will be welcome."

His voice was surprisingly light and pleasant, with a faint Austrian accent. He introduced himself as Herr El and his hand-shake was also reassuring. I knew I was in the presence of a man of substance. His dark green cape and hat were familiar enough clothing in Germany to cause no comment, but they also had the effect of disguising him, for the great collar could be pulled around the face and the brim tugged down to put what remained in shadow. There was something familiar about him and I was sure we had met at least once before, probably in Mirenburg.

"You're here to help me join the White Rose Society, I pre-sume?" I strolled with them through the ornamental shrubberies. "To fight against Hitler."

"We are certainly here to help you fight against Hitler," said the young woman, "since you, Count Ulric, are destined for spe-cific duties in the struggle."

She, too, gave me the impression that we had met before. I was surprised at her outlandish costume, which I would have thought would have attracted unwanted attention in the streets of the average German town, but guessed she was taking part in some celebration, some charade. Were they on their way to a party?

"Perhaps you know that I had a visit from my cousin Gaynor yesterday. He has Germanized his name and calls himself Paul von Minct. He's become a Nazi, though he denies it."

"Like so many, Gaynor sees Hitler and Company as furthering their own power. They cannot realize to what extent Hitler and his people are both fascinated by power and addicted to it. They desire it more than ordinary people. They think of nothing else. They are constantly scheming and counter-scheming, always ahead of the game, because most of us don't even know there's a game being played." He spoke with the urbanity of an old Franz Josef Viennese cosmopolitan. For me he represented a reassuring past, a less cynical time.

The young woman's face remained hidden, and she wore smoked glasses so that I could not see her eyes. I was surprised she could see at all as the dusk turned to darkness. She chose to sit on an old stone bench, she said, and listen to the last of the birdsong. Meanwhile Herr El and myself slowly walked amongst formal beds and borders which were just beginning to show the shoots of our first flowers. He asked me ordinary questions, mostly about my background, and I was happy to answer. I knew that the White Rose had to be more than careful. One informer and the best these people could hope for would be the guillotine.

He asked me what I hoped to achieve by joining. I said that the overthrow of Hitler was the chief reason. He asked me if I thought that would rid us of Nazis, and I was forced to admit that I did not.

"So how are we to defeat the Nazis?" asked Herr El, pausing beneath one of our old ornamental statues, so worn that the face was unrecognizable. "With machine guns? With rhetoric? With passive resistance?"

It was as if he was trying to dissuade me from joining, telling me that the society could not possibly have effect.

I answered almost unthinkingly. "By example, sir, surely?"

He seemed pleased with this and nodded slightly. "It is pretty much all most of us have," he agreed. "And we can help people escape. How would you function in that respect, Count Ulric?"

"I could use my house. There are many secret parts. I could hide people. I could probably hide a radio, too. Obviously, we can get people into Poland and also to Hamburg. We're fairly well positioned as a staging post, I'd say. I can only make these offers, sir, because I am naive. Whatever function you find for me, of course I will fulfill."

"I hope so," he said. "I will tell you at once that this house is not safe. They are too interested in it. Too interested in you. And something else here . . ."

"My old black sword, I think."

"Exactly. And a cup?"

"Believe me, Herr El, they spoke of a cup, but I have no idea what they meant. We have no legendary chalice at Bek. And if we had, we would not hide our honor!"

"Just so," murmured Herr El. "I do not believe you have the chalice either. But the sword is important. It must not become their property."

"Does it have more symbolic meaning than I know?"

"The meanings to be derived from that particular blade, Count Ulric, are, I would say, almost infinite."

"It's been suggested that the sword has a power of her own," I said.

"Indeed," he agreed. "Some even believe she has a soul."

I found this mystical tenor a little discomforting and attempted to change the subject. The air was growing cold again and I had begun to shiver a little. "My visitors of yesterday, who left this morning, looked as if they could use a soul or two. They've sold their own to the Nazis. Do you think Herr Hitler will last? My guess is that his rank and file will pull him down. They are already grumbling about betrayal."

"One should not underestimate a weakling who has spent most of his life dreaming of power, studying power, yearning for power. That he has no ability to handle power is unfortunate, but he believes that the more he has, the easier it will be for him to control. We are dealing with a mind, Count Ulric, that is at once deeply banal and profoundly mad. Because such minds are beyond our common experience, we do our best to make them seem more ordinary, more palatable to us. We give them motive and meaning which are closer to our own. Their motives are raw, dear Count. Savage. Uncivilized. The naked basic greedy primeval stuff of existence, unrefined by any humanity, which is determined to survive at any cost or, if that is its only option, to be the last to die."

I found this a little melodramatic for my somewhat puritanical education. "Don't some of his followers call him Lucky Adolf?" I asked. "Isn't he just a nasty little street orator who has, by sheer chance, been elevated to the Chancellory? Are his banalities not simply those you will find in the head of any ordinary Austrian petite bourgeois? Which is why he's so popular."

"I agree that his ideas mirror those you'll find in any small-town shopkeeper, but they are elevated by a psychopathic vision. Even the words of Jesus, Count Ulric, can be reduced to sentimental banalities. Who can truly describe or even recognize genius? We can judge by action and by what those actions accomplish. Hitler's strength could be that he was dismissed too readily by people of our class and background. Not for the first time. The little Corsican colonel appeared to come from nowhere. Successful revolutionaries rarely announce themselves as anything but champions of the old virtues. The peasants supported Lenin because they believed he was going to return the Tsar to his throne."

"You don't believe in men of destiny then, Herr El?"

"On the contrary. I believe that every so often the world creates a monster which represents either its very best or its very worst desires. Every so often the monster goes out of control and it is left to certain of us, who call ourselves by various names, to fight that monster and to show that it can be wounded, if not destroyed. Not all of us use guns or swords. We'll use words and the ballot box. But sometimes the result is the same. For it is motive, in the end, which the public must examine in its leaders. And, given time, that is exactly what a mature democracy does. But when it is frightened and bullied into bigotry it no longer behaves like a mature democracy. And that is when the Hitlers move in. The public soon begins to see how little his actions and words suit their interest and his vote is dwindling by the time he makes his final lunge for power and, through luck and cunning, suddenly he finds himself in charge of a great, civilized nation which had failed once to understand the real brutality of war and desired never to know that reality again. I believe that Hitler represents the demonic aggression of a nation drowning in its own orthodoxies."

"And who represents the angelic qualities of that nation, Herr El? The communists?"

"The invisible people mostly," he replied seriously. "The ordinary heroes and heroines of these appalling conflicts between corrupted Chaos and degenerate Law as the multiverse grows tired and her denizens lack the will or the means to help her renew herself."

"A gloomy prospect," I said quite cheerfully. I understood the philosophical position and looked forward to arguing it over a glass or two of punch. My spirits lightened considerably and I suggested that perhaps we could go discreetly into the house and draw the curtains before my people turned on the lamps.

He glanced towards the pale young "Diana," who had still to remove her dark spectacles, and she seemed to acquiesce. I led the way up the steps to the veranda and from there through French doors into my study, where I drew the heavy velvet curtains and lit the oil lamp which stood on my desk. My visitors looked curiously at my packed bookshelves, the clutter of documents, maps and old volumes over every surface, the lamplight giving everything golden warmth and contrast, their shadows falling upon my library as gracefully they moved from shelf to shelf. It was as if they had been deprived of books for too long. There was an almost greedy darting speed about the way they reached for titles that attracted them and I felt oddly virtuous, as if I had brought food to the starving. But even as they quested through my books, they continued to question me, continued to elaborate as if they sought the limits of my intellectual capacity. Eventually, they seemed satisfied. Then they asked if they could see Ravenbrand. I almost refused, so protective had I become of my trust. But I was certain of their credentials. They were not my enemies and they meant me no ill.

And so, overcoming my fear of betrayal, I led my visitors down into the system of cellars and tunnels which ran deep beneath our foundations and whose passages led, according to old stories, into mysterious realms. The most mysterious realm I had encountered was the cavern of natural rock, cold and strangely dry, in which I had buried our oldest heirloom, the Raven Sword. I stooped and drew back the stones which appeared to be part of the wall and reaching into the cavity, brought out the hard case I had commissioned. I laid the case on an old deal table in the middle of the cave and took a key on my keychain to unlock it.

Even as I threw back the lid to show them the sword, some strange trick of the air caused the blade to begin murmuring and singing, like an old man in his dotage, and I was momentarily blinded not by a light, but by a blackness which seemed to blaze from the blade and was then gone. As I blinked against that strange phenomenon I thought I saw another figure standing near the wall. A figure of exactly the same height and general shape as myself, its white face staring hard into mine, its red eyes blazing with a mixture of anger and perhaps mocking intelligence. Then the apparition had gone and I was reaching into the case to take out the great two-handed sword, which could be used so readily in one. I offered the hilt to Herr El but he declined firmly, almost as if he was afraid to touch it. The woman, too, kept her distance from the sword and a moment or two later I closed the case, replacing it in the wall.

"She seems to behave a little differently in company," I said. I tried to make light of something which had disturbed me, yet I could not be absolutely sure what it was. I did not want to believe that the sword had supernatural qualities. The supernatural and I were best left to meet once a week, in the company of others, to hear a good sermon from the local pastor. I began to wonder if perhaps the couple were tricking me in some way, but I had no sense of levity or of deception. Neither had wanted to be near the blade. They shared my fear of its oddness.

"It is the Black Sword," Herr El told the huntress. "And soon we shall find out if it still has a soul."

I must have raised an eyebrow at this. I think he smiled. "I suppose I sound fanciful to you, Count Ulric. I apologize. I am so used to speaking in metaphor and symbol that I sometimes forget my ordinary language."

"I've heard many claims made for the sword," I said. "Not least by the one whose family almost certainly forged it. You know von Asch?"

"I know they are smiths. Does the family still live here in Bek?"

"The old man left just before the beginning of the War," I said. "He had some important journey of his own to make."

"You asked no questions?"

"It isn't my way."

He understood this. We were walking out of the chamber now, back up the narrow twisting stair that would take us to a corridor and from there to a door and another flight or two of steps where, if we were lucky, the air would become easier to breathe.

The scene felt far too close to something from a melodramatic version of Wagner for my taste and I was glad to be back in the study where my guests again began to move amongst my books even as we continued our strange conversation. They were not impolite, merely profoundly curious. It was no doubt their curiosity which had brought them to their present situation, that and a common feeling for humanity. Herr El was impressed by my first edition of Grimmelshausen. *Simplicissimus* was one of his favorite books, he said. Was I familiar with that period?

As much as any, I said. The Beks appeared to have shifted their loyalties as thoroughly as most families during the Thirty Years War, fighting originally for the Protestant cause but frequently finding themselves side by side with Catholics. Perhaps that was the nature of war?

He said he had heard a rumor that my namesake had written an account of those times. There were records in a certain monastery which referred to them. Did I have a version of it?

I had never heard of it, I said. The most famous memoirs were the fabrications of my scapegrace ancestor Manfred, who claimed to have gone to faraway lands by balloon and to have had supernatural adventures. He was an embarrassment to the rest of us. The account still existed, as I understood, in a bad English version, but even that had been heavily edited. The original was altogether too grotesque and fantastic to be even remotely credible. Even the English, with their taste for such stuff, gave it no great credence. For such a dull family, we occasionally threw up the most peculiar sorts. I spoke ironically, of course, of my own strange appearance.

"Indeed," said Herr El, accepting a glass of cognac. The young woman refused. "And here we are in a society which attempts to stamp out all difference, insists on conformism against all reality. Tidy minds make bad governors. Do you not feel we should celebrate and cultivate variety, Count Ulric, while we have the opportunity?"

While in no way antagonistic to them, I felt that perhaps these visitors, too, had come for something and been disappointed.

Then suddenly the young woman still cowled and wearing dark glasses murmured to the tall man who put down his unfinished drink and began to move rapidly, with her, towards the French doors and the veranda beyond.

"One of us will contact you again, soon. But remember, you are in great danger. While the sword is hidden, they will let you live. Fear not, Herr Count, you will serve the White Rose."

I saw them melt into the darkness beyond the veranda. I went outside to take a last breath or two of clear night air. As I looked down towards the bridge I thought I saw the white hare running again. For a flashing moment I thought she followed a white raven which flew just above her head. I saw nothing, however, of the man and the woman. Eventually, losing hope of seeing the hare or the bird again, I went inside, locked the doors and drew the heavy curtains.

That night I dreamed I again flew on the back of a dragon. This time the scene was peaceful. I soared over the slender towers and minarets of a fantastic city which blazed with vivid colors. I knew the name of the city. I knew that it was my home.

But home though it was, sight of it filled me with longing and anguish and at length I turned the dragon away, flying gracefully over the massing waters of a dark and endless ocean. Flying towards the great silver-gold disk of the moon which filled the horizon.

I was awakened early that morning by the sound of cars in the drive. When I was at last able to find my dressing gown and go to a front window I saw that there were three vehicles outside. All official. Two were Mercedes saloons and one was a black police van. I was familiar enough with the scene. No doubt someone had come to arrest me.

Or perhaps they only intended to frighten me.

I thought of leaving by a back door but then imagined the indignity of being caught by guards posted there. I heard voices in the hallway now. Nobody was shouting. I heard a servant say they would wake me.

I went back to my room and when the servant arrived I told him I would be down shortly. I washed, shaved and groomed myself, put on my army uniform and then began to descend the stairs to the hall where two Gestapo plainclothesmen, distinguished by identical leather coats, waited. The occupants of the other vehicles must, as I suspected, have been positioned around the house.

"Good morning, gentlemen." I paused on one of the bottom stairs. "How can we help you?" Banal remarks, but somehow appropriate here.

"Count Ulric von Bek?" The speaker had been less successful shaving. His face was covered in tiny nicks. His swarthy companion looked young and a little nervous.

"The same," I said. "And you, gentlemen, are—"

"I'm Lieutenant Bauer and this is Sergeant Stiftung. We understand you to be in possession of certain state property. My orders, Count, are to receive that property or hold you liable for its safety. If, for instance, it has been lost, you alone can be held to account for failing in your stewardship. Believe me, sir, we have no wish to cause you any distress. This matter can be quickly brought to a satisfactory conclusion."

"I give you my family heirloom or you arrest me?"

"As you can see, Herr Count, we should in the end be successful. So would you like to reach that conclusion from behind the wire of a concentration camp or would you rather reach it in the continuing comfort of your own home?"

His threatening sarcasm made me impatient. "I would guess my company would be better in the camp," I told him.

And so, before I had had my breakfast, I was arrested, handcuffed and placed in the van whose hard seats were constantly threatening to throw me to the floor as we bumped over the old road from Bek. No shouts. No threats of violence. No swearing. Just a smooth transition. One moment I was free, captain of my own fate, the next I was a prisoner, no longer the possessor of my own body. The reality was beginning to impinge rapidly, well before the van stopped, and I was ordered far less politely to step into the coldness of some kind of courtyard. An old castle, perhaps? Something they had turned into a prison? The walls and cobbles were in bad repair. The place seemed to have been abandoned for some years. There was new barbed wire running along the top and a couple of roughly roofed machine-gun posts. Though my legs would hardly hold me at first, I was shoved through an archway and a series of dirty tunnels to emerge into a large compound full of the kind of temporary huts built for refugees during the War. I realized I had been brought to a fair-sized concentration camp, perhaps the nearest to Bek, but I had no idea of its name until I was bundled through another door, back into the main building and made to stand before some kind of reception officer, who seemed uncomfortable with the situation. I was, after all, in my army uniform, wearing my honors and not evidently a political agitator or foreign spy. I had been determined that they should be confronted by this evidence since, to me at least, it advertised the absurdity of their regime.

I was charged, it seemed, with political activities threatening the property and security of the State and was held under "protective custody." I had not been accused of a crime or allowed to defend myself. But there would have been no point.

Everyone engaged in this filthy charade knew that this was merely a piece of playacting, that the Nazis ruled above a law which they had openly despised, just as they despised the principles of the Christian religion and all its admonishments.

I was allowed to keep my uniform but had to give up my leather accoutrements. Then I was led deeper into the building to a small room, like a monk's cell. Here I was told I would stay until my turn came for interrogation.

I had a fair idea that the interrogation would be a little less subtle than that I'd enjoyed from Prince Gaynor or the Gestapo.

# CHAPTER FOUR

# Camp Life

etter writers than I have experienced worse terrors and anguish than I knew in those camps and my case was, if anything, privileged compared to poor Mr. Feldmann with whom I shared a cell during a "squeeze" when the Gestapo and their SA bullyboys were busier than usual.

Of course, I lost my uniform the first day. Ordered to shower and then finding nothing to wear but black and white striped prison clothes, far too small for me, with a red "political" star sewn on them, I was given no choice. While I dressed, bellowing SA mocked me and made lewd comments reminding me of their leader Röhm's infamous proclivities. I had never anticipated this degree of fear and wretchedness, yet I never once regretted my decision. Their crudeness somehow sustained me. The worse I was treated, the more I was singled out for hardship, the more I came to understand how important my family heirlooms were to the Nazis. That such power should still seek more power revealed how fundamentally insecure these people were. Their creed had been the rationalizations of the displaced, the cowardly, the unvictorious. It was not a creed suited for command. Thus their brutality increased almost daily as their leader and his creatures came to fear even the most minor resistance to their will. And this meant, too, that they were ultimately vulnerable. Their children knew their vulnerability.

My initial interrogation had been harsh, threatening, but I had not suffered much physical violence so far. I think they were giving me a "taste" of camp life in order to soften me up. In other words, I still might find an open gate out of this hell if I learned my lesson. I was, indeed, learning lessons.

The Nazis were destroying the infrastructure of democracy and institutionalized law which they had exploited in order to gain their power. But without that infrastructure, their power could only be sustained by increased violence. Such violence, as we always see, ultimately destroys itself. Paradox is sometimes the most reassuring quality the multiverse possesses. It's a happy thought, for one of my background and experience, to know that God is indeed a paradox.

As a relatively honored prisoner of the Sachsenburg camp, I was given a shared cell in the castle itself, which had been used as a prisoner-of-war camp during the Great War and was run on pretty much the same lines. We "inside" prisoners were given better treatment, slightly better food and some letter-writing privileges, while the "outside" prisoners, in the huts, were regimented in the most barbaric ways and killed almost casually for any violation of the many rules. For "insiders," there was always the threat of going "outside" if you failed to behave yourself.

Give a German of my kind daily terror and every misery, give him the threat of death and the sight of decent human beings murdered and tortured before his helpless eyes, and he will escape, if he can escape at all, into philosophy. There is a level of experience at which your emotions and mind, your soul perhaps, fail to function. They fail to absorb, if you like, the horror around them. You become a kind of zombie.

Yet even zombies have their levels of feeling and understanding, dim echoes of their original personalities—a whisper of generosity, a passing moment of sympathy. But anger, which must sustain you at these times, is the hardest to hold on to. Some zombies are able to give every appearance of still being human. They talk. They reminisce. They philosophize. They show no anger or despair. They are perfect prisoners.

I suppose I was lucky to share a cell first with a journalist whose work I had read in the Berlin papers, Hans Hellander, and then, by some bureaucratic accident when the "in" cells were filling too fast for the "out," Erich Feldmann, who had written as "Henry Grimm" and had also been classified as a political, rather than with the yellow star of the Jew. Three philosophizing zombies. With two bunks between us, sharing as best we could and sustaining ourselves on swill and the occasional parcel from the foreign volunteers still allowed to work in Germany, we relived the comradeship we had all known in the trenches. Beyond the castle walls, in the "out" huts of the compounds, we frequently heard the most bloodcurdling shrieks, the crack of shots, and other even more disturbing sounds, less readily identified.

Sleep brought me no benefit, no escape. The most peaceful dream I had was of a white hare running through snow, leaving a trail of blood. And still I dreamed of dragons and swords and mighty armies. Any Freudian would have found me a classic case. Perhaps I was, but to me those things were real—more vivid than life.

I thought that I began to see myself in these dreams. A figure almost always in shadow, with its face shaded, that regarded me from hard, steady eyes the color and depth of rubies. Bleak eyes which held more knowledge than I would care for. Did I look at my future self?

Somehow I saw this doppelgänger as an ally, yet at the same time I was thoroughly afraid of him.

When it was my turn for a bunk, I slept well. Even on the floor of the prison, I usually achieved some kind of rest. The guards were a mixture of SA and members of the prison service, who did their best to follow old regulations and see that we were properly treated. This was impossible, by the old standards, but it still meant we occasionally saw a doctor and very rarely one of us was released back to his family.

We already knew we were privileged. That we were in one of the most comfortable camps in the country. Although still only hinting at the death factories of Auschwitz and Treblinka, Dachau and some of the other places were becoming recognized as murder camps and this, of course, long before the Nazis had ever considered making the Final Solution a reality.

I was not to know my own "lesson" was only just beginning. After about two months of this, I was summoned from my cell one day by SA Hauptsturmführer Hahn whom we'd come to fear, especially when he was accompanied, as now, by two uniformed thugs we knew as Fritzi and Franzi, since one was tall and thin while the other was short and fat. They reminded us of the famous cartoon characters. Hahn looked like most other SA officers, with a puffy face, a toothbrush mustache, a plug of a nose and two or three tiny receding chins. All he lacked to make him identical to his leader Röhm were the hideous scarred face and the rapacious proclivities which would make men hide their sons when he and his gang came to town.

I was marched between Fritzi and Franzi up and down stairs, through tunnels and corridors until I was brought at last to the commandant's office where Major Hausleiter, a corrupt old drunk who would have been drummed out of any decent army, awaited me. Since my reception, when he had seemed embarrassed, I had only seen him at a distance. Now he seemed nervous. Something was in the air and I had a feeling that Hausleiter would be the last to know what was really going on. He told me that I was being paroled on "humanitarian leave" under the charge of my cousin, now Major von Minct, for a "trial period." He advised me to keep my nose clean and cooperate with people who only had my good at heart. If I returned to Sachsenburg, it might not be with the same privileges.

Someone had found my clothes. Doubtless Gaynor or one of his people had brought them from Bek. The shirt and suit hung on my thinner than usual body, but I dressed carefully, tying the laces of my shoes, making a neat knot of my tie, determined to look as well as possible when I confronted my cousin.

Escorted into the castle courtyard by Fritzi and Franzi, I found Prince Gaynor waiting beside his car. Klosterheim was not with him, but the glowering driver was the same.

Gaynor raised his hand in that ridiculous "salute" borrowed from American movie versions of Roman history and bid me good afternoon.

I got into the car without a word. I was smiling to myself.

When we were driving through the gates and leaving the prison behind, Gaynor asked me why I was smiling.

"I was simply amused by the lengths of playacting you and your kind are willing to allow yourselves. And apparently without embarrassment."

He shrugged. "Some of us find it easier to ape the absurd. After all, the world has become completely absurd, has it not?"

"The humorous aspects are a little wasted on some of those camp inmates," I said. In prison I had met journalists, doctors, lawyers, scientists, musicians, most of whom had been brutalized in some way. "All we can see are degenerate brutes pulling down a culture because they cannot understand it. Bigotry elevated to the status of law and politics. A decline into a barbarism worse than we knew in the Middle Ages, with the ideas of that time turned into 'truth.' They are told obvious lies—that some six hundred and forty thousand Jewish citizens somehow control the majority of the population. Yet every German knows at least one 'good' Jew, which means that there are sixty million 'good' Jews in the country. Which means that the 'bad' Jews are heavily outnumbered by the 'good.' A problem Goebbels has yet to solve."

"Oh, I'm sure he will in time." Gaynor had removed his cap and was unbuttoning his uniform jacket. "The best lies are those which carry the familiarity of truth with them. And the familiar lie often sounds like the truth, even to the most refined of us. A resonant story, you know, will do the trick with the right delivery . . ."

I must admit the spring air was refreshing and I thoroughly enjoyed the long drive to Bek. I scarcely wanted it to end, since I had anxieties about what I might find at my home. After asking me how I had liked the camp, Gaynor said very little to me as we drove along. He was less full of himself than when I'd last seen him. I wondered if he had made promises to his masters which he'd been unable to keep.

It was dusk before we passed through Bek's gates and came to a stop in the drive outside the main door. The house was unusually dark. I asked what had happened to the servants. They had resigned, I was told, once they realized they had been working for a traitor. One had even died of shame.

I asked his name.

"Reiter, I believe."

I knew that feeling had returned. My spirits sank. My oldest, most faithful retainer. Had they killed him asking him questions about me?

"The coroner reported that Reiter died of shame, eh?"

"Officially, of course, it was the heart attack." Gaynor stepped out into the darkness and opened my door for me. "But I'm sure two resourceful fellows like us will be able to make ourselves at home."

"You're staying?"

"Naturally," he said. "You are in my custody, after all."

Together we ascended the steps. There was a crude padlock on the door. Gaynor called the driver to come forward and open it. Then we stepped into a house that smelled strongly of damp and neglect and worse. There was no gas or electricity, but the driver discovered some candles and oil lamps and with the help of these I surveyed the wreckage of my home.

It had been ransacked.

Most things of value were gone. Pictures had vanished from walls. Vases. Ornaments. The library had disappeared. Everything else was scattered and broken where Gaynor's thugs had clearly left it. Not a room in the house was undamaged. In some cases where there was nothing at all of value, men had urinated and defecated in the rooms. Only fire, I thought, could possibly cleanse the place now.

"The police seem to have been a little untidy in their searches,"

Gaynor said lightly. His face was thrown into sharp, demonic contrast by the oil lamp's light. His dark eyes glittered with unwholesome pleasure.

I knew too much self-discipline and was far too weak physically to throw myself on him, but the impulse was there. As anger came back, so, in a strange way, did life.

"Did you supervise this disgusting business?" I asked him.

"I'm afraid I was in Berlin during most of the search. By the time I arrived, Klosterheim and his people had created this. Naturally, I berated them."

He didn't expect to be believed. His tone of mockery remained.

"You were looking for a sword, no doubt."

"Exactly, cousin. Your famous sword."

"Famous, apparently, amongst Nazis," I retorted, "but not amongst civilized human beings. Presumably you found nothing."

"It's well hidden."

"Or perhaps it does not exist."

"Our orders are to tear the place down, stone by stone and beam by beam, until it is nothing but debris, if we have to. You could save all this, dear cousin. You could save yourself. You could be sure of spending your life in contentment, an honored citizen of the Third Reich. Do you not yearn for these things, cousin?"

"Not at all, cousin. I'm more comfortable than I was in the trenches. I have better company. What I yearn for is altogether more general. And perhaps unattainable. I yearn for a just world in which educated men like yourself understand their responsibilities to the people, in which issues are decided by informed public debate, not by bigotry and filthy rhetoric."

"What? Sachsenburg hasn't shown you the folly of your childish idealism? Perhaps it's time for you to visit Dachau or some camp where you'll be far less comfortable than you were in those damned trenches. Ulric, don't you think those trenches meant something to me, too!" He had suddenly lost his mockery. "When I had to watch men of both sides dying for nothing, being lied to for nothing, being threatened for nothing. Everything for nothing.

Nothing. Nothing. Nothing. And seeing all that nothing, are you surprised someone like myself might not grow cynical and realize that nothing is all we have in our future."

"Some come to the same realization but decide we still have it in us to make a life on earth. Through tolerance and good will, cousin."

He laughed openly at that. He waved a gauntleted hand around the ruins of my study.

"Well, well, cousin. Are you pleased with everything your good will has brought you?"

"It has left me with my dignity and self-respect." Sanctimonious as that sounded, I knew I might never have another chance to say it.

"Oh, dear Ulric. You have seen how we end, have you not? Writhing in filthy ditches trying to push our own guts back into our bodies? Shrieking like terrified rats? Climbing over the corpses of friends to get a crust of dirty bread? And worse. We all saw worse, did we not?"

"And better, perhaps. Some of us saw visions. Miracles. The Angel of Mons."

"Delusions. Criminal delusions. We cannot escape the truth. We must make what we can of our hideous world. In truth, cousin, it's safe to say that Satan rules in Germany today. Satan rules everywhere. Haven't you noticed? America, where they hang black men on a whim and where the Ku Klux Klan now puts state governors into office? England, which kills, imprisons and exiles thousands of Indians who naively seek the same rights as other citizens of the Empire? France? Italy? All those civilized nations of the world, who brought us our great music, our literature, our philosophy and our sophisticated politics. What was the result of all this refinement? Gas warfare? Tanks? Battle airplanes? If I seem contemptuous of you, cousin, it is because you insist on seeking the delusion. I have respect only for people like myself, who see the truth for what it is and make sure their own lives are not made wretched by allegiance to some worthless principle, some noble ideal, which could well be the very ideal which sends us into the next war, and the next. The Nazis are right. Life is a matter of brute struggle. Nothing else is real. Nothing."

Again, I was amused. I found his ideas worthless and foolish, entirely self-pitying. The logic of a weak man who arrogantly assumed himself stronger than he was. I had seen others like him. Their own failures became the failures of whole classes, governments, races or nations. The most picturesque were inclined to blame the entire universe for their own inability to be the heroes they imagined themselves to be. Self-pity translated into aggression is an unpredictable and unworthy force.

"Your self-esteem seems to rise in direct proportion to the decline of your self-respect," I said.

As if from habit, he swung on me, raising his gloved fist. Then my eyes locked with his and he dropped his arm, turning away. "Oh, cousin, you understand so little of mankind's capacity for cruelty," he hissed. "I trust you'll have no further experience of it. Just tell me where the sword and cup are hidden."

"I know nothing of a cup and sword," I said. "Or its companion blade." That was the closest I came to lying. I wanted to go no further than that. My own sense of honor demanded I stop.

Gaynor sighed, tapping his foot on the old boards. "Where could you have hidden it? We found its case. No doubt where you left it for us. In that cellar. The first place we searched. I guessed you'd be naive enough to bury your treasures as deep as you could. A few taps on the wall and we found the cavity. But we had underestimated you. What did you do with that sword, cousin?"

I almost laughed aloud. Had someone else stolen Ravenbrand? Someone who held it in no particular value? No wonder the house was in such a condition.

Gaynor was like a wolf. His eyes continued to search the walls and crannies. He paced nervously as he talked.

"We know the sword's in the house. You didn't take it away. You didn't give it to your visitors. So where did you put it, cousin?"

"The last I saw Ravenbrand was in that case."

He was disgusted. "How can someone so idealistic be such a

thoroughgoing liar. Who else could have taken the sword from the case, cousin? We interrogated all the servants. Even old Reiter didn't confess until his confession was clearly meaningless. Which left you, cousin. Not up the chimneys. Not under the floorboards. Not in a secret panel or a cupboard. We know how to search these old places. Not in the attics or the eaves or the beams or the walls, as far as we can discover. We know your father lost the cup. We got that out of Reiter. He heard one name, 'Miggea.' Do you know that name? No? Would you like to see Reiter, by the way? It might take you a while to spot something about him that you recognize."

Having nothing to gain from controlling my anger, I had the satisfaction of striking him one good blow on the ear, like a bad schoolboy.

"Be quiet, Gaynor. You sound as banal as a villain from a melodrama. Whatever you did to Reiter or do to me, I'm sure it's the foulest thing your fouler brain could invent."

"Flattering me at this late stage is a little pointless." He grumbled to himself as, rubbing his ear, he marched about the ruins of my study. He had become used to brutish power. He acted like a frustrated ape. He was trying to recover himself, but hardly knew how anymore.

At last he regained some poise. "There are a couple of beds upstairs which are still all right. We'll sleep there. I'll let you consider your problem overnight. And then I'll cheerfully give you up to the mercies of Dachau."

And so, in the bedroom where my mother had given birth to me and where she had eventually died, I slept, handcuffed to the bedpost with my worst enemy in the other bed. My dreams were all of pale landscapes over which ran the white hare who led me to a tall man, standing alone in a glade. A man who was my double. Whose crimson eyes stared into my crimson eyes and who murmured urgent words I could not hear. And I knew a terror deeper than anything I had so far experienced. For a moment I thought I saw the sword. And I awoke screaming.

Much to Gaynor's satisfaction.

"So you've come to your senses," he said. He sat up in a bed covered with feminine linen. An incongruous sight. He jumped to the floor in his silk underwear and rang a bell. A few moments later, Gaynor's driver arrived with his uniform almost perfectly pressed. I was uncuffed and my own clothes were handed to me in a pillowcase. I did my best to look as smart as possible while Gaynor waited impatiently for his turn in the only surviving bathroom.

The driver served us bread and cheese on plates he had evidently cleaned himself. I saw rat droppings on the floor and recalled what I had to look forward to. Dachau. I ate the food. It might be my last.

"Is the sword somewhere in the grounds?" asked Gaynor. His manner had changed, had become eager.

I finished my cheese and smiled at him cheerfully. "I have no idea where the sword is," I said. I was lighthearted because I had no need to lie. "It appears to have vanished on its own volition. Perhaps it followed the cup."

My cousin was snarling as he stood up. His hand fell on the holstered pistol at his belt, at which I laughed more heartily. "What a charlatan you have become, Gaynor. Clearly you should be acting in films. Herr Pabst would snap you up if he could see you now. How can you know if I'm telling you the truth or not?"

"My orders are not to offer you any kind of public martyrdom." His voice was so low, so furious, that I could hardly hear it. "To make sure that you died quietly and well away from the public eye. It's the only thing, cousin, that makes me hold back from testing your grip on the truth myself. So you'll be returned to the pleasures of Sachsenburg and from there you'll be sent on to a real camp, where they know how to deal with vermin of your kind."

Then he kicked me deliberately in the groin and slapped my face.

I was still handcuffed.

Gaynor's driver led me from my house and back into the car.

This time Gaynor sat me in front with the driver while he lounged, smoking and scowling, in the back. As far as I know, he never looked at me directly again.

His masters were no doubt beginning to think they had over-estimated him. As he had me. I guessed that the sword had been saved by Herr El, "Diana" and the White Rose Society and would be used by them against Hitler. My own death, my own silence, would not be wasted.

I made the best use I could of the journey and slept a little, ate all that was available, dozed again, so that we had driven back through the gates and were in the great black shadow of Sachsenburg Castle before I realized it.

Fritzi and Franzi were waiting for me. They came forward almost eagerly as I stepped from the car.

They were clearly pleased to see me home.

They had clubbed me to the ground, in fact, and were in the process of beating my skinny body black and blue before Gaynor's car had gone roaring back into the night. I heard a voice from a window above and then I was being dragged, almost insensibly, back to my cell where Hellander and Feldmann attempted to deal with the worst of my bruises as I lay in agony on a bunk, con-vinced that more than one bone had been broken.

The next morning they didn't come for me. They came for Feldmann. They understood how to test me. I was by no means sure I would not fail.

When Feldmann returned he no longer had any teeth. His mouth was a weeping red wound and one of his eyes seemed per-manently closed.

"For God's sake." He spoke indistinctly, every movement of his face painful. "Don't tell them where that sword is."

"Believe me," I told him, "I don't know where it is. But I wish with all my soul that I held it in my hands at this moment."

Small comfort to Feldmann. They took him again in the morning, while he screamed at them for the cowards they were, and they brought him back in the afternoon. Ribs were broken. Several fingers. A foot. He was breathing with difficulty, as if something pressed on his lungs.

He told me not to give up. That they were not defeating us. They were not dividing us.

Both Hellander and I were weeping as we did our best to ease his pain. But they took him again for a third day. And that night, with nothing left of him that had not been tortured, inside and out, he died in our arms. When I looked into Hellander's eyes I saw that he was terrified. We knew exactly what they were doing. He guessed that he would be next.

And then, even as Feldmann gave out his last, thin gasp of life, I looked beyond Hellander and saw, distinct yet vaguely insubstantial, my doppelgänger. That strange, cloaked albino whose eyes were mine.

And for the first time I thought I heard him speak.

"The sword," he said.

Hellander was looking away from me, looking to where the albino had stood. I asked him if he had seen anything. He shook his head. We laid Feldmann out on the flagstones and tried to say some useful service for him. But Hellander was wretched and I didn't know how to help him.

My dreams were of the white hare, of my doppelgänger in his hooded cape, of the lost black sword and of the young woman archer whom I had nicknamed Diana. No dragons or ornamented cities. No armies. No monsters. Just my own face staring at me, desperate to communicate something. And then the sword. I could almost feel it in my hands.

Half-roused, I heard Hellander moving uncomfortably. I asked him if he was all right. He said that he was fine.

In the morning I awoke to find his hanging body turning slowly in the air above Feldmann's. He had found his means of escape as I slept.

A full twenty-four hours passed before the guards removed the corpses from my cell.

# CHAPTER FIVE

# Martial Music

ritzi and Franzi came for me a couple of days later. Without bothering to move me, they took out their blackjacks and beat me up on the spot. Fritzi and Franzi enjoyed their work and had become very expert at it, commenting on my responses, the reaction of my strange, pale body to their blows. The peculiar color of my bruises. They complained, however, that it was hard to get sounds out of me. A small problem they thought they would solve over time.

Shortly after they left, I received a visit from Klosterheim, now an SS captain, who offered me something from a hip flask which I refused. I had no intention of helping him drug me.

"A sequence of very unfortunate accidents, eh?" He looked around my cell. "You must find all this a bit depressing, Herr Count."

"Oh, it means I don't have to mix too much with Nazis," I said. "So I suppose I am at an advantage."

"Your notion of advantage is rather hard for me to grasp," he said. "It seems to get you in this sort of predicament. How long did it take our SA boys to finish off your friend Feldmann? Of course, you could be a little fitter, a little younger. How long was it? Three days?"

"Feldmann's triumph?" I said. "Three days in which every word he had written about you was proven. You confirmed his judgment in every detail. You gave extra authority to everything he published. No writer can feel better than that."

"These are martyr's victories, however. Intelligent men would call them meaningless."

"Only stupid men who believed themselves intelligent would call them that," I said. "And we all know how ludicrous such strutting fellows are." I was glad of his presence. My hatred of him took my mind off my injuries. "I'll tell you now, Herr Captain, that I have no sword to give you and no cup, either. Whatever you believe, you are wrong. I will be happy to die with you believing otherwise, but I would not like others to die on my behalf. In your assumption of power, sir, you have also assumed responsibility, whether you like it or not. You can't have one without the other. So I present you with your guilt."

I turned my back on him and he left immediately.

A few hours later Fritzi and Franzi arrived to carry on their experiments. When I passed out, I immediately had a vision of my doppelgänger. He was speaking urgently, but I still couldn't hear him. Then he vanished and was replaced by the black sword, whose iron, now constantly washed with blood, bore the same runes but they were alive—scarlet.

When I woke I was naked with no blanket on my bed. I understood at once that they meant to kill me. The standard method was to starve and expose a prisoner until they were too weak to withstand infection, usually pneumonia. They used it when you refused to die of a heart attack. Why this charade was perpetuated I was never sure. I guessed this "message" was a bluff. If they still thought I could lead them to the sword or the cup they set such store by, they wouldn't kill me.

In fact Major Hausleiter came to my cell himself at one point. He had Klosterheim with him. I think he attempted to reason with me, but he was so inarticulate he made no sense. Klosterheim reminded me that his patience was over and made some other villainous, ridiculous threat. What do you threaten the damned with? I was too weak to offer any significant retort. But I managed something like a smile with my broken mouth.

I leaned forward, as if to whisper a secret, and watched with satisfaction as, drop by drop, my blood fell upon his perfect uniform. It took him a moment to realize what had happened. He pulled back in baffled disgust, pushing me away so that I fell to the floor.

The door slammed and there was silence. Nobody else was being tortured tonight. When I tried to rise I saw another figure sitting on my bunk. My doppelgänger made a gesture and then seemed to fold downwards onto the bare mattress.

I crawled to the bunk. My double had gone. But in his place was the Ravenbrand. My sword. The sword they all sought. I reached out to touch the familiar iron and as I did so it, too, vanished. Yet I knew I had imagined nothing. Somehow the sword would find me again.

Not before Fritzi and Franzi had returned once more. Even as they beat me they discussed my staying power. They thought I could take one more "general physical" and then they would let me rest up for a day or two or they would probably lose me. Major von Minct was arriving later. He might have some ideas.

As the door slammed and was locked, leaving me in darkness, I saw my doppelgänger clearly framed there. The figure almost glowed. Then it crossed to the bunk. I turned my head painfully, but the man was gone. I knew I was not hallucinating. I had a feeling that if I had the strength to get to my bed I would see the sword again.

Somehow the thought drove me to find energy from nothing. Bit by bit I crawled to the bunk and this time my hand touched cold metal. The hilt of the Raven Sword. Fraction by fraction I worked my fingers until they had closed around the hilt. Perhaps this was a dying man's delusion, but the metal felt solid enough. Even as my hand gripped it, the sword made a low crooning noise, one of welcome, like a cat purring. I was determined to hang on to it, not to let it vanish again, even though I had no strength to lift it.

Strangely the metal seemed to warm, passing energy into my hands and wrists, giving me the means to raise myself up onto the bunk and lie with my body shielding the sword from anyone looking into the cell. There was a fresh vibrancy about the metal. As if the sword were actually alive. While this thought was disturbing, it did not seem as bizarre as it might have a few months earlier.

I do not really know if a day passed. My own head was full of images and stories. The sword had somehow infected me. It could have been later that night Franzi and Fritzi arrived. They had brought some prison clothes and were yelling at me to get up. They were taking me to see Major von Minct.

I had been gathering my strength and praying for this moment. I had the sword gripped in both hands and as I turned I lifted the blade and threw my body weight behind it. The point caught short fat Franzi in the stomach and slid into him with frightening ease. He began to gulp. Behind him Fritzi was transfixed, unsure what was happening.

Franzi screamed. It was a long, cold, anguished scream. When it stopped, I was standing on my feet, blocking Fritzi from reaching the door. He sobbed. Clearly something about me terrified him. Perhaps my sudden energy. I was full of an edgy, unnatural power. But I was glad of it. I had sucked Franzi's lifestuff from him and drawn it into my own body. Disgusting as this idea might be, I considered it without emotion even as, with familiar skill, I knocked Fritzi's bludgeon from his red, peasant hand and drove the point of my sword directly into his pumping heart. Blood gushed across the cell, covering my naked flesh.

And I laughed at this and suddenly on my lips there formed an alien word. One I had heard only in my dreams. There were other words, but I did not recognize them.

"*Arioch!*" I shrieked as I killed. "*Arioch!*"

Still naked, with broken ribs and ruined face, with one leg which would hardly support my weight, with arms that seemed too thin to hold that great iron battle blade, I picked up Franzi's keys and padded down the darkness of the corridor, unlocking the cell doors as I went. There was no resistance until I reached the guardroom at the far end of the passage. Here a few fat SA lads sat around drowsing off their beer. They only knew they were being killed as they awoke to feel my iron entering their bodies and somehow adding to the power which now raged through my veins, making me forget all pain, all broken bones. I screamed out that single name and within moments turned the room into a charnel house, with bodies and limbs scattered everywhere.

Once the civilized man would have known revulsion, but that civilized man had been beaten out of me by the Nazis and all that was left was this raging, bloodthirsty, near-insensate revenging monster. I did not resist that monster. It wanted to kill. I let it kill. I think I was laughing. I think I called out for Gaynor to come and find me. I had the sword he wanted. Waiting for him.

Behind me in the corridors, prisoners were emerging, clearly not sure if this was a trick of some kind. I flung them every key in the guardroom and made my way out into the night. Even as I reached the courtyard, lights began to come on in the castle. They heard unfamiliar screams and disturbing noises from the prison quarters. I loped like an old, wounded wolf across the compound towards the ranks of huts where the less fortunate prisoners were kept. Anything that threatened me or tried to shoot at me, I killed. The sword was a scythe which swept away wooden gates, barbed wire and men, all at once. I hacked down the wooden legs of a machine gun post and saw the thing collapse, bringing down the wire, making escape far easier. In no time at all I was at the huts, striking the padlocks and bolts off the doors.

I don't know how many Nazis I killed before every hut was opened and the prisoners, many of them still terrified, began to pour out. Up on the castle walls they had got a searchlight working and I heard the pop of their shots as they aimed into the prisoners, apparently at random. Then I saw a group of stripe-uniformed inmates swarm up the wall and reach the searchlight. Within seconds the compound was in darkness as other lights were smashed. I heard Major Hausleiter's voice, crazed with a dozen different kinds of fear, yelling over the general melee.

God knows what any of them made of me, holding a great leaf-bladed longsword in one ruined hand, with my bone-white skin covered in blood, my crimson eyes blazing with the ecstasy of unbridled vengeance as I called out an alien name.

*Arioch! Arioch!*

Whatever demon possessed me, it did not have my feelings about the sanctity of life. Had this monster always lain within me, waiting to be awakened? Or was it my doppelgänger, whom I confused with the sword itself, who drew such wild satisfaction from my unrelenting bloodletting?

Machine gun fire now began to spatter around me. I ran with the other prisoners for the safety of the walls and huts. Some of the prisoners, who had clearly had experience of street fighting, quickly collected the weapons of the men I had killed. Soon shots were spitting back from the darkness and at least one machine gun was silenced.

The prisoners had no need of me. Their leaders were well-disciplined and able to make quick decisions.

With the camp now in total confusion, I went back into the castle and began to climb stairs, looking for Gaynor's quarters.

I had barely reached the second floor when ahead of me I met the same hooded huntress, whom I had seen earlier with Herr El, that mysterious "Diana" who had also appeared in my dreams. Her eyes, as usual, were hidden behind smoked glasses. Her pale hair was loose. She, like me, was an albino.

"You have no time for Gaynor," she said. "We must get away from here soon or it will be too late. They have a whole garrison of storm troopers in Sachsenburg village, and someone is bound to have got through on the telephone. Come, follow me. We have a car."

How had she got inside the prison? Had she brought me the sword? Or was it my doppelgänger? Did they work together? Was she my rescuer? Impressed by the White Rose's powers, I obeyed her. I had already put myself at the society's service and was prepared to follow their orders.

Some of the battle lust was leaving me. But the strange, dark energy remained. I felt as if I had swallowed a powerful drug which could have destructive side effects. But I was careless of any consequences. I was at last taking revenge on the brutes who had already murdered so many innocents. I was not proud of the new emotions which raged through my body, but I did not reject them either.

I followed the hooded woman back into the melee of the compound towards the main gate. The guards were already dead. The huntress stopped to pull her arrows from their corpses as she unlocked the gates and led me through, just as the emergency lighting system began to flicker on. Now the freed prisoners flooded towards the gates and rushed past us into the night. At least some of them would not die nameless, painful and undignified deaths.

As we reached the open roadway, I heard a motor bellow into life. Headlights came on and I heard three short notes on a horn. My huntress led me towards the big car. A handsome man of about forty, wearing a dark uniform I couldn't identify, saluted from behind the steering wheel. He was already driving forward as we climbed in beside him. He spoke good German with a distinctly English accent. It seemed the British Secret Service was already in Germany. "Honored to meet you, dear Count. I'm Captain Oswald Bastable, LTA, at your service. Business has improved in this region lately. We've got some clothes for you in the back, but we'll have to stop later. The schedule's looking a bit tight at the moment." He turned to my companion. "He means to bring them to Morn."

A few shots spat up dirt around us and at least one bullet struck the car.

My battle rage was passing now and I looked down at my ruined body, realizing that I was a mass of blood and bruises. Stark naked. With a bloody longsword in the broken fingers of my right hand. I must have been a nightmarish sight. I tried to thank the Englishman, but was thrown back in my seat as with her famous roar the powerful Duesenberg bore us rapidly along a country road, straight towards a mass of approaching headlights. No doubt these were the storm troopers from Sachsenburg town.

Captain Bastable seemed unperturbed. He was slipping Nazi armbands on his sleeves. "You'd better act as if you're knocked out," he said to me. As the first truck approached, he slowed down and waved a commanding hand from the car. He gave the Hitler salute and spoke rapidly to the driver, telling him to be careful. Prisoners were escaping. They had taken many guards captive and forced them to wear prison stripes before turning them loose into the countryside. There was every chance that if they shot at a man without being sure who he was, they could be killing one of their own.

This preposterous story would create considerable confusion and probably save a few prisoners' lives. Saying he had urgent business in Berlin, Bastable convinced the storm troopers, who were rarely the brightest individuals, and they roared off into the night.

Bastable kept up his own high speed for several hours, until we were climbing a narrow road between masses of dark pines. I was reminded of the Harz Mountains where I had often hiked as a boy. At last I saw a sign for Magdeburg. Thirty kilometers. Sachsenburg lay, of course, to the east of Magdeburg, which was north of the Harz. Another sign at a crossroads. Halberstadt, Magdeburg and Berlin one way, Bad Harzburg, Hildesheim and Hanover the other. We took the Hanover road but, before Hildesheim, Bastable drove into a series of narrow, winding lanes, switching off his car's lights and slowing down. He was buying time, he hoped.

Eventually he stopped near a brook with wide shallow sides where I could easily climb down and wash myself thoroughly in the icy water. Cold as I was, I felt purified and dried myself with the towels Bastable had provided. I hesitated a little when I realized that the clothes he had brought for me were my own, but of the kind one wore for hunting, even down to the knee-high leather boots, tweed breeches and a three-eared cap—what they call a deerstalker in England—which I fastened under my chin. I must have looked like a whiteface clown posing as a country gentleman, but the cap covered my white hair and I could be less readily identified by anyone who had been given a description of us. I pulled on the stout jacket and was ready for anything. Psychologically, the clothes made me feel much better. I wasn't too sure they would look as good with a longsword as with a twelve-bore, but perhaps if I wrapped the sword in something it would be less incongruous.

Bastable had the manner and appearance of an experienced soldier. He was reading a map when I came back and shaking his head. "Every bloody town begins with an 'H' around here," he complained. "I get them mixed up. I think I should have taken a right at Holzminden. Or was it Höxter? Anyway, it looks as if I overshot my turning. We seem to be halfway to Hamm. It'll be daylight fairly soon and I want to get this car out of sight. We have friends in Detmold and in Lemgo. I think we can make it to Lemgo before dawn."

"Are you taking us out of the country?" I asked. "Is that our only choice?"

"Well, it will probably come to that." Bastable's handsome, somewhat aquiline face was thoughtful. "I'd hoped to get all the way tonight. It would have made a big difference. But if we hole up in Lemgo, which is pretty hard to reach, we'll still have a chance of getting clear of Gaynor. Of course, Klosterheim will probably guess where we're eventually heading if the car has been recognized. But I took roads that were little traveled. We'll sleep in Lemgo and be ready for the next part of our journey tomorrow evening."

I fell into an exhausted doze but woke up as the car began to bounce and flounder all over a steep, badly made road full of potholes, which Bastable was negotiating as best he could. Then suddenly, outlined against the first touch of dawn on the horizon, I saw the most extraordinary array of roofs, chimneys and gables, which made Bek look positively futuristic. This was an illustration from a children's fairy tale. We seemed to have driven in our huge modern motorcar to the world of Hansel and Gretel and entered a medieval fantasy.

We had arrived, of course, in Lemgo, that strangely self-conscious town which had embellished every aspect of its picture-book appearance in the most elaborate ways. Its quaintness disguised a dark and terrible history. I had been here once or twice on walking holidays but had stayed only briefly because of the tourists.

Our route from Sachsenburg had been circuitous and could well have thrown any pursuers off our scent. I asked no questions. I was too exhausted and I understood the White Rose Society needed to be discreet with its secrets. I was content at that moment to be free of what had been an extended nightmare.

I wondered if Lemgo had any significance for my liberators. It was the essence of German quaintness. A fortified town, a member of the Hanseatic League, it had known real power, but now it was almost determinedly a backwater, still under the patronage of the Dukes of Lippe, to whom we were distantly related. Its streets were a marvel, for the residents vied with one another to produce the most elaborate housefronts, carved with every kind of beast and character from folklore, inscribed with biblical quotations and lines from Goethe, painted with coats of arms and tableaux showing the region's mythical history.

The bürgermeister's house had a relief depicting a lion attacking a mother and her child while two men vainly tried to frighten the creature away. The house known as Old Lemgo was festooned with plant patterns of every possible description, but the most elaborate house of all, I remembered, was called the Hexenbürgermeisterhaus, the sixteenth-century House of the Mayor of the Witches in Breitestrasse. I glimpsed it as the car moved quietly through the sleeping streets. Its massive front rose gracefully in scalloped gables to the niche at the top where Christ held the world in his hands, while further down Adam and Eve supported another gable. Every part of the woodwork was richly and fancifully carved. A quintessentially German building. Its sweetness, however, was marred a little when you knew that its name came from the famous witch-burner, Bürgermeister Rothmann. In 1667 he had burned twenty-five witches. It was his best year. The previous bürgermeister had burned men as well as women, including the pastor of St. Nicholas's Church. Other pastors had fled or been driven from the town. The fine house of the hangman in Neuestrasse was inscribed with some pious motto. He had made a fat living killing witches. I could not help feeling that this place was somehow symbolic of the New Germany with its sentimentality, its folklore versions of history, its dark hatred of anything which questioned its cloying dreams of hearth and home. The town would never have seemed sinister to me before 1933. What should have been innocent nostalgia had become, in the present context, threatening, corrupted romanticism.

Bastable drove the car under an archway, through a double door and into a garage. Someone had been waiting and the doors were immediately closed. An oil lamp was turned up. Herr El stood there, smiling with relief. He moved to embrace me, but I begged him not to. The energy I seemed to have derived from the sword was still with me, but my bones remained broken and bruised.

We crossed a small quadrangle and entered another old door. The lintels of the doors were so low I had to bend to get through them. But the place was comfortable and there was a relaxing air to it, as if some protective spell had been cast around it. Herr El asked if he could examine me. I agreed and we went into a small room next to the kitchen. It seemed to be set up as a surgery. Perhaps Herr El was the doctor to the White Rose. I imagined him treating gunshot wounds here. As he examined me, he commented on the expert nature of the beatings. "Those fellows know what to do. They can keep a fit man going for a long time, I'd imagine. You yourself, Count von Bek, were in surprisingly good condition. All that exercise with your sword seems to have paid dividends. I'd guess you'll heal in no time. But the men who did this were scientists!"

"Well," I said grimly, "they're passing their knowledge on to their fellow scientists in Hell now."

Herr El let out a long sigh. He dressed my wounds and bandaged me himself. He clearly had medical training. "You'll have to do your best with this. Ideally, you should rest, but there'll be little time for that after today. Do you know what's happening?"

"I understand that I'm being taken to a place of safety via some secret underground route," I said.

His smile was thin. "With luck," he said. He asked me to tell him all that I could remember. When I remarked how I had become possessed, how some hellish self had taken me over, he put a sympathetic hand on my arm. But he could not or would not reveal the mystery of it.

He gave me something to help me sleep. As far as I knew that sleep was dreamless and uninterrupted until I felt the young woman shaking me gently and heard her calling me to get up and have something to eat. There was a certain urgency in her voice which made me immediately alert. A quick shower, some ham and hard-boiled eggs, a bit of decent bread and butter, which reminded me suddenly how good ordinary food could be, and I was hurrying back to the garage where Bastable waited in the driving seat, the young woman beside him. She now carried her arrows in a basket and her bow had become a kind of staff. She had aged herself by about seventy years. Bastable wore his SS-style uniform and I was back in my country clothes, with a hat hiding my white hair and smoked glasses hiding my red eyes.

The young woman turned to me as I climbed into the Duesenberg. "We can deceive almost anyone but von Minct and Klosterheim. They suspect who we really are and do not underestimate us. Gaynor, as you call him, has a remarkable instinct. How he found us so quickly is impossible to understand, but his own car has already passed through Kassel and it's touch and go who'll reach our ultimate destination first." I asked her where that was. She named another picturesque town which possessed an authentic legend. "The town of Hameln, only a few miles from here. It's reached by an atrocious road."

Some might almost call it the most famous town in Germany. It was known throughout the world, and especially in England and America, for its association with rats, children and a harlequin piper.

Again we drove frequently without lights, doing everything we could to make sure that the car was not recognized. A less sturdy machine would have given up long since, but the American car was one of the best ever produced, as good as the finest Rolls-Royce or Mercedes and capable of even greater speeds. The thump of its engine, as it cruised at almost fifty miles an hour, was like the steady, even beat of a gigantic heart. Admiring the brash, optimistic romanticism of its styling, I wondered if America was to be our eventual destination, or if I was to learn to fight Hitler closer to home.

Crags and forests fled by in the moonlight. Monasteries and hamlets, churches and farms. Everything that was most enduring and individual about Germany. Yet this history, this folklore and mythology, was exactly what the Nazis had co-opted for themselves, identifying it with all that was least noble about Germans and Germany. A nation's real health can be measured, I sometimes think, by the degree in which it sentimentalizes experience.

At last we saw the Weser, a long dark scar of water in the distance, and on its banks the town of Hameln, with her solid old buildings of stone and timber, her "rat-catcher's house" and her *Hochzeitshaus* where Tilly is said to have garrisoned himself and his generals the night before they marched against Magdeburg. My own ancestor, my namesake, fought with Tilly on that occasion, to our family's shame.

We turned a tight corner in the road and without warning encountered our first roadblock. These were SA. Bastable knew if we were inspected, they would soon realize we were not what we seemed. We had to keep going. So I raised my arm in the Nazi salute as our car slowed, barked out a series of commands, referring to urgent business and escaped traitors while Bastable did his best to look like an SS driver. The confused storm troopers let us pass. I hoped they were not in regular communication with anyone else on our route.

With no way of bypassing Hameln, and I even doubted that an old bridge could take as large a car as ours across the Weser, we had no choice. Bastable slowed his speed, put on his cap and became stately. I was an honored civilian, perhaps with his mother. We reached the ferry without incident but it was obvious that nothing could take the weight of our car. Bastable drove the machine back to the nearest point to the bridge and led us over on foot. We had no weapons apart from the woman's bow and the black sword I held on my shoulder as I limped in the rear.

We crossed the bridge and soon Bastable was leading us along a footpath barely visible in the misty moonshine. I caught glimpses of the river, of the lights of Hameln, clumps of tall trees, banks of forest. Perhaps the distant headlamps of cars. We seemed to be pursued by a small army. Bastable increased his pace, and I was finding it difficult to keep up. He knew exactly where he was going but also was becoming increasingly anxious.

From somewhere we heard the roar of motor engines, the scream of Klaxons, and we knew that Gaynor and Klosterheim had anticipated our destination. Was there a route by road to where Bastable led us? Or would they have to follow us on foot? I panted some of these questions to Bastable.

He replied evenly. "They'll have split into two parties, is my guess. One coming from Hildesheim and the other from Detmold. They won't have our trouble with the river. But the roads are pretty bad and I don't know how good their cars are. If they get hold of a Dornier-Ford-Yates, for instance, we're outclassed. Those monsters will roll over anything. We're almost at the gorge now. We can just pray they haven't anticipated us. But Gaynor really can't be underestimated."

"You know him?"

"Not here," was Bastable's cryptic reply.

We were stumbling into a narrow gorge which appeared to have a dead end. I'd become suspicious. I thought for a moment that Bastable had brought us into a trap, but he cautioned us to silence and led us slowly along the side of the canyon, keeping to the blackest shadows. We had almost reached the sheer slab of granite which closed us in when from above and to the sides voices suddenly sounded. There was some confusion. Headlamps came on and went out again. A badly prepared trap.

"The sword!" Bastable shouted to me, flinging his body

against the rock as the beams of flashlights sought us out. "Von Bek. You must strike with the sword."

I didn't know what he meant.

"Strike what?"

"This, man. This wall. This rock!"

We again heard the roar of engines. Suddenly powerful head-lamps carved through the darkness. I heard Gaynor's voice, urging the car forward. But the driver was having difficulty. With an appalling scraping of gears, whining and coughing, the car rolled forward.

"Give yourselves up!" This was Klosterheim from above, shouting through a loud-hailer. "You have no way of escape!"

"The sword!" hissed Bastable. The young woman put her quiver over her shoulder and strung her oddly carved bow.

Did he expect me to chop my way through solid granite? The man was mad. Maybe they were all mad and my own disorientation had allowed me to believe they were my saviors?

"Strike at the rock," said the young woman. "It must be done. It is all that will save us."

I simply could not summon enough belief, yet dutifully I tried to lift the great sword over my shoulders. There was a moment when I was sure I would fail and then, again, my doppelgänger stood before me. Indistinct and in some evident pain, he signed to me to follow him. Then he stepped into the rock and vanished.

I screamed and with all my strength brought the great black battle-blade against the granite wall. There was a strange sound, as if ice cracked, but the wall held. To my astonishment, so did the sword. It seemed unmarked.

From somewhere behind me a machine gun rattled.

I swung the blade again. And again it struck the rock.

This time there was a deep, groaning snap from within the depths of the granite and a thin crack appeared down the length of the slab. I staggered back. If the sword had not been so perfectly balanced I could not have swung it for a third time. But swing it I did.

And suddenly the sword was singing—somehow the vibrating

metal connected with the vibrating rock and produced an aston-ishing harmony. It bit deep into my being, swelling louder and louder until I could hear nothing else. I tried to raise the sword for a fourth time but failed.

With a deafening crack, the great slab parted. It split like a plank, with a sharp crunching noise, and something cold and ancient poured out of the fissure, engulfing us. Bastable was pant-ing. The young woman had paused to send several arrows back into the Nazi ranks, but it was impossible to see if she had hit any-one. Bastable stumbled forward and we followed, into a gigantic cave whose floor, at the entrance, was as smooth as marble. We heard echoes. Sounds like human voices. Distant bells. The cry of a cat.

I was terrified.

Did I actually stand at Hell's gates? I knew that if somehow that wall of rock closed behind me, just as it had in the Hameln legend, I would be buried alive, cut off forever from all I had loved or valued. The enormity of what had happened—that I had some-how created a resonance with the blade which had cracked open solid rock to reveal a cave—supported a bizarre legend which everyone knew had grown out of the thirteenth century and the Children's Crusade. I think I was close to losing consciousness. Then I felt the young woman at my elbow and I was staggering forward, every bruise, fracture and break giving me almost unbearable pain. Into the darkness.

Bastable had plunged on and was already lost from sight. I called out to him and he replied. "We must get into the stalagmite forest. Hurry, man. That wall won't close for a while and Gaynor has the courage to follow us!"

A great shriek. Blazing white light as Gaynor's car actually reached the entrance of the cave and drove inside. He was like a mad huntsman in pursuit of his prey. The car was a living steed. No obstacle, no consideration was important as long as he held to our trail.

I heard guns sound again. Something began to ring like bells, then tinkle like glass. A heavy weight came whistling down out of the darkness and smashed a short distance from me. Fragments powdered my body.

The shots were disturbing the rock and ice formations typical of such caves. In the light from Gaynor's car I looked upwards. Something black flew across my field of vision. I saw that Bastable and the young archer were also watching the ceiling, just as concerned for what the gunfire might dislodge.

Another spear of rock came swiftly downwards and bits of it struck my face and hands. I looked up again, lost my footing and suddenly was sliding downwards on what appeared to be a rattling slope of loose shale.

Above me I heard Bastable yelling. "Hang on to the sword, Count Ulric. If we're separated, get to Morn, seek the Off-Moo."

The names were meaningless, almost ludicrous. But I had no time to think about it as I did my best to stop my slide and hold on to Ravenbrand at the same time. I was not about to let go of that sword.

We had become one creature.

Man and sword, we existed in some unholy union, each dependent upon the other. I thought that if one were destroyed the other would immediately cease to exist. A prospect which seemed increasingly likely as the slope became steeper and steeper and my speed became a sickening fall, down and down into impossible depths.

# CHAPTER SIX

# Profundities of Nature

 was weeping with anguish as my body came to rest at last. Somehow I had bonded my hand to the hilt of the sword. Instinctively I knew that the black blade was my only chance of survival. I could not believe I had an unbroken bone. I had no real business being alive at all. The tough, padded deerstalker had saved my head from serious injury. The peak had come down over my eyes but when I at last pushed it up I lay on my back looking into total darkness. Shouts and the occasional shot were far distant, high above. Yet they were my only contact with humanity. I was tempted to shout out, to tell them where I was, even though I knew they would kill me and steal my sword.

Not that I could have shouted. I was lucky still to have my sight. I watched their lights appear on the distant rim. This gave me some hint of the height of the cliff. I could not be sure I was at the bottom. For all I knew I would walk a foot or two and step into a cold, bottomless abyss and fall forever in limbo, held always in that eternal moment between life and death, between consciousness and bleak oblivion. A fate hinted at in those terrible dreams. Dreams which now seemed to have predicted this increasingly grotesque adventure.

But now, with some relief, I could see an end to it. None would find me here. I would soon sleep and then I would die. I would have done what I could against the Nazis and given my life in a decent cause. Dying, moreover, with my sword, my duty and my defender, unsurrendered, as I had always hoped I would die, if die I must. Few men could hope for more in these times.

Then something touched my face. A moth?

I heard the young woman's voice. A murmur, close to my ear. "Stay silent until they're gone."

Her hand found mine. I was surprised how much this comforted me. I took shuddering, painful breaths. There was not a centimeter of my body which did not in some way hurt, but her action allowed the pain no effect. I was instantly heartened. I sensed feelings towards this half-child which were hard for me to identify—feelings of comradeship, perhaps. Only mildly did I feel sexually attracted towards her. This surprised me, for she had a sensuality and grace which would have drawn the attention of most men. Perhaps I was beyond passion or lust. In circumstances like mine, such needs become neurotic and self-destructive, or so it has always seemed to me by observing the erotomanes in my own family. For them the stink of gunpowder was always something a little delicious.

I asked her if, under the circumstances, she would mind telling me her name. Was it really "Gertie"? I heard her laugh. "I was never Gertie. Does the name Oona sound familiar to you?"

"Only from Spenser. The Lady of Truth."

"Well, perhaps. And my mother? Do you not remember her?"

"Your mother? Should I have known her? In Bek? In Berlin? Mirenburg?" Ridiculously, I felt as if I had made a social faux pas. "Forgive me . . ."

"In Quarzasaat," she said, rolling the exotic vowels in a way that showed some familiarity with Arabic. It was not a place I recognized and I said so. I sensed that she did not entirely believe me.

"Well, I thank you, Fräulein Oona," I said, with all my old, rather stiff courtesy. "You have brought me many blessings."

"I hope so." Her voice from the darkness had grown a little abstracted, as if she gave her attention to something else.

"I wonder what's happened to Bastable?" I said.

"Oh, that's not a problem. He can look after himself. Even if they capture him, he'll get free one way or another. For a while at least his part in this is over. But I have only his instructions for finding the river which he promises will lead us eventually to the city of Mu Ooria."

The name was faintly familiar. I remembered a book from my library. One of those unlikely memoirs which enterprising hacks turned out in the wake of Grimmelshausen's *Simplicissimus* and Raspe's *Munchausen*. The author, perhaps the pseudonym for an ancestor, claimed to have visited an underground kingdom, a refuge for the dispossessed, whose natives were more stone than flesh. I'd enjoyed the tale as a boy, but it had become repetitive and self-referencing, like so much of that fantastic stuff, and I had grown bored with it.

I pointed out that I was in rather poor shape for a long walk. I was already surprised by the immensity of the cave system. Did she know how far it extended?

This seemed to amuse her. "Some think forever," she replied, "but it has never been successfully mapped." She told me to wait and went off into that cold darkness. I was astonished by the ease with which she seemed to find her way. When she came back I heard her working at something. At length, I felt her lift me under the shoulders and drag me a few feet until I was lying on cloth. She placed my sword beside me.

"Thank the Nazis for starving you," she said, "or I wouldn't have the strength for this." I felt the cloth rise and tauten under me. I could now feel the sides, like long, smooth saplings, but not wood. And then we were moving forward. Oona the Bow-woman was actually dragging me on a kind of travois.

I noticed with a certain dismay that we were still going downwards, rather than back up towards the crevice I had created with the sword's harmonics. Although never very conscious of it before, even in the dugouts of Flanders, my tendency to claustrophobia was growing. Yet I knew even Oona wasn't strong enough to drag me back to the surface. She seemed to have some sense of what lay ahead. Trying to reach a place of safety which she knew of either from her own experience or from what Bastable had told her. I hoped that Bastable himself had not been captured. No civilized man can imagine the tortures those brutes invented. I shuddered at the thought of Gaynor finding me in this condition. I tried to speak to Oona but became dizzy just from the effort. Soon it scarcely mattered to me, for I passed out at last.

I awoke with a sense that something had changed. The silence around me had become peaceful rather than sinister. There was a whispering, as of a wind through leaves, and I realized that I could see a dim band of light in the distance, as if we faced a horizon.

Oona was faintly visible to me as a dark shape against a darker background. She had prepared food. Something which smelled like turnip, tasted like mashed gingerroot and had an unpleasant slimy texture; but I felt invigorated by it. She told me our breakfast was made from local food. She was used to foraging down here.

I asked her if this cave system was like the famous catacombs of Rome and elsewhere, where victims of religious persecution had hidden, sometimes developing whole communities.

"The victimized do sometimes arrive here," she said, "and find a certain sanctuary, I suppose. But there is a native race, who never venture close to the surface, who are the dominant people."

"Do you mean an entire civilization dwells in this cave system?"

"Believe me, Count Ulric, you will find much more than one civilization down here."

Rationally, I refused to accept this fantastic claim. Even the recently explored caverns of Carlsbad were not so vast.

And yet something in me was prepared to believe her. I sensed an echo of a mysterious truth, something that perhaps I had once known, or that an ancestor had experienced and which was imprinted in my race memory. I knew of the fashionable fascination amongst German bohemians who spoke of a world within the world, whose entrance lay at the North Pole, and I knew some of this nonsense had been given credence by Nazis like the vegetarian crank Hess, but I had never suspected that such an underworld existed beyond the fantasies. Probably it did not. This system, though vast, was bound to be finite and so far there had been no evidence of it being populated by any kind of human settlement. Perhaps Oona herself was one of those who believed the myth. I had no choice but to trust her judgment. She had, after all, saved my life more than once.

I was convinced that Gaynor and Klosterheim were still in pursuit, that my sword meant too much to them. They would follow it, if necessary, into Hell.

As the light grew less faint, I could make little of my surroundings. The echoes told me that the roof of the cavern was very distant, and I began to wonder how much farther we could go down before gravity began to crush us. Mostly what I saw was a kind of reflected glow from icicles and stalagmites. We seemed to be following a smooth road of igneous rock, perhaps some ancient lava path, which wound down towards the shining horizon. As we got nearer, we became aware of a rushing sound which grew louder until it was a distant roar. I could not imagine what was causing the sound. Neither could I guess the source of the light.

We made increasing stops as Oona rested. She was growing tired and the roaring was so loud, so unbroken that we could hardly hear each other. Yet she was determined to continue. Fifteen minutes and she was up again, dragging me and the travois down the gleaming slope until at last the ground leveled out and we were standing on a kind of hillock, looking towards a band of pale pewter light which danced forever ahead of us.

I had tried to ask her what it was, but she couldn't hear me. She was almost as exhausted as I was. I could tell by the way she moved the poles onto her shoulders, settled the makeshift harness around her, and plodded on.

My strength had hardly returned. If I did not see a doctor soon, many of my broken bones would not heal properly and a split rib might pierce some internal organ. I had no special fear for myself, but I acknowledged this reality. I was already reconciled to death. It would give me great satisfaction if I and the sword were lost forever to my enemies.

We kept moving, meter by painful meter, towards the source of the light and the sound. Now, every hour or so, Oona would pause and take a drink from the flask she carried. Then she would force me to swallow some of the ill-smelling stuff. A witch's brew, I said. If you like, she replied.

I had no idea how far or for how long we traveled. The sound grew louder and louder until it pounded like blood in my eardrums. My own skull seemed to have become a vast auditorium. I was aware of nothing else. And, though still dim by ordinary standards, the light was growing so bright it had begun to hurt my eyes. I found it hard to turn my head, but when I did so I saw that the band of sparkling brilliance had grown much higher and was rising into the darkness, illuminating every kind of grotesque shape. I saw frozen rock that seemed organic, that assumed the shapes of fabulous beasts and buildings, of people and plants. Etiolated crags. A silvery light contrasting with the utter blackness of the farther reaches. A place of deep, alarming shadows. A monochrome world in extremes of black and white. A mysterious spectacle. I could not believe it had not been discovered or written about before now. I had no idea of its history or geography. It seemed somehow obscene that the Nazis should be obsessed with exploring and no doubt conquering this weird unspoiled territory. They had a natural affinity, I suppose, for darkness. They sought it out.

For my own part, though it was a wonderful revelation to know that such a world existed, I longed to be free of it. Half-dead as I was, this world shared too much with the grave.

Yet it was clear I was in some ways restored. Whatever remedy Oona had forced me to drink had reinvigorated me in a way that the sword could not. Even the pain of broken bones and torn muscles and flesh was reduced to a single, dull, acceptable ache. I felt fresher and cleaner, as I used to feel when I took an early swim in the river at home.

I wondered if I still had a home. Had Cousin Gaynor fulfilled his promise to pull the place down stone by stone?

Perhaps he now thought me in possession of both cup and sword and would do no further damage to Bek or its inhabitants. But that meant he would be here, somewhere, determined to claim the sword for himself, certain in his madness that I knew the whereabouts of a mythical and probably nonexistent Holy Grail.

The roar seemed to absorb us. We became part of it, drawn closer and closer to its source as if hypnotized. We made no resistance, since this was our only possible destination.

Using the poles of the travois and with the sword slung over my back on a piece of queerly tough fiber Oona had given me, I was now able to hobble forward beside her. The light had the brilliance of the flash powder cameramen use. It blinded and dazzled, so that Oona soon replaced her smoked glasses and I drew the peak of my deerstalker down over my eyes. Effectively we were blind and deaf and so moved even more slowly and carefully.

The phosphorescence curved in a wide ribbon that stretched across our horizon and fell, almost like a rainbow, downwards into sparking blackness. Farther away one could just make out another glowing area, much wider than the great band of light which pierced the darkness of the vast cavern. None of this light revealed a roof. Only the depth of the echo gave any notion of height. It might have been a mile or two up. The roar, of course, was coming from the same source as the light. And so, I now began to notice, was the heat.

If complex life did exist so far below the surface of the earth, I now knew at least how it survived without the sun.

From the humidity I guessed us to be approaching the river Bastable had mentioned. I was unprepared for the first sign that we were near. Like winking fireflies at first, the rocks soon became alive with the same silvery blaze we could see ahead. Little stars blossomed and faded in the air and began to fall on our bodies.

Liquid. I thought at first it must be mercury but realized it was ordinary water carrying an intense phosphorescence, no doubt drawn from a source closer to the surface, perhaps under the sea.

Oona was more familiar with the stuff. When she found a pool, she cupped her hands and offered some to me. The water was fresh. Her hands now glowed, so that she resembled some garish saint from a commercial Bible. Where she pushed back her hair, her head was briefly surrounded by a halo. Wherever the water clung to us, we were jeweled in pewter and glinting quicksilver. She signed that I could drink if I wished. She bent to her hands and sipped a little. For an instant, her lips glowed silver and her ruby eyes regarded me with enthusiastic glee. She was enjoying my astonishment. For a few seconds the water passing down her throat illuminated veins and organs so that she seemed translucent.

I was entranced by these effects. I longed to know more about them, but the roar continued to deafen us and it was still hard to look directly at the horizon.

As the phosphorescent water fell on our heads and bodies, covering us with tiny fragments of stars, we ascended smooth, slippery rocks at the point where the great wall of light began its gentle downward curve.

At last we could see the reason for the roaring. A sight which defied anything I had witnessed in all my travels. A wonder greater than the seven which continue to astonish surface dwellers. I have often said that the wonders of the world are properly named. They cannot be photographed or filmed or in any way reproduced to give the sense of grandeur which fills you when you stand before them, whether it be Egypt's pyramids or the Grand Canyon. These unknown, unnamed falls were like something you might discover in Heaven but never on our planet. I was both strengthened and weakened by what I observed. To describe it is beyond me, but imagine a great glowing river widening across a falls vaster than Victoria or Niagara. Under the roof of a cavern of unguessable height, whose perimeters disappear into total darkness.

A vast tonnage of that eerie water crashed and thundered, shaking the ground on which we stood, rushing down and down and down, a mighty mass of yelling light and wild harmonies that sounded like human music. Throwing monstrous shadows everywhere. Revealing galleries and towers and roads and forests of rock, themselves throwing out soft illuminating silver rays like moonbeams. Relentlessly carrying the waters of the world down to the heart of creation, to renew and be renewed.

Something about that vision confirmed my belief in the existence of the supernatural.

I felt privileged to stand at the edge of the mighty cataract, watching that fiery weight of water tossing and swirling and sparking and foaming its way down a cliff whose base was invisible, yet which became a river again. We could see it far below, winding across a shallow valley and forming at last the main mass of shining water which I now realized was a wide underground sea. At least this geography followed surface principles. On both sides of the river, on the rising banks of the valley, were slender towers of white and gray light so varied they might have been the many-storied apartment blocks of the New York skyline. The formations were the strangest I'd ever experienced. My geologist brother, who died at Ypres, would have been astonished and delighted by everything around us. I longed to be able to record what I was seeing. It was easy to understand why no explorer had brought back pictures, why the only record of this place should be in a book by a known fantast, why sights such as these were incredible—until witnessed.

In the general yelling turbulence and showering silver mist, I had not considered what we would do next and was alarmed when Oona began to point down and inquire, through signs, if I had enough energy to begin a descent. Or should we sleep the night at the top?

Although weak, I did everything I could to move under my own volition. I still felt Gaynor had a chance of catching us. I knew I would feel more secure when I had put a few more miles between us. On the other hand, I was deeply uncomfortable with my circumstances and longed to begin the climb back to the surface, to get to a place where I could continue the common fight against Adolf Hitler and his predatory psychopathic hooligans.

I didn't want to continue that descent, but if it was the only way, I was prepared to try. Oona pointed through the glittering haze to a place about halfway down the gorge, where I saw the outlines of a great natural stone bridge curving out over the water, apparently from bank to bank. That was evidently our destination. I nodded to her and prepared to follow as she began to make her way carefully down a rough pathway which appeared to have been covered with droplets of mercury. The roaring vibrations, the long fingers of stone which descended from the roof or rose from the ground, the light, the massive weight of water, all combined to half mesmerize me. I felt I had left the real world altogether and was in a fantastic adventure which would have defeated the imagination of a Schiller.

In all directions the rock flowed in frozen, organic cascades. Every living thing on earth seemed to have come here and fused into one writhing chimera so that trees turned into ranks of bishops and bishops into grinning gnomes. Ancient turtle heads rose from amongst nests of crayfish and their eyes were the eyes of basilisks. You felt they could still reach you. Gods and goddesses like those intricate carvings on the pillars of Hindu temples or Burmese pagodas. I found it impossible to believe at times that this was not the work of some intelligence. It reproduced every aspect of the surface, every human type and every animal, plant and insect, sometimes in grotesque perspective or magnified twenty times. As if the stuff of Chaos, not yet fully formed, had been frozen in the moment of its conception. As if an imagination had begun the process of creating an entire world in all its variety—and been interrupted.

This vision of a not-quite-born world made me long for a return to the darkness which had hidden it from me. I was beginning to go mad. I was coming to realize that I did not have the character for this kind of experience. But something in me pushed me on, mocked me to make me continue. This is what they had tried to reproduce in Egypt and in Mexico. This is what they remembered in their Books of the Dead. Here were the beast-headed deities, the heroes, the heroines, angels and demons and all the stories of the world. There was no evident limit to these statues and friezes and fields of crystal looming over us, no far wall which might help us get our bearings. I had begun to understand that we had passed beyond any point where a compass could help us. There were no conventional bearings here. Only the river.

Perhaps those Nazi pseudoscientists had been right and our world was a convex sphere trapped in an infinity of rock and what we perceived as stars were points of light gleaming through from the cold fires which burned within the rock.

That I was experiencing full proof of their theory was no comfort. Without question we explored an infinity of rock. But had that rock once lived? Or did it merely mock life? Had it been made up of organic creatures like us? Did it strive to shape itself into the life of the surface as, in a less complex way, a flower or a tree might strive through the earth to reach the light? I found it easy to believe this. Anyone who has not had my experience need only find a picture of the Carlsbad Caverns to know exactly what I mean.

Pillars looked as if they had been carved by inspired lunatics so that you saw every possible shape and face and monster within them, and each rock flowed into another and they were endless in their variety, marching into the far darkness, their outlines flickering into sharp relief and dark shadow from the white fire flung up by that enormous phosphorescent river as she heaved herself endlessly into the heart of the world. Like Niagara turned into moonlit Elfland, an opium-eater's dream, a glorious vision of the Underworld. Did I witness the landscapes and the comforts of the damned? I began to feel that at any moment those snaking rocks would come alive and touch me and make me one of themselves, frozen again for a thousand years until brought to predatory movement only when they sensed the stray scuttling of creatures like ourselves, blind and deaf and lost forever.

The beauty which the river illuminated inspired wonder as well as terror. High above us, like the delicate pipes of fairy organs, were thousands and thousands of hanging crystal chandeliers, all aflame with cool, silvery light. Occasionally one of the crystals would catch a reflection and turn whatever color there was to brilliant, dazzling displays which seemed to travel with the water, flickering, through the haze, following the currents as that huge torrent endlessly roared, flinging its voice to the arches and domes above even as it fell.

I could not believe that the system could go so deep or, indeed, be so wide. It seemed infinite. Were there monsters lurking there? I remembered an engraving from Verne. Great serpents? Gigantic crocodiles? Descendants of dinosaurs?

I reminded myself that the real brutes were still somewhere behind us. Even Verne, or indeed Wells, had failed to anticipate the Nazi Party and all its complex evil.

No doubt Gaynor and his ally, Klosterheim, had more ambitious motives than helping the Nazi cause. My guess was that if the Nazis were no longer useful to them, the two men would no longer be Nazis. This made them, of course, an even greater threat to us. They believed in no cause but their own and thus could appear to believe in all causes. Gaynor had already showed me both his charming and his vicious side. I suspected there were many shades of charm and, indeed, viciousness which others had seen. A man of many faces. In that, he reflected some of Hitler's qualities.

I cannot explain how I inched down that long, slippery pathway, much of it with Oona's help, constantly aware of the broken bones in my foot but, thanks to her potion, in no severe pain. I knew my ruined body couldn't support me for much longer.

We at last reached the extraordinary bridge. It rose from the surrounding rock with that same sinuous dynamic as if something living had been frozen only moments before. Against the glowing spray its pale stone columns were outlined before us in all their cathedral-like beauty. It reminded me of a fantasy by the mad Catalan architect Gaudi or our own Ludwig of Bavaria, but far more elaborate, more delicate. Flanked on both sides by tall spires and turrets, all formed by the natural action of the caverns and again bearing that peculiarly organic quality, its floor had not been naturally worn but smoothed to accommodate human feet. The delicate silvery towers marched across the gorge through which the glowing river ran in caverns "measureless to man, down to a sunless sea." Had the opium poets of the English Enlightenment seen what I was now seeing? Had their imaginations actually created it? This disturbing thought came more than once. My brain could scarcely understand the exact nature of what my eyes witnessed and so I was inclined, like any ordinary lunatic, to invent some sort of logic, to sustain myself, to stop myself from simply stepping to one unguarded edge of that great bridge and leaping to my inevitable death.

But I was not by nature suicidal. I still had some faint hope of getting medical assistance and a guide back to the surface where I could do useful work. The roar of the water in the chasm below made it impossible to ask Oona questions and I could only be patient. Having rested, we began to hobble slowly across the bridge, I using my sword as a rough crutch and Oona using her carved bow-staff.

The foam from the torrent below engulfed the bridge in bright mist. I slowly became aware of a figure, roughly my height, standing in my path. The fellow was a little oddly shaped and also seemed to support himself on a staff. Oona pressed forward, clearly expecting to be met.

When I drew close, however, I realized the figure who waited to greet us was a gigantic red fox, standing on his hind legs, supporting himself with a long, ornamental "dandy pole" and dressed elaborately in the costume of a seventeenth-century French nobleman, all lace and elaborate embroidery. Awkwardly removing his wide-brimmed feathered hat with one delicate paw, the fox mouthed a few words of greeting and bowed.

With some relief, as if escaping a nightmare, I lost consciousness and fell in a heap to the causeway's quivering floor.

# CHAPTER SEVEN

## People of the Depths

nable to accept any further assault on my training and experience, my mind did the only thing it could to save itself. It had retreated into dreams as fantastic as the reality, but dreams where I appeared at least to have some control. Again I experienced the exultation of guiding not just one great sinuous flying reptile but an entire squadron of them. Racing up into cold, winter skies with someone held tight against me in my saddle, sharing my delight. Someone I loved.

And there stood my doppelgänger again. Reaching towards me. The woman had vanished. I was no longer riding the dragon. My double came closer and I saw that his face was contracted with pain. His red eyes were weeping pale blood. At that instant I no longer feared him. Instead I felt sympathy for him. He did not threaten me. Perhaps he tried to warn me?

Slowly the vision faded and I knew a sense of extraordinary, floating well-being. As if I was being reborn painlessly from the womb. And as I relaxed, my rational mind slowly came awake again.

I could accept the existence of an underground kingdom so vast as to seem infinite. I could accept and understand the effects of its weird formations on my imagination. But a fox out of a fairy tale was too much! In my feverish attempts to absorb all those alien sights, it was quite possible I'd imagined the fellow. Or else had become so used to the fantastic that I had failed to recognize an actor dressed up for a performance of *Volpone.*

Certainly the fox was nowhere to be seen when I opened my eyes. Instead, looming over me, was the figure of a giant, whose head resembled a sensitive version of an Easter Island god. He looked down on me with almost paradoxical concern. His uniform alarmed me until I realized it was not German. I hardly found it extraordinary that he was wearing the carefully repaired livery of an officer in the French Foreign Legion. An army doctor, perhaps? Had our journey brought us up into France? Or Morocco? My prosaic brain jumped at ordinary explanations like a cat at a bird.

The large legionnaire was helping me to raise myself in the bed.

"You are feeling well now?"

I had answered, rather haltingly, in the same language before I realized we were speaking classical Greek. "Do you not speak French?" I asked.

"Of course, my friend. But the common tongue here is Greek and it's considered impolite to speak anything else, though our hosts are familiar with most of our earthly languages."

"And our hosts are what? Large, overdressed foxes?"

The legionnaire laughed. It was as if granite cracked open. "You have met Milord Renyard, of course. He was eager to be the first to greet you. He thought you would know him. I believe he was friendly with an ancestor of yours. He and your companion, Mademoiselle Oona, have continued on urgently to Mu Ooria, where they consult with the people there. I understand, my friend, that I have the honor to address Count Ulric von Bek. I am your humble J.-L. Fromental, lieutenant of France's Foreign Legion."

"And how did you come here?"

"By accident, no doubt. The same as M'sieur le Comte, eh?" Fromental helped me sit upright in the long, narrow bed, whose shallow sides tightly gripped even my half-starved body. "On the run from some unfriendly Rif, in my case. Looking for the site of ancient Ton-al-Oorn. My companion died. Close to death myself I found an old temple. Went deeper than I suspected. Arrived here." Everything in the room seemed etiolated. The place felt like certain Egyptian tombs I had seen during that youthful trip with my school to the ancient world and the Holy Land. I half expected to see cartouches painted on the pale walls. I was dressed in a long garment, a little on the tight side, rather like a nightshirt, which they call a djellaba in Egypt. The room was long and narrow, like a corridor, lit by slim glasses of glowing water. Everything was thin and tall as if extended like a piece of liquid glass. I felt as if I was in one of those "Owl Glass Halls" of mirrors which were such a rage in Vienna a few years ago. Even the massive Frenchman seemed vaguely short and squat in such surroundings. Yet strange as everything was, I had begun to realize how well I felt. I had not been so fit and at one with myself since the days of my lessons with old von Asch.

The silence added to my sense of well-being. The sound of water was distant enough to be soothing. I was reluctant to speak, but my curiosity drove me.

"If this is not Mu Ooria, then where are we?" I asked.

"Strictly speaking this is not a city at all, but a university, though it functions rather more variously than most universities. It is built on both sides of the glowing torrent. So that scientists can study the waters and understand their language."

"Language?"

That was the nearest translation. "These people do not believe that water is sentient as animals are sentient. They believe everything has a certain specific nature which, if understood, allows them to live in greater harmony with their surroundings. It's the purpose of their study. They are not very mechanically minded, but they use what power they discover to their advantage."

I imagined some lost oriental land, similar to Tibet, whose peoples spent their lives in spiritual contemplation. They had probably come here, much as we had come, hunted by some enemy, then grown increasingly decadent, at least by my own rather puritanical standards.

"The people here brought you back to health," Fromental told me. "They thought you would rather wake to a more familiar type of face. You will meet them soon." He guessed what I had been thinking. "There are practical advantages to their studies. You have been sleeping in the curing ponds for some long time. Their bonesetters and muscle-soothers work mostly in the ponds." At my expression he smiled and explained further. "They have pools of river water, to which they have added certain other properties. No matter what your ailment, be it a broken bone or a cancerous organ, it can be healed in the curing ponds, with the application of certain other processes specific to your complaint. Music, for instance. And color. Consequently, timeless as this place is, we are even less aware of the familiar action of time as we know it on the surface."

"You do not age?"

"I do not know."

I was not ready for further mysteries. "Why did Oona go on without me?"

"A matter of great urgency, I gather. She expects you to follow. A number of us are leaving for the main city, which lies on the edge of the underground ocean you saw from above."

"You travel together for security?"

"From a habit of garrulousness, no more. Expect no horrid supernatural terrors here, my friend. Though you might think you've fallen down a gigantic rabbit burrow, you're not in Wonderland. As on the surface, we are at the dominant end of the food chain. But here there is no hot blood. No conflicts, save intellectual and formal. No real weapons. Nothing like that sword of yours. Here everything has the quiet dignity of the grave."

I looked at him sharply, looking for irony, but he was smiling gently. He seemed happy.

"Well," I admitted, "bizarre as their medicine might be, it seems to work."

Fromental poured me a colorless drink. "I have learned, my friend, that we all see the practice of medicine a little differently. The French are as appalled by English or American doctoring as the Germans are by the Italians and the Italians by the Swedes. And we need not mention the Chinese. Or voodoo. I would say that the efficacy of the cure has as much to do with the analysis and treatment as it does with certain ways of imagining our bodies. What's more, I know that if the cobra strikes at my hand, he kills me in minutes. If he strikes at my cat's neck, my cat might feel a little sleepy. Yet cyanide will kill us both. So what is poison? What is medicine?"

I let his questions hang and asked another. "Where is my sword? Did Oona take it with her?"

"The scholars have it here. I'm certain they intend to return it to you now that you are well, They found it an admirable artifact, apparently. They were all interested in it."

I asked him if this "university" was the group of slender pillars I had seen from the distance and he explained that while the Off-Moo did not build cities in the ordinary sense, these two groups of pillars had been adapted as living quarters, offices and all the usual accommodation of an active settlement, though commerce as such was not much practiced by them.

"So who are these utopians? Ancient Greeks who missed their way? Descendants of some Orpheus? The lost tribe of Israel?"

"None of those, though they might have put a story or two into the world's mythologies. They're not from the surface at all. They are native to this cavernous region. They have little practical interest in what lies beyond their world but they have a profound curiosity, coupled with habitual caution, which makes them students of our world but instinctively unwilling to have intercourse with it. When you have lived here for a while you'll understand what happens. Knowledge and imagination are enough. Something about this dark sphere sets people to dreaming. Because death and discomfort are rare, because there is little to fear from the environment, we can cultivate dreaming as an art. The Off-Moo themselves have little desire to leave here and it's a rare visitor who is willing to return to the upper world. This environment makes intellectuals and dreamers of us all."

"You speak of these people as if they were monks. As if they believed there was purpose to their dreaming. As if their settlements were great monasteries."

"So they are in a way."

"No children?"

"It depends what you mean. The Off-Moo are parthenogenetic. While they often form lasting unions, they do not need to marry to reproduce. Their death is also their birth. A rather more efficient species than our own, my friend." He paused, putting a gentle hand on my shoulder. "You'd best prepare yourself for many surprises. Unless you decide to jump in the river or go so far you fall into the lands that are called Uria-Ne by the Mu Oorians. The Lands Beyond the Light is what we would call them, I suppose. Or perhaps just the Dark World. These people do not fear that world as much as we do. But only a desire for painful death would take you there."

"Is that not our own world they describe?"

"It could be, my friend. There are few simplicities in this apparently black and white environment. You and I do not have the eyes to see the beauties they perceive, nor the subtleties of tone and shade which to them are vivid as our surface roses or sunsets. Soon you could become as obsessed as I with understanding the sensibilities of this gentle and complex people."

"Perhaps," I said, "when the time comes for me to want peace. But meanwhile in my own country there is a ruthless enemy to be fought, and fight him I must."

"Well, every man must be able to look his best friend in the eye," said Fromental, "and I will not dissuade you. Can you walk? Come, we'll seek what advice we can from Scholar Fi, who has taken a strong interest in your welfare."

I found that I could walk easily with a great sense of energy. I followed Fromental, who had to squeeze his massive body through some of the doors, down a sinuous spiral walkway and at last into the street. I was almost running as I reached the cool, damp outside air. Yet the nature of that dreaming town, apparently bathed in perpetual moonlight, with spires so slender you would think the slightest sound would shatter them, with its basalt pathways and complex gardens of pale fungi whose shapes echoed those of the rocks, made me walk slowly with respect. As we left our elongated Gothic doorway behind, I smelled a dozen delicious, delicate, warm scents, perhaps of prepared food. And the plants had a musty perfume you sometimes find above ground. The delicate aroma you associate with certain truffles.

The towers themselves were of basalt fused with other kinds of rock to produce the effect of creatures trapped behind thick glass, perpetually staring out at us. This natural architecture, which intelligent creatures had fashioned to their own use, was of extraordinary beauty and delicacy and sometimes, when a faint shudder from the river shook the ground, it would sway and murmur. Buildings suddenly brought to life. All this pale wonder framed against the shifting glow of the blazing river and the more distant light from the lake. I suddenly saw the river as their version of the Nile, the mother of all civilizations. Was that why I made that instinctive connection with the builders of the pyramids?

As we walked I asked Fromental if he knew Bastable. Fromental had met him once at this very university. He understood that Bastable regularly visited the main city of Mu Ooria.

"So it is possible to come and go?"

Fromental was amused. "Certainly, my friend. If you're Bastable. That Englishman belongs to a somewhat exclusive group of people who are able to travel what some call the moonbeam roads. It's a talent denied me. He can move from one sphere to another at will. I understand he believes you to be a very important fellow."

"How could you know that?"

"From Ma'm'selle Oona. Who else?"

"I think he values my sword more than he values me."

"Scholar Gou knows him. I've heard him speak about it. I think Bastable values both."

And then we had stepped through another archway and

entered a house that seemed made of flesh and blood internal organs yet was cold marble to the touch.

We were in a very high chamber lit by a chandelier containing dozens and dozens of the same long, slender light bottles I had seen earlier. Around the walls of the chamber were charts, diagrams, pictures in many languages. The dominant script reminded me of the most beautiful Arabic in its flowing, elaborate purity. Clearly the written speech of the Off-Moo. All in what to my eye was monochrome, as if I had entered a film set and was trapped in a wild adventure serial.

Fromental's voice seemed even deeper and more resonant. "Count von Bek, may I present my good friend and mentor Scholar Fi, who directed the team which healed you."

My voice sounded coarse and heavy in my own ears. I could scarcely open my mouth and not gape. At first I thought I had come upon my doppelgänger, but this figure was far taller and thinner, even though his long, thin triangular features were an exaggerated version of my own. He too was an albino. But his skull must have been at least twice the length of mine and about half the width and was framed by a conical headdress that went to a point, exactly mirroring the length and shape of the scholar's face. The hat fanned over his shoulders across a garment identical to my own, with long "mandarin" sleeves and a hem that trailed the floor. I could not make out the size or shape of his feet. His robe, however, was woven from the same fine silk as the one I wore. His slanting ruby eyes, his long ears and strangely shaped brows all made his face a parody of my own. Were people like this my ancestors? Was it Off-Moo genes which made me an earthly outcast? Had I found my own people? The sudden sense of belonging was overwhelming and I almost wept. I recovered myself and thanked him gravely for his hospitality. And for bringing me back to life.

"You are most welcome." As soon as the creature spoke in the beautiful, liquid formality of Greek, I knew that my preconceptions had been nonsense. "It's only rarely I have the privilege of serving one of your particular physiology, which has much in

common with our own." His voice was gentle, precise, lilting—
almost a song. His skin was if anything paler than my own and
much thinner. His eyes were a kind of rosy amber, and his ears
slanted back from his head, ending in points. My own ears,
though not as exaggerated, were similar to his. They were called
"devil's ears" in my part of the world.

Scholar Fi seemed an enthusiastic host. He asked after my
well-being and said if I had any questions he would answer them
as best his poor powers allowed. I had a feeling Fi spoke with the
modesty of genius. First he took me to an alcove and showed me
my sword resting there. Fromental, perhaps discreetly, said he had
some business on the outskirts of the city and would rejoin us
later.

Scholar Fi suggested we stroll in the shade-flower forest,
which was restful and aromatic, he said. Gently he led me from
his house through serpentine streets where orderly natural rows
of gigantic pagoda stalagmites marched into the distance, all illuminated by the glow from the river. As I looked closer I realized
the vast pillars were thoroughly occupied. Such glorious architecture would touch a chord in any romantic, finding that
authentic frisson the poets entreated us to seek. What would
Goethe, for instance, make of all this extraordinary, pale beauty?
Would he be as overwhelmed, both aesthetically and intellectu-
ally, as I?

Scholar Fi led me through a series of twitterns to a wall and a
gateway. We passed into an organic world of pale grey and silver—
an astonishing spectacle of huge plants which grew from a single
massive stem and opened like umbrellas to form a canopy displaying delicately shaded membranes. The giant plants also
resembled living organs, like a cross section in a medical book.
They gave off a heavy, narcotic scent which did not so much
sedate as excite. My vision seemed to improve. I noticed more
detail, more shades. Fi told me that in Mu Ooria there were gardens like this as large as earthly countries. The flowers and their
stalks were important sources of nutrients and remedies, as well as
materials from which to make their furniture and so on. They

grew in rich silt which the river brought from the surface. "The river brings us everything we need. Food, heat, light. Originally we lived in towers and galleries already hollowed by the water's action but gradually, as our numbers expanded—we occasionally give birth to twins—we learned to fashion houses from within, using chiefly elemental methods."

Although not entirely understanding some of his answers, I asked him how old their civilization was. I could not believe a human traveler had never visited this place and returned with his story. Scholar Fi was regretful. He was not an expert in time, he said. But he would find someone who could probably translate for me. He thought his people had probably existed for about as long as our own. The journey between one world and the other was a matter of luck, since it involved crossing the Lands Beyond the Light, and the methods we used on the surface to measure space were less than helpful there. That is why they never felt curious enough to visit what Scholar Fi called "the Chaos side," presumably the surface. Their notions of the natural universe were as alien as their ideas of medicine. I could only respect them. I was getting a glimmering of their logic, beginning to understand the way the Off-Moo perceived reality. I could understand Fromental's fascination. As I walked in that narcotic mist, the huge veins and sinews of the plate plants vibrating overhead, I casually considered the idea of forgetting Hitler and staying here, where life was everything it should be.

"Fromental and a party of others leave for Mu Ooria when the current turns to the fourth harmony. You will be wanting to go with them? Can you hear the harmonies, Count Ulric? Are you familiar with"—a glint of dry humor—"our aural weather?"

"I fear not," I said.

He produced a small piece of metal from his sleeve, holding it in those incredibly long fingers that seemed too delicate to grasp a bird feather. He then blew on the metal, producing a sweet vibration.

"That is the sound," he said.

I think he expected me to remember it after hearing it only

once. I decided that my best chance was to stay with Fromental at all times and depend upon his experience and wisdom.

"I am hoping to get help in Mu Ooria," I said. "I need to return to my own world. I have a duty to perform."

"There you will find our wisest people who will help you if they can."

I remembered to ask him more about the creature who had met us on the bridge. Lord Renyard was an explorer and a philosopher, said Scholar Fi. His old home had been destroyed in a supernatural battle and his current home was under threat, but he was a regular visitor. "He has never known others of his own kind. You are probably lucky that he wasn't able to pump you on your knowledge of the thinkers and scholars he admires. He has a great enthusiasm for one of your philosophers. Do you know Voltaire?"

"Only as well as the average educated man."

"Then you are probably fortunate."

I had not expected sarcastic humor from such a being as Scholar Fi and again I was charmed. There were more and more reasons why I should stay here.

"He wanted to greet you so badly." Scholar Fi led me around a great piece of bulbous root that seemed to rise and fall like a creature breathing. "He was acquainted apparently with one of your ancestors, a namesake, whom he had known before his fiefdom was destroyed by warfare. He had considerable praise for this Count Manfred."

"Manfred!" The family had always considered him an embarrassment. A liar on the scale of Munchausen. A scapegrace and turncoat. A spy. A Jacobin. A servant of foreign kings. An adventurer with women. "His name is never mentioned."

"Well, Lord Renyard seemed to think he was a fair scholar of the French Enlightenment, by which he sets great store."

"My ancestor Manfred was a scholar only of the street song, the beer stein and the good-natured strumpet." He had brought such shame to the family that a later ancestor of mine destroyed many of his accounts and suppressed others. Manfred had been the hero of a famous burlesque opera: *Manfred; or, The Gentleman*

*Houri.* There had been some attempt by his contemporaries to have him declared insane but after escaping the French Assembly, of which he had briefly been a member, he kept his head and disappeared into Switzerland. The last anyone heard, he had appeared in Mirenburg in the company of a Scottish aerial engineer by the name of St. Odhran. They had made claims for an airship which they could not substantiate. Eventually they escaped from angry investors in their vessel. Apparently they turned up again later in Paris selling a similar scheme. By that time, to our family's intense relief, the name von Bek was no longer used. He was also known as the Count of Crete, and rumor had it that he was hanged as a horse thief in the English town of York. Other stories claimed he had lived near Bristol as a woman for the rest of his life, broken by love. And another story told how he had tracked a piper out of Hameln, never to be seen again. I became disturbed. Was I following in the footsteps of legendary ancestors whose lives had been so secret even their nearest and dearest did not know who they really were? And was it my destiny to be destroyed by the knowledge which had almost certainly destroyed them?

Scholar Fi was baffled by my opinion of Manfred. "But I am learning more and more about your perceptions."

I tried to explain how we no longer believed the old myths and folktales of our ancestors and he continued to be mystified. Why, he wondered, would one idea have to be rejected in favor of another? Did we only have room in our heads for one idea at a time?

Scholar Fi trembled all over with laughter. He trilled appreciatively at his own wit. This was completely charming and I found myself joining in. Even in motion there was a quality about the Mu Oorian which made it seem a delicate stone figure had become animated.

Suddenly my host cocked his head to one side. His hearing was far more acute than mine. He began to turn.

In time to see Fromental walking rapidly towards us.

"Scholar Fi, Count Ulric. Citizens reported their approach. I went to verify it. I can now tell you that a party of about a hundred armed men, equipped with the latest technical help, have crossed the bridge and now wait at the outskirts. They're demanding to speak to our 'leader.'"

I had no time to explain the notion to the bewildered scholar. Fromental turned to me. "I think it's your particular nemesis, my friend. His name is Major von Minct and he seems to believe you are a criminal of some kind. You stole a national treasure, is that it?"

"Do you believe him?"

"He seems a man used to power. And used to lies, eh?"

"Did he threaten you?"

"His language was relatively diplomatic. But the threats were implicit. He's used to getting his way with them. He wants to speak to you. To persuade you to do your duty and turn yourself over to the forces of law and order. He says he has not much time and will only use enough violence to demonstrate his power." Clearly Fromental had not believed a word of Cousin Gaynor's story. But a hundred swaggering storm troopers could do considerable damage to creatures with no understanding of war or any other form of aggression. I feared for Scholar Fi's people more than I feared for myself.

"Do you wish to speak to this man?" asked Scholar Fi.

I did my best to explain what had happened and in the end he raised one long-fingered palm. Did I mind, he asked, if he came with me to meet Gaynor? Uncertainly, I agreed.

Gaynor and his army of uniformed ruffians were lounging about near the bottom of the bridge. The sound of the water was louder here, but Scholar Fi's voice carried through it. He made a small speech of welcome and asked Gaynor their business. Gaynor uttered the same nonsensical claims. And Scholar Fi laughed in his face.

Klosterheim, beside Gaynor, instantly drew his Werther PPK from its holster and pointed it at Scholar Fi. "Your creature had best show more respect for an officer of the Third Reich. Tell him to be careful or I'll make an example of him. To quote the

Führer—'Nothing is so persuasive as the sudden overwhelming fear of extinction.'"

"I am serious about the sword." Gaynor's terrible eyes looked straight into mine. The little sanity he had when he entered the caverns had been driven out of him by what he had experienced here. "I will kill anyone who stops me from holding her. Where have you hidden her, cousin? My love. My desire. Where's my Ravenbrand?"

"She's hidden herself," I said. "You'll never find her here and I'll never tell you where she is."

"Then you are responsible for this monster's death," said Klosterheim. He leveled his pistol straight at the gentle scholar's domed forehead and pulled the trigger.

# BOOK TWO

*Gone to the world beyond the world,*
*Gone to the sea beyond the sea.*
*Orpheus and his brothers*
*Seek wives amongst the dead.*

—LOBKOWITZ, "Orpheus in Auschwitz," 1949

# CHAPTER EIGHT

# The Arms of Morpheus

t that moment, as Klosterheim squeezed his automatic's trigger, I understood profoundly how I'd left my familiar world far behind and was now in the realm of the supernatural.

Klosterheim's gun barked for the briefest moment and there was no echo. The sound was somehow absorbed into the surrounding atmosphere. Then I watched as the bullet stopped a few inches from the barrel, and was *swallowed* in the air.

Klosterheim, an oddly fatalistic expression on his face, lowered his arm and holstered his useless weapon. He glanced meaningfully at his master.

Gaynor swore. "God be damned—we're in the Middlemarch!"

Klosterheim understood him. And so did I. A memory as ancient and mysterious as my family's blood.

The surrounding landscape, alien as it was, felt far too solid for me to believe myself dreaming. The only other conclusion had been edging at the corners of my mind for some time. It was as logical as it was absurd.

As Gaynor had guessed, we had entered the mythical

Mittelmärch, the borderlands between the human world and Faery. According to old tales, my own ancestors had occasionally visited this place. I'd always assumed that realm to be as real as the storybook world of Grimm, but now I was beginning to wonder if Grimm was no more than a recollection of my present reality. Hades, too, and all the other tales of underworlds and other worlds? Was Mu Ooria the original of Alfheim? Or Trollheim? Or the caverns where the dwarfs forged their magic swords?

As the strange scene unfolded before me, all these images and thoughts passed through my mind. Time really did seem to have an indescribably different quality in this twilight realm. A foreign *texture*, a sense of richness, even a slight instability. I was sensing a way of living simultaneously at different speeds, some of which I could actually manipulate. I'd already experienced a hint of this quality in my recent dreams, but now I was certain that I was more awake than I had ever been. I was beginning to sense the multiverse in all her rich complexity.

Now that he had an idea of his geography, Klosterheim seemed more at ease than any of us. "I have always preferred the night," he murmured. "It is my natural element. When I am at my predatory best." A long, dry tongue licked thin lips.

Scholar Fi offered Klosterheim a shadowed smile. "You could try to kill me by some other means, but I can defend myself. It would be unwise to pursue your present aggression. We have countered violence before in our history. We have learned to respect all who respect life. We do not show the same respect for those who would destroy life and take all with them into the oblivion they crave. Their craving we are able to satisfy. Though it is a journey that can only be made alone."

I cast my eye over the Nazi ranks to see if any of them but their leaders understood the scholar's Greek, but it was clear all they heard were threatening foreign sounds. My attention was caught by a figure at the back of the party and to the right, standing beside a tall stalagmite, like a set of giant dishes stacked one on top of the other. The figure's face was obscured by an elaborate helmet and its body was clad in what appeared to be armor of coppery silver, gleaming like dull gold in the semidarkness. The baroque armor was almost theatrical, like something designed by Bakst for a fantastic Diaghilevian extravaganza. I felt I had glimpsed Oberon in Elfland. I turned to ask Fromental if he had seen the figure, but the Frenchman's attention was on Gaynor again.

My cousin had scarcely been listening to Scholar Fi. He drew the ornamental Nazi dagger from its scabbard at his belt. Pale steel and polished ebony, the hilt reflected the dancing, misty light. The blade's gleam seemed to pierce the atmosphere, challenging the whole organic world around us.

Balancing the dagger on the flat of his hand, Gaynor thrust it out to his side. His eyes challenged mine. Without turning his head he called behind him in German. "Lieutenant Lukenbach, if you please."

Proud of his master's recognition, a tall brute in SS black stepped forward and closed his fingers almost voluptuously around the dagger. He waited like an eager hound for his orders,

"You have the temerity to speak of aggression." Gaynor took a cigarette from his case. "You shall know that you challenge the authority of the Reich. Whether you realize it or not, my undernourished friend, you are now citizens of the Greater Germany and bound by the laws of our Fatherland." This speech was spoiled by his failure to ignite his cigarette. He threw both lighter and cigarette to the ground. "And some of your own laws, too, it seems . . ."

He was mocking himself. I admired his coolness, if not his folly, as he signed Lieutenant Lukenbach forward. "Show this fellow how sharp our old-fashioned Ruhr steel can be."

I became increasingly fearful for Scholar Fi, who lacked the physical strength to defend himself against the Nazi. Fromental, too, was looking a little worried, but motioned me back. He was prepared to trust the Off-Moo's sense of survival.

Neither Scholar Fi's expression nor his stance had changed as he watched this threatening drama. He seemed completely unmoved, murmuring in Greek as the SS man approached.

I would have been terrified by what I saw in Lukenbach's eyes
alone. They held that familiar dreaming glaze I had seen so many
times in recent months—the look of the sadist, of a creature
allowed to fulfill its most vicious yearnings in the name of a higher authority. What had the Nazis awakened in the world?
Between relativism and bigotry, there is no room for the human
conscience. Perhaps without conscience, I thought, there could
only be appetite and ultimate oblivion—an eternity of unformed
Chaos or petrified Law, which found such excellent expression in
the lunacy of communism and fascism whose grim simplifications
could only lead to sterility and death and whose laissez-faire cap-
italist alternative also brought us ultimately to the same end. Only
when the forces were in balance could life flourish at its finest.
The Nazi "order," however, was a pretense at balance, a simplified
imposition on a complex world—the kind of action which always
brought the most destruction. The fundamental logic of reaction.
I was about to witness another example of that destructive power
as the SS officer came slowly on.

Lukenbach's eyes were greedy for butchery. He drew back his
arm and began to take the last few paces towards us, grinning into
Scholar Fi's extinction.

Unable to restrain myself as the Off-Moo's life was threatened,
I sprang forward, ignoring Fromental and the scholar. But before I
could reach Lukenbach, another man appeared between us. This
figure was also clad from head to foot in armor as baroque as the
other I had seen, but his was jet black. Unfamiliar as his costume
was, the face was all too familiar. Gaunt, white, with blazing eyes
hard as rubies. It was my own. It was the creature I had already
seen in my dreams and later in the concentration camp.

I was so shocked by this that I was stopped in my tracks, too
late to grapple with the Nazi. "Who are you?" I asked.

My doppelgänger was prepared to reply. He mouthed some
words, though I heard nothing. Then he moved to one side. I tried
to see where he went, but he had vanished.

Lukenbach was almost on his victim. I could not reach him in
time.

Slowly Scholar Fi raised a long, slender arm, perhaps in warning. Lukenbach continued to advance, as if he were himself
entranced. His grip on the swastika dagger tightened as he prepared to aim his first blow.

This time both Fromental and I instinctively moved to defend
the scholar but he gestured us back. As Lukenbach came within
striking distance the Off-Moo opened his mouth wider than any
human's, almost as if he unhinged his jaw like a snake, and
shrieked.

The sound was at once hideous and harmonious. A ululation,
it seemed to weave its way through the quivering stalactites overhead, threatening to bring them all down on us. Yet I had the
impression the shriek was directed very precisely and pitched in a
specific way.

Overhead crystal began to tinkle and murmur in sympathetic
vibration. Yet none broke free.

The shriek seemed endless, as melodic as it was controlled.
High above, the crystals continued to rustle and chime until gradually they formed a single sweet harmonic whose note, surprisingly
harsh, ended with a sudden *snap*.

A single slender spear had broken clear of its companions, as
if the Off-Moo had selected it, and was dropping down towards
the threatening Nazi whose grin broadened as he anticipated his
pleasure. Clearly he thought Scholar Fi was shrieking with fear.

The crystal shaft hesitated a short distance above
Lukenbach's head. The Off-Moo was controlling the thing with
sound alone.

The shriek ended. Scholar Fi made a tiny movement of his lips.
In response to a murmured command, the crystal lance changed its
angle and rate of descent. Then the scholar gestured very carefully.
The stalactite described a gentle arc and then, with an almost elegant impact, struck deep, precisely into the Nazi's heart.

That shriek continued to echo through the endless caverns
while Lukenbach's death throes took their rapid course.

He lay still on the rocky surface, his blood welling up around
the crystal spear jutting from his chest. Fromental and I were

shocked by this death as much as we welcomed it. Gaynor was clearly revising his strategy.

My cousin bent forward and retrieved his dagger from Lukenbach's stiffening fingers. With some distaste he stepped back, straightening and looking directly into my eyes.

"I'm learning not to underestimate you, cousin. Or your comrades. Are you sure you won't throw in with us? Or failing that give me the Raven Sword and I'll promise to harass you no further."

I allowed myself to smile at his knowing effrontery while Fromental declared, "You're in a rather weak bargaining position at the moment, my friend."

"I have a habit of strengthening my position." Gaynor was still looking directly at me. "What d'you say, cousin. Stay here with your new friends and I'll take the sword back to the real world to carry on the fight against the forces of Chaos."

"You're not the forces of Chaos?" My amusement grew.

"They are exactly what I fight. Which is why I must have the Black Sword. If you return with me, you'll have honors, power— power to make the kind of justice the world is crying out for! Hitler is merely a means to this end, believe me."

"Gaynor," I said, "you've given yourself in service to the Beast. You'll bring nothing but chaos to the world."

It was my cousin's turn to laugh in my face. "Fool. Have you no idea how wrong you are? You're duped if you believe I serve Chaos. Law's my master and ever will be! What I do, I do for a better, more stable, predictable future. If you also believe in such a future, come over to our side while you can, Ulric. It's you who serves the cause of Chaos, believe me."

"This sophistry's unworthy of a Mirenburger," I said. "You have demonstrated your loyalty to evil. You are wholly selfish, I've witnessed your cruelty, heard your callousness too often, to be persuaded of any sincerity you protest, other than a sincere need to devour us all. Your love of Law's no more than a madman's obsession with tidiness, Gaynor. That's not harmony. Not true order."

A strange expression crossed Gaynor's handsome features as if he recalled memories of better times. "Ah, well, cousin. Ah, well."

"They're dupes, my lord," said Klosterheim suddenly. He looked troubled. "There's no convincing them."

"And do you, Herr Klosterheim, regard yourself a noble servant of Law?" asked Fromental.

Klosterheim turned his barren eyes on the Frenchman. He smiled his bleak, loveless smile. "I serve my own master. And I serve the Grail, whose guardian I shall again become. We shall meet again, gentlemen. As I told you, I am at last in my element. I have no fear of this place and shall eventually conquer it." He paused and looked around him in joy. "How often I have yearned for the night and resented the interruption of day. Sunrise is my enemy. Here I can come into my own. I am not defeated by you."

Gaynor seemed surprised by this outburst.

"A somewhat old-fashioned view," I said. "You sound as if you've been reading far too much romantic poetry, Herr Major."

He leveled glowering eyes at me and said flatly: "I am an old-fashioned man, a cruel and vengeful man." For a moment his voice was filled with poisoned dust.

"You must go now," said Scholar Fi suddenly. "If you are found in the light, our guards will kill you."

"Go? Go where? What guards?"

"Go into the dark. Beyond the light. Our guards are many." Scholar Fi gestured and it seemed the pointed rocks all around moved slightly. In each one I saw the face of an Off-Moo. "Time is not our master, the way it is yours, Prince Gaynor."

Gaynor and Klosterheim had underestimated us. I don't believe we underestimated them. Gaynor von Minct had become a handsome, watchful snake. "If we go back, we can return with an army."

"More than one army has been lost here," said the scholar casually. "Besides, you are unlikely to get back to the place you left and equally unlikely to find an entrance to our world again. No, you will journey to the darkness, beyond the river, and there you will learn to survive or perish, as fate decides. There are many others of your kind out there. Remnants of those same armies. Whole tribes and nations of them. Men as resourceful as yourselves should survive well and no doubt discover some means of flourishing."

Gaynor was contemptuous, disbelieving. "Whole nations? What do they live on?"

Scholar Fi began to turn towards the settlement. His patience had expired. "They are primarily cannibals, I understand."

He paused as we joined him. He looked back. Gaynor and the Nazis had not moved.

"Go!"

He gestured.

Gaynor continued to defy him.

Scholar Fi moved his mouth again, this time in a kind of echoing whisper. About a dozen crystal spears came crashing down a foot or two from the Nazis. We stood there and watched as Gaynor gave the command to retreat. Slowly the party disappeared into the darkness.

"We are unlikely to see them again," said the Off-Moo. "Their time will be taken up with defending themselves rather than attacking us."

Fromental's eyes met mine. Like me, he did not share the scholar's confidence.

"It's perhaps as well we're traveling to Mu Ooria," he said. "We should at least report this."

"I agree," said the scholar. "And because of the circumstances, I suggest you take the *voluk,* rather than go on foot. We have no clear idea how closely the time flows coincide in this season, so it is as well to be cautious." He was not expressing anxiety, rather common sense.

Fromental nodded his huge head. "It will be interesting," he said.

"What is the *voluk?*" I asked him, after we had parted from Scholar Fi.

"I have never seen it," he said.

When he returned me to my quarters, Ravenbrand was waiting for me. My hosts were telling me to be prepared for the worst.

I slept fitfully for what seemed a few hours, but my dreams were confused. I saw a white hare running across the underground landscape, running through sharp crags and looming inverted pillars, running towards the towers of Mu Ooria, pursued by a red-tongued, jet-black panther. I saw two horsemen riding across a frozen lake. One horseman wore armor of silvered copper, glaring in the light from a pale blue sky. The other, who challenged him, wore armor of black iron, fashioned in fantastic forms, with a helm on his head that resembled a dragon about to take flight. The face of the black-clad horseman was my twin. I could not see the face of the other horseman, but I imagined it to be Gaynor, perhaps because I had encountered him most recently. As I fell in and out of these dreams, I wondered about my doppelgänger, who had clearly not wanted me to interfere in the Off-Moo's defense. Was I deluded? Was it only I who could see him? Was there some Freudian explanation to my dreams and visions? And if what I saw was real, how was it possible? I consoled myself that in Mu Ooria I might learn a little more of the truth. Oona, for instance, would be glad to educate me. And there, I decided, I would ask for help in returning to my own Germany, to join in the fight against an evil which must soon engulf the whole of Europe and perhaps the world.

I had been awake for only a short time when Fromental called for me. I was surprised to see that he was carrying a sword at his hip and a bow and quiver of arrows on his back.

"You're expecting attack?" I asked.

"I see no point in not being ready for trouble. But I believe Scholar Fi's optimism is probably well founded. Your cousin and his band will have much to occupy them in the Lands Beyond the Light."

"And why do you travel to Mu Ooria?" I asked him.

"I hope to meet with some friends of Lord Renyard's," he said. And would not be drawn further.

I had wrapped my sword in a cloth and bound it up so that I, too, could sling it over my back. I had a few provisions and changes of clothing and was now wearing my own familiar outfit, complete with deerstalker, which looked even more incongruous than Fromental's kepi.

After we had breakfasted on some rather bland broth, he led me through the twisting streets until we stood at last on the banks of the river, in a kind of cut where the waters were calmer. Scholar Fi and a group of Off-Moo were already on the harborside, apparently in lighthearted conference.

My own astonished attention was drawn to what was moored there. At first I thought the thing alive, but then I guessed it to be cunningly fashioned from some kind of crystalline stone, predominantly of dark marOone and crimson. The massive vessel seemed to have been carved from a single ruby. Yet the stone was light as glass and sat easily in the waters like a ship. The *voluk* looked like some mythical sea beast drawn up from the depths where it had long since petrified. As I regarded its fishy, reptilian face, all flared nostrils and jowls and coiling tendrils, I imagined that it looked at me. Was it alive? I had a nagging memory . . .

On the *voluk*'s back was a large, flat area, created by a kind of enormous saddle, making a platform, a raft large enough to take fifteen or twenty passengers and steered by two massive sweeps, one on each side.

I was impressed by the size as well as the complexity of the carving and remarked on it to Fromental as we followed the Off-Moo crew up the gangplank to where they took their places at the oars.

The Frenchman was amused by this. "It's nature's hand, not the Off-Moo's, you must blame for this monster. They draw these remains from their lake and find that with only minor modification, they can employ them as rafts. But, of course, they're rarely used, since they have to be dragged back upstream. Clearly, by putting a *voluk* at our disposal, our hosts are showing they believe the situation to be serious."

"They expect attack from Gaynor, when they are so easily able to defend themselves? Have they a means of seeing into the future?"

"They can see a million futures. Which in some ways is the same as not seeing any. They trust their instincts, I suspect, and know Gaynor's type. They know he will scarcely sleep until he has been revenged for what happened out there. They have survived for so long, my friend, because they anticipate danger and are ready to counter it. They will not underestimate men such as Gaynor. Whatever lives out there in the Lands Beyond the Light seems dangerous enough, from what I've learned. But the Off-Moo know that periodically one of the creatures unites the others in a truce, long enough to try to attack Mu Ooria. They can see that Gaynor and Klosterheim have the intelligence and motive to succeed in creating some kind of alliance of the darklands tribes. All hate Mu Ooria because at some stage Mu Ooria has welcomed them and then banished them to the outer darkness."

"Are we all eventually banished there?"

"By no means. Wait until you get to Mu Ooria herself!" Fromental clapped me on the back, clearly relishing the wonders he would soon be showing me.

Scholar Fi approached us as we settled into the shallow seats at the center of the raft. He was gracious. He hoped we would return, he said, and let them all know how we fared. Then he went ashore, the gangplank was raised, and the slender Off-Moo, in their nodding conical cowls and their flowing pale robes, lent their strength and experience to the sweeps, guiding us out of the calm water and into the black, star-studded channel of the main river.

At once the current caught us. The crew had little to do but keep the monstrous hull on course. We moved with alarming speed, sometimes striking white water as the river narrowed between high banks and seemed to pour even deeper into the core of the planet.

Not, of course, that we were any longer on the planet, as we knew it. This was the Mittelmärch, which obeyed the laws of Elfland.

The dark waters were surprisingly clear and it was often possible to see to the bottom, where the rock had been worn to an artificial smoothness. I wouldn't have been surprised to learn that we were actually moving along a man-made canal. The light grew increasingly bright as we neared the lake and the temperature also grew warmer, suggesting that this inland sea was the source of the Off-Moo civilization. It was to them what the sun and the Nile were to Egypt.

Although both banks were visible most of the time, the shadows and strange shapes of the rocks, the way the light from the water constantly varied, made it seem that the river course was populated with all kinds of monsters. Gradually I became used to the phantasmagoric nature of the swiftly passing landscape. But then, as I admired a grove of slender stalagmites which grew just on the edge of the water, like Earthly reeds, I was sure I saw an animal of some kind.

It was not a small animal. The light had caught its eyes, emerald green, glaring at me from the darkness. I turned to Fromental, asking him if he knew what creature it might be. He was surprised. There were usually no animals about larger than the Off-Moo themselves. Then, in a length of bank where the light flickered strongly, I saw it again.

I'd seen it once before. In my dream. A gigantic cat, far larger than the largest tiger, jet black, its red tongue lolling from a jaw filled with sharp, white fangs, and two enormous curving incisors. A saber-toothed panther, its long tail lashing even as it ran, was keeping pace with us. A creature of my dreams. Running beside the raft as the current bore us towards the Off-Moo capital!

Now Fromental could see the beast. He knew what it was. "Those cats are never normally found this close to the river, as they loathe and fear it. They hunt the Lands Beyond the Light. The cannibals are their natural prey. They're greatly feared because they can see in the dark, if not in the conventional sense. Though it seems those eyes look at you, in fact the beasts are completely blind."

"How do they hunt? How is that beast able to follow us?"

"The Off-Moo tell me it is heat. Somehow the eyes see heat rather than light. And their sense of smell is extraordinary. They can pick up certain scents that are a mile or more away. The dark-landers live in terror of them. The Off-Moo believe the cats are their greatest single protection against threats from the cannibals."

"The cannibals don't hunt the panther?"

"They can hardly protect themselves against it. Superstition and fire are about all they have in their defense, for they, too, are largely blind. They instinctively fear the creatures, for whom they are relatively easy prey."

But the Off-Moo were alarmed now that they could see the cat. They spoke in high-pitched Greek which was almost impossible for me to understand. Fromental told me that this sign increased their anxiety, their sense of danger. Why had the cat come so close to the river?

"Perhaps nothing more than curiosity," suggested my friend.

He signaled to Scholar Brem, an acquaintance, and went to talk to him. When he came back he seemed disturbed. "They fear that some powerful force drives the cats away from their usual hunting grounds. But there again it might just be an isolated young male looking for a mate." I didn't see the great, black saber-tooth again. We were already slowing as the thrust of the river met the embrace of the blazing lake, whose further shores were lost in the pitch-darkness beyond.

Gradually, just as one might from a ship or a train entering the outskirts of a mighty city, we began to notice that the formations around us had given way to the slender living towers of the Off-Moo. These towers often reflected soft shades, the merest wash of color, which added to their mysterious beauty. Curious Off-Moo began to appear on the banks and on their balconies while our steersmen strained against their sweeps, catching the current which bore us gracefully in towards a harbor, where several similar petrified sea monsters were moored.

With considerable skill, the sweepsmen brought the raft alongside a quay of elaborately carved rock. On it a small crowd waited to greet us. For the most part they were Off-Moo, subtly individual in their conical hoods, but then I recognized a shorter figure standing to one side and knew such pleasure, such relief, that I was surprised by the depth of my own emotion. I had come to care very much for Oona. Her pale, albino beauty gave her an even more ethereal quality in this world than it had in my own. But that was not what gladdened my heart. It was a feeling far more subtle. A sense of recognition, perhaps? I hurried off the bizarre raft and onto the basalt of the quayside, running to greet her, to embrace her, to feel the warmth, the reality, the profound familiarity of her.

"I am glad you are here," she murmured. She embraced Fromental. "You have arrived in time to meet Lord Renyard's friends. They bring desperate news. As we suspected, our foes attack three realms at least, all of them strategic. Your own world is in mortal peril. Tanelorn herself is again under deep siege, this time from Law, and could fall at any moment. And now, it seems, Moo Uria herself faces her greatest threat. This is not coincidence, gentlemen. We have a very powerful opponent." She was already leading us away from the docked raft, through twisting, narrow streets.

"But Tanelorn can't be conquered," said Fromental. "Tanelorn is eternal."

Oona turned serious eyes up towards his distant face. "Eternity as we understand it is in jeopardy. All that we take for granted. All that is permanent and inviolable. Everything is under attack. Gaynor's ambitions could bring about the destruction of sentience. The end of consciousness. Our own extinction. And possibly the extinction of the multiverse herself."

"Perhaps we should have killed him when he first threatened us," said Fromental.

The young huntress shrugged her shoulders as she led us into one of the slender buildings. "You could not kill him then," she said. "It would be morally impossible."

"How so?" I asked.

Her tone was matter-of-fact, as if I had missed the most obvious answer in the world.

"Because," she said, "at that point in your mutual histories he had yet to commit his great crime."

# CHAPTER NINE

# A Conference of Spheres

I was having difficulties with Mittelmärch notions of time. It seems we were all fated to live identical lives in billions of counterrealities, rarely able to change our stories, yet constantly striving to do so. Occasionally, one of us was successful, and it was the effort to change that story which somehow helped maintain the balance of the universe—or rather the multitude of alternate universes Oona called "the multiverse," where all our stories were being played out in some form.

Oona was patient with me but I was of a prosaic disposition and such notions didn't sit easily with my ideas of common sense. Gradually I began to see the broader vision, which helped me understand how our dreams were simply glimpses of other lives, often at their most dramatic, and how it was possible for some of us to move between these dreams, these other lives, and even sometimes change them.

She spoke of these matters after she had taken me to my quarters and allowed me to refresh myself. Then, when I was reinvigorated, she led me out into the sinuous streets of Mu Ooria, a vital, crowded city which was far more cosmopolitan than I had anticipated. Clearly not all humans were banished into the darkness. Entire quarters were filled with people of many different races and creeds, evidence of a great mingling of cultures, including that of the Off-Moo. We passed through street markets which might have flourished in modern Cologne, between houses which would not have been out of place in medieval France. Clearly the Off-Moo had a long history of welcoming refugees from the surface, and these people had kept their habits and customs, blending happily with the others.

As well as the familiar, there was also the exotic. Oona led me past reflective jet and basalt terraces festooned with pale lichens and fungi, balconies of sinuous limestone whose occupants were sometimes indistinguishable from the rock. This eternal, sparkling night had a luring beauty of its own. I could understand how so many chose to settle here. While you might never know sunlight and fields of spring flowers, neither would you know the kind of conflict which could rob you of both in an instant.

I understood and sympathized with the people who had chosen to live here, but I longed to see again the familiar, robust, cherry cheeks of our honest Bek peasantry. Not one of the inhabitants of this place looked entirely alive, though they obviously took pleasure in their existence and enjoyed a high level of complex civilization, despite the sense of the crushing weight of rock overhead, the knowledge of this land's dark boundaries, the hush which seemed to settle everywhere, the slightly exaggerated courtesy you didn't expect to find in a busy metropolis. I had every admiration for it but would never choose to settle here myself. Would I ever now find my way back to my fatherland?

Again I was filled with a sense of desperate frustration. I loved my country and my world. All I wanted was the opportunity to fight for what was decent and honorable in both. I needed to take my place with those who resisted a cowardly terror. Who encountered cruelly philistine forces wishing to destroy everything that had ever been valuable in our culture. I told Oona this, as we continued to stroll through the winding canyons of the city, admiring gardens and architecture, exchanging pleasantries with passersby.

"Believe me, Count Ulric," she assured me, "if we are successful, you will have every opportunity to fight the Nazis again. But there is much to be done. The same battle lines are being drawn on at least three separate planes and at this stage it looks as if our enemies are stronger."

"You're suggesting I fight for the same cause by taking part in your struggle?"

"I am saying that the cause is the same. How you serve it will ultimately be your decision. But it will be simultaneous with other decisions." She smiled at me and put her delicate hand into mine, leading me eventually into a great, natural circle, slightly con- cave, close to the city's center. Here there were no stalagmites, and the stalactites in the roof were hidden by the deep shadow created by the lake's glare.

I thought at first this was an amphitheater, but there was no evidence that it accommodated any kind of audience. Leading out of the circle was one wide main thoroughfare which seemed to go directly to the lake. If the Off-Moo were a different people I would have assumed it was designed to display some kind of mil- itary triumph—a returning navy might parade up this avenue and its victorious forces present themselves to the people in the great, shallow bowl.

Oona was amused by my stumbling suggestions, my noticing that the floor seemed to have been worn smooth by thousands of feet, that there was a faint, familiar smell to the place.

"This is the only chance you will have to come here," she said. "Assuming the tenant returns."

"Tenant?"

"Yes. He has lived with the Off-Moo for as long as their his- tory. Some think they came to this world together. There is even evidence that the city was created around him. He is very old indeed and sleeps a great deal. Periodically, perhaps when he is hungry, he leaves this place and travels down there"—she point- ed to the broad avenue—"to the lake. The times of his disappear- ances vary, but he has always returned."

I looked around for some kind of dwelling. "He lives here without furniture or shelter?"

She was enjoying my mystification.

"He is a gigantic serpent," she said. "In appearance not unlike the *voluk,* but much bigger. He sleeps here and offers no harm to the Off-Moo. He has been known to protect them in the past. They believe that he goes into the lake to hunt. A strange beast, with long side fins, almost like the wings of a ray, but primarily reptilian. Some believe he has vestigial limbs secreted within his body, that he is in fact more lizard than snake. Not unlike those resurrected husks they turn into rafts, though much larger, of course."

"The World Serpent?" Half amused, half in awe, I referred to the mythical Worm Oroborous, said by our ancestors to guard the roots of the World Tree.

Surprisingly her tone was sober when she replied. "Perhaps," she said. Then, deliberately, she lightened her mood and took my hand again.

I was suddenly conscious that I was trespassing and was glad to let her laugh and lead me through another series of winding twittens to show me the pastel glories of the water gardens, fashioned from natural stone and cultivated fungi. Glimmering points of light from the misty miniature falls reflected all the subtle colors of the bizarre underground fauna. My guide was delighted at my enchantment, taking proprietorial pride in the wonders of Mu Ooria.

"Could you not learn to love this place?" she asked me, linking her arm in mine. With her I felt a friendliness, a comfortable closeness which I had never experienced with another woman. I found it relaxing.

"I love it already," I told her, "and I think the Off-Moo a civil and cultivated race. An exemplary people. I could stay here for a year and never experience all the city has to offer. But it isn't in my nature, Fraülein Oona, to take exotic holidays while my nation is threatened by a monster far more dangerous than Mu Ooria's adopted serpent!"

She murmured that she understood my concern and that she would do everything she could for me. I asked after Captain Bastable, the mysterious Englishman, but she shook her head. "I believe he's engaged elsewhere."

"So will you, who clearly can come and go at will, lead me out of here?"

"There are dream roads," she said. "Finding them isn't difficult. But getting you back to where you came from can sometimes prove impossible." She raised a hand to forestall my anger. "I have promised you that you'll have the chance to fight your enemies. Presumably you would like to be as successful as possible?"

"You are telling me to be patient. What else can I be?" I knew she was sincere. I gave her arm an affectionate squeeze. I felt I had known her all my life. She might have been one of my more attractive relatives, a niece perhaps. I recalled her rather odd expectation that I would know her. Now I understood that, in the conflicting time streams of the multiverse, it was possible for something to be both mysterious and familiar. She had no doubt mistaken me for someone else, even one of my myriad "other selves" who, if she and the Off-Moo were to be believed, proliferated throughout a continuously branching multiverse.

I was not comforted by her assurance that I had not one doppelgänger but an infinite number. Which reminded me to ask her about the two bizarre figures I had seen earlier. One of them had been my double.

She found my news disturbing, rather than surprising. She asked me precise questions and I did my best to answer. She shook her head. "I did not know there were such forces at work," she said. "Not such great forces. I pray some of them choose to ally their cause with our own. I might have misused or misunderstood my mother's skills."

"Who were those armored men?"

"Gaynor, if he wears the armor you describe. The other is his mortal enemy, one of the greatest of your avatars, whose destiny is to change the very nature of the multiverse."

"Not an ancestor, then, but an alter ego?"

"If you like. You say he was asking you for something?"

"My guess."

"He is desperate." She spoke affectionately, as if of a very familiar friend. "What did Fromental see?"

"Nothing. These were glimpses only. But not illusions. At least, not in any sense I understand."

"Not illusions," she confirmed. "Come, we'll confer with Fromental and his friends. They've had long enough without us."

We crossed a series of canals rather like those of Venice, one narrow bridge after another, following natural gullies and fissures employed as part of the city's water system. I was impressed by how the Off-Moo adapted to the natural formations of the earth. Goethe, for instance, would have been impressed by their evident respect for their surroundings. Ironically, those surroundings, if described in my own world, would have been taken for the fantasies of some opium-addicted Coleridge or Poe. A tribute to the majority's capacity to deny any truth, no matter how monumental, which challenges its narrow understanding of reality.

Eventually we entered a small square and Oona led me into a doorway and up a twisting, asymmetrical staircase until we came into a large room, surprisingly wide for an Off-Moo apartment. The place was furnished more to human taste, with large couches and comfortable chairs, a long table loaded with food and wine. Evidently a meal had been eaten while Fromental conferred with Lord Renyard and the three strangers who rose to greet us as we entered the room.

I had never, outside of a comic opera, seen such a collection of swaggering fantasticoes. Lord Renyard wore the lace and embroidery of a mid-seventeenth-century fop, balancing his slightly unsteady frame on an ornamental "dandy pole." A scarlet silk sash over his shoulder held the scabbard of a slender sword. His eyes narrowed in pleasure as he recognized us. "My dear friends, you are most welcome." He bowed with an awkward grace. "May I introduce my fellow citizens of Tanelorn—Baron Blare, Lord Bragg and Duke Bray. They seek to join forces against the common enemy."

These three were all dressed in the exaggerated uniforms of Napoleonic cavalry officers. Baron Blare had huge side-whiskers and a wide, horsey grin displaying large, uneven teeth. Lord Bragg was a glowering, self-important cockerel, all blazing wattles and comb, while Duke Bray had a solemn, mulish look to his huge face. Although not as distinctly animal-like as Lord Renyard, they all three had a slight air of the farmyard about them. But they were cordial enough.

"These gentlemen have come by a hard and circuitous route to be with us," Fromental explained. "They have walked the moonbeam roads between the worlds."

"Walked?" I thought I had misheard him.

"It's a skill denied to many." Lord Renyard's voice was a sharp, yapping bark. He spoke perfect classical French but he had to twist his mouth and vocal cords to get some of his pronunciations. "Those of us who learn it, however, would travel no other way. These are my good friends. When we understood the danger, we all left Tanelorn together. Our Tanelorn, of course. We were separated some while ago, during an alarming adventure. But they came here at last and brought fresh news of Tanelorn's plight."

"The city is under siege," said Fromental. "Gaynor, in another guise, attacks it. He has the Higher Worlds on his side. We fear it will soon fall."

"If Tanelorn falls, then all falls." Oona was pacing. She had not expected such dramatic news. "The doom of the multiverse."

"Without help Tanelorn will most certainly perish," said Lord Bragg. His flat, cold voice held little hope. "The rest of our world is already conquered. Gaynor rules there now in the name of Law. His patron is Lady Miggea the Mad. And he draws on the power of more than one avatar."

"We came here," said Duke Bray, "searching for those avatars in the hope that we could stop them combining. In our world it has happened already. Here, Gaynor has barely begun to test his power."

I didn't understand. Oona explained. "Sometimes it is possible, with immortal help, for two or more avatars of one person to be combined. This gives them considerably greater power, but they lose sanity. Indeed, such an unnatural blending threatens the stability of the entire multiverse! The one who draws on the souls of his avatars in this way takes terrible risks and can pay a very great price for the action."

Something in the way she glanced at me caused me to shudder. The chill went deep into my bones and would not leave me.

"We can't let Mu Ooria be attacked because of us," I said. "Why don't we lead an expedition into the Dark Land and strike at them first? It will take Gaynor months to marshal a force."

Oona smiled grimly. "We cannot anticipate the rate at which time passes for him."

"But we know we can defeat him."

"That depends," said Lord Renyard, apologetic for interrupting.

"On what?"

"On the quality of help we can summon. I would remind you, dear Count von Bek, that in our world all that remains unconquered is Tanelorn herself. Gaynor has mighty help. The help of at least one goddess."

"How has Tanelorn resisted up to now?" I asked.

"She is Tanelorn. She is the city of eternal sanctuary. Usually neither Chaos nor Law dare attack here. She is the embodiment of the Grey Fees."

Oona came to my rescue. "The Grey Fees are the lifestuff of the multiverse—you could call them the sinews, muscles, bones and sap of the multiverse—the original matter from which all else derives. The original home of the Holy Grail. Although creatures can meet in the Grey Fees, even dwell there if they choose, any attack on them, any fight that takes place within the Fees, is an affront to the very basis of existence. Some would call it an affront to God. Some believe the Grey Fees to be God, if the multiverse itself is not God. I prefer to take a more prosaic view. If the multiverse is a great tree, forever growing, shedding limbs, extending roots and branches in all directions, each root and branch a new reality, a new story being told, then the Fees are something like the soul of the entity. However crucial the struggle, we never attack the Grey Fees."

"Is attacking Tanelorn the same as attacking the Grey Fees?" I asked.

"Simply call it an alarming precedent," said Lord Bray, showing more irony than I first suspected in him.

"So Gaynor threatens the fundamental fabric of existence. And if he succeeds?"

"Oblivion. The end of sentience."

"How might he succeed?" My habits of logic and strategy were returning. Old von Asch had taught me how to reason.

"By recruiting the help of a powerful Duke of Law or Chaos. There are elements in either camp who believe that if they control everything, the multiverse will accord better with their own vision and temperament. The lives of the gods have cycles when senility and bigotry replace sense and responsibility. Such is the case with Gaynor's ally in our realm."

"A god, you said?"

"A goddess, as it happens." Lord Blare uttered an unruly laugh. "The famous Duchess Miggea of Dolwic. One of the most ancient of Law's aristocrats."

"Law? Surely Law resists such injustice?"

"Aggressive senility isn't only a characteristic of Chaos in its decline. Both forces obey the laws of the multiverse. They grow strong and virile, then decline and die. And, in their dying, they are often desperate for life. At any price. All past loyalties and understanding disappear, and they become little more than appetites, preying upon the living in order to sustain their own corrupted souls. Even the noblest Lords and Ladies of Law can suffer this corruption, often when Chaos is at her most vigorous and dynamic."

"Don't make my mistake," murmured Fromental to me, "and confuse Law and Chaos with Good and Evil. Both have their virtues and vices, their heroes and villains. They represent the warring temperaments of mankind as well as the best we might become, when the virtues of both camps are combined in a single individual."

"Are there such individuals?"

"A few," said Lord Bray. "They tend to arise as the occasion demands."

"Gaynor's not one of those?"

"He's the opposite!" Lord Renyard yapped indignantly. "He combines the vices of both sides. He damns himself to eternal despair and hatred. But it's in his nature to believe he acts from practical necessity."

"And he has supernatural help?"

"In our world, yes." Lord Bragg's long face became briefly animated. "At his side rides Lady Miggea. The Duchess of Law has all the powers of her great constituency at her command. She could destroy whole planets if she wished. The hand of Law is deadly when it serves unthinking destruction rather than justice and creativity. We had hoped Lord Elric . . ."

Lord Blare had begun to pace about the room. He was all urgent blue eyes, rattling spurs and jingling harness. "Much as I enjoy a good chin-wag, gents, I'd remind ye that we're all in immediate danger and our journey here was to seek the help of the Grey Lords, whom we understood these Off-Moo fellers to be."

"But they can't offer much in the way of practical help, I gather. Gaynor threatens your world, too." Lord Bragg fingered his muttonchops. "So we must look elsewhere for salvation."

"Where would you go?" asked Fromental.

"Wherever the moonbeam roads lead us. They are the only way we know to travel between the realms." Lord Bray seemed almost apologetic. "With Elric duped and charmed . . ."

"Would you teach me to walk those roads if I came with you?" Fromental asked quietly.

"Of course, my friend!" Lord Renyard responded with a generous yap. A clap of his paw upon Fromental's vast arm. "I for one would be proud to have the company of a fellow citizen of France!"

"Then I'm your man, *monsieur*!" The legionnaire straightened his cap and saluted. He turned to me. "I hope, my friend, that you don't feel I desert you. My quest was always for Tanelorn. Perhaps in my search I will learn something that will help us all fight Gaynor. Be assured, my friend, if you are ever in danger, I will help you if I can."

I told him much the same. We shook hands. "I'd go with you," I said, "only I have sworn to return home as soon as possible. So much is threatened at this moment."

"We have our separate destinies," said Lord Renyard, as if to console us. "All are threads in the same tapestry. I suspect we shall all meet again. Perhaps in happier circumstances."

"The Off-Moo are populous and resourceful, even when supernatural forces are brought against them." Oona stepped amongst the huge, beastlike military dandies to make her own farewells. "We each serve the Balance best by serving our own realms." She, too, shook Fromental's hand.

"Do you think Gaynor will attack the city?" asked the big legionnaire.

"This is his story," she said a little mysteriously, "his dream. I would not be entirely surprised if his great campaign has already begun. This is the adventure which will earn him his best-known sobriquet."

"And what is that?" asked Fromental, trying to smile.

"The Damned," she said.

When we had parted from the Tanelornians (of whom I could not help thinking in my own mind as "the Three Hussars"), I asked Oona how she understood so much.

She smiled and again settled her small body comfortably against mine as we walked through the twilight canyons in which so many commonplace activities were no doubt taking place.

"I am a dreamthief's daughter," she said. "My mother was a famous one. She stole some mighty dreams."

"And how are dreams stolen?"

"Only a dreamthief knows how. And only a dreamthief can safely carry one dream into another. Use one dream against another. But that is how she earned her riches."

"You could steal a dream in which I was emperor and place me in another where I was a pauper?"

"It's a little more complicated than that, I understand. But I did not receive my mother's training. The great school in Cairo was closed during my time in the city. Besides, I lacked the patience."

She paused in her step, bringing me to a halt. She said nothing, merely stared up into my face. Ruby eyes met my own. I smiled at her and she smiled back. But she seemed a little disappointed.

"So you are not the thief your mother was?"

"I didn't say I was a thief at all. I inherited some of her gifts, not her vocation."

"And your father?"

"Ah," she said, and began to laugh to herself, looking down at the jade-green street which reflected our shadowy figures. "Ah, my father."

She'd not be drawn further on that matter, so instead I asked her about her journeyings in other worlds.

"I've traveled very little compared to Mother," she said. "I spent some while in England and Germany, though not in your history. I must say I have something of a fascination with the worlds that would be most familiar to you, perhaps because my mother had such affection for them. And you, Count von Bek, do you miss your own family?"

"My mother died giving birth to me. I was her last child. Her hardest to bear."

"And your father?"

"A scholar. A student of Kierkegaard. I think he blamed me for my mother's death. Spent most of his time in the old tower of our house. He had a huge library. He died in the fire which destroyed it. Dark hints of madness and worse. I was away at school, but there were some strange tales told of that night and what the people of Bek believed they witnessed. There was a grotesque and sensational story spread about my father's refusing to honor some family 'pact with the devil' and losing an heirloom that was his trust."

I laughed, but not with my companion's spontaneity. I found it difficult to grieve for a man so remote from me, who would not, I suspect, have grieved if I had died in that fire. He found my albinism repulsive. Disturbing, at least. Yet my attempts to distance myself from my parents and their problems had never been wholly successful. He expected me to carry the family duty but could not love me as he loved my brothers. Oona did not press me further. I was always surprised by the levels of emotion such memories revealed.

"We share a complicated family life," she murmured sympathetically.

"For all that," I insisted, "I still intend to return to Bek. Is there no way you can get me home soon?"

She was regretful. "I journey between dreams. I inhabit the stories, they say, which ensure the growth and regeneration of the multiverse. Some believe we dream ourselves into reality. That we are yearnings, desires, ideals and appetites made concrete. Another theory suggests the multiverse dreams us. Another that we dream it. Do you have a theory, Count von Bek?"

"I fear I'm too new to these ideas. I'm having some trouble believing the basic notions behind them." I put my arm around her because I sensed a kind of desperation in her. "If I have a faith, it's in humankind. In our ultimate capacity to pull ourselves from the mud of unchecked appetite and careless cruelty. In a positive will to good which will create a harmony not easily destroyed by the brutes."

Oona shrugged. "Anxious dogs overeat," she said. "And then they usually vomit."

"You are a cynic?"

"No. But we have a long battle, we Knights of the Balance, to achieve that harmony."

I'd heard that phrase earlier. I asked her what it meant.

"A term some use to describe those of us who work for justice and equity in the world," she explained.

"And am I one of those knights?" I asked.

"I believe you know," she said. Then she changed the subject, pointing out the flowing cascades of what she called moonflowers, pouring down the slender terraces of Mu Ooria's spires.

In spite of all the dangers and mysteries I had known, it was a privilege to witness such beauty. It defied anything I had ever anticipated. It had an intensity, a tactile and ambient reality, that even an opium-eater could not understand. I knew that, whatever I experienced, I was not dreaming. There was no denying the absolute reality of this gloomy, rocky world.

Oona clearly wished to answer no further questions, so we spent the next while in silence, admiring the skills of the Off-Moo architects who blended their own creations with the natural, giving the city an organic wholeness I had never seen in a place of that size before.

As we turned from admiring a fluted curtain of transparent rock appearing to undulate in the light from the lake, I saw a man standing not four feet from me. I felt sick and silenced by the shock. Again this was my doppelgänger, still clad in the baroque black armor, his face an exaggerated likeness of my own, with high cheekbones, slightly slanting brows and glaring red eyes, his skin the color of fresh ivory. Screaming at me. Screaming at me and understanding that I could not hear a word.

Oona saw him, too, and recognized him. She began to approach him, but he moved away down an alley, signaling me to follow. His pace increased and we were forced to run to keep up with him. Twisting, turning, dipping down into narrow tunnels, ascending steps, crossing bridges, we followed the armored man to the outskirts of the city, until we were some distance inland. He remained ahead of us, moving steadily up the bank of the river, in and out of the constantly changing shadows, the flickering, silvery light. Every so often he glanced back and the black metal helmet framed a face filled with urgency. I was certain that he wished us to follow him.

Momentarily blinded, I lost track of him. Oona began to run ahead of me. I think she could still see him. I hurried in her wake.

Then, from ahead, I heard a sudden, agonized scream, a wail of grief and terror combined. Rushing forward I found the young woman kneeling on the ground beside what I took at first for the corpse of the black-armored stranger.

The stranger had vanished. The carcass was that of the great saber-toothed panther who had kept pace with our raft as we sailed towards the city.

Oona raised her weeping eyes to mine.

"This can only be Gaynor," she said. "Murdering for pleasure."

I looked up, hoping to see the stranger, wondering if he had killed the cat. I thought I caught a glimpse of coppery silver, heard a mocking note in the current of the river, but there was no sign of my doppelgänger.

"Did you know the animal?" I asked Oona, kneeling beside her as she wrapped her arms around its huge body.

"Know her?" Oona's slender frame shivered with unbearable emotion. "Oh, yes, Count von Bek, I know her." She paused, trying to take control of her grief. "We are more than sisters." The tears began to come now, streaming silver against her bone-white skin.

I thought I'd misheard her.

"Only Gaynor," she whispered, rising and looking about her. "Only he would have the cruel courage and cleverness to attack our cats first. They are crucial to Mu Ooria's defense."

"You say she's your sister?" I looked wonderingly down at the massive black cat, her curved, white tusks the length of swords. "This beast?"

"Well," she said abstractedly, still trying to recover herself. "I am, after all, a dreamthief's daughter. I have some choice in the matter."

Then Gaynor, still in his SS uniform, stepped from behind a pillar. Incongruously he had a short, bone bow in one hand. With the other, he was drawing back a string. Nocked to it was a slender silver arrow aimed directly at Oona's heart.

She reached for her own weapon but then froze, realizing that Gaynor had the complete advantage.

"I've been having some interesting adventures and encounters, cousin," he said. "Learning some good lessons. Time's simply zipped by. How has it been for you?"

# CHAPTER TEN

## Rippling Time

y Raven Blade was where I had left it in my new lodgings. Oona could not use her bow and was otherwise without arms. Gaynor was choosing which one of us to shoot. His aim wavered, but he was too far distant for me to be able to attack him.

Then reason reminded me that he could not afford to kill us. He wanted my sword. He also seemed to have forgotten the still, slow-time Off-Moo sentinels.

"You'll recall, cousin, that not all who guard this place are immediately detectable," I said.

His smile was dismissive. "They're no danger to me. I've had many ordeals, many adventures and encounters since we last met. I have more powerful help now, cousin. Supernatural help. We already lay siege to Tanelorn. The Off-Moo's defenses are unsophisticated in comparison. This is a wonderful realm, once you find your way around in it. I have learned much that will be useful when I have the Grail."

"You think that it will be easy for you to return?"

"For me, cousin, yes. You see, I've made some fine new friends since we parted on such bad terms. Once you meet them, you'll soon be enthusiastically apologizing to me. And only too pleased to run home to fetch the Raven Sword while I entertain your pretty young friend, eh?"

I recognized an element of bravado in him, an unsteadiness about his eyes. I replied contemptuously. "If I had the sword with me, cousin, I suspect you'd be a little more civil. Lower your bow. Was it you who killed the panther?"

"I'll keep the bow strung and maintain our equilibrium for the moment, cousin. Is the big cat dead? An epidemic, no doubt? One of those dreadful plagues which sometimes attacks the feline world . . ." His arrow was still level with my heart, but the verbal barb was intended for Oona.

Oona did not respond. What was meant to goad her, only drove her to take further charge of herself. "Your claims are illegitimate, Prince Gaynor. Your own cynicism will defeat you. All the future holds for you is an eternity of despair."

His amusement increased. Then he frowned, as if he brought himself back to business. "True, I'd hoped to find you here with your sword, Ulric. So I'll strike that bargain—bring me the blade and I'll spare the girl's life in exchange."

"The sword is my charge," I said. "I can't give it up. My honor depends upon my stewardship . . ."

"Bah Your father's honor also depended upon a stewardship— and we know how thoroughly he defended his trust!" Now he was contemptuous.

"Stewardship?"

"Fool! The von Beks had the most powerful combination of supernatural artifacts in the multiverse. Your weakling father, degenerated to mumbling voodoo spells and other witcheries, let one fall from your possession. Because he feared it would be stolen! Your family doesn't deserve its destiny. From now on, I and mine will keep those objects of power together. Forever."

I was baffled. Had he gone mad? Though he seemed to think I understood him, I could scarcely make sense of a word he said.

"Quickly." He drew the bowstring back a little farther.

"Which one will get the sword, which one will stay here as hostage for it?"

Oona suddenly clutched her head and staggered. Gaynor turned the bow on her.

At Oona's feet, the shining black body quivered. Huge muscles flexed. A tail lashed. Vast whiskers twitched. Jade eyes gleamed. A great, black nose made a single, searching snort.

Oona was disbelieving, but Gaynor was cursing as the saber-tooth climbed slowly to its feet, its glaring eyes casting around for an enemy, its huge ivory tusks glinting in the riverlight. And then, standing shoulder to shoulder with the gigantic cat, I saw another human figure.

My doppelgänger.

Had he brought the cat back to life? Gaynor barely disguised his own terror. Oona had the common sense to drag us behind the shelter of a nearby stalagmite so we could watch from cover.

The other albino seemed to be talking to Gaynor. He gestured. Suddenly both he and the cat vanished. Gaynor unnocked the arrow, stuck it in his belt and ran into the darkness.

I was completely mystified by the exchange. I tried to ask Oona if she understood any better, but she was grim, hurrying back to the interior of the city. "We must warn them of what's happening. This will take all their resources."

"What does it mean? Who is that bizarre version of myself?"

"Fairer to say that you are a version of him," she said. "He's called Elric of Melniboné and he carries the greatest burden of us all."

"And he's from another—what—? One of these alternatives to our own reality?"

"Some call them 'branches' or 'branes.' Or 'the realms,' or 'the scales,' but they are all versions of our universe." She was still intent on negotiating the winding lanes of Mu Ooria, heading deeper and deeper into the city.

"And like you, this doppelgänger of mine travels between these worlds? And he knows you?"

"Only in his dreams," she said.

We were both out of breath. I had no idea where she was lead-ing us, but she would not rest. While the immediate danger was in the forefront of my mind, I still seethed with a thousand unan-swered questions. Questions so numinous I could not begin to frame them in words.

She had led us through a high doorway, down a long corridor and up a short winding ramp until we stood in a low-ceilinged hall full of long benches of carved stone arranged around a large, glassy circular area.

I was reminded of monks' communal quarters. The hall was lit by the tall, watery glasses. An air of tranquillity hung about the place. The shadows were soft. The circular area at the center stirred occasionally, its shades shifting from jet black to dark grey.

Oona led me behind the main rank of benches. As she did so, the first Off-Moo began to arrive, their long faces grave, their odd eyes questioning. I hadn't seen the young woman give any signal. Our presence in the room must have been enough to bring the Off-Moo elders there immediately. Some had the air of people interrupted in important tasks. Clearly they believed the matter serious. How had she summoned them? Was she in telepathic communication with their group intelligence? Her face had a beautiful, open quality when she communicated with them. The gracious unhumanity of these creatures made me feel I was in the company of angels.

With murmured acknowledgment to us, they assembled around the obsidian circle and listened gravely as Oona told them what she had seen and what we had learned.

"Could be an army already marches against Mu Ooria." She spoke a little hesitantly.

Again, she was acknowledged. But the Off-Moo's concentra-tion had begun to focus on the reflective, glossy circle of rock around which they had gathered. I wondered what they saw there, if this were their version of a crystal ball? Some means of focusing their group consciousness?

Then I fell back, dazzled, throwing up my hands to protect my eyes. I thought the Off-Moo would be equally affected, but they

calmly held their ground. Still guarding my eyes, I found Oona. She
held her own hands before her face. "What's happening?" I asked.

I think they have a way of bending light," was all she could tell
me. Then the worst of the white-gold glare had gone and my eyes
had become accustomed to what remained. I could see the source
of the radiance. At the center the circle, it was three-dimensional
and thoroughly real—an ordinary block of stone suspended in
space and giving off a faint, sweet-sounding vibration which
brought strange memories, recollected moments of purity. When
thought, deed and idea were all in harmony. I half expected Sir
Parsifal, the pure knight, to appear kneeling before it. For the
stone had changed before my eyes.

I was now looking in absolute awe at what I had always
assumed to be nothing more than a beautiful legend. A great,
golden bowl, set with crystal and precious jewels and brimming
with thick, crimson wine which poured down the sides to be
absorbed by the light which darkened to deep gold and showed
the whole Off-Moo conference chamber in dramatic, organic
contrast, alive with dark, swirling color. My senses were barely
capable of registering so much at once. I felt oddly weak and
found myself, for no clear reason, longing to be united with my
Raven Sword. I felt that if only I could grasp the hilt, I would be
able to draw strength from the black blade. But the sword was still
in my chambers and I could not bear to leave the presence of that
extraordinary vessel. The bowl, this Grail, grew larger.
Everywhere the tall, conical hoods of the Off-Moo waved and
nodded, as if this sight was unusual, even to them. Angular shadows were softened by the rounded rock over which they fell.

The Off-Moo's voices began a single low note which became
a chant, a word, a mantra threatening to set the entire world
vibrating. Light and dark were shaken together and mingled. The
bowl then re-formed, rolling into itself until it was a golden, jeweled staff, rotating slowly in the air above the obsidian disk.

The Off-Moo chant changed and the staff expanded, grew.
Just for an instant it became the shape of a small child with a
round, beatific face. Then the staff returned and slowly changed

shape again until it was a single arrow. The sign of Law. Then it became a sheaf of arrows, fanning out and upwards above the glassy circle. Eight golden, jeweled arrows, spinning slowly overhead. Chaos.

The Off-Moo were concentrating on the field of glistening obsidian. Very quickly a three-dimensional picture began to form there. Riders seemed to be emerging from the rock and galloping towards us. The illusion was not unlike a very realistic cinema experience. But it was also a terrifying reality. Gaynor, in his bizarre armor, rode a great white stallion whose blind eyes stared upwards, yet whose footing was unconsciously sure. Behind him, also on pale, blind horses, still in their black and silver uniforms, came the majority of his SS followers, Klosterheim at their head. All were cloaked and armed with miscellaneous antique weaponry.

Behind these was as bizarre a collection of monsters and grotesques as ever came shuffling and hopping out of a picture by Bosch. Perhaps, after all, the painter had been drawing from experience rather than imagination? They were long-limbed, long-headed, with huge myopic eyes. They had snuffling, exaggerated snouts, showing that they used scent more than sight. These loose-limbed travesties were much larger than the men who rode ahead of them, like toy soldiers modeled to two different scales. They were clearly savages, armed with maces and axes. Archers were in their ranks, and swordsmen. A mob rather than a disciplined army. But there were thousands of them,

"Troogs," said Oona.

I could see why the Off-Moo had known they had little to fear from these denizens of the borderlands. The giants had neither the intelligence nor the ambition to attack Mu Ooria on their own accord.

One of the Off-Moo murmured something and Oona nodded. "All the panthers have disappeared," she told me. "They no longer control the troogs. We don't know if the cats are dead, charmed or have simply vanished."

"How could they vanish?"

"The workings of a powerful spell."

"Spell?" I was thoroughly skeptical. "Spell, *Fräulein?* Are we so desperate we rely on sorcery?"

She showed some impatience with me. "Call it what you like, Count von Bek, but that is the best description. They sense a Summoning. A being far more powerful than the kind which usually walks these caverns. Perhaps a Lord of the Higher Planes. Which means that Gaynor has somehow brought the Lords of the Balance out of their own realm and has given his allegiance. If they are able to bring all their power with them, they will be almost impossible to defeat. But some need the medium of a human creature like Gaynor and his army."

"Those troogs are huge."

"Only here," she said. "In certain configurations of the branches, they are tiny. They're just the creatures who inhabit the borderland between Mu Ooria and the Grey Fees. They are not of the Higher Planes but exactly what you know them to be, creatures of the lower depths. They're Gaynor's cannon fodder. If Gaynor's sorcery is successful against us, they will do the routine slaughtering."

"You seem to have experienced such an invasion before," I said.

"Oh, more than once," she said. "This struggle is constant, believe me. You cannot imagine what is beginning to happen in your own world."

Increasingly, I was feeling the need to have the Raven Sword at my side. While Oona continued to confer with the Off-Moo, I told them I would return soon.

I ran through serpentine streets, through the shifting light, finding my way as much by the muted colors as by the shape of the buildings, until I reached my quarters. I went to where I had left the sword. To my enormous relief it was still in the alcove near my bed. I unwrapped it, just to make sure it was my own beloved blade, and the dark, vibrating steel murmured to me in recognition.

Settling Ravenbrand in its makeshift scabbard, I left the room with it over my shoulder and once again made my way through the winding streets, recognizing how a shaft of silvery light fell here, how the shadows moved there, how the colors changed in a particular stretch of wall, what was contained in those weird gardens.

I crossed the central plaza again and was approaching the streets on the other side when I heard a mocking sound from behind me. Turning, I stared into the triumphant eyes of my cousin Gaynor. He was aiming an arrow directly at me.

It hadn't occurred to me that he would have the audacity to follow us all the way into the heart of Mu Ooria. I was still not used to seeing two versions of the same person—one leading a hideous army against a great city and the other already in the city.

Gaynor had a happy cruelty about him. "Surprised, I see, cousin. I have an alter ego taking care of one front, while I'm free to attack on another. Every general's greatest desire, eh?" He was salivating and his eyes kept moving towards the sword. He was fascinated—almost enraptured—by it.

Without thinking, I shifted my grip on the hilt and held it with the point down, against the counterweight of the pommel, so that it could come up rapidly, almost without any effort on my part, and send Gaynor's bow flying from his grasp. I only had to bring him in a little closer.

But he was wary. He stayed some distance off, the arrow still nocked against the string. He was clearly new to the art of archery but seemed to have mastered it well enough.

There was nothing else for it. I would have to close with him.

I began to move, very gradually, talking as I attempted to shorten the distance between us. But Gaynor was grinning and shaking his head from side to side. "Why on Earth would you think I had any reason to keep you alive now, cousin. You have what I need. All I have to do is kill you and take it from you."

"You could have shot me in the back to do that," I said, just as he loosed an arrow which caught me high in my left arm. I was surprised that I felt no pain, then I realized my sturdy Norfolk jacket's tweed had taken the arrow. I was untouched. Before he could fit another shaft to his bowstring, I took a few swift steps towards him and held the sword's needle-sharp point to his throat.

"Drop your weapon, cousin," I demanded.

I felt a sharp pain in my side, looked down and saw the blade of a Nazi dagger pressed against my rib cage. Looking up I stared into the lifeless eyes of the gaunt Klosterheim.

"So, you also have a twin." I shuddered.

"We are all the same," murmured Klosterheim. "All of us. Millions of us."

He seemed feverish, abstracted. Even nervous.

We were now in a stalemate, with my blade at Gaynor's throat and Klosterheim's at my ribs.

"Lower your sword, sir," he said. "And place it on the ground before you."

I laughed in his face. "I'm sworn to die before I give up Ravenbrand."

Gaynor was impatient. "Your father, too, was sworn to die to protect your family's inheritance. And die he did, sir. Ulric. Dear cousin. Give me the Black Sword and I guarantee that you will be allowed to live on at Bek, with all your villagers, your castle and everything back the way you're used to. No one will bother you. Believe me, cousin, there are those of us, quite as idealistic as you, who are prepared to get their hands dirty in order to plant the seeds of paradise. If you choose to keep clean hands, that is your decision. But I do not make that choice. I'm ready to accept the necessity, to establish order throughout the multiverse. Do you understand?"

"I understand that you're mad," I said.

He laughed aloud at this. "Mad? We're all that, cousin. The multiverse is mad. But we shall make it sane again. We shall make it whatever we wish it to be. Can't you feel yourself changing? It is the only way you'll survive. It's how I've survived. But no human brain can accept so much intellectual and sensory over-load without radically adapting. Do you really believe you're the same person who so recently fled a concentration camp?"

He spoke the truth. I could never be the same man. Yet he was still trying to confuse me.

"Herr Klosterheim will have to kill me," I said, "because I am not going to volunteer you my services or my sword."

We had reached a rough-and-ready stalemate. I looked past

Gaynor. Over his shoulder a familiar figure raced towards me across the smooth floor of the plaza. It wore ornate black armor, a complicated helm. Its red eyes blazed as its pale hands reached out. It ran straight through the unaware Gaynor. A mirror-ghost. It radiated a terrible, desperate urgency. My instinct was to pull back, but my intellect told me to hold my ground.

The figure charged at enormous speed. It must surely knock me down. But he did not stop. Neither did he run through me. Instead he ran directly *into* me. Armored body, helmed head, everything passed into my sensibly dressed twentieth-century person and was absorbed! A moment earlier I had been one individual. Now I was two.

I was two men in a single body. I did not for a second question this fact. How could I?

Suddenly I had two sets of memories. Two identities, each very distinct. Two futures. Two sets of emotions. But I also shared much with my doppelgänger. An overweening hatred for Gaynor, his brutal pack and all that it represented both here and in my own world. My double's resolve combined to strengthen my own, to complement my own anger. I knew at once that this was his intention. He had deliberately set out to achieve a combination of our power. And, because he was in so many ways myself, I could only trust him. He could not lie to me. Only to himself.

Now the Black Sword began to pulse and murmur, the red runes running like veins up and down her throbbing length. I felt her writhe in my hand. She rose under her own volition, rose in my fist until I held her shoulder-high. I cried out some savage battle shout as the sword set my body thrilling with power, with a thousand conflicting notions and feelings, with a cruel, unfamiliar death lust. I could taste the sweet blood and bitter souls my sword would soon devour. I licked my long lips. I was coming alive!

*The beast will return to the fold, the sparrow to the field. Swords to marry, souls to heal.*

I was speaking. A mantra. The end of some longer chant? A spell. In a language which one half of me did not understand at all, but the other half knew perfectly. It was not the language either of us habitually spoke. I could understand my thoughts in both languages and they were almost the same, save that the older tongue was full of throat-twisting glottal stops, clicks and hisses.

This other speech was far more liquid, immeasurably more ancient. Not human at all. Something that had to be learned, sound by sound, meaning by meaning. Something that had taken me many tortured years to come by.

*Two cups for justice. Two swords for harmony. Twin souls for victory. Lords and ladies walk on moonshine. Twins command the serpentine. Flows the blood and flows the wine. Flows the river to the sign. Twins in harlequin combine.*

My alter ego was concentrating on the mantra. It had enabled him to perform this astonishing magic. Of course, I understood everything at once, for we were now the same creature. And being two identities in a single body, I saw how it was possible to be many people. To be sane and conscious of many other identities all at the same time. So many decisions, choices, obstacles. To understand that, at every moment, a million other selves were determining a million subtly or radically different paths. To be able to see the multiverse in whole, to have no worlds hidden, no possibilities denied! A glorious gift. All you had to do was find the roads. Now I understood the lure of such a life and why Oona and her mother and her mother's mother had inevitably chosen it.

The immediacy of the moment was in no way lessened by this experience of infinity. I was able to defend myself, indeed to carry the attack if I so desired, for I had combined Elric's training with my own. I knew how to act in battle and concentrate on a spell at the same time, for I was of the pure, old blood of Melniboné and we nurtured such gifts in ourselves. Our ancient folk had forged many compacts with the elementals of the multiverse. With the powers of Earth, air, water and fire. And many of those compacts remained unbroken. I could call on all the powers of nature, though not all nature's power. To sense one's control of the wind, fire, the very form of the Earth and flow of the water, to have conversed with the great beast-gods, those archetypes from whom all other animals came and who could command legions should they desire: all this was indescribably marvelous. Few of these allies had more than a healthy beast's need for a sufficiency of things and so had few ambitions in the affairs of men or gods, though the Lords of the Higher Worlds respected them. Only when called would the elementals agree, occasionally, to concern themselves in mortal conflicts. And now I had all these powers, understood the price to be paid for exercising them and the need for a psychic and physical sustenance far greater than anything I had required in the world of Bek. The reality was more intense, the stakes far higher than anything I had ever guessed possible.

But it required fuel for my flexing muscles, my heaving lungs, fuel to power my warrior's body as well as my warlock's wisdom. Only two sources for that fuel existed. One was a combination of herbs and other ingredients which allowed me to lead an active life. The other was the sword. Understanding what the sword did, my ordinary human self was thoroughly repulsed. Yet I also understood that survival depended upon my using her and that she would not allow me to act against my own interest. My affection for Ravenbrand remained, but I had a new respect for her. Clearly this sword chose who would wield her.

All my lessons of swordsmanship came back to me as I prepared to do battle. I was not reluctant to fight. I panted to fight, I yearned to draw blood.

"Prince Gaynor." Elric's haughty formality made my Saxon manners seem loose. "Has your death time come so soon?"

The Hungarian's damaged face had a demented look. "What are you? Do you control that human?"

"You're impertinent, Prince Gaynor. Your questions are offensive and coarsely put. I am of the Royal Line of Melniboné and your superior. Throw down that bow. Or my sword drinks your soul."

Gaynor was frightened by the changes in me, even though he guessed the reason. He had not been prepared for anything like this. Klosterheim's knife no longer pressed against my side. Gaynor's cadaverous colleague was staring with dawning intelligence. He had seen Elric run through his master and be absorbed by my body. He knew what I was, and I frightened him.

The sword was hungry for their souls. I could feel her needs speeding from her hilt to my hands. I did all I could to resist, but she became increasingly demanding.

"Arioch!" The name formed on my lips. "Arioch!" It tasted like the most exquisite wine. I was one with a being for whom words had specific flavors and for whom music was also color.

"He'll not empower you here." Gaynor was recovering himself. He unstrung his bow. "Not in Mu Ooria. Law rules here now."

I took charge of the quivering blade. I replaced it firmly in the rough sheath I had made. Gaynor had revealed something. Perhaps a weakness. Were his own supernatural allies also unable to enter Moo Uria herself? Did she have subtler defenses?

"Only when the city's taken," I said on a hunch.

And then he realized what he had revealed to me and smiled a wry acknowledgment. I now thought he had slipped into the city with a few men, but could not draw on his ally's powers. It was a tribute to his daring that he came here with only Klosterheim to help him steal the Raven Sword.

"You understand much of the multiverse, cousin," said Gaynor.

"Only in my studies and dreams," I told him. "I am here at the request of my blood kin. Otherwise I'd have no part of this business."

"Blood kin?"

I became circumspect. I now knew what Ulric had previously not known.

I could scent familiar, ancient perfumes, traces of mustier smells. I began to take an interest in my surroundings.

With my attention off him, Gaynor made several rapid steps backwards, believing himself out of range of my sword. He yelled and gestured. Klosterheim drew his own sword and ran to join him. I began to smile. This promised tasty sport. My left hand closed over the scabbard and held it firmly so I could draw the sword rapidly if I had to. She was murmuring and quivering again. She echoed my own rapidly changing moods.

My ears were far sharper than when they belonged only to von Bek. I heard swift, slithering movements from the shadows. While

Gaynor's most powerful allies might not be able to help him here, his lowlier troops were all too evident. He had not, after all, braved the city with only Klosterheim's support. I could see them, closing in from all sides. Their fear of cats dispelled, they had gathered enough courage to obey Gaynor and follow him. The gigantic grotesques Oona had called troogs. They snuffled and grunted in anticipation of a flesh feast. I recalled that the Off-Moo had called them cannibals.

I began to laugh. "Here's an irony, gentlemen," I said. I made a fluid movement, and the black blade was loose again. The runes ran crimson up and down her length. The iron pulsed and crooned. I began to pad like a cat towards Gaynor and Klosterheim. I broke into a trot as I closed the distance between us. The dark iron lifted higher. At one with my blade and my doppelgänger I knew a sense of boundless power. My laughter filled those immeasurable caverns!

Gaynor shrieked for his followers to attack. I defended myself against a blizzard of iron. Maces and swords swung at me from all sides. I dodged them with preternatural instincts and reflexes. I had soon cleared a space around me, but they scarcely feared me. I saw their nostrils dilating as they sniffed. I suspected they could hardly see me. Even here, they had no need of eyes. They had numbers. They had my scent. They were waiting only for Gaynor's signal before moving in again. This time it seemed they must surely crush me.

Now the black blade was howling. The sword which I called Ravenbrand and my alter ego called Stormbringer would not let me sheathe her again until she had been blooded. Her song blended with the delicate chimes of the crystal above. Her song was a hungry one. In her time, she had slain whole armies. She demanded her feast. She had moaned and lusted so long for satisfaction.

At last she could take her pleasure. At last she could feed. And deliver to me the energy I would need for my next Summoning.

# CHAPTER ELEVEN

# The Power of Two

aynor shouted an order and the monsters were upon me. Seconds later I was carrying the attack. The sword was alive. She possessed an intelligence of her own. She slashed red gouting trails into the surrounding air, slid through flesh and bone and sinew and drew deep of this crude lifestuff, the souls of the slain. Every soul went to satisfy my own flagging substance. I had a taste for the work. I hacked my way through to where Gaynor and Klosterheim stood, on the edge of the square, goading the troogs and savages to kill me. I cleared a path towards the two leaders as another might clear his way through tall grass. They began to be afraid of me.

I was used to that fear. I expected little else. All humans had it. I despised it. No such weakness was allowed to infect the blood of a Melnibonéan. My folk had ruled the world for ten thousand years. They had determined the histories of the Young Kingdoms, those nations of humankind. My race was older, wiser and infinitely crueler than men. We knew nothing of the softer ways, the cruder ways of creatures we regarded as scarcely higher than apes. In my bones I had only contempt for them.

I was a Melnibonéan aristocrat. I had known more terror in

the training for my sorcerous powers than these creatures had capacity or senses to experience. I had earned my alliances with the elementals and the lesser Lords of Chaos. I could raise the dead. I could force my will on any natural creature and could destroy an enemy with nothing but my black runeblade.

I was Elric of Melniboné, Last of the Sorcerer-Emperors, Prince of Ruins, Lord of the Lost. Called Traitor and Womanslayer. Wherever I went I was feared and courted, even by those who hated me, for I had a power no human could begin to control.

Even amongst my own people, I had only ever had one living rival. My family had kept its power down the millennia by cultivating its traditional learning and constantly making new alliances with Chaos. Our household gods were Dukes of Hell. Our patron was Lord Arioch of Chaos, whose fiefdom included a million supernatural realms. Whose power was vast enough to destroy them all. Those of my blood could call casually upon such forces for help. A handful of us had controlled the world for ten thousand years. We might have continued to rule, had I not betrayed that blood and made myself an outlaw everywhere.

"Arioch!" Again the name came readily to my lips. Arioch was my own patron Lord of Chaos, whose power was shared by the Black Sword, who fed from the same souls which fed me and the sword. Were we one creature—sword, god and mortal—truly potent only when all parts came together? These were easy, casual thoughts for a Melnibonéan. What were less familiar were the notions of morality, of right and wrong, which now contaminated my brain and had done, it seemed, from childhood. A burden I had as yet not managed to abandon. My father had loathed me for this. My other relatives had been embarrassed. Many supported my cousin Yyrkoon's desire to replace me.

"Arioch!"

He could not or would not manifest himself here.

I heard a murmur in the back of my brain, as if that great Duke of Hell tried to speak, but then even that became faint.

Gaynor was growing more confident.

Recklessly he yelled for his remaining forces to attack me.

There was every chance I could be borne down under the weight of their numbers. Even the sword, which seemed to have a life of its own, could not kill them all. With desperate clarity my mind began to project a different quality of thought, like rapidly growing tendrils, into the surrounding supernatural realms, those infinite worlds the Off-Moo called the multiverse.

I was not sure I would be answered. I knew Duke Arioch could not aid me. But I had considered all the likely dangers I would have to face when I accepted the dreamthief's help. And while this human brain might lack some of the subtlety of my own, it was a good one. There was every chance I would be successful.

I began to murmur the deceptively simple mantra which helped my mind follow certain paths, engage with the stuff of the supernatural, speak a language which no living creature on the Earth could understand. The verses were plain enough. They connected me to the complexities of the elemental spheres, where I might, if luck was on my side, find the means of escaping an increasingly likely fate.

I fought on, pushing back first one wall of battling flesh and then another. Yet I never gained ground, was always threatened with losing the last few meters I had cleared. The bodies became a barrier which I could use to my advantage. Never once did I lose that special concentration which continued to send tentacles of thought through all planes of the multiverse until, just for a second, I seemed to touch an alien intellect. One that recognized me.

And one I, too, recognized.

I sensed a world of water. Universe upon universe of water. Populated water. Water that coursed from one plane of existence to another. Ancient water. Newborn water. Swirling and still, wild and tranquil. Water lapped my face, even as a score of monsters fell to my hungry sword.

I began to sing—

*King of all oceans; king of all the waters of the worlds;*
*King of the deep darkness, king of silence, king of pearls;*

*King of washed bones, king of all our drowned;*
*King of sadness, of sinking souls unfound,*
*Revive our ancient friendship, our enemies confound.*
*As your old tides curl their currents like woven threads,*
*Recollect our bargains. Recall our sacrificial dead.*
*Bring honor to those compacts, and bind them fresh around,*
*Tie stronger still the white knots and the red,*
*Two kingdoms and two wounds. A mutual victory.*
*A memory, a means to meet our double destiny.*

A tide suddenly swirled around me, passed and was gone. I looked for water but saw only the glittering faraway lake, the long prospect which stretched towards it from the square said by Oona to be the lair of the great World Worm. All of this I took for granted, for I had seen more monsters and miracles than most mortals, but, as the cannibals formed a circle around me and began to press in again, I knew I was lost if King Straasha, my old ally, avatar of all the gods of all the oceans of the multiverse, could not hear me, or did not wish to hear me.

Gaynor saw the thing first. My cousin whirled and pointed, as he signaled Klosterheim to flee. Gaynor had no disrespect for my powers of sorcery. He had counted on my not being able to use them here.

Beyond the quays and the tethered boats, the water was rising. It formed a towering wall, did not move like a tidal wave, but stayed in place, quivering, threatening. The wall grew higher. If it fell, it would extinguish the whole city.

Now the help I had summoned threatened to kill my friends as well as my enemies. I knew a sardonic moment. This seemed to be my perpetual destiny.

Yet I was sure the Off-Moo were not as vulnerable as they appeared. They must know by now that I fought Gaynor and his minions in the square. Had they fled? Or were they preparing defenses?

The wall of water began to move. It gathered itself together. It started to form a shape. And soon, in shimmering outline, I distinguished the bulky figure of a giant. He was all shifting, swirling pale green water, never stable, never completely still, with pale blue eyes that searched the city and, at length, found mine.

Gaynor's followers fell back screaming for orders. Gaynor knew he could not possibly begin to fight King Straasha. A heavy, wet movement brought water running around our feet. King Straasha stepped ashore. His huge body walked, step by liquid step, up the great prospect towards us. If that weight of water should lose its form, it would drown us entirely.

As Gaynor searched for the swiftest escape route, another human figure appeared on the far side of the square and ran towards me.

Oona, the dreamthief's daughter.

"Warn the Off-Moo," I said. "They are in danger."

"They know of their danger," she said.

"Then save yourself."

"I'm safe enough, Lord Elric." She addressed me casually by this name, as if she had always known it. "But you must go. You have achieved your purpose here. The rest is work for me and the others to do. At least for now."

I began to suggest she stay with me for safety, but Klosterheim flung a dagger at me. I was distracted by its clattering to the ground a few meters away. When I looked up again, Oona had gone.

King Straasha was still wading towards me. I could tell the action was painful to him, but he was genial enough. "Well, little mortal, I am here because I have never yet broken a bargain and I have a certain affection for your kind. What would you have me do? Does this city have to be destroyed?"

"I need your help, sire. I need to move through the realms of water. I need to find the realm I left—the realm where my mortal form remains."

He understood.

"Water to water," he said, "and fire to fire. For the respect your ancestors showed my folk, I will do, Prince Elric, as you desire."

A vast watery hand descended towards me. I gasped, sensing that I was drowning as I struggled in King Straasha's grip. I feared he would kill me by accident.

Then I was engulfed in a bubble of air, held by a gigantic hand. I knew a sudden sense of peace, of absolute security. I was in the safekeeping of the king of water elementals. We flew over the crags and spires of Mu Ooria, until all I could see was the glowing lake surrounded by a mighty darkness. That part of me which was von Bek would have been incredulous, had not that part of me which was Elric shown such familiarity with the supernatural. Within me, even as I experienced the impossible, I could sense that von Bek believed in a world where all was Law, save for occasional upheavals of Chaos, and I believed in a multiverse where all was Chaos, where Law was something carved from that stuff and maintained by the will of mortals and the designs of the Lords of the Higher Worlds. Chaos was clearly the dominant force in all the realms, natural and supernatural. Two fundamentally opposed views of existence, yet in balance within the single body, the only mind. The harmony of opposites, indeed!

Von Bek neither hesitated nor questioned what I as Elric determined. For this was a world I understood and which had been a total mystery to him. Of course, he had all my memories, as I had all of his. For the moment the dominant me was the sorcerer-king, calling upon a great manifestation of an elemental, who served neither Law nor Chaos, nor any other thing, but lived to exist and perpetuate that existence endlessly.

The city was lost to sight. King Straasha hesitated, contemplating what he must do next. He and I had already communicated something which could not be represented by spoken language.

Unlike most sorcerer races, Melnibonéans had deliberately cultivated alliances with the elementals. With those great, old beings who were the embodiment of familiar and unfamiliar animals—with Meerclar of the Cats and even Ap-yss-Alara, Queen of the Swine, who was said to refuse all mortal advances and would continue to do so while one of them still ate pork.

Since pork was not eaten by any Melnibonéan of the higher castes, my folk had first made their accommodation with the queen.

The blood fever was dying away in me. For the moment Stormbringer was satiated. The energy we had acquired was crude and would not last long, but it enabled me to do what I must. I delighted in the knowledge that I was thwarting Gaynor not on one plane, but on two or more.

We came to rest in the center of the lake. For a second I looked on a placid stretch of sparkling water: moonlight illuminating a Mediterranean idyll. Then King Straasha made a gesture with his other watery hand. He was laughing. Instantly I stared down into the wide mouth of a raging maelstrom. It sent clutching, foamy tendrils up towards me. It roared and lusted for my life and soul. It swirled and eddied and whispered for me to jump from King Straasha's protecting hand, down into the sublime rapture of its heart. That hypnotic sound, at once shriek and murmur, drew me helplessly towards it. My animal instinct was to resist, but I knew I must not.

The surrounding bubble had burst. I stood there on the sea king's palm. Without further thought, I secured the runesword and dived into the howling vortex.

I was caught like a speck of dust and drawn deeper and deeper towards the infinite. I knew that I was whirling to my death, but I had no fear.

I knew what I was doing, where I was going, just as had King Straasha. There was still a chance I could lose my way and be carried off by my enemies. Both Chaos and Law, in this current battle, had much at stake and could be ruthless in their self-protection.

I heard the sea king's roaring voice fade into the shout of the great maelstrom and I gathered all my resources, attempting to make my way through, to find the one pathway I needed.

It became almost impossible to breathe. The water began to fill my lungs. I wondered how much longer I could survive before I drowned. Then the sword stirred at my belt. Some instinct made me reach for her blindly, drag her free of her scabbard and then let her pull me through the wild swell. Her course took me first up, then down, then deep within those watery walls.

Whole cities, continents, races swirled around me. All the oceans of all the worlds had combined into one. I passed through universes of water. Blind instinct guided me while the sword pointed like a lodestone, pulling me deeper and deeper down into the maelstrom.

My feet touched something solid. I could stand upright, though water still flowed. I could feel its pressure on my legs and torso. The great underground ocean stopped its agitation. Overhead was blackness, before me was more water. I was standing waist-high in it.

Warily I sheathed my sword. I began to move forward, expecting at any moment to find the ground give way beneath my feet. At last I trod on fine gravel. There was a cool, steady breeze on my cheek. Somewhere, in the distance, a fox barked.

I was no longer in Mu Ooria but did not know if I had found my destination. As I emerged completely from the water, I looked up at a familiar sky, at familiar stars. Near the horizon was the thin outline of a gibbous moon. Growing accustomed to the faint light, I made out the steep roofs and spires of a city I recognized. A quiet place, with few monumental buildings, no great architecture. Like one of the more ordinary medieval German towns I had seen on our dash towards Hameln. I hoped I had returned to the right time as well as place.

A wide moat surrounded the island on which the city was built. The island had not always been there. I had created the moat in one of my first attempts to defend the city, which no longer existed in exactly the same position as when I had first arrived there. I had used all the forms of sorcery I knew to save her from conquest, but every spell had been countered. And he had defeated me.

Elric's personality was now paramount. As I waded ashore, I hoped no one had guessed my strategy, though it was clear Gaynor had been able to manifest himself concurrently on at least three different planes, no doubt with the help of his supernatural mistress. Miggea, Duchess of Law. Lady Miggea.

In Mu Ooria she had been unable to break through, but here

she dominated the world. Only here, beyond the moat, was there any safety from Miggea's cold, relentless rule, and that safety was already threatened.

I was soaked and shivering. My clothing made movement difficult. I pulled off the cap and squeezed water from my long hair. I moved warily up the bank, my senses alert, my hand ready to pull my sword free in an instant.

Only now did I realize how weary I was. I found it difficult to put one heavy foot in front of another. I still did not know if I had reached my desired destination. Everything looked right. But a fundamental of the illusionist's art is that everything should look right . . .

I had become too used to deception. For all I knew I was quite alone in a world bereft of men and gods. Or did a thousand eyes even now watch me from the darkness?

I thought I heard a footfall. I paused. I could see very little. Just the outlines of shrubs and trees, the silhouette of the city ahead of me. Automatically I brought up my sword. All the energy we had stolen together, all the souls we had eaten, had dissipated in that journey through the vortex. I felt weak again. I was dizzy.

Voices. I prepared myself for battle.

I think I fell backwards. I still had some hold on my senses. I was aware of faces looking down at me. I heard my name spoken.

"It can't be him. We were told nothing could lift the enchantment. Look at its bizarre garments. This is a demon, a shapechanger. We should kill it."

I tried to join in the argument, to assure them that despite my costume I was truly Elric of Melniboné. Then my senses completely failed me. I fell into dreaming, urgent shadows. I struggled to get back. But it was useless. I was too weak to resist or to flee.

I thought I heard mocking laughter. The laughter of my enemies.

Had I been captured? After all my efforts, was I doomed never to reach my city again?

Darkness encircled my brain. I heard the whispering of my captors. Consciousness began to fade.

I knew I had failed.

I tried to lift my sword. Then I was engulfed.

Dreams fled away from me. Important dreams. Dreams which could save me. A white hare on a white road.

I tried to follow. I woke up in a clean bed, looking around at a familiar room. In front of me stood a stocky redheaded fellow with a wide mouth and freckled skin, dressed simply but with a certain style, in green and brown.

"Moonglum?"

The redheaded man grinned.

"So, Prince Elric, you know who I am?"

"It would be strange if I did not." I was weeping with relief. I had managed to return. And Moonglum, who had accompanied me on more than one recent adventure, was waiting for me. Foolish as it was, I felt more than comradeship for the loyal swordsman.

"True, my lord." He grinned and swaggered forward, a little puzzled. "But I wonder what exotic creature you robbed for your clothes."

"They're conventional," said von Bek, "in my time. His time."

I knew exactly where I was. In the Tower of the Hand in Tanelorn. A Tanelorn whose ruin was almost certain. And if she perished, all that she stood for would perish, too. It was for her that I had risked so much and had accepted the dreamthief's help. Not, she insisted, that Oona was a dreamthief. She was merely a dreamthief's daughter.

"And my body?" I asked, rising.

His face darkened and his eyes took on a certain expression, familiar to me when he believed sorcery to be involved. "Still in its place," he said. He grinned, but refused to meet my gaze. "Still sleeping. Still breathing." He paused. "Where, might I ask, my lord, did you acquire this new body? Is it something fashioned of sorcery?"

"Only of dreams," I said, and promised to answer him further when I knew more.

He led me from that simple bedroom to another. There in the

gloom lay a sleeping man. I was not prepared for the sight of my own naked body lying stretched out before me, hands folded across my chest, which rose and fell with slow regularity. My eyes were open. Twin rubies staring into the void. I slept. I was not dead. But neither could I be awakened. I was, after all, dreaming this dream. I reached to close my eyes.

Gaynor had brought great power against me. I knew the enchantment. I had used it myself, to ill effect. It threatened all I loved.

Now he gathered his strength to finish us. And if he finished Tanelorn, then all the worlds of all the realms were in danger.

I looked up from my sleeping self. Through the window, the sun was beginning to rise. Its first golden light slipped above the horizon. I held up my hand in the faint rays and compared it to that of the sleeping man. Essentially we seemed to be the same creature. It had taken great sorcery and the work of a dreamthief to achieve this, but now both my body and my sword were restored to me.

There might yet be time to rescue Tanelorn.

# CHAPTER TWELVE

## The Word of Law

few weeks earlier, Moonglum and I had come down out of the hills on the other side of Cesh, following any goat trail we could, having left the employ of the Cesh of Cesh in bad faith. In return for the destruction of a small supernatural army, we had been promised a treasure horde. The army destroyed, the horde was found to be two coins, one of them forged. I had left the Cesh on display at the city gates, as a warning to others not to waste our time or our good will. I had been weak before I left the place and in no condition to confront the war party sent to pursue us by the Cesh's blood relatives, duty-bound to kill us.

With imperfect maps we lost ourselves in the rocky terrain but lost our pursuers as well. We had certainly not expected to come upon Tanelorn so soon after finding our way down from the hills. We had expected to cross a desert before we found any form of civiliza-tion. We knew that it was in the nature of this city to manifest her-self occasionally in another place, so we did not challenge our luck. Without hesitation, we led our exhausted horses down towards the city walls. We were grateful for sight of the ancient, welcoming buildings, the gardens and tall trees, the red brick, black beams and thatch, the orchards and fountains, the twisting timbers of the gables. I, for one, had become weary of the fantastic and looked forward to the common human comforts I'd become used to.

Our habit, when our travels took us here, was for Moonglum and myself to rest until we were ready to wander on, seeking fresh employment, new masters. Ours were the lives of mercenary swordsmen and, if sometimes short of wages, we were rarely short of work. Tanelorn, we consoled ourselves, would give us credit. We had acquaintances in the city. We occasionally met enemies there. But there was no conflict. Tanelorn was the haven to which all weary people could come, to rest, to stand outside the wars of men and gods. Here, with the necessary drugs, I could enjoy a certain peace.

I had hoped to lodge with my old friend Rackhir of Phum, the Red Archer, but he was gone on an adventure of his own. And he had left something in his house he did not want disturbed.

An acquaintance of mine, Brut of Lashmar, who had been a professional soldier, was the first familiar face to greet us. He was tall with close-cropped hair and scarred, handsome features. He wore dark linen and wool, seeming more monkish than soldierly, as a sign of his retirement. He seemed troubled. He was not an eloquent man, and it was difficult for him to find appropriate words to describe his feelings. He took us to his rambling house, gave us rooms there, an entire wing, and made us welcome. As we ate, he told us that there seemed to be sorcerous currents in the air. "Wizardry buzzing everywhere. Strange, powerful magic, my friends. Perilous magic."

I asked him to be specific, but he could not. I told him that I always knew when Chaos was present. I assured him there was no smell of Chaos here, unless about my own person. He was not happy, he said, that the city had moved. Usually moving was something she did to save herself only when in the worst danger.

I told him that he had become timid in his retirement. Tanelorn was safe. We had already fought for and won her security. Perhaps we should have to do so again some day, for Tanelorn, like all fragile ideas, had to be perpetually defended. Still, it was highly unlikely that Chaos would attack her again.

In good faith I was not as certain as I sounded. I told Brut that no being in all creation would be foolish enough to risk the destruction of the Balance itself. But in my heart I knew there were always such beings. We had already defended the city against them once. But it would be madness to assume Chaos would attack again, so soon after we had driven her back. I refused to become anxious. I intended to make the most of my stay, I said, and restore myself as best I could.

Most of our talk was reminiscence. It was the nature of the place. We discussed old fights, old threats, legendary battles of the past and speculated upon the nature of our sanctuary.

We were in Tanelorn less than a week, however, before the city came under direct threat. And, of course, I had not sniffed Chaos. I had never anticipated that Law would be taking her turn as aggressor. My world had little stability. Did it go back to that one moment in my past, that moment when I killed the only woman I truly loved? Had I set these events in motion, all that long time ago?

Meanwhile, again Tanelorn was threatened. And by Law gone mad. That these besieging powers must be particularly corrupt and manipulated by a creature whose ambitions were unusually determined was no comfort. Such mindlessness was always the most destructive. It had nothing to lose but its own threatened oblivion.

I knew we were being challenged by unusual wizardry one afternoon when the whole surrounding landscape melted even as we watched from the battlements and old walls. The land turned to glaring ash flats studded with wind-carved limestone crags—a world of crystalline whiteness. The inhabitants of Tanelorn were astonished and alarmed. This was the work of the gods. Or demons. Even I was not capable of such sorcery.

What fresh interest did the Lords of the Higher Worlds have in Tanelorn? Everything but Tanelorn was now the color of wind-scarred bone. Her gentle trees and pretty houses were made vulgar by all that starkness.

The moon must look like this, I said. Everything scoured

away. Was that where we were now? Tanelorn's wise men thought we had merely been shifted to an alternative world from our own, which had already been conquered.

I was capable of one last Summoning. I begged the Earth elementals to dig a defensive moat around the city walls. It was the best I could do and it exhausted me.

We could not imagine the madness of a creature capable of reducing a world to such barren horror.

There were scholars of every kind in Tanelorn. I sought their best wisdom. Who had moved us to this world?

"My Lady Miggea of Law," I was told. "Almost certainly. She has already reduced several more realms to similar nothingness." She had immense supernatural resources and commanded more. I knew my gods and goddesses. I knew she had her own cycle of myth and legend which empowered her on earth, but she had to have mortal agents or she could not break through into these spheres.

At least one mortal was serving her here. My Lord Arioch of Chaos was equally helpless without mortal compliance. My patron, impulsive as he could be, had learned never to attempt the conquest of Tanelorn.

Our first attackers were mostly half-armored foot soldiers, oddly identical. They marched out of nowhere and did not stop marching until they reached our moat and then did not stop marching, over the backs of drowning comrades, until they were at our walls. Thousands and thousands were thrown against us daily and were so incapable of individual decision that we killed them effortlessly with few losses to our side.

The soldiers attacked again. We defended Tanelorn. We debated plans for her salvation. But we hardly knew what we were defending against, who our enemy really was. None knew how far the ash desert extended. A manifestation of Lady Miggea had been seen by some who recognized it, confirming that she was indeed in this realm now and watching from afar. At least this is what I was told. Some of our newer inhabitants had fled realms where she already ruled, had come here because of the terror they had left behind. But we still did not know the name of the mortal who served the Lady Miggea. And we wondered why the city did not shift herself away from danger, as we thought she could.

The marching minions of Law were easy enough to defeat. They had no true will and seemed almost drugged. They were mechanically predictable. They used identical tactics every time they tried to take the city. It was nothing to slaughter them in hundreds as they swam over or attempted to bridge the moat. I began to believe that their only function was to distract us while larger plans were hatched.

Warfare at its most boring.

Then Lady Miggea herself came to look at Tanelorn.

At first even I didn't understand the significance of the visit.

One morning I took my usual walk around the wall and to my astonishment saw that the surrounding horizon was filled with the pennants and lances of a vast mounted army. Everywhere their outlines signified our annihilation. These were not Law's cannon fodder, but her finest knights, drawn from all over the multiverse.

I threw up my hand to defend my eyes and saw, as if emerging from a shimmering mirage, a massive she-wolf, the size of a large mare, all caparisoned with pretty silks and beaded leather, with painted leather saddle, with brass and silver and glinting diamonds in her harness. Her deep-set eyes were mysterious as she came racing towards the city at the head of a pack of human knights. Her white, fanged muzzle twitched a little, as if she scented prey. Perhaps the wolf had been caught in Melniboné, I thought, for like me she was a pure albino. Her red eyes glared from bone-white fur, streaming behind her as she ran.

Even more bizarre was her rider. An armored man whose glittering silver helm completely hid his face. Whose lance shimmered the color of pewter. Whose metal was festooned with fluttering silks, with cloaks and scarves of a thousand colors.

I saw him turn, stand in his stirrups, and raise something to his helm. I heard the sound of his horn.

They came on and on. Thousands of white horses and their

silver-armored riders. Surely they meant to trample Tanelorn beneath their hooves.

Then I saw what the wolf pursued.

A hare, as white as winter, raced over the pale ash ahead of that whole thundering army. Racing for our gates. A thousand spears poised to pierce her.

Too late.

The hare reached the moat and plunged into the water. She swam to the city gates and sped through a narrow gap, disappearing at once into the streets.

Only when the little animal found the safety of the city, did the hunt quickly disperse, fanning to both sides around Tanelorn's wide moat. They had lost their prey. A distant horn called them away.

But they had impressed us with their armor. Their shining armor. Their faceless, enigmatic helms. And their numbers.

I knew their kind. The Knights of Law served a holy cause. Summoned to the standard of their mistress, the Lady Miggea, I knew they would fight to the death for her. They did not and could not question her. Their nature was to serve the office, no matter how warped it had become. They clung to a single idea, just as she did, unable to imagine more than one thing, one future, which they must create. They disguised their natural rapacity as their quest for Order.

But it had been the hare they intended to destroy that morning, not us. Their horses' hooves churned the ashy desert as from her huge pale throat, the white she-wolf voiced her angry frustration at losing her quarry. A chilling growl.

Again the horn sounded.

The mounted knights began to reorder themselves, turning and moving back towards the horizon.

Moonglum stepped up beside me. He had been commanding a group of fighters farther along the wall.

"What's this?" He sniffed and rubbed at his sleeve, as if to remove a stain. "Were they simply out for a gallop? Did you see the quarry they followed, my lord? The little hare?"

I had seen her and I wondered why she was so important to a Duchess of Law. What had held them back from pursuing her into the city? Some understanding that by entering eternal Tanelorn they threatened the fundamental order of all our realms?

Madness is what I witnessed. I had seen it more than once when Law became corrupted and decadent. For that reason alone my people preferred the uncertainties and wildness of Chaos. Law gone rotten was a far more perilous prospect. Chaos did not pretend to logic, save the logic of temperament, of feeling.

The she-wolf had turned and was loping back towards us, bearing her arrogant rider, who now, apparently relaxed, held his lance easily in its stirrup.

I heard a noise from within the helm. I heard a voice. I heard my own name.

"Prince Elric, called Traitor. Is that you?"

"You have me at a disadvantage, sir."

"Oh, you'll soon be familiar enough with one or another of my names, sir."

"Why," I asked, "do you attack our Tanelorn? What do you want from it?"

"What, my lord, do you defend? Do you know? Have you never questioned your actions? You defend nothing. You defend an innocent idea. Not a reality."

"I have seen many an idea made reality," I replied. "I'll defend Tanelorn or sack her, should I feel the urge. I have nothing better to do, sir. And I would like a chance to kill you."

He laughed within his helm. An easy laugh. A familiar laugh. He ignored my taunt. "Prince Elric, I have a bargain to make with you. All in Tanelorn will be saved if you simply give me your sword. Upon my word, I will then leave you in peace. All of you. There's enough physic in the city to keep you alive and well. It's a fair bargain, Prince Elric. You save all your comrades and lose nothing but a useless blade."

"I have more care for my sword than for most of my comrades, sir. So the offer has no attraction for me. You are welcome to the city. I shall enjoy killing a vast number of you before you take it.

If you know me well, sir, you know that I am only replenished by the work of slaughter. Sir, if you'll forgive me for repeating myself, have you the courage to accept a challenge? I would enjoy the pleasure of killing you. And the overlarge beast you ride."

At this the beast turned her head and her red eyes met my own. There was a kind of threatening mockery in her expression.

"You will have considerable difficulty killing a Duchess of Law, Prince Elric," she said. She grinned, her pale tongue lolling amongst her sharp, yellow teeth.

I returned her stare. I said, "But a wolf might kill a wolf."

She made no answer, though it seemed she was off before her rider was ready. It amused me that she chose that particular form and pretended that the man on her back was her master. Another sign of her monstrous delusion. I had ventured into supernatural realms where logic of her sort ruled. Nothing was more hideous. Even a Melnibonéan could not take pleasure in the wretchedness which the likes of Miggea created. Her half-dreaming mind was scarcely aware of the consequences of her actions. She believed that she ordered and protected, that she sacrificed herself to the common good. Her knights, of course, would obey her without question. Duty and loyalty were all. Virtues unto themselves. They were as mad as she.

I began to wonder if, after all, the object of their assault was not the city? What if they only wanted my sword? What if they directed all this vast sorcery upon Tanelorn merely in order to strike a bargain with me? A bargain I had refused. And would continue to refuse.

They would never compromise me. I would hold firm against them. And ultimately I would overcome them.

For the next few days the whole besieging army withdrew to below the horizon. Life in Tanelorn returned to something approaching normal. Not a single citizen attempted to leave as there was nowhere to go. The armies of Law had retreated, but the surrounding landscape had not returned to its natural state. For as far as the eye could see were bleak ash flats relieved by grotesque columns of clinkered limestone. A landscape of petrified death. I grew increasingly miserable with just that glinting desert for a view. I began to consider taking a horse and riding out to explore this world.

At night I began to dream again of different worlds. Worlds hardly distinguishable from my own. Worlds hideously or beautifully or subtly different. I dreamed of Bek, though I did not recognize it. I dreamed of uniformed men who stole my sword and tortured me. I dreamed of battles won and lost loves, of loves won and battles lost. I dreamed of terrifying landscapes and breathtaking natural visions. I dreamed of impossible futures and possible pasts. I dreamed of Cymoril, my murdered betrothed, pleading with me as her soul-stuff poured into mine. I woke sobbing.

Moonglum, in the next room, took to wrapping his bedclothes around his ears.

I was dreaming, of course, of my past as well as my near future. I dreamed of the world I would find. The world of my nightmares made reality.

This strategy of Law's was probably merely a pause while our enemies gathered strength to crush us. We discussed the nature of our predicament but had no precedents for it. I failed in my attempts to summon any further supernatural aid. Lady Miggea obviously controlled almost everything in this realm. We were dumbfounded. We hardly knew how to counter Law. Chaos had attempted to take Tanelorn more than once, but never, as far as we knew, the forces of Order.

For some reason not one of us believed we would all die. Perhaps Tanelorn had already demonstrated her invulnerability, when the White Hunt had divided around the city. Perhaps they could not enter. Some greater force prevented them. Or, perhaps like many gods and elementals, they needed to be invited by mortal agents into mortal realms? And, strictly, Tanelorn was not in this realm.

Our speculation was of little use to us. It was impossible to anticipate Law's next move. Impossible to understand their intentions.

We made some attempt to discover the white hare, but clearly she had waited for the hullabaloo to die down and gone back to her own territory.

I confided to Moonglum that I was growing bored. If no attempt was made on the city soon, I had it in mind to ride on. He did not offer to join me. I think he had some notion that I planned to betray Tanelorn.

Then one afternoon when the sun stained the ash flats scarlet, an armored rider on a white wolf came down the hills towards Tanelorn and sat yelling before our causeway gates, demanding that I be summoned.

The swaggering silver knight had draped himself in even more gaudy silk, as if in defiance of Law's cold taste. He sat arrogantly in his saddle. The water of the moat reflected his armor. He seemed made of mercury.

Still nameless.

He recognized me the moment I appeared on the eastern keep and stepped up to the battlements. He gestured elaborately. Some unknown form of greeting.

"Good morning, Prince Elric."

"Good morning, Sir No Name."

Easy laughter came out of that helm, as if I'd made a rich joke. This creature used every weapon in his arsenal, including subtle flattery and charm.

This morning he presented himself as being in a bluff, commonsensical kind of mood.

"I'll not waste your time, my lord," he said, "but as a Knight of the Balance and a servant of Law, I have come to take you up on a challenge. Hand-to-hand combat, as you said. And what's more I offer you a bargain." He had that half-belligerent tone you often hear amongst merchants and office-seekers, forever trying to sell you something you don't want or need.

"I understand those roles to be contradictory," I said mildly. While I exulted at the chance to fight him, I had, of course, become immediately suspicious of his motives. "A Knight of the Balance serves only the Balance."

"Aye," says he, almost impatiently, "that's the old thinking on it. But Chaos threatens and will engulf all unless we guard against her."

"Well," says I, "as one who serves Chaos, I can only speak for myself: I have no plans to engulf anything or anyone."

"Then you're a liar or a dupe, sir," says he.

"I've often wondered the same," I admitted easily. I knew he attempted to goad me, but there were few who could match the cruel wit of the average Melnibonéan aristocrat. "What would you sell me this morning, sir?"

"If you'll grant me a little hospitality, I'll tell you over breakfast. It's not my way to speak of private matters so publicly."

"We do not have private matters here in Tanelorn, sir. It's a communal place. We bother neither with secrets nor postmortems. It is part of our way of life."

"I have no wish to disturb that way of life, sir." The wolf moved suddenly as if not entirely in agreement with her rider. "And you can easily ensure your tranquillity. I came, after all, to accept your challenge. A duel. One to one. To decide the issue. Or, if you no longer feel you wish to settle this as a matter of honor, I'll take token tribute. All I seek is that old sword you carry. Give me the runeblade and I'll take my men away. You have seen the weight of armor we can bring against you. You know you would be crushed in an hour. Wiped out of existence. A few forgotten whispers on an ancient wind. Give me the sword and you'll all be immortal. Tanelorn will remain something more than a memory."

"Metaphysical threats," I said. "I've heard them echoing out of steel helmets all my life, sir. They always have the same apocalyptic ring to them. And they're exceedingly hard to prove . . ."

"There's nothing vague about my threats, sir," says the Knight of the Balance, shifting impatiently and pushing almost fussily at his errant silks. "Nothing insubstantial. They are backed by a hundred thousand lances."

"Not one of which can enter this city, I'd guess." I began to turn away. "Without being invited. You have nothing to offer me, sir, except the boredom I seek to escape. Even your unsavory, near-senile mistress Miggea cannot stride unasked into Tanelorn. Those mortal soldiers we fought were recruited here. Most are dead. Anything supernatural still must beg to be admitted. And you, sir, have already demonstrated your belligerence. I do not believe you have any intention of fighting me fairly."

"My tone was a mistake, I'll grant you, Prince Elric. But you will find me a more reasonable Champion of Law today. Willing to meet you man-to-man. Here's what I offer: I'll fight you fairly for the sword. Should you defeat me, all Law retreats from Tanelorn and you are returned to your natural condition, the city untouched. Should I defeat you, I take the sword. And leave you to defend yourselves as best you can."

"My sword and I are bonded," I said simply, "we are one. If you held the sword she could destroy you. And eventually she would return to me. Believe me, Sir Secret, I would not have it thus by choice. But it is so. And we are full of energy now. We have feasted well on your opposition. You have made us strong."

"Then let's test the strength. You have nothing to lose. Let me in and we'll fight for all to see—in the public square."

"Fighting is forbidden in Tanelorn." I said only what he already knew.

His voice was all mellow mockery. "What forces threaten your right to fight?" The knight's tone became openly challenging. "What power nursemaids an entire metropolis? Surely you are not going to let yourself be dictated to by meaningless custom? No free man should be forbidden the right to defend his life. To carry his weapons with pride and use them when he has to. That is how we of Law think now. We have rejected the great weight of ritual and look to a cleaner, fresher, more youthful future. Your rituals and customs are rules that have lost their meaning. They are no longer connected to the harsh realities of survival. Today the battle is to the strong. To the cunning. Those who do not resist Chaos are doomed to be destroyed by it."

"But if you destroy Chaos?" I asked. "What then?"

"Then Law can control everything. The unpredictable will be

banished. The numinous will no longer exist. We shall produce an ordered world, with everything in its place, and everyone in their place. We will know at last what the future brings. It is man's destiny to finish the gods' work and complete the divine symphony in which we shall all play an instrument."

In my mind I was thinking I had rarely heard such pious lunacy expressed so perfectly. Perhaps my overfondness for reading, as a child, had made me too familiar with all the old arguments used to justify the mortal lust for power. The moment the moral authority of the supernatural was invoked, you knew you were in conflict with the monumentally self-deceiving, who should not be trusted at any level.

"Man's destiny? *Your* destiny, I think you mean!" I leaned on the battlements like a householder enjoying a chat across the fence with his neighbor. "You have a strong sense of what is righteous, eh? You know there is only one path to virtue? One clean, straight path to infinity? We of Chaos have a less tidy vision of existence."

"You mock me, sir. But I have the means of making my vision real. I suspect that you do not."

"Neither the means nor the desire to do so, sir. I drift as the world drifts. We have no other choice. I don't doubt your power, sir. Law has driven my own allies away from this realm. All that stands between us and your total conquest of us is my sword and this city. But somehow, I know, we can defeat you. It's in the nature of those of us who serve Chaos to trust a little more to luck than you do. Luck can often be no more than the mood of a mob, running in your favor. Whatever it is, we trust to it. And in trusting to luck, we trust ourselves."

"I'm not one to argue with Melnibonéan sophistry," said the Silver Knight, fussing with his fluttering scarves and flags. "The ambitions of your own patron, Duke Arioch, are well known. He would gobble the worlds, if he could." A cool, morning breeze stirred the surrounding desert. Our visitor seemed almost bound up by those long scarves. Hampered by them, yet unwilling to be rid of them. As if he could not bear the idea of wearing undecorated steel. As if he yearned for color. As if he had been denied it for an eternity. As if he clutched at it for his life. Sometimes when the sun caught his armor and the fluttering silk, he seemed to be on fire.

I knew I could defeat him in a level fight. But if the Lady Miggea helped him, it would be more difficult, perhaps impossible. She still had enormous powers, many of which I could not even predict.

There was no doubt, when I looked back on that morning, that my enemies knew me in some ways better than I knew myself. For they were playing on my impatience, on my natural boredom. I had very little to lose. Tanelorn was tired. I did not believe she could be defeated by this beribboned knight, nor even by Miggea of Law. I was anxious for the siege to end, so that I could continue about my restless and, admittedly, pointless business. I was constantly reminded of my beloved cousin Cymoril, who had died by accident as Yyrkoon and I fought. All I had wanted was Cymoril. The rest I was willing to give up to my cousin. But because Cymoril loved me, Yyrkoon needed also to possess her. And as a result of my own pride, my folly and passion, and of Yyrkoon's overweening greed, she had died. Yyrkoon, too, had died, as he deserved. She had never deserved such awful violence. My instincts were to protect her. I had lost control of my sword.

I had sworn never to lose that control again. The sword's will seemed as powerful as my own sometimes. Even now, I could not be entirely sure whether the energy I felt coursing through me was mine or the blade's.

Grief, anger and desperate sadness threatened to take hold of me. Every habit of self-discipline was strained. My will battled that of the sword and won. Yet I became determined to fight this stranger.

Perhaps my mood was encouraged by a clever enemy. But it seemed that I was offering to fight him on my terms.

"The she-wolf must leave," I said. "The realm—"

"She cannot leave the realm."

"She can have no hand in this. She must give me the word, the holy word of Law, that the wolf will not fight me."

"Agreed," he said. "The wolf shall have no part in our fight."

I looked at the wolf. She lowered her eyes in reluctant compromise.

"What guarantee is there that you and she will keep your word?"

"The firm word of Law cannot be broken," he said. "Our entire philosophy is based on that idea. I'll not change the terms of the bargain. If you defeat me, we all leave this realm. If I defeat you, I get the sword."

"You're confident you can defeat me."

"Stormbringer will be mine before sunset. Will you fight me here? Where I stand now?" He pointed back behind him. "Or there, on the other side?"

At this I began to laugh. The old blood-madness was gripping me again. Moonglum recognized it. He came running up the steps. "My lord—this has to be a trick. It stinks of a trap. Law grows untrustworthy. Everything decays. You are too wise to let them deceive you . . ."

I was grave when I put my hand on his shoulder. "Law is rigid and aggressive. Orthodoxy in its final stages of degeneration. She clings to her old ways, even as she rejects what is no longer useful to her. She'll keep her word, I'm sure."

"My lord, there is no point to this duel!"

"It might save your life, my friend. And yours is the only life I care for."

"It could bring me torment, and the same to all others in Tanelorn."

I shook my head. "If they break their word, they can no longer be representatives of Law."

"What kind of Law do they represent, even now? A Law willing to sacrifice justice for ambition." Moonglum dragged at my arm as I began to descend the steps back to the ground. "And that's what makes me doubt everything they promise. Be wary of them, my lord." He gave up trying to persuade me and fell back.

"I'll be watching for any signs of their treachery and I'll do what I can to ensure the duel's fair. But I say again—it's folly, my friend. Your mad, old blood has seized your brain again."

I was amused by this. "That mad blood has found us many ways out of trouble, friend Moonglum. Sometimes I trust it better than any logic." But I could not raise his spirits.

A dozen others, including Brut of Lashmar, begged me to be cautious. But something in me was determined to break this stalemate, to follow my blind instincts and embrace a story that was not inevitable, that took a fresh direction. I wanted to prove that it was not the working-out of some prefigured destiny. As I'd told Moonglum, this was by no means the first time I had let the old blood blaze through my veins, sing its song in me and fill my being with wild joy. If I lived, I swore it would not be the last time I felt that thrill.

I was entirely alive again. I was taking risks. My life and soul were the stakes.

I marched down the steps, shouted for the gates to be raised. Demanded that the she-wolf be gone. That the faceless knight meet me alone.

When I had put Tanelorn's walls at my back and stepped across the causeway out into that barren world, the she-wolf had vanished. I looked into a mirror. I saw my own blazing features, my glaring ruby eyes, my fine, white hair whipping about my shoulders as the wind continued to blow across the ash desert.

The dismounted knight's helm and breastplate reflected everything they faced. Seemingly an advantage in battle. It would feel as if you were fighting yourself!

The knight stood with a silvery steel broadsword in his gauntleted hands. I was disturbed by the sight of it. He had not carried it earlier. This sword was a mirror of Stormbringer in everything but color. A negative image. I could easily recognize the symbols of sorcery, and that silver sword had no magical properties to speak of. I would have smelled them. Instead it exuded a deadness, a negativity.

No sorcery. Or sorcery so subtle even I couldn't detect it? A slow chill passed through me, leaving me wary and briefly weaker.

I felt a frisson of déjà vu.

Something chuckled from within the silver helm. A different note, almost a whisper.

"We act out our stories many times, Prince Elric. And occasionally we are granted the means to change them. You will understand, I hope, that in some of those stories, in some of those incarnations, you lose. In some, you die. In others, you suffer more than death."

Again that mysterious chill.

"I think this will be one of those other stories, my lord."

Then the gleaming blade was rushing down on me.

I barely blocked it in time. Stormbringer growled as she clashed with that white steel. She was expressing hatred. Or was it fear? Not a sound I had heard from her before.

I felt energy flowing out of me. With every countered blow, I found it harder to lift my sword. I peered into the silver helm as we fought but could see no hint of the features within.

I was horrified. I relied on my sword's strength to sustain my own. And now instead Stormbringer was sapping my strength. What aided this mysterious warrior? Why had I not smelled sorcery? I was clearly the victim of some supernatural force.

The knight was not an expert swordsman, as I had expected. He was rather clumsy. Yet every blow of mine was met. Only rarely did the knight feint back at me. He seemed to be playing an entirely defensive role, This, too, made me suspicious. If I had not agreed to the fight, I would have ended it there and then and returned to the city.

I was used to the wild song of my sword as I fought, but now Stormbringer merely vibrated with her blows. And those vibrations seemed feebler for every passing moment.

Moonglum had been right. I was the victim of a trap. I had no choice but to fight on.

Two more blows of mine were met by two of the knight's and then I was staggering, my knees buckling. I could barely lift my sword, which increasingly became a dead weight in my hands. I was baffled. The urgency of my movements tired me further. I had been completely outmaneuvered.

Again a low unfamiliar chuckle came from the depths of that helm.

I rallied everything I had. I tried to call on Arioch for help, but I was overwhelmed with tiredness. An unnatural tiredness. I used all my sorcerer's disciplines to bring my mind back into control over my body, but it was no use. The heavy pall of enchantment seeped through my being.

Within a few minutes of that fight beginning I lost my footing, and fell backwards onto the harsh, white ground. I saw the armored figure stoop and take Stormbringer and I was horrified. I had no means of resistance. I tried to struggle up and failed. Few could handle that sword without evil consequences, yet my opponent was casually able to pick her up. My certainties were collapsing around me. I feared I was going mad.

As my vision began to blur, I grew aware of the armored figure looking down on me, still laughing.

"Well, Prince Elric. Our bargain and our duel are settled and you are free to return to Tanelorn. We'll not harm the city, have no fear. I have what we came for."

The knight then lifted the helm for the first time. A woman looked down at me. A woman with pale, radiant features, with blond hair and glaring black eyes. A woman whose teeth were pointed, whose lips were on fire.

I knew immediately how I had been deceived.

"Lady Miggea, I presume." I could barely whisper. "You gave your word. The word of Law."

"You didn't listen carefully enough. It was the wolf who swore not to fight. Your blood is wise," she said softly, "but it informs your heart, not your mind. These are urgent times. There is much at stake. Sometimes the old rules no longer sustain the reality."

"You'll not keep your word? You said you'd leave the city in peace!"

"Of course, I shall. I'll let it die of natural causes."

"What do you mean?" My words were a dry gasp. I was beginning to realize the folly of my decision. Moonglum was right. I had brought untold disaster both to myself and my world. All because I had followed wild "instinct" rather than logic. There are times when faith provides only further catastrophe.

"There's no more water in this realm. Only what you see. Nothing to sustain your gardens. Nothing for you to drink." She smiled to herself as she held up Stormbringer by the blade, clutching it in a fist which seemed to grow larger as she spoke. "Nothing to help you. No supernatural aid. You cannot return to your own realm. It took my power to bring you here and keep you here. Few are as powerful as Miggea of Law. No human aid will save you. In time you'll wither away and that will be the end of you and your stories. But I have been merciful. You'll know none of this, Prince Elric, for you will be asleep."

As my sight faded and the last of my strength went out of me, I made one last attempt to rise. "Sleep?"

Her horrid crazed face came close to mine. She pursed her lips and blew into my eyes.

And then I descended into dreaming darkness.

# CHAPTER THIRTEEN

# The Dreamthief's Daughter

I became dimly aware of my friends from the city carrying me back. I was entirely incapable of movement, drifting in and out of an enchanted sleep, only vaguely conscious of the surrounding world, sometimes completely oblivious to it. I knew my friends, especially Moonglum, were concerned. I tried to rouse myself, to speak, but every effort took me deeper into my dreamworld.

I did not want to go deeper. I feared something there. Something which Miggea had prepared for me.

The only course open to me was the interior. Incapable of movement or communication, yet aware of my own condition, I finally let myself slip slowly down, afraid that I might never emerge again from the pit of my own complex psyche. Drowning in my own dark dreams.

The last of my will deserted me. I began to fall. Away from Tanelorn. Away from all the fresh dangers of the future. Dangers I would not be able to face without my sword. And how would the sword be used? To destroy the Balance itself? My mind was in a turmoil. Falling at last into oblivion was a relief.

I was unconscious for seconds, and then I began to dream. In

my dream I saw a man clothed in rags, standing with his face
turned from his own house, a book in his hand and a great bun-
dle on his back. I wanted to ask him his name, but his eyes were
filled with tears and he could not see me. For a moment I thought
when he turned towards me his face would be mine, but it was a
plain, round human head. He hesitated and then began to return
to his house where his wife and children waited for him, glad he
had not left them. They had not seen how distressed he was. For
one of my kind to feel sympathy for such ordinary souls was almost
disgusting, yet I longed to help these people in their misery.

Time passed. At last I saw the man leave his house with his
burden and walk away until he was out of sight. I began to follow
him, but when I reached the crest of the hill he had gone. I saw a
valley and in that valley a number of different battles were being
fought. Men burned castles, villages and towns. They slaughtered
women and children. They killed everything that lived, and then
they turned on one another and began to kill again. The only road
took me through this valley. Reconciled, I began my descent.

I had not gone very far, however, before a small, hunched figure jumped from a rock onto the path in front of me and, grinning, offered me an elaborate bow. He spoke to me, but I could
not hear him. He became frustrated, signing and gesturing, but
still I could not understand him. Eventually he took me by the
hand and led me around a corner of the rock. There ahead was
what seemed like an ocean, rising vertically to form a wall in front
of me. Through the ocean ran a gleaming road of dappled light,
like one ray of sunshine falling on water.

So strange was the perspective that I felt almost ill. Yet the
crooked little man continued to lead me until we had stepped
onto that dappled road and were walking up its steep surface. I
had the strong smell of ozone in my nostrils. The road then
straightened and became a silver moonbeam in a complex lattice
of moonbeams, like the roadways through the realms. My guide
was gone.

I was alarmed. At the same time I realized I had a feeling of
physical well-being. I had never known it before. I had only ever

experienced pain or relief from pain, but never a body that did not know pain at all. All my life I had had to deal with some weakness, either physical or moral. Now I began to feel fresh, elated, even relaxed. Yet I knew that in reality I had no physical body at all, that it was only my dreaming soul which wandered these worlds of enchantment.

The conflicting emotions within me did nothing to help my condition. I did not know if this was part of Miggea's trap. I did not know which path to choose. I looked up into all that vast complexity and I saw a million roads, each one like a ray of light, on which creatures of every kind walked. I knew that there was no such thing as a multiversal vacuum, that every apparently empty space was populated. I saw the roadways as branches of a great silver tree, whose roots somehow went deep down into my own brain. I knew that this was the fundamental structure of the multiverse. I decided, in spite of recent experience, to trust my instincts and to follow a small branch running off a more substantial limb.

I set foot on the pale road and it gave slightly to my step. It made walking a pleasure. In no time I had passed half a dozen branches, heading for my chosen path. But as I did so, I realized that the weave of the branches was more complicated than I had originally seen. I found myself in a tangle of minor brambles, which blocked my way and which I could not easily push aside. My body felt so light, so insubstantial that there was no danger of my breaking the branches. It seemed to me that tiny figures moved along other branches, just as I moved along mine.

Eventually I found ways of passing through the branches so that I disturbed very little. I had the impression that somewhere up there might be another creature, far bigger than myself, perhaps a version of myself, who was carefully trying to avoid knocking me from my branch.

At one point I paused. I was no longer dressed in my ordinary clothes but wore full Melnibonéan war armor. Not the elaborate baroque of ceremonial plate, but the efficient, blade-turning protection a man needed in battle. I had no sense of weight to the armor, any more than there was to my body. I half assumed I had died and become some kind of wandering ghost. If I remained here for a long time, I would gradually grow amorphous and merge with the atmosphere, breathed in like dust by the living.

Having lost my original direction, I found myself wandering down increasingly narrow and twisting branches. I thought I must soon step upon the last twig at the farthest edge of the multiversal tree. I was beginning to despair when I saw that the track led through a tunnel formed of willow boughs. On the other side of that tunnel was a weirdly shaped cottage, thatched with the straw of centuries, its bricks apparently borrowed from every source in existence, its windows at peculiar angles and of odd sizes, its door narrow and tall, its chimneys fantastically curled. From the roof of the small porch hung several baskets of blooming flowers and a birdcage. Under the birdcage sat a black and white sheepdog, her tongue lolling as if she had just come in from a day's work.

The pleasant pastoral scene made me oddly wary. I had become used to traps and delusions. My enemies seemed to enjoy making promises they had no intention of keeping, as if they had just discovered the power of the lie. If this image were a lie, it was a clever one. Everything looked perfect, including the plume of smoke coming from the chimney, the smell of baking, the domestic clatter from within.

I glanced back. Behind me, dwarfing everything, was the multiverse. Its great lattice filled all the myriad dimensions, its branches stretched into infinity. And its light shone down on this little cottage which sat exactly on the edge of the abyss, a great dark wood behind it. I tried to move forward and to my astonishment had some difficulty. The armor was heavy. My body, though feeling fit, was weary. In an instant I had become full corporeal!

I opened the gate of the cottage and dragged myself up the slate path to knock on the door. I remembered to remove my helmet. It was an awkward thing to carry under one's arm, all angles and filigree.

"Come in, Prince Elric," called a cheerful young voice. "You have trustworthy instincts, it seems."

"Sometimes, madam." I passed through the narrow doorway and found myself in a low-ceilinged room with black beams and white plaster. On the floor was luxurious carpet and on the walls were tapestries, living masterpieces showing every manner of human experience. I was astonished at the opulence, which seemed in contrast to the domestic atmosphere.

A young woman came from the next room, evidently the kitchen, wiping flour from her hands and arms. The powder fell in a silvery shower to the rich maroon carpet. She sniffed and then sneezed, apologizing. "I have waited for you for what seems an eternity, my lord."

I could not speak. I looked at one of my own kind. She had extraordinary, aquiline beauty, with slanting eyes and delicate, small, slightly pointed ears. Her eyes were red as fresh strawberries in a skin the color of bleached ivory. Her long, bone-white hair fell in soft folds down over her shoulders. She wore a simple shirt and breeches, over which she had thrown a rough linen apron. And she was laughing at me.

"My friend Jermays put you on the right road, I see."

"Who was that little man?"

"You'll meet him again in time, perhaps."

"Perhaps."

"We all do. Often when our stories start to alter. Sometimes one's destiny changes radically. A new tale is born. A new myth to weave in with the old. A new dream."

"I am dreaming this. I am dreaming you. Therefore I am dreaming this conversation. Does this mean that I am mad? Has the enchantment which holds me in sleep also attacked my brain?"

"Oh, we all dream one another, Prince Elric, in some ways. It is our dreams and our demands upon them which have made us so various and at odds with so much and so many."

The young woman even had gestures which I recognized.

"Would you do me the honor, madam, of telling me your name."

"I'm called White Hare Sister by the dreamthieves and shape-changers amongst whom I was raised. But my mother calls me Oona, after the custom of her folk."

"Her name is Oone?"

"Oone the Dreamthief. And I am Oona, the dreamthief's daughter. And Oonagh will be my daughter's name."

"Oone's daughter?" I hesitated. "And mine?"

She was laughing openly now as she came towards me. "I think it likely, don't you?"

"I did not know there was—issue."

"Oh, quite spectacular 'issue,' I assure you, Father."

The word struck at me with the force of a tidal wave. Father! An emotional blow worse than any sword stroke. I wanted to deny it, to say anything which would prove me to be dreaming. To make this fact disappear. But my eyes could not deceive me. Everything about her showed that she was my daughter and Oone's. I had loved Oone briefly. We had sought the Fortress of the Pearl together. But as I remembered this, another thought occurred to me. More deception!

"Not enough time has passed," I said. "You are too old to be my daughter."

"In your plane, perhaps, my lord, but not on this one. Time is not a road. It's an ocean. I believe you and my mother celebrated your friendship here in this realm."

I liked her irony.

"Your mother—?" I began.

"Her interests are no longer in these worlds, although she occasionally visits the End of Time, I understand."

"She gave birth to you here?"

"I was one of twins, she said."

"Twins?"

"So she told me."

"Your sibling died?"

"My twin didn't die when we were born. But something happened which mother could not explain, and I was soon separated from my sibling. Gone. Gone. My mother's words. I know nothing else."

"You seem very casual about your twin's fate."

"Reconciled, my lord. I thought, until recently, you had found that twin to raise as your own, but, of course, I now know that is not the case." She turned urgently, disappearing back into the kitchen. The smell of greenberry pie came to me in a single, delicious wave. I had forgotten the simple pleasures of human life.

Because this was a dream I saw nothing strange about being invited to sit down at a kitchen table and enjoy a meal of good, new bread, fresh-churned butter, some chandra and a bottle of goldfish sauce, with the prospect of the pie, and perhaps a puff of glas to complete my pleasure.

Not once, for all the trickeries of Law, did I further suspect this young woman. Nor the sense of sanctuary which came from her cottage. It was impossible. I knew she was of my blood. If she had been a lie, a shape-changing creature of Chaos, I should have guessed it immediately.

Yet a voice in the back of my mind told me I had not smelled sorcery when Law had so successfully defeated me and essentially committed me to my present fate. Had I lost my powers? Was I only now beginning to realize it? Was this another illusion to steal what was left of my soul?

My temperament was such that I could not go cautiously. Nothing was to be gained from caution. I had few choices in this extraordinary cottage at the center of the silvery matrix of moonbeams.

"So you have no idea what became of your sister?"

"My sister?" She smiled. "Oh, no, my dear father. It was not my sister. It was my brother we lost."

"Brother?" Something in me shuddered. Something else exulted. "My son?"

"Maybe it's as well you did not know, my lord. For if he is dead, as I suspect, then you would be grieving now."

I reflected that I had only known I had a son for a few seconds. I was in shock. It would be a moment or two before I came to the grieving stage!

I looked wonderingly at my daughter. My feelings were both

direct and complex. On an impulse which would have shocked and disgusted a Melnibonéan, I stepped forward and embraced her. She returned my embrace awkwardly, as if she, too, was not used to such customs, She seemed pleased.

"So you are a dreamthief," I said.

She shook her head fiercely. I saw a dozen honest emotions flit across her features. "No. I am a dreamthief's child. I have the experience and some of the skills, but not the vocation. In fact, to tell you the truth, Father, I'm somewhat divided. Part of my character vaguely disagrees with the morality of Mother's profession."

"Well, your mother was of great help to me when we sought the Fortress of the Pearl together." I myself was overfamiliar with matters of moral and emotional division.

"It is one of the few adventures she retold. She was unusually fond of you, given the number of lovers she has known down the centuries and over the whole of the time field. I suspect you are the only one by whom she had children."

"Special affection or special resentment?"

"She bore you no ill will, sir. Far from it. She spoke of you with pleasure. She spoke of you as a great warrior. As a brave and courteous knight of the limits. She told me you would have made the most gorgeous dreamthief of them all. That was her own special dream, I think. What do you think dreamthieves dream of most, Father?"

"Perhaps of dreamless sleep," I said. I was still surprised by the discovery of my child. A child whose beauty was stunning and whose character seemed, as far as I could tell, complex and full of intelligence. A child who had brought me here to her little Earth on the very edge of time. Her birthplace, she told me as we ate.

The forest, which looked threatening to me, she assured me was full of amiable wonders. She had enjoyed a perfect childhood, she said. The forest and the cottage were protected in some way, much as Tanelorn was protected, from the rapacity of either Law or Chaos. The place was far from lonely. Many of her mother's friends traveled between the worlds, as she did, and they loved nothing better than bringing back stories to tell in the evening around the fire.

When she was fifteen, she had gone with her mother to those worlds where Oone intended to retire, but she had not liked them. She decided to find her own vocation. Meanwhile she, too, would wander the myriad realms of the multiverse for a time. To give her travels some purpose, she tried to discover if her brother were still alive, but the only albino she heard of was her father, the feared and hated Elric of Melniboné. She had felt no great desire to meet him.

Then, later, she had discovered others. A bloodline, of sorts, which she was still trying to trace. She hoped this might provide a better means of finding her brother. She believed he had settled in one particular realm, similar to the kind her mother favored. Not only had he settled there, he had absorbed himself in his host culture, married and produced offspring.

I was feeling older by the moment. While I could grasp the notion of time having passed in different ways in different realms, it was still hard for me, a relatively young man, to see myself as the patriarch of generations. The responsibility alone made me uncomfortable. I felt a certain wariness overcome me, and I wondered if this were not part of Law's complicated deception, part of some greater cosmic plot in which I played a minor role. I again began to feel like a pawn in a game. A game the gods played merely to while away their boredom.

This thought fired me to quiet anger. If that were the case, I would do everything I could to defeat their plans.

I called you here, Father, not from curiosity, but out of urgency. I know how you were duped. And why." She seemed to sense my mood. "Miggea and her minions threaten Tanelorn and several other realms, including the one inhabited by your descendants."

"A race resembling Melniboné's?"

"Resembling their last emperor, at any rate. Fighting the same forces we both fight, sir. They are our natural allies. And there is one who can help us defeat Law."

"Madam," I said with every courtesy, "you are aware perhaps that beyond this realm I have no true physical form. I am a shade. A ghost. Outside this environment I am a spirit. I am, madam, as good as dead. I could not hold a cup if it were not for whatever temporary physicality you or this place has bestowed on me. My body lies in a deep, unwakable slumber in the doomed city of Tanelorn, while Miggea, Duchess of Law, now holds the Black Sword and can do with it whatever she likes. I am defeated, madam. I have failed in every venture. I am a dream within a dream. All this can be nothing but dream. A useless, pointless dream."

"Well," she said, picking up the dishes, "one person's dream is another's reality."

"Platitudes, madam."

"But truths, too," she said. A kind of confident stillness had come upon her as she undid her apron and hung it up. "Well, Father, are you pleased to see me?"

Her eyes, humorous and inquiring, looked frankly into mine.

I began to smile. "I believe I must be," I said. "Though no royal Melnibonéan would admit it."

"Well," she said, "I am glad I am not a royal Melnibonéan."

"I'm the last of those," I said, "or so I understand."

"Aye," she said, "that seems to be the truth. Melniboné falls, but the blood continues. Ancient blood. Ancient memory."

"Forgive me if I seem brusque," I said, "but I understood you to say, Lady Oona, that you guided me here as a matter of some urgency." I could not bring myself to address her informally.

"With my skill I can help you, Father," she said. "I can help you get your sword back and possibly even be revenged on the one who stole it from you."

Again, I should have suspected a trick, but my daughter convinced me completely. I knew that this entire episode could be a development of the same enchantment under which Law had put me. But it seemed I had no other course of action to take. I had to trust her or remain frozen on my couch in Tanelorn, unable to retrieve my sword or claim vengeance on the one who had stolen it.

"You know the future?" I challenged.

She replied quietly, "I know more than one."

She explained how the multiverse is made up of millions of worlds, each only a shade different from our own. In each of those worlds certain people struggle eternally for justice. Sometimes for Law. Sometimes for Chaos. Sometimes simply for equilibrium. Most people do not know that other versions of themselves are struggling, too. Each story is a little different. And very occasionally a major change can be made to the story. Sometimes their strengths can be combined. Which was exactly what we hoped to achieve through my daughter's extraordinary strategy.

She believed it was possible for two or more avatars to occupy the same body, if the body was of like blood. I needed a physical body and a physical sword. She believed she had found both.

She told me of von Bek, of his blade and his own fight against corrupted authority. She said she believed our fates were intertwined at this particular configuration of the cosmic realms. He and I were both avatars of the same being. I could help him, and he could help me, by lending me his body and his sword.

I said that I had to think.

Dreamlessly, perhaps because I now lived a dream, I rested at Oona's cottage on time's borderlands in the so-called Mittelmärch. While I rested, my daughter taught me more of the dreamthief's secrets. How to travel the roads between the realms. The realms we thought supernatural but which were perfectly mundane to their inhabitants. She had her mother's library and was able to show me old tales, current scientific ideas, the theories of philosophers, all of which spoke of dreams as being glimpses of other times and places. Some of them understood what Oona understood—that the worlds of our dreams have physical reality and cannot be easily manipulated, that each one of us has a version of themselves in all these billions of alternative worlds and that somehow all our actions are interlinked to make a grander cosmic whole whose scale is inconceivable, a pattern of order which we either support or threaten, depending on our loyalties and ambitions.

One morning, looking at a book of watercolors done by an ancestor of Oona's, I asked my daughter if she really believed that somehow we might dream one another. Did we exist entirely as a result of our own wills? Did we bring ourselves and our worlds into reality because of some mighty desire, stronger than the physical universe? Or was it possible we had already created the universe? The multiverse, even. Was the great tree something which mortals had nurtured until it was no longer in their control?

If so, had we also created the gods, the Cosmic Balance, the elementals? I could not bring myself to believe that. It would suggest we had forged our own chains, as well as creating the means of our salvation! It would mean that the gods were just symbols of our own strengths, weaknesses and desires!

I offered this speculation to my daughter, but she dismissed it. She had heard it all too often. There was little point to it, she seemed to say. We are here. Whatever the causes or the reasons, we now exist and have to make the best of it. She reminded me of her purpose in bringing me here.

"Once you are free," she said, "you will be able to do everything you could do before. In Mu Ooria you will not be blocked from your elemental allies. Von Bek has one of Stormbringer's manifestations. He is the only way you can recover your own blade. With von Bek's help, you might get your sword back and save Tanelorn. I will help you as best I can, but my powers are limited. I have my mother's skills, but not her temperament."

The next morning I stood beside her as she locked her door and gave last instructions to her dog and bird, who listened intelligently.

"No." She turned to me as if we were going on a family outing to the country. "We'll take the moonbeam roads which will lead us to the heart of the multiverse. To the Grey Fees. And thence to Moo Uria, dear Father, and your continuing destiny."

The Grey Fees? I shall not attempt to describe that place which is, most believe, the origin of all things, the fundamental stuff of the multiverse, misty fields where you glimpse ribbons of

basic matter creating cryptic arabesques, perpetually writhing and
pulsing, forming and re-forming, becoming whole worlds, dissipating again, and, perhaps most bizarrely, inhabited by mad adven-
turers with loyalty neither to Law nor to Chaos, only to their own
idiosyncratic mathematics. Amiable enough fellows, and magnifi-
cently intelligent, able to sail anywhere in the multiverse by
means of "scale ships" but warped by their environment in mind
and body. We avoided these Lords and Ladies of Sublime Disorder
whenever possible, Even they were aware that some great disaster
threatened us all. That Law had gone mad.

The Chaos Engineers guided us through the bewildering Grey
Fees to the terrifying world of the Nazis. Thereafter, I was with
von Bek most of the time, though he could rarely see me. I
became his guardian angel; his life was very important to me. By
following Oona's instructions I was able to help my doppelgänger
von Bek in the camps and later in the caverns of Mu Ooria, where
I discovered that what my daughter had said was true. It was possible to blend my own substance with von Bek's.

My powers had some small potency even before I bonded with
von Bek. But with von Bek to help, they were now completely
restored. We were more than the sum of our parts. We were
stronger when we came together although it was not easy to
achieve the bonding or to make it last.

I tried more than once to merge with him but either he had
resisted or the time had not been right. Twice I almost succeeded, but lost him again. Eventually, when he needed my help
most and was prepared to accept what I could offer him, I
stepped into his body, just as Oona had taught me, and immediately we became the single creature I have already described. I
merged with him, blending his skills and character with my own.
And now I had the benefit of von Bek's wisdom and swordsmanship. That was how I had been able to return to Tanelorn.
That was the only possible way to thwart the enchantment put
upon me.

There was precious little time. Although we had returned
rapidly, Lady Miggea and her knights could have left this world

and, with Stormbringer to help them, even now be conquering Mu Ooria.

Brut gave us his best horses. Moonglum and I rode out of Tanelorn onto those unforgiving ash flats whose sentinels of limestone were a constant reminder of our mortality. On Oona's advice and my own impulse, determined to achieve the impossible, we were going hunting.

Hunting for a goddess.

# CHAPTER FOURTEEN

# Fresh Treacheries

 deep chill had settled on this world. Nothing was alive. When the breeze stirred the ash drifts or flaked the crags so it seemed to snow, a complete absence of vitality was evident in the landscape.

Miggea's was no ordinary desert. It was all that remained of a world destroyed by Law. Barren. No hawks soared in the pale blue sky. There were no signs of animal life. Not an insect. Not a reptile. No water. No lichen. No plants of any kind. Just tall spikes of crystallized ash and limestone, crumbling and turned into crazy shapes by the wind, like so many grotesque gravestones.

Law's cold hand had fallen on everything. Law achieved this desolation at her worst. This tidiness of death. Mankind inevitably achieves the same when it seeks to control too much.

Moonglum had insisted on accompanying me and I had not refused. Unusually, I felt the need for company. Moonglum's comradeship was something I valued. He recognized when I was at my most negative, my most self-pitying, and would say something sardonic to remind me of my stupidity. He was also a brilliant swordsman, who had fought sorcerers as well as soldiers, the steadiest man to have at one's side in any kind of fight.

As we rode, I tried to explain to my somewhat repulsed friend how I was now two people—two entirely different identities but of the same blood, locked together in one near-identical body. By this combination we had thwarted Lady Miggea's enchantment. By entering the world of dreams and finding an alternative version of myself.

All this made my friend very uncomfortable. "Two people warring inside you?" He shuddered. "To be joined physically, by the head, say, is one thing. But to be joined in the mind! Forever in conflict . . ."

"We are not in conflict," I explained. "We are one. Just as, say, a playwright will invent a character and that character will live within him, quite comfortably. So it is with von Bek and myself. Where his world is the most familiar, he will take the ascendancy, but here, within an environment I understand a little better, I am in command. We have shared memories also—the entire creature from birth to present. And believe me, my friend, there is less conflict between von Bek and myself than there is between me and myself!"

"That's easy enough to believe, my lord," said Moonglum, staring with half-seeing eyes out at the forest of stones.

We could ride only so far without water. We had large canteens, enough to last for several days, but no certainty that any of our enemies were still here. Indeed, Lady Miggea had a use for the sword, no doubt as part of her plans for further conquest. All we could do was follow the faint trails marked by her army, hoping they had left some clue behind that would lead us to discover where she had gone with my sword.

The sky was a stark eggshell blue. We had no means of keeping our direction except by noting the shapes of the different rocks we passed, hoping to recognize them on our return.

Less than a day from the city we began to descend into a wide shallow valley which stretched for several miles on all sides. When we were halfway down and rounding a great bulk of tattered rock, we saw some distance ahead of us a grotesque building, clearly the work of intelligent beings, but reeking of mad cruelty.

Dry wind whispered through a palace built of bones. Many of those bones still had rotting flesh clinging to them: The bones of horses. The bones of men. From the evidence, the bones of all those Knights of Law who had so recently threatened us. Who had thundered so forcefully past us in pursuit of the little white hare. Their silver armor was scattered around the building, thousands of breastplates, helmets, greaves, gauntlets. Their lances and swords lay half-buried in the pale ash. Miggea had expected the ultimate sacrifice from her loyal followers, and she had received it.

But what had she built her fortress against?

Or was it a fortress? Did it now function as a prison?

As we drew nearer, the wind began to sough more miserably than ever through those half-picked bones, turning to a mournful howling that filled the world with despair. We slowed our horses and moved more cautiously, searching the low surrounding hills for the sight of wolves. There were none.

We moved closer to the towering palace of bones. Keeps and domes and battlements and buttresses were shaped from the recently living bodies of men and horses from which strips of flesh and fur and linen fluttered like banners in the erratic wind. And the terrible howling continued. All the grief in all the realms of the multiverse. All the frustration. All the despair. All the wounded ambition.

So dense were the bones packed to form the walls of the palace that we could not see inside. But we thought we saw a movement behind the palace. A solitary figure. Perhaps an illusion.

"The howling's coming from inside the bones, my lord." Moonglum cocked his head to one side. "From deep within that house of bones. Listen."

He was better able to locate the source of sounds than I, though my hearing was more acute. I had no reason to disbelieve him.

Whatever was howling was either trapped in the bone palace or was defending it. Was Miggea still here, still in the shape of a wolf? That would explain the howling and also the frustration. What could have thwarted her plans?

Again we glimpsed movement, this time from within the palace, as if something paced back and forth. We moved closer still until the vast construction loomed over us. And now we could smell it. Sweet, cloying, horrible, It stank of rotting flesh.

We hesitated before the great central entrance. Neither of us had any desire to confront what was within.

Then, as we made up our minds to dismount and enter, another human figure came around one of the bone buttresses. Colored rags still clung to him. He carried a sword in either hand. Leaf-bladed broadswords. One was a shade of diseased ivory with black runes running its length. The other was Stormbringer, all pulsing black iron and scarlet runes.

The man who bore them was Prince Gaynor of Mirenburg. He was wearing a mirror breastplate over the torn remains of his SS uniform.

He was laughing heartily.

Until I drew my Ravenbrand.

Then his breath hissed from him. He looked about, as if for allies or enemies, then he faced me again. He forced a grin.

"I did not know there was a *third* sword," he said. I could see from his eyes that he was attempting a new calculation.

"There is no third sword," I told him, "or second sword. You are disingenuous, cousin. There is only one sword. And you have stolen it. From your mistress, eh?"

He looked down at both hands. "I seem to have two swords, cousin."

"One, as you know, is a *farun*, a false sword, forged to attract the properties of the original and absorb them. It can steal the souls of men as well as swords. It's a kind of mirror, which absorbs the essence of the thing it most resembles. No doubt Miggea made it for you. Only a noble of the Higher Worlds can forge such a thing. Foolishly I did not anticipate such elaborate conjuring.

"That was how you two tricked Elric. And were able to capture first my energy, then the power of my blade and then the blade itself. I name your second sword 'Deceiver' and demand you return its stolen power. You defeated me by trickery, cousin, with words and illusions."

"You always were too wild-blooded, cousin. I relied on you being unable to resist a challenge."

"I shall not be foolish again," I said.

"We'll see, cousin. We'll see." He was eyeing Ravenbrand. Looking from it to Stormbringer, as if alarmed by what might happen if the two should meet in battle. "You say there's only one sword, yet—"

"Only one," I agreed.

He understood the implications of my words. While he had not studied as I had and did not possess my skills or learning, he had masters whose casual knowledge was far more profound than all my wisdom. Yet he was impressed. His answering grimace was almost admiring. "Powerful sorcery," he said. "And clever strategy. You've had unanticipated help, eh?"

"If you say so, cousin." I was reluctant to use the blade. I had no idea what the consequences might be. I had a sense of extraordinary supernatural movement all around me, unseen, not yet expressed. An imminence of sorcery. It was easy, in that atmosphere, to feel little more than a desperate pawn in a vast game played by the Lords of the Higher Worlds, who some said were also ourselves at our most powerful and least sane. I took control of myself. Slowly, with all the habits of discipline learned from Bek as well as Melniboné, I extended my mind to include as many of the supernatural realms as I could, sensing unexpected friends as well as mighty enemies.

Gaynor's answer was drowned by a vast, mournful howl from within the palace of bones. He laughed richly in response. "Oh, she is an unhappy goddess," he said jubilantly. "Such a sad old she-wolf. A prisoner of her own forces. A pretty irony, eh, cousin?"

"You did this to her?"

"I arranged it, cousin. Even I cannot control a Duchess of the Distance, a Denizen of the Higher Worlds." He paused, as if with modesty. "I only helped. In a small way."

"Helped what? Whom?"

"Her old enemy," he said. "Duke Arioch of Chaos."

"You serve Law! Arioch is my patron!"

"Sometimes these alliances are convenient," he said, shrugging. "Duke Arioch is a reasonable fellow, for a Lord of Hell. When it became evident that my patroness was no longer in charge of her sanity, I simply made a bargain with that Master of Entropy to deliver my erstwhile mistress into his keeping. Which I shall do as soon as I can deliver her to him. Tricking her, Prince Elric, was even easier than tricking you. The poor creature is senile. She has lost all judgment. She brought no honor to her cause. Only defeat. I had to save the good name of Law. It was time she sought dignified retirement. Her followers were no longer useful to her. And so they became her home. She believed she was going to the Isle of Morn . . ."

"She doesn't seem to appreciate it greatly," said Moonglum. "Indeed she appears to be acting as if you have imprisoned her."

"It's for her own good," said Gaynor. "She was becoming a danger to herself, as well as to others."

"Such a high moral purpose," I said. "And meanwhile you steal from her the sword she fought me for."

"The plan was mine and the sword is mine," he said. "Only the magic was hers."

He held the white sword by the hilt and stripped off the last of his colored scarves, as if he had no further need of them.

"Her ambitions were unrealistic. I, on the other hand, am the ultimate realist. And soon I shall have everything I have sought. All the old, mystic treasures of our ancestors. All the great objects of power. All the legendary treasures of our race. Everything that guarantees us victory and security for the next thousand years. Herr Hitler's time will soon be over. He'll be recognized as the flawed knight, my precursor."

He gave me a mad, knowing look, as if I were the only creature who could possibly understand his intelligence and the logic of his ambition.

"I shall prove their Parsifal. Their true Führer. For by then I will have the sword and the cup, and I will be able to show the world proof of my destiny to rule. All Christendom, East and West, will rally to my banner. Arioch has promised me this. I shall have no challengers, for my power shall be both temporal and spiritual. I will become the true blood leader of the Teutonic peoples, cleansing the world in the name of our holy discipline. Then the Golden Age will begin. The Age of the Greater Reich."

I was familiar with such nonsense. I had heard a hundred like him in those years before and after Hitler ascended to the chancellorship. For all his bombast, he seemed to be playing a tyro's game. Such games often progress rapidly, whether in chess or with worlds for stakes, because of the very lack of sense behind their strategies. They can't be anticipated or countered logically. They eventually doom themselves and are always overcome. I was far more interested in what he had said earlier. "How," I asked him, "did you strike a bargain with my own patron, Arioch of Chaos?"

"Miggea was no longer trustworthy and therefore no longer useful to my plans. For an eternity Arioch has yearned for vengeance on his old enemy. I sought him out and offered to help him reach this plane. He could do so only with human agency. He agreed happily to the bargain and trapped her here. She cannot leave. For she has no one left to help her. Should you attempt to free her, you will be betraying your trust, flaunting the will of your patron demon." He raised his voice in malevolent glee, to be heard by his prisoner as well as by me.

Once more the air was filled with that terrible howling.

Furious, I raised my black sword and spurred my horse towards my cousin.

He began to laugh at me again. Standing his ground as I rode down on him.

"One other thing I forgot to mention, cousin." He crossed the two blades in front of him, as if for protection against me. "I am no longer part of your dream."

The blades formed an X as a strange yellow and black light began to pulse from them, half blinding me so that I could no longer see Gaynor clearly. I held up one hand to shade my eyes, my sword ready. But he had become a rapidly moving shadow, racing away from me with violent light flickering all around him. He passed between two great crags and disappeared.

I spurred after him around the great bone palace while the she-wolf kept up her perpetual howling, and I almost caught him. Again the two swords were crossed and again they fluttered with that confusing black and yellow light.

Blinded by the light, deafened by the howling, I once more lost sight of Gaynor. I heard Moonglum yelling something. I looked around for my friend but could not see him. More shadows ran back and forth in front of me.

The horse balked, reared and began to whinny. I tried to control him but only barely managed to get him steadied. He was still uneasy, shifting his feet and snorting. Then there was an explosion of silver, soft, all-engulfing, narcotic. And a sudden silence.

I knew Gaynor was gone.

After a while, the she-wolf began her howling again.

Moonglum suggested that I summon Arioch. "It is the one move you can make to allow us to pursue Gaynor. Arioch can come and go as he pleases here now. Miggea's power no longer opposes his."

When I pointed out that Arioch habitually demanded a blood sacrifice as the price of his summoning and that he, Moonglum, was the only other living mortal soul in the vicinity, my friend put his mind to alternative schemes for our salvation.

I suggested that rather than remain and listen to Miggea's eternal lament, we should return to Tanelorn and seek the advice of the citizens. Should a blood sacrifice still be necessary, at least I could kill an exiled witch-lawyer and win easy popularity with the majority.

So we turned our horses, hoping to reach the city by dark.

By nightfall, however, we were hopelessly lost. As we feared, it had been impossible to tell one pillar of ash from another. The wind recarved them by the moment.

With some relief, therefore, a few hours later, with the stars our only light, we heard someone calling our names. I recognized it at once. My daughter's voice. Oona had found us. I congratulated myself on the intelligence of my relatives.

Then I thought again. This could be another deception. I cautioned Moonglum to ride forward carefully in case of a trap.

In the starlight, reflecting the glittering desert, I saw the silhouette of a woman on foot, bow and arrows slung over her shoulder. I had begun to guess that Oona had a more supernatural means of traveling than by horseback.

Once again I was looking at her intensely.

Her white skin had a warmth to it which my own lacked. Her soft hair glowed. She had much of her mother in her, a natural vitality I had never enjoyed. I had admired, respected and loved Oone the Dreamthief for a brief time when our paths had crossed. We had risked our lives and our souls in a common cause. And we had grown to love and ultimately lust for each other. But this feeling for my daughter was a different, deeper emotion.

I felt a peculiar pride in Oona, a gladness that she so resembled her mother. I imagined that her human characteristics sat better than those of her Melnibonéan ancestry. I hoped she had less conflict in her than did I. I suppose I envied her, too. It could be, of course, that all of us were doomed eternally to conflict, but maybe Fate granted a few a little more tranquillity than others. What I chiefly felt, even in these dangerous circumstances, was a quiet affection, a sense that whatever virtues I had were being passed by my blood from one soul to another. That perhaps my vices had atrophied and been lost from the blood.

Surging up from the ancient layers of my breeding came the utterly Melnibonéan response to one's children, to cut off all feelings of affection lest they weaken us both, to turn away from them. I resisted both impulses. My self-discipline was constantly being tested, constantly being tempered and retempered.

"I thought you had again fallen prey to Gaynor." She sounded relieved. "I know he was here until a short while ago."

I told her what had happened to Miggea. I spoke grimly of Gaynor's trick with the swords, his escape. I cursed him for a traitor, betraying his mistress to my patron, Duke Arioch. Whom he would doubtless betray as well, should it suit him.

At this Oona began to laugh heartily. "How thoroughly he behaves according to type," she said. "There is no hope for that poor soul. No redemption. He races towards his damnation. He embraces it. Betrayal is becoming a habit with him. Soon it will become an addiction and he will be wholly lost. Declaring it mere common sense, he betrays Law in the name of the Balance and betrays the Balance in the name of Entropy. Inevitably he will betray Arioch. And then what a sad renegade he will be. For the moment, admittedly, he achieves a certain power."

"Then there is no defeating him," I said. "He will destroy Mu Ooria and then his own world."

She held my reins as I dismounted. Somewhat awkwardly, I embraced her. She seemed in good spirits. "Oh," she said, "I think we still have a good chance of thwarting Gaynor's ambition."

Moonglum began to grin. "You're an optimist, my lady, I'll say that. You must own a strong belief in the power of luck."

"Indeed I do," she agreed, "but I think we'd be wiser for the moment to rely upon the power of dreams. I shall visit the imprisoned goddess while you make haste for Tanelorn. You are free to inhabit your own form now, Father, and leave poor Count von Bek the privacy and sanctity of his overworked body."

With that she loped off the way we had come and was soon out of sight. The sun began to pour its scarlet light over the forlorn horizon. It revealed in the distance the gables and turrets of our doomed, beloved Tanelorn.

Riding out to greet us was as odd a group of warriors as I had seen. The leader was Fromental, still in his Foreign Legion uniform. Behind him rode the three beastly lords Bragg, Blare and Bray, while on all fours, and looking a little odd in all his fineries, trotted Lord Renyard. He was the first to greet us. They had heard of our quest and had come to aid us.

I told them of our adventures and suggested we all turn back to Tanelorn for some food and rest, but that motley party was adamant. They had come all the way from the Stones of Morn to settle with Gaynor. They could find a way to follow him. Perhaps Miggea would help them.

Resignedly I gave them directions and wished them good fortune. My purpose was to save Tanelorn, not pursue Gaynor, but I had no objection if they wished to take their revenge on him. My thoughts were elsewhere.

Soon it would be time for me to return to my own body and allow von Bek to make what he could of his destiny in our fight against the common enemy.

# BOOK THREE

*Two long songs for the pale lord's brood*
*Two short lies disguise them,*
            *Sing true, true, true for the snow-white bird.*
*Dead now lies my ivory child,*
*Emptied of sadness, his eyes defiled;*
            *Sing lie, lie, lie for the ivory child.*
*The white hare's fleet against the falling sun.*
*Two dark shadows she'll embrace;*
*One in shoddy, one in lace.*
*She speeds the lost old river's course,*
*Fleet against the falling sun,*
*The sweet beast runs*
*Where the ashy wastelands toss,*
            *To where the wasteland's ashes flow.*
            *Wild against the fallen sun.*

—WHELDRAKE, "The Wild Hare"

# CHAPTER FIFTEEN

# Where the Multiverse Begins

anelorn was a triumphant stain of warm life upon the endless ash. I wondered how long she would be trapped in this dead realm, conquered by Law, all traces of Chaos thoroughly extinguished. Eventually Miggea's spell would fade and the city must return to her natural place. My feelings were mixed as Moonglum and I rode through the low gates to be greeted by our friends. We told them we believed Tanelorn no longer to be in danger. But the dangers to other places to which we'd given our love and loyalty were considerable. Mu Ooria was still threatened, perhaps conquered by now. And my Germany was still in the grip of a mad tyrant. It was hard to retain one's focus when so many issues remained unresolved.

With deep anxiety I dismounted outside Brut of Lashmar's house and gave my reins to his ostler. I hoped Fromental and his strange band would be successful, but I doubted it. Gaynor was playing a far more ambitious game than I had guessed. It was never wise, as we of Melniboné had discovered to our cost, to set Law against Chaos in the hope of achieving one's mortal ends.

No creature, human or Melnibonéan, could ever command or contain the kind of power the gods commanded. To become involved in their struggles in this way was certain destruction. Part of me cared little if these inferior beings lived or died, but another part of me understood that there was a common bond, a common threat, and that my fate was closely bound up with the fate of the race which had founded the Young Kingdoms. I also understood that commonality was not a matter of race, but of intellect and disposition, that while my own culture was so alien to these humans, yet as an individual I made more friendships with them than I did with my own kind.

Melniboné's isolation and arrogance created within me a per-petual conflict. Like the multiverse itself, my mind was rarely at rest. I felt torn constantly between the opposing forces which bound reality, the eternal paradoxes of life and death, of war and peace. Yet if peace was all I sought, then why had I never settled in beguiling Tanelorn, where I had friends, books, music and mem-ories? Why did I lust sometimes for the next conflict and the next? For the dreaming violence, the bitter oblivion of the battlefield?

We were greeted by Brut, ill-at-ease but glad to see us. "How long must we suffer this damned enchantment?"

"Miggea's power's defeated. Or at least contained. It should not be long before you see your familiar surroundings once more." Brut's question seemed a minor problem, given Gaynor's growing power.

We stayed long enough at Brut's to refresh ourselves, then Oona came back, hard-faced and speaking little. "We must begin this at once," was all she would say. We went with somewhat mixed feelings to the Tower of the Hand, that queer red building whose battlements resembled a palm held outward in a gesture of peace. Where my body still lay in conjured slumber.

Acknowledged by the guard, we entered the low doorway and began to climb a steep staircase which let onto a warren of corri-dors. Oona led the way, her step light and sure. I came behind, a little less speedily, and Moonglum brought up the rear. He had the air of a man who had seen far too much sorcery and was not look-ing forward to witnessing any more. He was babbling about our need to leave Tanelorn as soon as possible, to get back on our

original course, to put all this behind us and return to the solid
realities of the Young Kingdoms, whose sorcery, by and large, was
of human proportions.

Oona was grim. "There will be precious few solid realities if
Gaynor brings Arioch to the Stones of Morn." Again she fell into
an unresponsive silence. I had heard her and Fromental refer earlier to the Stones of Morn but had no clear idea what they were.

At the end of a narrow passage we found another guarded
door. I stopped to draw breath while Moonglum exchanged a conventional word or two with the man on duty.

Pretending to have trouble with the door lock, I continued to
hesitate. I felt Moonglum's hand on my arm. Oona smiled at me
with diffident encouragement.

I pushed open the door.

The long body of a Melnibonéan noble lay before me. Aside
from its colorless skin, it could have been one of a hundred ancestors. The refined features were in contrast to the vulgarity of the
costume. The hands were longer and more slender than von
Bek's, the bones of the face more sharply defined, the ears taper-
ing slightly, the mouth sensitive, sardonic. The clothing was that
of a barbarian from the South; that alone identified it as mine. For
some time I had chosen not to wear my traditional costume. Even
the milky hair, pinned at the nape of the neck, was a barbarian
fashion. The figure lay dressed just as it had fallen. Nobody had
wished, Oona said, to disturb anything, in case I should awaken
suddenly. The knee-length boots of doeskin, the baroque silver
breastplate, the checkered jerkin of blue and white, scarlet leg-
gings, heavy green cloak. Even the empty scabbard lay beside him.
A far better scabbard than the rough-and-ready thing I had made
for Ravenbrand.

Though the figure was mine and familiar to the half of me
which was Elric, I observed it with a certain detachment, until
suddenly I was filled with a surge of emotion and, darting forward,
kneeled beside the bed, mutely grasping the limp, corpselike
hand, unable to express the feeling of intense sympathy which
consumed me. I was weeping for my own tormented soul.

I tried to pull myself together, embarrassed by my unseemly response. I took Ravenbrand and placed it in the cold hand. I began to rise, to say something to my friends, when suddenly the sleeping man's other hand closed on my own and kept me firmly where I was. He was still, as far as I could tell, in a deep, enchanted slumber. Yet there was no denying the power of his grip.

As I struggled to free myself, my eyelids grew heavier and what remained of my energy seeped away. I wanted only to sleep. This feeling was unnatural. I could not afford to sleep. What enchantment had Gaynor left behind for me?

I could not see that it mattered now whether I continued or whether I rested. It seemed perfectly logical, in the circumstances, to lie down beside the bed and join my other self in a much-needed slumber. I heard Moonglum's anxious voice in the deep distance. I heard Oona say something about our safety and the Stones of Morn.

And then I slept.

I was naked.

I stood with my feet planted in blackness. Filling the horizon ahead was a tall silver tree, its roots twisting about itself, the tips of its branches lost in the distance. I had never seen anything so delicate, so intricate. I stood outside existence and looked upon all the branches of all the branches of the multiverse, constantly growing, constantly dying. Like a piece of the most intricate filigree, that silver tree, the complexity so great that it was impossible to see and understand the whole. I knew that what I looked upon was immeasurable, infinite. And what if this were only one of many such trees? I began to move towards it until I could no longer see the tree itself, but only the nearest branches, on which figures moved, back and forth, walking between the worlds.

At last I was standing on a branch, and I felt the comfort of familiarity. I had no memory, either as Elric or Ulric, of these roads. Instead I had a sense of connection with countless other selves with endless pain, with indescribable joy, and I felt that I was walking home.

One branch met a wider branch and then wider still and I met more and more people walking, like me, on the silver roads between the worlds, seeking, like me, some desperate goal, some lost reality. Our greetings were brief. Few lasting friendships were ever made on the silver roads.

After walking awhile, I began to notice a certain familiarity about those I passed. In some it was striking, in others subtle. Every one of these solitary men and women was myself. Thousands upon thousands of versions of myself. As if I were drawing in the vast single personality that was the sum of our parts, swiftly losing my own identity to the greater whole, performing some mysterious dance or ritual, making patterns which would ultimately determine the fate of all.

In this second journey, my dream quest did not take me to Oona's cottage on the borderland. It took me step by step towards a number of circular branches curving around one upon the other, evidently in an agitated condition.

Using the disciplines I had learned in the art of sorcery, I made myself advance.

The silver threads broadened to ribbons and then to wide roads so complicated in their design that it was impossible to guess which direction they would take. All seemed ultimately to return to wherever I happened to pause. I was glad, therefore, to find a fellow traveler, but a little astonished to look on a face that bore no resemblance to my own yet which was familiar.

As happens in dreams, I felt no special surprise at meeting Prince Lobkowitz here. The distinguished older man, who used the nom de guerre of Herr El, gravely shook hands with me, as if we had met on a country road. He seemed comfortable in his natural environment. I remember the warmth and firmness of his grip, his reassuring presence.

—My dear Count! Lobkowitz seemed casually delighted — I was told I might run across you out here. Are you familiar with these crossroads?

—Not at all, Prince Lobkowitz. And I'll admit I don't seek to become familiar with them. I am merely trying to get home. I have, as I'm sure you're aware, many reasons for returning to Germany.

—But you cannot return, can you, without the sword?

—The sword is in better hands than mine now. I shall not have any particular need of it, I suspect, in my fight against Hitlerism, which is why I wish to return home.

Lobkowitz's sad, wise eyes took on an ironic glint. —I think we are all wishing that, my lord. Here, on the moonbeam roads, we occasionally encounter this phenomenon, where branches appear to curve in on themselves, swallow themselves, reproduce themselves in peculiar ways and grow increasingly complex and dysfunctional. The theory goes that such places are a kind of cancer, where Law and Chaos are no longer in equilibrium but maintain form in their mutually destructive conflict. They can be dangerous to us—their paradoxes are perverse, unnatural and have age not wisdom. They only lead towards further confusion.

—But my path takes me this way. How can I avoid it?

—You can't—but I can help you, if you wish.

Quite naturally, I accepted his offer and he fell in beside me, staring up at the lattice of silvery roads all around us and remarking on their beauty. I asked him if these were the Grey Fees. He shook his head.

—These are roads we ourselves make between the realms. Just as generations tread footpaths across familiar countryside until those footpaths turn to highways, so do our desires and inventions create familiar paths through the multiverse. You could say we create a linear way of traveling through nonlinearity, that our roads are entirely imaginary, that any form we believe we see is simply an illusion or a partial vision of the whole. The human psyche organizes Time, for instance, to make it navigably linear. They say human intelligence and human dreams are the true creators of what we see. I have great faith in the benign power of dreams and am myself partial to that notion—that in effect we create ourselves and our surroundings. Another of the paradoxes which bring us closer to an understanding of our condition.

The maze of roads had tangled all around us now and I knew a slight sense of alarm.

—Then what does this nest of silver threads represent?

—Linearity turned in on itself? Law gone mad? Chaos unchecked? At this stage it scarcely matters. Or perhaps these shapes are like blossoms on a tree, creating in turn whole new dimensions? I believe some call this junction *The Chrysanthemum* and avoid it.

—Why so?

—Because you become truly lost, truly cut off from any familiar reality. Or perhaps if they are cancers . . . ?

—Does no one know their true origin or function?

—Who can? They could be all of those things or none of those things.

—So we could be trapped. Is that what you're saying?

—I did not insist on it as a certainty. Here the philosophical idea can turn out to be a concrete reality. And vice versa . . .

Lobkowitz smiled a thin smile.

—Here it is best to have only informed theories—realities and certainties are unreliable at best. It is harder to be betrayed by a theory. They say that if you would understand the multiverse, you must change from the conceptual state to the perceptual—from manipulation to understanding, and from understanding to action.

I was taught something similar as a young student of sorcery. Yet I feared to let this silvery tangle of roads absorb me. The Austrian seemed almost amused.

—What were you hoping to find here?

I laughed. —Myself, I said.

—Look. Lobkowitz pointed. A small straight branch led out of the tangle into glinting blackness. —Would you go this way?

—Where does it lead?

—Where you have the will and the courage to go. Whatever you have the will and the courage to make.

I had hoped for rather more specific advice, but understood why it was not possible in a multiverse so malleable, so susceptible to mortal demands and so treacherously unstable. Nonetheless I had an uneasy feeling I had become trapped in some peculiar parable.

These dreams I dreamed as both von Bek and Elric. They were profound dreams, hard to recollect. Elric's dreams were the deepest and he would come to remember them only as nightmares amongst other, equally disturbing, nightmares. The kind that made him wake screaming in the night. That drove him to more and more desperate adventuring as he sought to escape the faintest memory of them.

Now, however, links with von Bek seemed increasingly tenuous as I stepped onto the new straight road. "You ultimately need to reach the Isle of Morn." Prince Lobkowitz wished me good-bye and turned back towards the dense tangle of paths.

I drew further away and looked over my shoulder. "Morn?" I could no longer see the mysterious Prince Lobkowitz, Herr El. The great complex now resembled an impeccably carved ivory chrysanthemum, so perfect it was possible to imagine it made by a mortal craftsman. I understood why it had acquired the name. Were there people who actually mapped these routes? Who could make identical journeys over and over again?

Why had Lobkowitz set me on this path to risk the danger he had described? Why had he, too, mentioned Morn? For a moment it occurred to me to wonder if he had deceived me, but I put the thought aside. I must trust the few I had learned to trust or I would be truly lost.

My road joined with another and another until I was again on a main branch of the multiverse, approaching a place where a silvery bough had turned upwards and then down to form a rough arch.

I had no choice but to go under this and find myself staring upwards into a glowing cauldron of white fire, which turned suddenly to shower me with flames the color of bone and pewter, absorbing me even as they fell and I fell with them—down for a thousand years, falling, falling for a thousand years. When I looked down I saw a vast field of ivory and silver flowers—of roses

and chrysanthemums, marigolds and magnolias—each one repre-
senting a different universe.

I feared that I would be drawn into one of the densely
woven universes, but gradually they began to form a simple
field of white in which two spots of ruby red glowed, until I realized I was staring into my own gigantic image and then instantly I was staring up at the anxious faces of Moonglum and my
daughter, Oona. I turned my head. On the floor beside me was
the sleeping body of Ulric von Bek. But there had been a fundamental change. Everything was most definitely not what it
had been . . .

As von Bek, however isolated I was from Elric and while he
would scarcely remember me once this dream was ended, I could
not rid myself of him. I remain both men. His story continues
within me. I shall never be free of him. I have no reason to believe
I was singled out for this fate and every reason to think it a mere
accident, for if I've learned nothing else from my experiences, it is
that luck has far more to do with one's fortune than any kind of
judgment and that to believe oneself in control of the multiverse
is to suffer the greatest delusion of all.

Since then I have heard of others who carry the identities of
a thousand souls within them, but at that moment I was horrified
by the notion. A simple Saxon landowner, I was bound by supernatural ties to the soul of a nonhuman creature separated from me
by untold distances of time and space. Even as I looked on his
face, I saw my own face looking back at me. It felt for a moment
as if I stared down an endless corridor of mirrors—thousands upon
thousands of selves reflected back at me. I rose with some difficulty from where I had fallen. I had the impression everything had
happened simultaneously. Moonglum was overjoyed by his
friend's restoration, and Oona took her father's hand as he stared
with disbelieving eyes at the scene before him.

Only I retained a conscious memory of the journey through
the moonbeam roads.

Elric looked at me. "I believe I have you to thank, sir, for waking me from that enchanted slumber?"

"I think the Lady Oona is to be thanked by both of us," I said. "She has her mother's skills if not her inclinations."

He frowned. "Ah, yes. I remember something." Then a shudder ran through him. "My sword—?"

"Gaynor has Stormbringer, still," said Moonglum quickly. "But your—this gentleman—has brought you another."

"I remember." Elric frowned. He looked down at Ravenbrand, which I had placed in his grasp. "Fragments. Gaynor won my sword, then I fell asleep, then I dreamed I found Gaynor and lost him again." He became agitated. "And he threatens—he threatens . . . No, Tanelorn is safe. Miggea's imprisoned. The Stones of Morn! Other friends are in danger. Arioch—my Lord Arioch—where is he?"

"Your Duke of Hell was here," said Moonglum. "In this realm. But we did not know it. Perhaps Gaynor went with him."

Elric clutched his head, groaning. "The sorcery is too much, even for me. No mortal can sustain sanity or life if exposed to it for long. Oh! I remember! The dream! The cottage! Those white faces. Caverns. The young woman . . ."

"You remember enough, Father," she said quietly. He looked up at her again. Startled. Baffled. Alarmed.

"Probably more than enough," I suggested. I was beginning to yearn for some natural, dreamless sleep.

Oona said quietly, "All is not over. Nor will it be until we have succeeded in getting rid of Gaynor. His strategy isn't clear. He still attacks on two fronts and becomes increasingly reckless—careless of all life, including his own."

"Where shall we seek him?" Elric made a careful inspection of the runesword. He seemed suspicious of it, yet the blade itself was clearly the one he was familiar with.

"Oh, there's no doubt," she said, "about where to find him. This Gaynor? He'll choose one of two places of power—Bek or Morn. How to fight him is the problem. If you are ready, Father, we should return as soon as we can to Mu Ooria, where there's still a great deal of work for us."

"How do you propose to get there?" I asked her. "I doubt if King Straasha can be prevailed upon to help me twice."

She smiled. "There are less dramatic means of travel. Besides, I think Miggea's spell has lifted. Now only she is trapped in the barren world she created for herself. Without human aid, there she stays. But while we can journey fairly easily between the worlds, Master Moonglum cannot. You must wait here, Moonglum, in Tanelorn, until Elric returns."

Moonglum seemed partially relieved at this news but he grumbled. "I've chosen to travel with you, Elric—to Hell, if necessary."

Elric stretched out his long, pale hand and placed it on Moonglum's shoulder. "It will not be necessary yet, old friend."

Moonglum took this well, but he was clearly saddened. "I'll wait a few weeks," he said. "And if you don't return by then, I might head back towards Elwher. I, too, have unfinished business. If I'm not here when you return, you'll find me there."

We left the little redheaded outlander in that room. He preferred, he said, to stay there until we had gone. He wished us luck. He was sure our paths would cross again.

Oona led us out of the Tower of the Hand into cheering streets and gentle sunlight. There, all around the city's walls, were familiar gentle green hills. Tanelorn had returned to her natural position in the multiverse.

Oona led us swiftly through the twittens and lanes of Tanelorn's most ancient districts until we entered a low house which had, by its condition, been abandoned years earlier. The upper floors were ruined but the basement was in good repair, its main room guarded by an iron-bound door which Oona, after checking that we weren't observed, opened with a surprisingly small key.

There seemed to be nothing especially valuable on the other side of the door. The room was furnished with a bed, working and cooking facilities, a desk, chair and several shelves of books and scrolls. It had the neat, well-used air of a nun's cell.

I didn't question her. This was one of her smaller surprises, after all.

Only when Elric was physically nearby did I not strongly

sense his mind. The albino seemed more ill at ease than anyone else, and I had no clear idea why. I think I assumed a sophistication in him. After all, my experience of the inventive twentieth century was not his. Indeed, he was often awkward in my presence, avoiding my eye and rarely addressing me directly. Clearly I made him deeply uncomfortable and would have left him, if I could. He had something of the air of a somnambulist. I began to wonder if he thought he dreamed all that was happening.

Perhaps he did dream? Perhaps he dreamed us all?

Now Oona crossed to the far wall and pushed back a tapestry hanging to reveal another door.

"Where does this lead?" I asked.

"It depends." She was smiling a little grimly.

"Upon what?"

"On whether Law or Chaos has control of certain realms."

"And how do you know?"

"You find out," she said, "by going through."

Elric was impatient. "Then let's go through," he said. "I've a mind to confront Cousin Gaynor on a number of issues." His hand was on the hilt of Ravenbrand. I admired his wild courage. We might have the same blood and some of the same dilemmas, but we were temperamentally very different. He sought oblivion in action, while I sought it in philosophy. I was reluctant to take decisions, whereas for Elric decisions were everything. He took them, as he took risks, habitually.

If he'd lived a prosaic life, with prosaic considerations, then prosaic things would chiefly have happened to him. But he was in no way prosaic, this wolfish whiteface, who relied on sorcery for his very sustenance.

Would I have been like him in his circumstances? I doubted it. But I had not known a childhood of sorcerous schooling and overbearing tradition. I had not, as a youth, stared into the most profound horror, and learned the skills of the dragonmasters, learned how magically I could manipulate the world. I knew everything about his past, of course, for his memories remained my memories, while he recalled nothing at all of me. In some ways I envied him his lack of consciousness.

With an air of impatience, Elric flung himself through the door and I followed. Oona closed the door behind us.

The three of us stood in a pleasant sunken garden. The kind of place one might seek rest and contemplation and exactly what one would have expected to find on the other side of that door. A comforting domesticity. The garden was surrounded by a high wall which was surrounded in turn by tall buildings, all of which had the effect of making it seem smaller than it was. Herbs and flowers, all sweet-scented, were laid out in formal beds. Peacocks and ornamental roosters strutted between the shrubs. At the center was a pool with a fountain. The fountain was ornate, of some dark, gleaming rock, and its sound added to the garden's sense of tranquillity.

Although pleasant, the scene was an anticlimax. We had expected something much more dramatic. Elric hesitated. He looked around him, suspiciously. I think he was trying to find something to kill.

Oona was relieved. She had clearly expected some less attractive scene. The garden had no exterior gate. The only way to get in or out was through the door we had just used.

"What now?" Elric glanced impatiently about. "Where do we go?"

"From Tanelorn to Mu Ooria and from Mu Ooria to Tanelorn," she said, "the way is always by water."

Elric dipped his hand into the ornamental pool. "By water? How? There's no room for a ship on this, madam." He stared with interest at the unusual fish swimming there, as if he expected to find some secret in the pool.

Smiling, Oona reached down with her curved bow and drew it gently across the surface, describing a circle. The circle remained visible. Within, the water became gradually more agitated, full of color and lilting ripples. Suddenly it began to funnel upwards, red and shining, like a fresh wound, a pillar of pulsing ruby light. The color was reflected in our three pale faces, giving our skin the appearance of bone stained with old blood.

Elric grinned his wolf's grin—the red light dancing in his eyes. "Is this the way?" he asked Oona.

She nodded.

Without a word or any further hesitation, the Melnibonéan flattened his body against the pillar. For a moment he jerked, like a frog on an electric fence, and then was absorbed.

I didn't move quite so readily and Oona laughed at me, taking my hand and stepping forward, leading me into the yielding, fiery light.

I felt something tugging at my body, pulling me away from her. I tried to hold on, but lost my grip. I was swimming through roaring, fluttering flames, down into a scarlet abyss which threatened to drown me in all the spilled blood of the multiverse. Fire which did not burn, but licked at the secret places of the soul. Fire which revealed gibbering faces, like the faces of the damned in Hell. Obscenely tortured bodies, a writhing ballet of torment. But I was not burned.

The fire had the quality of water, for I could swim through it easily. I hadn't drawn a single breath and felt no need for air. I was reminded of the thick, sluggish waters of the Heavy Sea which lay beyond Melniboné.

As I swam, I looked about for the others, but they had disappeared. Had this been a plan on the part of Elric and Oona to get rid of me now that I'd served my turn?

Behind me I had the sense of a malignant, monstrous presence. I swam faster than ever, even as the creature gathered speed. When I glanced back, seeking a glimpse of what pursued me, all I could see was a huge, shadowy white bulk, like the body of a shark seen through twilight seas. It seemed to carry the weight of the ages. It moved as in great pain. I heard it utter a peculiar groan. I felt something brush by me and then fall away back into the depths, as if it had attempted to attack me and failed.

I swam on through forests of identical ruby pillars. I swam between banks of blue flame and over fields of emerald and pearl. And I still had no need to draw breath, no need to defend myself.

I swam through cities in flames. I swam over battles between whole peoples and I swam over the destruction of worlds. I swam through tranquil woods and flowering fields and then, quite unexpectedly, I was inhaling liquid.

I coughed, flung myself upwards, and emerged into blazing blackness.

From somewhere in the darkness I heard an exultant voice. Oona was speaking to my doppelgänger. "Welcome, Father," she said. "Welcome to Mu Ooria. Welcome to your destiny."

# CHAPTER SIXTEEN

# The Greater Blasphemy

he other two were waiting for me as I waded to shore. It was bitterly cold. In that weird phosphorescent light from the lake, I saw the by now familiar outlines of Mu Ooria, but they seemed more ragged than before. Every so often a column of pale fire would rise for a moment, flutter into fragments and subside. While I had no idea of the cause, there was an ominous quality to the fire which made me fear the worst. I heard distant sounds, like the thin striking of a clock, *pnin, pnin, pnin,* a roar like a landslide, then laughter in the darkness. A crash. A panting noise, like the ardor of coupling dogs. The echo of what might have been a scream. A sense that something terrible was taking place, something obscene.

I did my best to keep my fears to myself. "On the evidence," I said, "Gaynor has been successful in his ambitions here."

As was his unconscious habit when disturbed, Elric put his hand on the pommel of Ravenbrand. "Then we had best go to see him at once."

I was beginning to understand that my near-twin was incautious by nature. What would seem insanity to an ordinary man was for Elric the logical course of action.

Oona smiled at this. "Perhaps we should first find out what his strength is. Remember, Father, that your sorcery could be limited here. Even the sword might lack her normal powers."

Elric shrugged at this but seemed willing to trust her judgment. After all, we were here largely at her volition and she knew far more about this world than either of us.

Making no effort to hide himself, Elric began to stride towards the city, following the curve of the shoreline. We could only continue in his wake.

Soon the signs of Gaynor's ambitions could be seen everywhere in that haunted, unsteady darkness. More than once we stumbled over the prone body of a giant black cat which had previously hunted this territory. Twice we found what were Off-Moo remains—crumpled corpses, hacked cartilage, but no bones. Did the Off-Moo have bones, in the conventional sense? We found one of their long, conical headdresses and still could not tell if they fitted the shape of the head or exaggerated it. We found signs of fires made from Off-Moo artifacts. We found the bodies of troogs and savages everywhere. Evidently some had fought amongst themselves for whatever prizes they discovered in Mu Ooria. I guessed there was little here they would value, which would make their destructiveness all the more frenzied.

How had they defeated the Off-Moo, who had been so well and cleverly protected? The dormant Off-Moo, those who had resembled statues and who guarded their borders, had clearly been caught unawares. They had never had a chance to wake. The Off-Moo's ability to direct deadly stalactites against their enemies had somehow been impaired. Initially knowing nothing of the Off-Moo, Gaynor had somehow learned much since I last visited their city.

Signs of savage, mindless cruel destruction were everywhere.

What had become of the Off-Moo? Had they fled? Were they in hiding in the city? Had they all been killed? Or captured? It was hard for me to remember that Gaynor had gathered supernatural allies since I had last visited this realm.

We saw a few silhouettes moving in the ruins. They had the

shambling walk of the troogs or the swagger of the half-blind savages who fought beside them.

As we drew nearer to them, even Elric began to keep to the
shadows, watching to see what they were doing. But it was clear
they were doing very little, save sifting through the ruins for the
loot they had hoped to find. I couldn't imagine what possessions
of the Off-Moo would be valuable to these semi-brutes. Where
was Gaynor's main army?

We were coming close to the great plaza of the city.
Everywhere the mysterious towers of the Off-Moo burned with
that strange fluttering white fire. What I had mistaken for their
screaming was the noise the towers made as they burned. The
sound of a mortal voice.

Where the towers burned, neither the conquerors nor the
conquered were in evidence.

We decided we would have to capture one of the savages and
interrogate him. Oona cocked her head, listening. She walked
rapidly towards a burning tower and peered in.

Seconds later a dark shape appeared in the doorway. Its own
robes flickered as the fire flickered and its eyes glittered. I saw no
welcome in them.

Oona exchanged a few words with the figure. Cautiously he
came out of the tower and glided towards us. It was hard to tell
from the long, stony face if we were recognized or not. The Off-
Moo spoke slowly, in Greek:

"Gaynor did this to us. He feared we would try to stop him in
his ambitions. And he feared rightly. But he has made exception-
al alliances with certain of the Lords of the Higher Worlds and so
gained the knowledge of how to defeat us and with what."

"How many of you has he killed?" Elric spoke with the direct
bluntness of a professional soldier.

"That remains to be seen, sir. I am Scholar Crina. I was not
here when Gaynor attacked. When I returned I found our city
much as you find it now. My departing colleagues were able to
inform me that the weight of barbarians overwhelmed them. But
before that something else occurred."

"Where are the barbarians now?" I asked. I was shivering, still soaked through. "Do you know?"

"They marched away," was all he would say.

"Where's this Gaynor?" Elric asked brusquely. "Presumably his will is what it always was?"

"He has done what he needed to do here."

"And what was that?"

"He has stolen our Great Staff and now marches against the Grey Fees."

"Impossible," said Oona. "The staff is useless in his blood-soaked hands. It could as easily destroy him as aid him. No one would take such a risk. Nobody would be so foolish as to chance such destruction."

"No one except Gaynor," said Elric.

"What does he expect to gain from invading the Grey Fees?" I asked.

Scholar Crina answered that question. "Enormous power. Power over the forces of creation themselves. This was what he first offered us, if we would help him. Naturally we refused him."

"The gods would never allow it."

Scholar Crina seemed amused. "No sane being would. But there is a theory that the Lords of the Higher Worlds themselves are no longer entirely sane, as disturbing changes take place throughout the multiverse. A conjunction comes. All the realms will realign within the great field of Time. New destinies will be decided. New realities. Yours is not the only story. There are others. Other lives. Other dreams. All lead to the same great supernatural moment. Nothing is as certain as it was. Even loyalties to Law and Chaos are no longer permanent. Look at Gaynor. He employs both Law and Chaos in his attempt to make himself the ruler of worlds. Once such things were impossible for mortals. But now, it seems, even mortal power increases and becomes less stable."

"Gaynor does not mean to destroy himself," said Oona. "He no doubt believes he is invulnerable now that he bears your Great Staff."

"He claims to be king of the world. And it is true that his possession of our Great Staff gives him the confidence to march upon the Grey Fees. But to what end? What can he hope to achieve, save complete destruction of the multiverse?"

"He reminds me of a certain dictator in my own country," I said mildly. "His madness, his poor grasp on reality seems to be what drives him. His addiction to power is so great, he will destroy whole realms in order to satisfy his craving."

Scholar Crina lowered his eyes. "He has no ordinary sense of self-interest. Those are the most dangerous people of all to gain control of a civilization."

"Echoes," said Oona thoughtfully to herself. "On how many planes, do you think, is a version of this story being played out? We believe we have volition, but we can do little to change the consequences or the direction of our actions, because those consequences and actions are taking place, with minuscule differences expanding to vast differences, on countless levels of the multiverse."

Elric showed no interest in her philosophy. "If Gaynor can be stopped on this plane," he said, "then presumably his defeat will be echoed, as his victories are?"

She smiled at him. "Well, Father, if anyone was best fitted to change his own destiny, then it is you."

Neither Elric nor I knew exactly what she meant, but I shared his sense of determination.

"Gaynor's power was too great for us," said Scholar Crina.

"But your Staff," said Oona. "How could he have taken that from you?"

"The Staff itself appears to have allowed it," said Scholar Crina simply. "We have always known it had volition. That is how it came to us."

They were referring to the malleable artifact—bowl, child, staff—I had witnessed the Off-Moo manipulating in that first ceremony. Or *had* they been the manipulators? Were they perhaps the manipulated? I remembered how it had changed shape. At whose volition?

"Does it always take the form of a staff?" I asked him. I recalled all the shapes it had made.

"We know it as the Runestaff," he said. "But it takes several forms. It is a staff and a cup and a stone and is one of the great regulators of our realities."

"Is that what my people know as the Grail?" I remembered von Eschenbach and some of our own family legends. "Were you its guardians?"

"In this realm," he said. "And in this realm we have failed."

"You mean various versions of the Grail inhabit other realms?"

Scholar Crina was regretful. "Only one Great Staff exists," he said. "It represents the Balance itself. Some say it is the Balance. Its influence extends far beyond any realm in which it is kept."

"My family was once said to guard the Grail," I told him. "But it was removed from our keeping. Presumably we also failed in our trust."

"The Runestaff has the power to change form and to move on its own volition," Scholar Crina told me. "Some say it can take the shape of a child. Why should it not, since it can presumably assume any form it likes? In this way it preserves and defends itself. And thus preserves those who respect and defend it. It is not always obvious what form it has taken."

"In what form does Gaynor possess it?" Oona wanted to know.

"The form of a cup," he said. "Of a fine drinking vessel. With that and the two swords he now carries, he has more power to change the destiny of worlds than any other mortal before him. And because the gods themselves hardly understand what is happening, he could succeed. For it is well known that a mortal will eventually bring about the destruction of the gods."

I paid little attention to this last. It had the smack of legend and superstition about it, yet at the same time a frisson of recognition went through my body. I tried to recall where I had heard a similar story, one which was couched in the mythology of my own age and people, the story of the Holy Grail and its ability to cure the world's pain. That legend also had a mortal changing the destiny of his world. I checked myself. I felt as if I was receiving an overdose of Wagner. My own tastes were for the clearer waters of Mozart or Liszt, whose appeal was as much to the intellect as to the emotions. Was that what I recognized? Had I somehow found myself in a very complicated Wagnerian opera? I shuddered at the thought. Yet even the momentous events of the Ring Cycle were as nothing compared to what I had already witnessed.

I turned to Oona. "You said something of my particular relationship with the Grail. What did you mean?"

"Not everyone is privileged to serve it," she said.

Her manner was grim. She did not seem optimistic. I think she had not expected Gaynor to get this far.

A strange stink filled the air. A mixture of a thousand different odors, none of them pleasant. The smell of evil.

I still could not see how Gaynor had so thoroughly defeated the Off-Moo and said as much to the scholar.

"You do not yet know," he said, "if Gaynor has defeated us. The game, after all, is not over."

I kept my own counsel, but as far as I could see this aspect of the game at least was well and truly won.

Elric wanted to know where Gaynor was, whether it was possible to catch up with him on foot.

"He moves towards the Grey Fees with his army. He believes he can take the power of the multiverse for himself. It is a delusion. But his delusion will destroy us all, unless someone challenges him." Scholar Crina seemed to glance inquiringly at me.

But it was Prince Elric who answered. "I have been insulted and humiliated by that creature. I have been deceived. Whatever power he now has, he will not escape my vengeance."

"You think not?" Oona stooped to run her hand through the sleek fur of one of the big cats, then drew it away again quickly, as if she did not wish to contemplate what had happened to the animal. Was it dead, or enchanted?

"Dream or no dream," said Elric quietly, "he shall be punished for what he has done."

I would not have believed another. Elric, however, was beginning to convince me that we might yet, somehow, defeat an entity who had become probably the greatest single force for evil in
the multiverse. As often happened between us, Elric replied to my
unvoiced ideas. "Melnibonéans believe that fate cannot be
altered. That each of us has a settled destiny. That to break free
of it—or attempt to break free of it—is an act of blasphemy. A
blasphemy I am prepared to commit. To prevent, perhaps, a
greater blasphemy."

He had the air of a man who wrestled with his own soul as
well as his conscience and background. I had the impression that
he might have spoken more, had he been able to put into words
the huge conflicts taking place within him.

We spent little time in Mu Ooria. The flames were already
beginning to die down and serious damage had been done. We
found no more Off-Moo. No sign of them. No piece of writing. No
clue. They had fled in defeat. I was disappointed in them. They
had no doubt become decadent, overconfident of their ability to
resist attack, relying, as Byzantium had done for so many decades,
on their ancient reputation. I had assumed them to be both
courageous and resourceful. Perhaps they had been once. Now, it
seemed, they had no capacity to resist Gaynor or anyone else who
chose to take their wealth and secrets.

"There is only one possible course of action," said Prince
Elric.

"Pursue Gaynor?" I asked.

"And hope to defeat him before he can reach the Grey Fees."

"He is almost there," said Scholar Crina. "He and his army
must even now be close to the borderland." For the first time he
appeared to show some kind of emotion. "The end for us," he
said. He lowered his cowled head. "The end for everyone. The
end of everything."

Oona was impatient with this. "Well, gentlemen, unless you
welcome the end as thoroughly as Scholar Crina, who seems to
derive some form of gloomy satisfaction from the situation, I suggest we rest for a while, eat well and then continue our pursuit."

"There's no time," said Elric, almost to himself. "We must eat on the move. And we must begin soon, for we have no mounts and must pursue Gaynor on foot."

"And when we catch up with him?" I said. "What will we do?"

"Punish him," said Elric simply. "Take back the sword he has stolen." He touched his hilt. He stroked it with his long fingers. He was beginning to grin. I found his humor alarming. "Use his own methods against him. Kill him."

A kind of lust smoldered in the Melnibonéan. He was longing for a bloodletting and did not much care how it was achieved. I began to fear for the safety of myself and his daughter. Scholar Crina sensed it, too. When I looked for him again, he was slipping back into the burning building. He seemed untroubled by the flames.

Wrapping my damp clothing about me and feeling the need for movement, I trudged towards the outskirts of the city, my companions behind me. I was convinced that I was likely to die in this adventure. I consoled myself that if Elric and Oona had not helped me escape the concentration camp, I would be dead by now anyway. At least I had had the chance to observe the suprareality that constituted the interlinked worlds of the multiverse.

We had retreated to the outer reaches of the city when suddenly the ground underfoot began to shudder. Pieces of stone whistled from above and crashed to the cavern's floor. Did an earthquake grip Mu Ooria? The rumbling staccato sound which followed the shock had the quality of mocking laughter.

I glanced a question to Oona, who shook her head. Elric, also, was baffled.

Another shock. More falling rock. As if a giant strode in our wake.

If I had not known better, I would have guessed that high explosives were being set off. I had experienced similar sensations and sounds when visiting the site of a new railway tunnel with my engineer brother, who had died while digging a trench three days after the outbreak of war.

I peered into the distance, between those vast columns of rock. It was impossible to see very far into that cavern or guess its dimensions. But now, far away, I caught glimpses of a flickering, raging fire. The phosphor from the lake had combined to form a whirlwind.

Several of these slender tornadoes were approaching us. Shrieking whirlwinds of whistling white light touched the ruins of the city and swirled them into new, even crazier patterns. Something about those thin twisters suggested they were sentient, or that they were at least controlled by a thinking creature.

We knew enough to run, seeking some kind of ditch or fissure into which we could climb in the hope that the tornadoes would bounce over us like their earthly counterparts, but it was a faint enough hope.

It was clear now what force Gaynor had used against our friends. Some fresh supernatural alliance, no doubt, brought him the strength of the *ishass*. Wind demons. Even in my earthly mythology I had heard of them. They figured largely in the folk-tales of desert peoples, usually as *ifrits*.

"Can they be harnessed by the likes of Gaynor?" Oona was asking Elric.

"Clearly," replied the albino laconically as he ran.

I brought up the rear, gasping for breath and unable to voice any of the questions rushing through my mind.

Oona signaled to us. She stopped and pointed. Ahead was the even darker mouth of a small cave. Hearing the advance of the *ishass* and not daring to look, without hesitation we squeezed into the hole, which was barely large enough to contain all three of us. The closeness of our bodies was a comfort to me. I felt as if the three of us had returned to some safe, defendable womb. Outside the shrieks and crashing grew louder and louder as the whirlwinds passed directly over us. Then came a lull. More twisters could be heard far away, but their sound was distant.

"This is a powerful force," Elric mused. "It requires enormous skill to summon it. Important bargains. I do not believe even your cousin, Count Ulric, with all his cleverness, could physically contain it. These demons are famous in the netherworlds. They are called the Ten Sons, the *ishass*. This means he keeps his alliances with Chaos, for the *ishass* will not serve Law and Law, save at its most unstable, would never employ them."

I felt guilty for judging the Off-Moo. No mortal creature could stand against such power. It would be like trying to confront an American twister with courage and moral integrity as your only weapons. And the Off-Moo, for all their sophistication, had nothing which would defend them against these *ishass*.

The wind demons were passing close by now. Yelping and shrieking and yapping like wild dogs, bringing ancient stones crashing down, uprooting columns which had taken a million years to grow. My fear took second place to my sense of outrage. What purpose could there be to such wild destruction? And why had Gaynor bothered to unleash the Ten Sons again upon a clearly defeated city? What was it in some mortals that gave them satisfaction in destruction? What terrible need did they satisfy by destroying the work and beauty of the centuries? Did they think they cleansed the world of something?

Only long after they passed, and we climbed out of our cramped little cave, did it occur to me that perhaps Gaynor did not command the Ten Sons. Perhaps they had escaped his control and now contented themselves with wreaking wholesale mayhem upon that once peaceful world? Or was this their reward for aiding him? They destroyed indiscriminately, not even sparing the few savages left rooting in the ruins who came into their path. They were caught up, arms and legs desperately flailing, swallowed, stripped of clothing and flesh, which was flung in all directions, their bones scattered. The bones fell like rain on a rooftop.

The Ten Sons were ahead of us now, forming a ragged line which could be followed easily. We came in their wake, stumbling along the wide path they had created and wondering what could lie before us that would be any more terrifying than what we had already witnessed.

Oona was frowning, She had had an idea, she said. "Perhaps they hurry to join Gaynor's army? Perhaps he has already reached the Grey Fees and summons them to his service once more. Does he think he can conquer Creation with a few wind demons?"

"I would imagine," I said, "that he has planned rather more thoroughly. What we can be sure of, I think, is that his power is the greatest granted to any human being before him."

"I think he will be hard to defeat," mused the Lord of Melniboné. "It's as well there are three of us. I am not sure I could do it alone."

We moved farther away from the city and into darkness which we illuminated with the barbarians' fallen brands. We had little chance of catching Gaynor's army quickly, but at least we were now safe from the Ten Sons, who leaped head of us, tiny now, glimpsed rarely amongst the massive tall stones which formed in this area a series of arches, like a huge rose arbor. We were grateful to them. They brought light to that aching distance. They gave us a clue to Gaynor's whereabouts. But it would be some time before we were able to get closer to them.

And, when we did, I was not at all sure we wouldn't be instantly killed. I had every reason to suspect Elric's determined optimism had much to do with his knowledge of sorcery but not a great deal to do with the vast numbers of soldiers Gaynor commanded, not to mention his evident supernatural allies.

We were lucky to come across the slaughtered corpse of a troog. The huge half-human still had its crude pouch on a belt about its misshapen waist. The pouch was full of miscellaneous and generally useless loot salvaged from Mu Ooria. But there was also food. Two solid loaves of bread, a couple of pots of preserved meats and bottles of pickled vegetables. He had also found from somewhere a leather bottle of wine. We had to pry it from his gigantic, scabby hand. An unpleasant task, but worth it in the end, for the wine was of good quality. I had a feeling it had originally belonged to one of Fromental's colleagues, perhaps even his friend the talking beast. This led me to wondering about the Frenchman's fate. I hoped he and his strange companions had been successful in finding the Tanelorn they sought.

We moved rapidly and eventually caught our first sight of Gaynor's terrible army.

In the far distance a band of grey formed a kind of horizon. Were we nearing the beginning of the mysterious Fees?

I turned inquiringly to Oona.

"The Forbidden Marches," she confirmed. "And beyond them, the Grey Fees."

# CHAPTER SEVENTEEN

# Careless Angels

ome peoples believe," said Oona conversationally, "that each of us has a guardian angel who discreetly looks after our interests, perhaps in the way we care for and protect a pet. The pet is barely conscious of what we do for it, just as we are hardly conscious of our guardian angel. And just as some pet animals have conscientious owners, others have bad owners. Therefore, though we are all assigned such an angel, the unlucky ones have careless angels."

We lay upon a broad terrace looking down into a valley that had probably never seen light before. It was illuminated by the marching twisters, the Ten Sons, which formed a loose line of whirling, shrieking light. They were clearly disciplined by something as they followed behind the brands of the blind cannibals with Gaynor. The torches were not for them, but for Gaynor and his Nazis, whose horses were equally blind. Every so often a vast shadow would be thrown upon a wall of ancient, fleshy rock. The gigantic troogs, the sightless savages, the Nazis in the remains of their black and silver uniforms. A foul alliance indeed. Beasts and men. Half-men and half-beasts. Shambling and lolloping, trudging and dancing, striding and riding. Some of them stumbling. Ironically, while they had learned to adapt themselves to the dark, they were often blinded by the light. A ragged army. An ugly army. A monstrous army, marching relentlessly towards the Grey Fees.

"Could be," I said, "that we're already deserted by our angels. Have you ever witnessed such grotesquerie?" I indicated Gaynor's army.

"Rarely," said Oona. Her sweet, beautiful face, framed by her long white hair, looked up at me with sardonic intelligence. For a moment I felt an extraordinary sensation as she glanced away. I believe I was falling in love with her. And already, of course, I was debating the morality of this.

Oona was not my daughter. She was Elric's. But at what point did a being conscious of its place in the multiverse choose to ignore the relationship it had in common with a million other beings? I could easily see the drawbacks of being fully conscious. Perhaps, years before, in his early sorcerous training Elric had been given the choice of being knowing or unknowing and had chosen to become unconscious of the multiverse. Otherwise he might never have been able to act at all.

What can it be like to be conscious that every action one performs has a consequence throughout time and space? One would become very circumspect about the company one kept. About the things one did or said. One could be frozen into complete inaction. Or returned to a state of absolute ignorance as the mind refused all information.

Or it could make one entirely reckless, willing, like Elric, to risk everything. For if one risked and lost, the reward was, after all, complete oblivion. And oblivion was what that poor, tortured soul longed for so frequently. This quality made him an unreliable ally. Not all of us sought or found oblivion in battle. Something in me still looked forward to a restoration of the tranquillity of my old estate, a return to the quiet pleasures of rural life. Not that the prospect seemed especially close at this particular moment.

Elric frowned to himself. He seemed to be calculating something. I looked at him nervously, hoping he would not decide on one of his reckless moves. We three could not stand alone against those strange forces.

Cautiously, using all the cover available, we gradually drew closer to Gaynor's horrible army. The wind demons seemed positioned to protect the flanks and rear. I could not guess how my cousin controlled them.

"How do you know these sentient tornadoes?" I whispered. "Have you encountered them before?"

"Not all ten," he said. He was impatient with my interruption. "I once summoned their father. They all command different aspects of the elements, these wind-beings. They are protective of their separate domains. They know strong rivalries. And they can be fickle. This is not work for the *sharnah,* makers of gales, but for the *h'Haarshann,* builders of whirlwinds."

I fell silent again. My instinct was to turn, to go back, to find the falls, the way through to Hameln. I would rather risk the horrors of a Nazi concentration camp than confront any more supernatural threats.

The marching army stopped. They pitched camp. Perhaps Gaynor needed to consider his next action? The Ten Sons became guardians of that vast horde by forming a rough circle around it. I studied the blazing whiteness as best I could, trying to see what really constituted the Ten Sons, but my vision began to blur immediately. I found it impossible to look at the wind demons for more than a few seconds.

I wondered if I tied a piece of gauze about my face it would be easier to make out whatever fundamental shape lay at the core of the Ten Sons. But perhaps I was deceiving myself. Perhaps there was no fundamental shape.

Elric murmured, "First the Ten, then my lady M."

He was speaking in rhyme. Indeed, even his breathing had a rhythmic quality I had not previously noticed. His movements took on a balletic air. He was scarcely aware of either Oona or myself. His eyes had a distant glaze.

I frowned and moved forward to touch him on the shoulder and ask him if he was all right, but Oona lifted a finger to her lips and motioned me away. She gave her father an expectant look, then, when she glanced back at me, she seemed to have a proud, proprietorial gleam in her eyes, as if to say "Wait. My father is a genius. Watch."

I had known him as intimately as it is possible to know another human being, from deep within, soul sharing soul. I had considerable respect and great sympathy for him. But only now did it occur to me that he might be a genius.

Elric warned us to speak softly, if we spoke at all. The Ten Sons had acute hearing.

All at once Elric was moving, climbing down the rocks nearby and, perhaps in answer to my unspoken question, muttering, "Oldfather. Oldfather needs a little fresh blood."

He disappeared for a moment. I heard a musical sound. Soft, menacing. I saw him below, walking cautiously towards Gaynor's camp. Ravenbrand was unscabbarded in his right hand.

Time passed. The camp slept. I continued to watch. Waiting for Elric to return. Oona, however, curled up and told me to wake her if I became sleepy.

Eventually I heard a noise below and saw the familiar outline. Elric was dragging something behind him. Something which grunted and groaned as it bumped over the rocky floor.

Next I saw him on the other side, still below me. Here the rocks formed a small natural amphitheater at the center of which Elric dumped his prize. It wriggled for a moment until he kicked it. I saw his face then. His eyes were glassy, blazing rubies. They looked into a world I could not begin to imagine. They looked into Hell itself. And his mouth was moving, his sword describing complicated geometries in the air, his whole body beginning to turn in ritual movements, a ghostly dance.

Oona awakened and lay beside me, watching Elric as he cut through the material binding his victim. I recognized the terrified human being. One of the Nazis who had originally come here with Gaynor. He was snarling like a trapped dog, but there was stark horror in his eyes and he could not control his trembling. He tried to strike out at Elric. Ravenbrand licked him. He pulled back his bleeding hand. Ravenbrand licked him again. His face carried a thin line of blood. And again. The ragged shirt covering his chest fell away to reveal another line from neck to navel.

The Nazi was whimpering, trying to find escape, allies, God, anything. The sword tasted him. Savored him. Relished his blood drop by drop. And while he played with the sniveling wretch, Elric crooned a haunting wordless song. The cadences rose and fell. I was astonished that they issued from a mortal throat. All the time they grew in intensity and bit by bit the Nazi died, pieces of his flesh falling away as he watched. The sword continued its delicate, terrible work.

Oona craned to see, fascinated. In this she was her father's child. She had the look of a cat. I, however, was forced to turn away more than once. Forced by the sound of that voice, rising and falling, growing stronger and stronger, by the sight of Elric himself, his wild, crimson eyes raised towards the upper darkness, his mouth open in something between a melody and a scream, his white flesh glinting and his great black runesword turning a human being to slivers before his own eyes.

The Nazi was still fully conscious, such was Elric's appalling artistry. The man still wore his black SS boots. He knelt before my doppelgänger and tears mingled with the blood from his eyes as Elric's blade teased them out until they hung by a few strands of muscle on his own cheeks.

Most of the time Elric's voice drowned the hideous screaming of the Nazi, his pleadings to spare him or kill him, and I was thankful for that.

Sword and man acted in unison—two intelligences in an unholy pact. I had never felt this of Ravenbrand before. Elric's use of the blade seemed to have awakened an evil in the very iron. Red runes slithered up and down its length, pulsing like veins. The sword seemed to relish the subtle, disgusting wounds which it now inflicted upon the Nazi's bloody flesh. It was without doubt the most loathsome sight I had ever seen.

Again I turned away. Then I heard Oona gasp and I looked back.

Another shape formed itself around the Nazi's tormented body. It twisted in and out, growing like something organic. Gradually, snakelike, it swallowed Elric's victim, then became increasingly agitated, and gouted up out of what remained of the corpse. Gushing towards the cavern's roof. Swirling like a cloud overhead. A cloud in which tiny strands of lightning seemed to flash and writhe, taking on the color of the Nazi's blood as the man squealed like a bled pig, realizing that there were worse fates than the one he had just endured. He finally gave himself up to the cloud.

I heard Elric's voice above all the other sounds. "Father of Winds. Father of Dust. Father of Air. Father of Thunder. H'Haarshann Oldfather. Oldest of fathers. H'Haarshann Oldfather, father of the first." I knew the language he spoke, because I knew all such things now, and I knew that he was delivering the wretched mortal up to the one he summoned.

"Oldfather! Oldfather! I bring you what the lord of the h'Haarshann demands. I bring thee the exotic meat thou craveth."

The cloud grunted. It was satisfied. It uttered a kind of soft whistle.

Now the scarlet lightning began to dance and skip again, forming a shape. I thought I saw the wizened face of a vindictive old man, long strands of lank hair hanging to his shrunken shoulders. A toothless mouth smacking lips as the last of the sacrifice was absorbed. Then the mouth grinned.

"You know how to feed an old friend, Prince Elric." The voice was a sighing breeze, a gale, a fluttering wind.

"As you have fed before, h'Haarshann Oldfather." My near-twin had sheathed the bloody black blade and now stood with arms outstretched in an attitude of respect. "As you will feed again, while I live. That is our bargain. Made with my ancestors a million years since."

"Ahaaaa . . ." A deep sigh. "So few remember. I have a mind to grant you my aid in return for that exquisite moment. What is it that you desire of me?"

"Someone has summoned your sons to this plane. They have misbehaved themselves. They have done great damage."

"It is in their nature. It is what they must do. They are so young, my ten sons. They are the ten great *h'Haarshann* that stride the worlds."

"That is so, Oldfather." Elric glanced down at the remains of the Nazi. As a hawk takes every part of the bird save the feathers, so Oldfather had taken the mortal, leaving nothing but the blood-soaked remains of his SS uniform. "They have been brought by my enemies from their place amongst the worlds. To threaten the lives of me and mine."

Oldfather quivered. "But without you I cannot know the exquisite taste of flesh. And my Ten Sons have business about the worlds, to breathe my will upon them."

"That is so, great Oldfather."

"None is left save you, sweet mortal. None who knows what Oldfather likes to eat."

At that moment Elric looked up. His eyes met mine. The sardonic mockery in his expression made me turn my head in disgust. I knew that Elric of Melniboné only resembled a man, that his blood was of an older, crueler kind than mine. In my own world such savage and sadistic sacrifice was only performed by the mentally ill. For Elric and his kind, those practices were a way of life, refined to an art and enjoyed as spectacle. In Melniboné praise was given to the victim who died with style and who best entertained his audience with his dying. What Elric had just done caused him no troubled conscience. The actions had been necessary and were natural to him.

Oldfather seemed to be debating the value of the sacrifice.

"Would you feast again, noble Oldfather?" Elric's voice was soft, coaxing. There was no threat in it, but Oldfather was remembering the taste of mortal flesh and was already yearning for more.

"I will see to my sons," said the apparition. "They, too, have eaten well."

The whirling scarlet fire swelled until it resembled circling cloud, sweeping up towards the cavern's faraway roof and then down into the darkness until it had disappeared, leaving the faintest of pink, dissipating light.

I looked towards Gaynor's camp. They had become aware of something. I saw troogs peering in our direction. One of them ran towards the center of the camp where Gaynor had pitched an ostentatious tent, its guy ropes secured by pegs hammered into the living rock.

I guessed the Nazi's death to have been pointless after all. Oldfather had gone. The ten whirling inverted cones of phosphorescent light still guarded the camp. Elric's filthy ritual had done nothing but attract the attention of Gaynor's horde.

A party of troogs lumbered in our direction. They had not seen us, but it would not take them long to find where we were. I looked around for some way of escape. Only Oona had a weapon. My sword was in the hands of my doppelgänger. I was not sure I would feel quite the same emotions towards the blade in the future. If I had a future to contemplate.

The troogs were beginning to climb the rocks towards us. They could smell us.

I looked around for something to throw. The rocks were the only weapons available to me.

Glancing back, I saw that Elric had sunk to his knees totally exhausted. I wondered if I could get to the sword before the troogs reached us. If I could ever handle that blade again.

Oona nocked an arrow to her bow and took aim.

She looked once or twice over her shoulder, unable to believe that Elric had failed, that Oldfather had taken his offering and left without giving us any of the help he had seemed to promise.

I caught a glimpse of something not far from the grey horizon. A scarlet flash which began to speed towards us, coming faster and faster and making a mighty thrum, as if someone plucked the strings of an enormous guitar whose sound was amplified through all creation.

Elric scrambled up to join us. He was grinning. He panted like a wolf. He had a look of wild lust in his eyes. A look of triumph, of hunger.

He said nothing to us but looked to where the scarlet cloud was approaching. To where the Ten Sons danced at the edges of Gaynor's camp.

Then he lifted his head, raised the black runesword in a victorious gesture and began to sing.

I knew the song. I knew Elric. I had been Elric. I knew what it meant. I knew what it said. But I could not know its effect. I do not believe I ever, in all my life of concert-going, heard such extraordinary beauty. If there was menace in it, if there was triumph in it, if there was cruel exultation in it, still, it was beautiful. I felt I heard an angel sing. More than one tune, many harmonies, were all carried on that strange voice. It brought tears to my eyes. It brought grief and mourning. I was mourning the death of the man I had seen killed. I was hearing the voice of a grief which had never filled the world before.

For a moment Elric's song stopped the troogs in their tracks.

I looked at Oona. She was weeping. She understood something in her father which mystified me and perhaps, therefore, him as well.

The song swelled and I realized Ravenbrand had joined with Elric. An almost tangible sound. I felt it embracing me. I felt the complexity of it, a thousand different sensations passing through my blood and nerves all at the same time. Something in me was strengthened by that song, but physically it weakened me, and I could barely stand.

Then another song joined in, from far away, near the grey horizon. I saw shreds of scarlet light radiating from a hidden source. Fingers of scarlet, like ropes, twisting around the rocky columns, reaching across the ranks of that vast army. A gigantic hand was stretching through the cavern. The hand of God. Or the hand of Satan. The flaming hand made a fist and that fist drew in each of the Ten Sons, who whirled and buzzed in sudden fury, resisting Oldfather's discipline. The white fire scattered and raced, but the hand extended to enfold it.

All the while Gaynor's camp was in uproar. I saw a figure emerge from his tent and mount one of the blind horses. I heard bugles sounding, drums beating. Confusion reigned as partially clothed men tried to control their mounts. The blind cannibals milled around gathering their weapons. Only the troogs were wide awake. Many of them were running back into the darkness, away from the Grey Fees, while the red hand of Oldfather gathered in his wild, squealing sons. The destruction they caused as they sought to avoid him brought more rocks crashing to the cavern floor, more stones whirling into the air.

A sea of brands moved chaotically in all directions as Gaynor demanded more light.

We could see him now, on his great albino horse, its blind red eyes rolling as it snorted and scented, its ears frantic as it tried to catch the source of the sounds. Yet Gaynor controlled the stallion with one hand and his knees. The other hand held the ivory sword— the sword Miggea's magic had made. He spurred in our direction, though I doubted he had any clear idea of what was happening. His main object was to turn the fleeing troogs and savages back to the camp. His men followed on their own horses, lashing out at the foot soldiers, yelling at them and causing further panic. Two of the Nazis rode up behind the troogs who were preparing to attack us.

They had no common language. The Nazis bellowed. The troogs bellowed back.

Elric suddenly rose from cover and began running at tremendous speed down the slope towards the Nazis.

Ravenbrand was still in his right hand. The sword howled with triumphant glee as it sliced into the neck of the first SS man. Elric dragged the corpse from its saddle and took the Nazi's place, spurring the blind horse directly at the other Nazi, who was already trying to flee the way he had come. Too late.

Elric swung Ravenbrand sideways, using the sword's wonderful balance to carry the weight of a blow which neatly took the Nazi's head from its shoulders as if it had been a cabbage on a stalk. He reached down to gather up the horse's reins and then rode back, scattering troogs as he came towards us.

"Here's a mount for one of you," he said. "The other must get their own."

I held the horse for Oona. She shook her head, grinning. "I can't ride," she said. "I've never had to learn." She replaced the arrow in her quiver. The troogs had given up any idea of attacking us.

I got into the saddle. It was a good, responsive horse. I told her to climb behind me, but she laughed. "I have my own ways of traveling," she said. "Though I thank you for the courtesy."

Gaynor had seen something and was charging towards us, his men at his back, Klosterheim by his side.

I looked forward at last to confronting him man-to-man.

Elric turned his horse, signaling that we should ride back the way we had come. He leaned down in his saddle and picked up one of the guttering brands. He handed it to me, then sought another for himself. The horses were excited. They wanted to gallop. I knew it would be dangerous in this darkness, but my cousin was gaining on us. He had become a far more expert rider in this bizarre landscape than I could hope to be.

I looked around for Oona. She had vanished.

Elric yelled for me to follow. I had no choice.

I cried out for him to stop, to wait for his daughter, but he laughed when he heard me and signaled me on.

He did not fear for her. I could only trust him.

We plunged into the booming darkness as the Ten Sons whirled their last ahead of us. All had been taken up in that one great red fist and were buzzing and whirring like wasps as the fingers molded and molded, turning the powerful, white light into something resembling a ball and hurling it upwards, higher and higher, until a moon hung overhead. Then it became a star. A point of light. And then it was gone.

A grumbling growl from the red cloud and Oldfather, too, vanished. Only Elric and myself remained, urging our horses into the blackness towards Mu Ooria, while Gaynor and his men, howling for our blood, came thundering behind us.

We followed the rough road the Ten Sons had carved, leaping broken columns, weaving between piles of rubble. Had I not known otherwise, I would have sworn the horses were sighted, they were so surefooted. Perhaps they had developed some of the qualities of bats. In a moment of humor I wished they had developed bat wings.

I was distracted by something white moving ahead of me along the broad road. The white hare raced as fast as it was possible to go. Towards the distant towers of Mu Ooria. I refused to let myself believe the obvious. I told myself that the white hare had found us again, that it had followed us from Tanelorn, when Miggea's hunt had chased it into our territory.

But Elric was grinning as he pursued it. For a moment I thought he was hunting it, but he kept behind it. He was following the beast.

Behind us came Gaynor, shouting like an angry ape, his own voice echoing in that mysterious helm, his cloak swirling about him like an agitated ocean, his horse's red eyes glaring sightlessly forward. He held up the ivory sword like a flag. The ragged remains of his SS guard were close behind him. Only Klosterheim, gaunt and hollow-eyed as ever, showed no emotion. At one moment, even that far away, I caught his grim, sardonic eye. In his own dark way, he was enjoying his master's discomfort.

"There's more to do yet," said Elric.

He looked back at the furious Gaynor and laughed.

For the first time I began to believe that perhaps he was not mad. At least, not in the way I had thought. His daughter thought him a genius. Presumably she believed him greater than most other sorcerers. His reckless courage might have been madness in another, but not in him. He could command power as no other mortal being could. And what was more, as I had witnessed, his alliances went back through generations upon generations, blood upon blood, when his own ancient people had been young and the world was not entirely formed.

For all his predatory skills, Elric was not by nature a predator. That differentiated him from his own people. Perhaps this was the bond all three of us shared.

"Fool!" Elric cried, dropping back to let my cousin gain on him. "Did you think I would allow an amateur sorcerer to invade

the Grey Fees? I am Elric, last Emperor of Melniboné, and I accept
no insult from a mere man-beast. Everything you believe you have
gained I will take from you. Everything you believe you have
destroyed will be restored. Every victory will become defeat."

"And I am Gaynor, who has mastered the Lords of Law and
Chaos! You cannot defeat me!"

"You are deluded," shouted my doppelgänger almost merrily.
"I care not what a man-beast calls itself. You have known a lucky
moment. You should have made better use of it while you had it."

Elric turned his back on Gaynor and urged his horse to a
faster pace. I was barely able to keep up with him but was astonished at the agility of my mount. It sensed all obstacles ahead. Our
brands guttered in a sudden current and threatened to go out
altogether, but the horses galloped on. Gaynor was fast catching
up with us, following the light we made. When the torches flared
back to life, I caught a sudden glimpse of Oona. The dreamthief's
daughter was standing to one side, gesturing to us. Elric extinguished his torch and gestured for me to do the same.

We heard Gaynor and his men galloping behind us. We saw
the ragged light of their torches. They were almost on us and I was
not sure Elric still had enough energy to engage so many. Without
a sword, I would be killed or captured immediately.

I saw the faintest circle of light ahead. I could still hear
Gaynor and his Nazi band. They were closer. Then, quite suddenly, the sound dropped away, distant, faint, and the light ahead
grew a little brighter. We were riding down a kind of natural tunnel, following the swift-footed white hare. The roof of the tunnel
reflected the light. It was mottled, like a book's marbling, like
mother-of-pearl. The noise of Gaynor and his army was gone
completely.

We had not come this way. I realized that Elric—or the white
hare—did not intend to return to Mu Ooria, at least not immediately. After a while, the Prince of Melniboné lit his torch again. I
lit my own. We were reaching the end of the tunnel.

The tunnel led downwards, opening into a great circular cavern which had clearly once been inhabited by human beings.

Rotting remains of clothing and old utensils suggested that the occupants had been killed while away from their home. It looked as if a whole tribe had lived here. Everything spoke of sudden disaster. But Elric was not interested in the previous tenants. He lifted his torch to inspect the cavern, seemed satisfied enough and dismounted.

I heard a movement behind me and looked back. Oona stood there, leaning upon her bow staff. I did not ask what magic had brought her here. Or what magic she had used to bring us here. I did not believe I needed to ask or to know.

Leaving the brands burning in the wall holes clearly designed for the purpose, Elric signaled for me to dismount and follow him back to the entrance of the tunnel. He wanted to be certain Gaynor had not found us. We moved cautiously, expecting to see our pursuers, but we had evaded them. Outside it was pitch-black. I heard Elric sniff. I felt his hand tugging me to go with him.

We moved through utter darkness, but Elric was surefooted, using his ears as well as his nose. I was again struck by our differences. He was Melnibonéan. His senses were far sharper than my own.

When he was entirely satisfied that Gaynor and his men had ridden on, with no idea of where we had hidden ourselves, he led me back to the tunnel and into the huge cave, where Oona was already busying herself with a fire and the food we had taken from the troog.

We ate sparingly. Elric sat some distance away. Frowning, wolfish. Clearly deep in thought, he did not wish to be disturbed. Oona and I exchanged a few words. She reassured me. We were not merely hiding, she said. We needed a place such as this. More sorcery was required. She was not sure how long her father could continue to find energy, from whatever source, to carry on. There was too much to be done, she murmured. She was careful to make sure that her father could not hear us.

When we had finished, Elric signed for us to get up and go outside. When he was sure Gaynor was no longer in the region, he told me to bring the horses. The three of us set off into the darkness, following a small, slow-burning taper which Elric held to guide us. We rode for miles over the rocky cavern floor until he stopped. Another cautious pause, then he took out one of our brands and lit it. This part of the underground world had not seen the movement of Gaynor's army. It was as still, as untouched, as it had always been. But where a group of stalagmites formed what looked like a circle of Off-Moo heads bent in prayer, I saw a body.

One of the big black cats the troogs feared, which Gaynor had somehow enchanted.

The thing was huge. Elric went up to it and attempted to lift it. Oona joined him, and then I. We were just able to get the beast off the floor of the cavern.

"We must take it back with us," the Melnibonéan said. "We'll use the horses."

The horses were not happy being so close to one of the panthers, let alone being used to transport it. We managed to make a sling and, with many minor pitfalls, finally succeeded in getting the huge body back to our hiding place.

Oona and I were exhausted, but Elric was filled with an edgy excitement. He anticipated what he had to do with some pleasure.

"Why have we brought this beast here?" I ventured.

His answer was dismissive.

"A further Summoning," he said. "But first we shall need an appropriate sacrifice."

I looked at Oona.

Did he intend to kill one of us?

# CHAPTER EIGHTEEN

## Old Debts and New Dreams

ona nodded briefly and ran from the cave. Elric let her go. He paid no attention to me. I wondered if this was because he did not wish to improve his relationship with one whom he might soon need to kill. Ironic, I thought, if my own sword drank my soul.

After a time, he got up, took a horse, and began to walk back towards the entrance.

"Do you wish me to stay here?" I asked him.

"As you please," he said.

So I followed him. My curiosity was far stronger than any fear that he might turn on me.

He had mounted and urged the horse forward through the darkness. Happily my own beast was inclined to follow its companion. By this means, I kept pace with the Melnibonéan.

At last the lights of Gaynor's camp could be seen again. It was still in confusion. We heard shouts and curses. Elric dismounted, handed me his reins and told me to wait. Then he made his way cautiously down towards the camp.

Fires had been extinguished and it was by no means as easy to see as it had been. But soon I began to hear shouts and the

wild, pleading cries, and I knew that Elric was replenishing his
energy.

Some while later, his white face suddenly appeared from the
darkness. His glittering, ruby eyes had a hot, satisfied look, and his
lips were partly open as he panted like a well-fed wolf. I could see
the blood on his lips.

Blood caked the black blade he held in his right hand. I knew
it had taken a score of souls to satisfy both flesh and iron.

We rode back in silence and were not followed. I had the
impression that Gaynor and his men were still riding the vast caverns of Mu Ooria, perhaps believing the last Lord of Melniboné to
have returned to the ruined city.

Elric said nothing as he led the way through the blackness. He
hunched over his saddle, still breathing slowly, a sated predator.
As close as we were, both in mind and blood, I found myself shuddering at this obscenity. Too much of my own blood was human,
not enough Melnibonéan, for me to relish the sight of my kinsman
or ancestor or whatever he was absorbing the souls he had stolen.

But what black souls they had been! I heard myself saying.
Did they not serve some better purpose now? Did they not
deserve to die in this perverse and terrible way, given the crimes
they had already committed, the blasphemies they had performed?

It was not in my civilized Christian soul to rejoice. I could only
mourn the destruction of so many in such an ungodly cause.

Once I thought I had lost Elric and lit my taper. Then I saw
the creature's demonic face, his glaring red eyes, his disgusted
mouth telling me to put the light out. He was irritated by me in
the way a man might be irritated by a badly trained dog. I saw
nothing human in that face. I had been stupid, nonetheless.
Gaynor must even now be returning from the city, having failed
to find us. A tiny light in this blackness would be seen for miles.

Only when we had found the tunnel again did Elric allow me
to light my way.

Oona had clearly been sleeping when we returned. She darted
a mysterious, concerned look at her father and another at me. I

could say nothing to her. I could tell her nothing. A vampiric sym-
biosis existed between man and blade. Who could tell which fed
the other? I guessed she was already familiar with these characteristics. Her mother would have told her, if she had not observed
them for herself by now.

Elric stumbled to the center of the cave where we had
arranged the huge bulk of the black cat. He pressed his head
against the body, against the thing's gigantic skull. He muttered
and busied himself. Oona could not answer my unspoken question. She watched in fascination as her father walked around the
great beast, muttering, making passages in the air with his hand,
as if trying to remember a spell.

Perhaps he was doing exactly that.

After a while he looked up, directly into our faces. "I shall
need your help in this." He spoke almost impatiently, in self-disgust. He must have been surprised by his own continuing weakness. Perhaps the kind of sorcery he had already performed
drained him more than he expected.

I knew I had no choice in the matter. "What do you want?"

"Nothing yet. I'll tell you when it's time." His expression,
when he looked at his daughter, was almost pitying. I'm not sure
if I imagined it, but I thought she moved a little closer to me for
comfort.

Elric seemed to be in pain. Every muscle on his body appeared
independently alive for a moment. Then he subsided into sweat-
ing stillness. His eyes glared up into worlds and creatures far
beyond my understanding. The words, as I heard them, meant little, even though another part of me knew their meaning all too
well.

One word had special resonance: Meerclar—Meerclar—
Meerclar—he repeated it over and over. A name. It meant more
than that. It meant a friend. A bond. Something resembling affection. Old blood. Ancient ties . . . And more. It meant bargains.
Bargains struck to last for eternity. Bargains struck in blood and
souls. Bargains between one unhuman creature and another.

Meerclar! The word was louder, sharper.

*MEERCLAR!* His face blazed like burning ivory. His eyes were living coals. His long, wild hair seethed about him like a living thing. One hand held Ravenbrand on high. The other clutched at the air, describing geometries which existed in a thousand dimensions.

*MEERCLAR!* GREAT LORD OF FANG AND CLAW! *MEERCLAR!* YOUR CHILDREN SUFFER. AID THEM, MEERCLAR! AID THEM IN THE NAME OF OUR ANCIENT COMPACT!

*MEERCLAR!* The vocal cords strained and twisted to pronounce the name. His body pitched and shook like a ship in a typhoon. He was hardly in control of it. Yet all the while he spoke and kept his grip on the Black Sword.

A yowl from somewhere. A deep animal stink. The thrumming of breath. A swish, as of a feline tail.

*MEERCLAR!* SEKHMET'S FAVORITE SON! BORN OF OUR UNION. BORN OF THE COMING TOGETHER OF LIFE AND DEATH. *MEERCLAR*, LORD OF THE CATS, HONOR OUR COVENANT!

The body of the huge panther in the center of the cavern twitched and stretched. A massive puff rolled from its chest. The whiskers straightened. But the eyes did not open and soon the cat was prone again, as if something had sought to animate it and failed.

*MEERCLAR!*

He summoned that most conservative of creatures, that least tractable of elementals, Meerclar, Son of Sekhmet, the archetype of all cats.

My doppelgänger howled like a gale. His voice rose and fell in a series of shrieks and groans which shook the walls of our cave and must surely be heard outside, where Gaynor searched for us.

I realized Oona had vanished. Had Elric taken his own daughter for a sacrifice? I would have believed anything at that moment.

The horses, already frightened, began to buck and whinny, retreating as far as they could from a dark shadow forming near the distant wall. A shadow that moved back and forth, like a pacing beast. A shadow that lifted a great head, gave voice, quintessentially feline, and began to harmonize with Elric.

A great black figure, tall and broad, but standing on two legs and looking down at us as it materialized, uttered a huge, growling purr and dropped to all fours. The eyes bore an intelligence older than Elric's. The handsome, wedge-shaped head was fierce with jutting whiskers, fangs and glowing yellow and black eyes. The monstrous tail lashed and threatened to destroy the remains of the abandoned living quarters. The huge claws flexed and withdrew, flexed and withdrew. I wondered if this mighty supernatural cat had eaten. For all my own natural affinity with the species, I was nervous. I knew that cats had little sense of regret or of consequence, and this one might eat us casually, without malice or even hunger.

This was Meerclar, Lord of the Cats. His image flickered a little, in and out of the various realities he inhabited. I had become used to witnessing this phenomenon in creatures which lived in more than one of time's dimensions.

I feared for Oona. She was nowhere to be seen. Lord Meerclar had the air of a cat which had recently feasted.

Had Oona not told me earlier that one of the great panthers was her avatar in this world? But what was the white hare?

How many avatars could a dreamthief possess?

How many lives?

Elric addressed Lord Meerclar. The great elemental's deep voice rumbled in response as Elric recounted what had happened. How Lord Meerclar's own kin had been entranced and put into a slumber that must ultimately kill them as they starved.

At this the mighty cat began to show some agitation. It paced on all fours, tail lashing, breath grumbling. Then it sat, in thought, claws flexing.

In the far corner, the terrified horses no longer snorted and dilated their eyes. They stood frozen, perhaps certain that they must soon become Lord Meerclar's prey.

I was scarcely more active. I watched as Elric reversed the sword. He placed his two hands on the hilt and stood with his legs wide apart staring up into the cat elemental's huge face, still speaking in those same strange tones.

I was shocked, therefore, when I felt something warm and damp upon my neck. Turning, I looked straight into the muzzle of the panther, which I had assumed was dead. The big cat narrowed his eyes and a vast purr vibrated from his chest. I felt his spittle on my face, felt the heat of him against my body.

In an extraordinary gesture of submission, the great panther crossed to Meerclar and Elric, laid his head between his paws, and looked up into Meerclar's face.

A mighty purr escaped the Lord of the Cats, as of profound satisfaction, and the panther rose, stretched, turned and trotted from the chamber. The beast looked as if it had just risen from a quick nap.

Oona was still nowhere to be seen. I had an impulse to follow the panther. Meerclar then stretched his huge muscles, his eyes narrowed, and he said something in his own language which I could not hear.

Elric was showing signs of considerable strain. His limbs shook. He could barely stand up. His eyes had begun to take on a glazed look. His face was harrowed. I moved towards him, to help him, but he saw me and signed me back.

The huge yellow eyes turned on me. They regarded me with dispassionate curiosity. I knew what it must be like to be a mouse in such a situation. All I could do was make a courteous bow and retreat.

This seemed to satisfy Lord Meerclar, who returned his attention to Elric. He was purring again, his pleasure the result of whatever it was Elric had done. He praised my doppelgänger. He expressed a kind of gratitude. Something seemed to embrace the Melnibonéan. And then the Lord of the Cats became smoke.

And vanished.

"Where is Oona?" I wanted to know. Elric tried to speak. His eyes lost focus. I caught him as he fell, the great iron sword clattering to the floor. I thought the spell-making had taken too much. I thought it had killed him.

But I found a pulse. I checked his eyes. He was in a swoon, perhaps a supernatural trance brought about by his contact with the elementals. He was breathing heavily, as if drugged. I had seen men in alcoholic stupor, and others who had imbibed the famous Mickey Finn, who seemed more lively. However, I was convinced he would not die immediately.

I considered going out of the cave again and seeking Oona, but common sense told me she was better able to look after herself. And if, as I suspected, she could change her shape—to that, specifically, of a white hare—she was out there somewhere. Unless she had, indeed, been given as hostage to Meerclar. He might regard her, after all, as one of his own. And he might have demanded that she return home with him.

A noise came from the tunnel. At first I assumed the panther had made it. Then I identified it more clearly. The sound of horses' hooves, the clatter of harness and weaponry, of metal and leather. Warriors riding towards us. Could they be the original inhabitants, come to reclaim their own quarters? It did not seem likely.

We had no other way out of the cave and the man who might have saved us lay in an exhausted slumber on the rocky floor. Oona, who could have defended us with her bow, was also gone. I had no weapon.

I knelt beside Elric, trying to wake him, but he would not stir. His breathing was long, like that of a hibernating animal, and I could not see his eyes. He was completely unconscious.

I reached reluctantly towards the Raven Blade, still lying near his right hand. Even as the tips of my fingers touched that strange, living iron, light came brawling into the cave. A mounted man with a brand. Another behind him. And another.

Our own horses whinnied and pranced in recognition. The other horses snorted and stamped on the floor of the cave. A coarse voice said something in German.

My fingers closed on the sword's familiar hilt. The torchlight half blinded me, but I climbed to my feet, using the sword to help me. I looked up and recognized the armored outline. Gaynor, of course, had found us. No doubt he or one of his men had seen my foolish light or the panther leaving the cave entrance and investigated.

Gaynor's unhappy laughter boomed in his helm. "This will make a splendid tomb for the pair of you. A shame you will lie here unknown and forgotten for the rest of eternity."

He was a splendid figure in his silvery armor, a black sword on his left hip and the mysterious ivory sword on his right. He had a glow about him that I could only believe was supernatural. His flesh had a look of exaggerated health. He swaggered in the joy of it all and mocked the feeble thing I was.

Or had been.

My anger outweighed my fear. I reached and drew Ravenbrand to me. I held my old sword in my two hands. I felt its familiar balance, coupled with an unfamiliar power. I snarled at him. As I gripped the sword, some of that filthy, stolen vitality coursed into me. It filled my veins with dark energy. It filled them with evil strength. Now I was laughing, also. Laughing back at my cousin Paul Gaynor von Minct and relishing his doom.

Part of me was troubled by how I was behaving, but something of Elric was in me now and the sword responded to that.

"Greetings, Gaynor," I found myself saying. "I thank you for your courtesy in saving me the trouble of tracking you down. Now I shall kill you."

Gaynor laughed in turn as he saw the prone Melnibonéan. I suppose I must have looked a little odd, dressed in my tattered twentieth-century clothes, holding the great iron battle blade in two hands. But his laughter wasn't as confident as it might have been and Klosterheim, beside him, was not at all amused. He had not expected to find two of us.

"Well, cousin," Gaynor said, leaning on his pommel, "you've come to prefer the darkness to the light, I see. Selective ignorance was always a trait of your side of the family, eh?"

I ignored this. "You have done a great deal of killing since we last met, Prince Gaynor. You appear to have slaughtered an entire race."

"Oh, the Off-Moo! Who's to tell, cousin? Who's to tell? They suffered the delusion common to all isolated peoples. They decided that because they had never been conquered, they were invulnerable. The British have the same delusion in your world, do they not?"

I was not here to discuss imperial delusions or the philosophy of isolationism. I was here to kill him. A completely unfamiliar bloodlust was rising in me. I felt it take me in its grip. Not a pleasant sensation for one of my basic disposition. Was it a response to Gaynor's threats? Or was the sword transferring to me what it had earlier transferred to Elric?

I trembled with the excess energy which pulsed through me. Now came unexpected desires of all kinds, all forming one single directive in my mind—kill Gaynor and any who rode with him. I anticipated the sweet slicing of the sword into flesh, the impact of the bone as it shattered under sharpened steel which slipped through muscles and sinew as smoothly as a spoon through soup, leaving red ruin behind. I anticipated the relish I would know as a human life was taken to feed my own greedy soul. I licked my lips. I regarded Gaynor's followers as so much food and Gaynor himself the tastiest choice of all. I could feel my own hot breath panting in my throat, the saliva, blood as salt, on my tongue and I had begun to scent at the men and beasts before me, recognizing each individual by their specific smell. I could smell their blood, their flesh, their sweat. I could even smell the tears as I took my first Nazi and he wept briefly for his mortal soul as I sucked it from him.

The yelling in the cave, the stamp of the horses and the clash of metal, echoed everywhere. It was impossible to tell where all my enemies were. I killed two before I realized it and their souls went to strengthen me, so that I moved with even greater speed, the sword writhing and turning in my hands like a living creature, killing, killing, killing. Killing, while I laughed my wolf's laugh and dedicated my victims to eternal service with Duke Arioch of Chaos.

Gaynor, typically, had thrown his men to the front. Within the confines of that cavern I could not easily reach either him or Klosterheim. I had to hack my way through men and horses.

I saw my cousin pull something from within his clothing. A golden staff, raging with fiery light, as if all the life of all the worlds was contained within. He held it before him as one might hold a weapon and then, from his scabbard, he drew Stormbringer, the blade he had stolen from my doppelgänger, brother to the Raven Sword I now held.

It did not alarm me. I leaped and sliced and was almost upon my cousin as he took in his reins, cursing at me, the Runestaff returned to his shirt, the black blade howling. I knew that the blade could not be resheathed until it had taken souls. That was the bargain one always made with such a sword.

Urging his men forward, the Knight of the Balance turned his great pale horse back into the tunnel and yelled for Klosterheim to follow. But I was between him and Klosterheim, who was grappling at his horse's reins. I swung my sword upwards, trying to get through his guard. Every time I struck, the Raven Sword was countered by Stormbringer. By now both swords were howling like wolves and shrieking as they clashed, their red runes rippling up and down the black iron like static electricity. And that hideous strength still flowed into my veins.

Gaynor was neither laughing nor cursing. He was screaming.

Something happened to him every time the two swords crossed.

He began to blaze with an eerie crimson fire. The fire burned only briefly, and when it went out, Gaynor looked even more drawn.

Metal met metal with a terrible clang and every time the same fire raged through Gaynor.

I did not understand what was happening, but I pressed my advantage.

Then, to my astonishment, my cousin let go of the Black Sword and his left hand reached for the ivory blade, scabbarded on his opposite hip.

For some reason this amused me. I swung a further arc of iron and he bent backwards, barely avoiding it. The ivory sword met the black and for a moment it was as if I had hit a wall at sixty miles an hour. I was instantly stopped. The Black Sword continued to moan and its remaining energy still passed into me, but the white sword had countered it. I swung again. Gaynor, untriumphant but clearly glad enough to survive, spurred his horse into the darkness of the passage, Klosterheim and the remains of his band fast behind him.

I was suddenly too weak to continue after them. My own legs buckled. I was paying the price for all that unexpected power.

I tried to keep my senses, knowing that Gaynor would immediately take advantage of me if he knew that I, like Elric, had collapsed.

I could do nothing to save myself.

I stumbled deeper into the cavern, now a charnel house of dead horses and human corpses, and tried to reach Elric, to revive him, to warn him of what was happening.

My pale hand reached out towards his white, unresponsive face, and then I was absorbed by darkness, vulnerable to anything that now desired my life.

I heard my name being called. I guessed it was Gaynor, returning to have his revenge upon me.

I took a fresh grip on the sword, but the energy no longer filled me. I had paid my price for what it had given me. It had paid its price to me.

I remember thinking, sardonically, that the account was now fully closed.

But I looked up into Oona's face, not Gaynor's. Had any time passed? I could still smell the blood and torn flesh, the ordure of savage battling. I could feel cold iron against my hand. But I was too weak to rise. She lifted me. She gave me water and some kind of drug which set my veins to shaking before I drew a long, deep breath and was able to get to my feet.

"Gaynor?"

"Already witnessing the destruction of his army," she said. She had an air of satisfaction. I had the impression her lips were bloody. Then she licked them, like a cat, and they were clean.

"How so? The Off-Moo?"

"Meerclar's children," she said. "All the panthers were revived. They wasted no time hunting down their favorite prey. The troogs are dead or fled and most of the savages have gone back to their old territories. Gaynor can no longer protect them against their traditional enemies. They would be going to their instant doom if they followed him into the Grey Fees."

"So he cannot conquer the Grey Fees?"

"He believes he has the power to do it without his army. For he has the white sword and he has the cup. These he believes contain the power of Law, and he believes the power of Law will give him the Grey Fees."

"Even I know that's madness!" I began to walk unsteadily to where the Melnibonéan was still lying. Now, however, he had the air of a man experiencing ordinary sleep. "What can we do to stop him?"

"There's a chance," she said quietly, "that he cannot be stopped. Just by introducing those two great objects of power into the Grey Fees he could unbalance the entire multiverse, sending it spinning to its eternal destruction and all living, feeling creatures with it."

"One man?" I said. "One mortal?"

"Whatever happens," she said, "it is predicted that the fate of the multiverse shall depend upon the actions of one mortal man. That encourages Gaynor. He thinks he is the mortal chosen for that honor."

"Why should he not be?"

"Because another has already been chosen," she said.

"Do you know who it is?"

"Yes."

I waited, but she said no more. She leaned over her father, testing for his pulse, checking his eyes, just as I had earlier. She shook her head. "Exhausted," she said. "Nothing else. Too much sorcery, even for him." She rolled up a cloak and put it under his head. It was a strange, rather touching gesture. All around us was death and destruction. Spilled blood was everywhere, yet Elric's daughter behaved almost as if she kissed a child good night in its own bed.

She picked up Stormbringer and resheathed it for him. Only then did I realize I still held Ravenbrand in my hand. Oona had found Elric's sword where Gaynor had hurled it when it turned on him and instead of giving him strength, burned up what remained of his energy.

"Well," I said, "at least we have the stolen sword back."

Oona nodded reflectively. "Yes," she said, "Gaynor must change his plans."

"Why didn't Stormbringer feed off him earlier?"

"By betraying Miggea, he also lost her help. He seemed to think he would be able to keep it, in spite of her being a prisoner. She has to be able to exert her will in order to aid him, and he ensured that she could not."

I heard a mumble and looked to where Elric lay. He stirred. His lips formed words, tiny sounds. Troubled sounds. The sounds of a distant nightmare.

Oona laid her cool hand upon her father's forehead. The Melnibonéan immediately breathed more regularly and his body no longer twitched and trembled.

When, eventually, he opened his eyes, they were full of wise intelligence.

"At last," he said. "The tide can be turned." His hand went to the handle of his runesword and caressed it. I had the feeling she had somehow communicated everything that had happened to him. Or did he get it telepathically from me?

"Perhaps it can be, Father." Oona looked around her, as if seeing the signs of battle for the first time. "But I fear it will take more resources than we can summon now."

The Prince of Melniboné began to rise. I offered him my arm. He hesitated, then took it with an expression of profound irony on his face.

"So now we are both whole men again," he said.

I was impatient with this. "I need to know what unique qualities that staff or cup or whatever it is and that white sword have.

Why are we fighting for possession of them? What do they represent to Gaynor?"

Elric and Oona stared at me in some surprise. They had con-
cealed nothing deliberately from me. They had simply not
thought to tell me.

"They exist in your own legends," said Oona. "Your family
protected them on your plane. That is your traditional duty.
According to your legends the Grail is a cup with magical properties, which can restore life and can only be beheld in its true, pure
form by a knight of equally true and pure soul. The sword is the
traditional sword which bestows great nobility upon its wielder, if
used in a noble cause. It has been called many names. It was lost
and Gaynor sought it. Klosterheim got it from Bek. Miggea told
him that if he bore both the black sword and the white and took
them, together with the Grail, into the Grey Fees, he would be
able to set his will upon existence. He could re-create the multiverse."

I found this incredible. "He believed such nonsense?"

Oona hesitated. Then she said: "He believed it."

I thought for a moment. I was a twentieth-century man. How
could I give any credibility to such mythical tomfoolery? Perhaps
all I was doing was dreaming after hearing some overblown piece
of *Sturm und Drang.* Was I trapped in the story of *Parsifal, The
Flying Dutchman* and *Götterdämmerung* all at the same time? Of
course it was impossible to pursue such logic. Not only had I been
party to Elric's past, his entire experience of the sorcerous realms,
but I recollected everything I had seen since escaping from the
Nazi concentration camp. From the moment my sword clove the
cliff of Hameln, I had accepted the laws of wizardry.

I began to laugh. Not the mad laughter I'd offered Gaynor, but
natural, good-humored self-mockery.

"And why should he not have done?" I said. "Why should he
not believe anything he chooses?"

# CHAPTER NINETEEN

# Beyond the Grey Fees

e must follow Gaynor," said Oona. "Somehow we must stop him."

"His soldiers are scattered or destroyed," I said. "What harm can he do?"

"A great deal," she said. "He still has a sword and the Grail."

Elric confirmed this. "If we are swift, we could stop him reaching the Grey Fees. If we do that, we shall all be free of his ambitions. But the Fees are malleable—subject to human will, it's said. If that will is complemented with Gaynor's new power . . ."

Oona was striding for the tunnel. She disappeared into the shadows. "Follow me," she said. "I'll find him."

We mounted wearily, Elric and I. Each of us had a black runesword at his belt. For the first time since this affair started, there was real hope we could capture Gaynor before he did further damage. Perhaps I was stupid to believe that the ownership of a sword conferred a sense of self-respect upon me, but I now felt Elric's equal. Not just the sword, but what I had done with it made me proud to ride beside the gloomy Prince of Ruins in pursuit of a kinsman still capable of destroying the fundamental matter of existence.

That I should feel self-respect as a result of killing almost half-a-score of my fellow human beings was a mark of what I had become since my capture by the Nazis. I, who in common with most of my family, abhorred war and was disgusted by mankind's willingness to kill their own so readily, in such numbers and with such abandon, was now as thoroughly blooded as any of the Nazis we fought here in the world of Mu Ooria. And the strongest thing I felt was satisfaction. I looked forward to killing the rest.

In a way the Nazis' rejection of traditional humanism led to their appalling fates. It is one thing to mock the subtle infrastructures of a civil society, to claim they serve no purpose, but quite another to tear them down. Only when they were gone did we realize how much our safety and sanity and civic well-being depended on them. This fascist lesson is learned over and over again, even into modern times.

Emerging from the tunnel with guttering torches we saw ahead of us one of the panthers awakened by Elric's sorcery. The beast turned bright knowing eyes on us. It was leading us through the caverns, searching, I was certain, for my cousin Gaynor.

Was the panther Oona? Or was the beast mentally controlled by my doppelgänger's daughter? Mystified, we could do nothing save trust the beast as it padded ahead of us, occasionally looking back to make sure we followed.

I was half expecting another ambush from a furious Gaynor. My cousin would be considering his revenge on us already. But I soon realized he would no longer be flinging an army into the Grey Fees. His army had been destroyed.

As if to demonstrate this destruction, the panther led us straight through Gaynor's camp. The big cats had done their work swiftly and efficiently. Ruined troog bodies lay everywhere, most with their throats torn out. The savages had also been attacked, but clearly a great many of them had fled back to their own territories. I doubted if Gaynor would be able to raise another army from their ranks.

A weird howling came from behind us, as if jackals mourned their own kind, and then, from around a huge stalagmite rode

Gaynor. Klosterheim and the remains of his men followed him, though not with enthusiasm. Gaynor whirled the great ivory runesword around his head, bearing down on us with single-minded hatred. I could not tell if the sounds came from him or the blade.

Elric and I acted as one.

Our swords were in our hands. Their murmuring became a shrill whine modifying to a full-throated howl which made the white blade's sound seem feeble.

Gaynor had become used to unchallenged power. He seemed surprised by this resistance, in spite of his recent experience. He tugged on his reins, bringing his horse to a skidding turn and urged his men towards us.

Once again I felt the battle frenzy in my veins. I felt it threatening to take over my entire being. Beside me Elric was laughing as he spurred towards the leading rider. The howling of his sword changed, first to triumph as it bit into its victim's breast, then to a satiated murmur as it drank the man's soul.

My own black battle blade twisted in my hand, thrusting forward before I could react, taking the next rider in the head, shearing off half his skull in the process. And again the sword drank, uttering a thirsty croon as the Nazi's life essence poured into it and mixed with mine. Those who lived by the sword, I thought . . . The idea took on an entirely new meaning. I saw Klosterheim and urged my horse towards him. Elric and Gaynor were fighting on horseback, sword against sword. Two more of Gaynor's men came at me. I swung the heavy sword—it moved like a pendulum—and took the first rider in the side, the second, as I swung back behind me, in the thigh. As the first died, I finished the second. Their soulless remains slumped like so much butcher's meat in their saddles. I found myself laughing at this. I turned again and met the crazed ruby blaze of Elric's own eyes, my eyes, glaring back at me.

Gaynor jumped his horse over a pile of bodies and turned, the Runestaff held in his gauntleted hand. "You cannot kill me while I hold this. You are fools to try. And while I hold this—I hold the key to all Creation!"

Elric and I did not have horses capable of jumping so high. We were forced to ride around the pile of corpses while Klosterheim and the three remaining Nazis interposed themselves between us and our quarry.

"I'm no longer Knight of the Balance," Gaynor raved, "I am Creator of All Existence!" Lifting the white sword and the Runestaff over his head, he spurred his horse, galloping off into the misty blackness, leaving his followers to slow our pursuit.

I took no pleasure in that killing. Only Klosterheim escaped, disappearing soundlessly amongst the great pillars. I made to go after him, but Elric stopped me. "Gaynor must be our only prey." He pointed. "Let her guide us. She can follow his scent."

The panther padded on without pause and our tireless blind horses trotted behind it.

Once I thought I heard Gaynor's laughter, the galloping of hooves, and then I saw a blaze of golden light as if the Grail signaled its own abduction. The pearly grey of the horizon grew wider and taller ahead of us until its light spread like a gentle blanket of mist over the whole vast forest of stone. The air had grown noticeably cooler and there was a clean quality to it I could not identify. For a while that featureless grey field filled me with utter terror. I looked upon endless nothingness. The finale of the multiverse. Limbo.

The calmness of it frightened me. But the fear began to disappear and was replaced by an equally strong sense of reconciliation, of peace. I had been here before, after all. None of these emotions affected the course of our actions, however, for the blind horses bore us relentlessly on. The panther continued to lead us and gradually, without any dramatic event, we found ourselves slowly absorbed into the gentle grey mist.

The mist had a substantial quality to it. I could not rid myself of the sense that Gaynor and Klosterheim might rush on us suddenly from ambush. Even when, for a few brief moments, the air ahead of us was filled with the brilliant scarlet and green of huge, delicate amaryllis blooms and creamy iris, I did not drop my guard.

"What was that?" I asked Elric.

The sorcerer offered me a crooked smile. "I don't know. Someone's sudden thought?"

Had those shapes been formed spontaneously by the strange, rich mist? I felt the stuff could create recognizable shapes at any moment. While I had expected something more spectacular from the legendary Grey Fees, I was relieved that it was not the roiling tangled strands of Chaos others had led me to expect. I had the feeling I would only have to concentrate to see my own most bizarre imaginings made concrete. I scarcely dared think of Gaynor and Klosterheim for fear of conjuring them into being!

The sound of our horses, of our harness, of our very breathing, seemed amplified by the mist. The panther's outline was half-hidden by it, but remained just in view, a shadow. Whether we rode on rock or hard earth was impossible to tell now, for the pewter-colored fog engulfed the horses to their bellies, washing around them like quicksilver.

The ground beneath us became softer, a turf, and the sounds were more muffled. A silence was gradually dominating us. The tension was still considerable. I spoke briefly to Elric. My voice seemed to be snatched away, deadened.

"We've lost him, eh? He's escaped into the Fees. And that, I understand, is a disaster."

When he replied I was not sure if he spoke or if I read his mind. "It makes the task more difficult."

Everything was becoming less certain, less defined, no doubt a quality of the Grey Fees. It was supposed to be, after all, the unformed fundamental stuff of the multiverse. But no matter how obscured, the panther remained in sight. Our path remained constant. Gaynor remained a threat.

The panther stopped without warning. It lifted its handsome face, sniffing, listening, one paw raised. The tail lashed. The eyes narrowed. Something perturbed the great, black cat. It hesitated.

Elric dismounted, wading chest-high through the mist to where the panther stood. The mist thickened and I lost sight of him for a moment. When I next saw him he was talking to a human figure. I thought at first we had found Gaynor.

The figure turned and came back with him. Oona carried her bow and her quiver over her shoulder. She might have been taking a casual stroll. Her grin was challenging and told me to ask no questions.

I still did not know if she was a sorceress, an illusionist, or if she merely controlled the movements of the panther or the hare. I had no clear idea of the magic involved. I was now perfectly prepared to accept that it was indeed magic that I witnessed. These people manipulated the multiverse in ways which were normal for them but which were totally mystifying to me. Once I realized that my own familiar twentieth century seemed a world of bizarre, chaotic mechanical invention to others, as mysterious to them as theirs was to me, that it still represented a terrifying conundrum to demigods able to manipulate worlds with their own mental powers, I began to accept for its own sake everything I experienced. I did not attempt, as some lunatic mapmaker might, to impose the grid of my own limited experience and imagination upon all this complexity. I had no wish, indeed, to make any mark on it. I preferred to explore and watch and feel. The only way to understand it at all was to experience it.

The pearly mist continued to swirl around us as I joined Oona and Elric. The Grey Fees I had crossed before had been more populous. She frowned, puzzled. "This is not," she said almost disapprovingly, "my natural element."

"Which way have they gone?" I asked. "Do you still have their scent, Lady Oona?"

"Too much of it," she said. She dropped to one knee and made a sweep with her left hand, as if clearing a window. Her gesture revealed a bright, sunny scene. "See!"

A scene I immediately recognized.

I gasped and moved forward, reaching towards that gap in the mist. I felt I'd been given my childhood back. But she restrained me. "I know," she said. "It is Bek. But I do not think it is your salvation, Count Ulric."

"What do you mean?"

She turned to her right and cleared another space in the mist.

All was red and black turmoil. Beast-headed men and man-headed beasts in bloody conflict. Churned mud almost as far as the eye could see. On the horizon the ragged outline of a tall-towered city. Towards it, in triumph, rode the figure of Prince Gaynor von Minct—the one who would come to be called Gaynor the Damned.

Elric craned forward this time. He recognized the city. It was as familiar to him as Bek was to me. Familiar to me, too, now that our memories and minds had bonded. Imrryr, the Dreaming City, capital of Melniboné, the Isle of the Dragon Lords. Flames fluttered like flags from the topmost windows of her towers.

I looked back. Bek was still there. The green, gentle hills, the thick, welcoming woods, the old stones of the fortified manor farm. But now I saw that there was barbed wire around the walls. Machine-gun emplacements at the gates. Guard dogs prowling the grounds. SS uniforms everywhere. A big Mercedes staff car drove into view, speeding down the road to my old home. The driver was Klosterheim.

"How—?" I began.

"Exactly," said Oona. "Too much spoor, as I said. He took two paths and there he is in two different worlds. He has learned more than most of us can ever know about existing in the timeless infinity of the multiverse. He still fights on at least two fronts. Which could be his weakness . . ."

"It seems to be his strength," said Elric with his usual dry irony. "He is breaking every rule. It's the secret of his power. But if those rules no longer have meaning . . ."

"He has won already?"

"Not everywhere," said Oona. But it was clear she had no idea what to do next.

Elric took the initiative.

"He is in two places—and we can be in two places. We have two swords now and sword can call to sword. I must follow Gaynor to Melniboné and you must follow him to Bek."

"How can you see these places?" I asked her. "How do you select them?"

"Because I desire it?" She lowered her eyes. "We are not told," she said. "What if the Grey Fees are created by the will and imaginations of mortals and immortals? What they most wish for and most fear are therefore created here. Created over and over again. Through the extraordinary power of human memory and desire."

"Created and re-created throughout eternity," mused Elric. He laid his gauntleted hand on the pommel of his runeblade. "Always a little different. Sometimes dramatically so. Memory and desire. Altered memories. Changing desires. The multiverse proliferates, growing like the veins in a leaf, the branches in a tree."

"What we must not forget," said Oona, "is that Gaynor has in his hands the power to create almost any desired reality. The power of the Grail, which is rightfully yours to protect but never directly use."

In spite of our bizarre circumstances, I found myself laughing. "Rightfully mine? I would have thought such power was rightfully Christ's or God's. If God exists. Or is He the Balance, the great mediator of our creativity?"

"That's the cause of much theological discussion," said Oona, "especially amongst dreamthieves. After all, they live by stolen dreams. In the Grey Fees, they say, all dreams come true. And all nightmares."

I felt helpless, staring around me in that void, my eyes constantly returning to those two scenes. They only reminded me of our quandary. They, too, could be an illusion—perhaps created by Oona herself, using the arts she had learned from her mother? I had no reason to trust her, or to believe she acted from altruism, but no reason not to either.

I felt a frustrated fury building in me. I wanted to draw my sword and cut through the mist, cut my way through to Bek, to my home, to the more peaceful past.

But there was a swastika flag flying over Bek. I knew that scene was no lie.

Elric was smiling his old, wan smile. "Difficult," he said, "to follow a man who travels in two directions at once. Reluctant as we are to accept this, I do not believe we can continue this adventure together, my friends. You two must follow him one way—I'll seek to stop him the other."

"Surely we weaken our power by doing that?" We knew we fought against the Lords of the Higher Worlds as well as Gaynor and Klosterheim.

"We weaken our power significantly," agreed Elric, "perhaps impossibly. But we have little choice. I shall go back to Imrryr to fight Gaynor there. You must go to your own realm and do the same. He cannot have the Grail in two places at once. That is a certain impossibility. He will have it, therefore, where it will serve him best. Whoever finds it first must somehow warn the others."

"And where might such a place be?" I asked.

He shook his head. "Anywhere," he said.

Oona was less uncertain. "That is one of many things we do not know," she said. "There are two places he might go. Morn, whose stones he needs to harness the power of Chaos, or Bek."

Elric remounted his blind horse. The beast whinnied and snorted, stamping at the mist. He urged it forward, towards the scene of turmoil which opened to absorb him. He turned, drawing his great blade and saluted me. It was a farewell. It was a promise. He then rode into the battling beasts, his black sword blazing in his right hand as he urged the horse towards Imrryr.

With a touch of her staff Oona sent my horse racing back into the mist. The beast would have no trouble getting home. Taking my arm Oona led me forward until we stood smelling the summer grass of Bek, looking down at my ancient home and realizing, for the first time, that it had been turned into a fortress. Some kind of important SS operations center, I guessed.

We dropped to the ground. I prayed we had not been seen. SS people were everywhere. This was no ordinary establishment. It was thoroughly guarded, with machine-gun posts and heavy barbed wire. Two crude barbicans of wire surrounded the moat.

We crept down the hills away from Bek's towers. I was easily able to guide Oona through the dense undergrowth of our forest-land. I knew as many trails as the foxes or rabbits who inhabited these woods when Beks had cleared the land to build their first house. We had lived in harmony, for the most part, down all those centuries.

My home had become an obscenity, a shameful outrage. Once it had stood for everything Germans held to be of value—prudent social progress, tradition, culture, kindness, learning, love of the land—and now it stood for everything we had once loathed; intolerance, disrespect, intemperate power and harsh cruelty. I felt as if I and my entire family had been violated. I knew full well how Germany had already been violated. I knew the nature of that evil and I knew it had not been spawned from German soil alone, but from the soil of all those warring nations, the greed and fear of all those petty, self-serving politicians who had ignored the real desires of their voters, all those opposing political formulae, all those ordinary citizens who had failed to examine what their leaders told them, who had let themselves be led into war and ultimate damnation and who still followed leaders whose policies could only end in their destruction.

What was this will to death which seemed to have engulfed Europe? A universal guilt? Its utter failure to live up to its Christian ideals? A kind of madness in which sentiment was contrasted by action at every turn?

Night came at last. Nobody hunted us. Oona found some old newspapers in a ditch. Someone had slept on them. They were yellow, muddy. She read them carefully. And, when she had finished, she had a plan. "We must find Herr El," she said. "Prince Lobkowitz. If I am right, he's living quietly under an assumed name in Hensau. Time has passed here. We are several years further on than when you left Germany. Hensau is where he will be. Or was, the last time I was in 1940."

"What do you mean? You are a time traveler, too?"

"I once thought so, until I understood that time is a field, and the same event takes place over and over again within that field, all at the same time. How we select from that field gives us a sense of the multiverse's mortality. We are not really time-traveling but shifting from one reality to another.

"Time is relative. Time is subjective. Time alters its qualities.

It can be unstable. It can be too stable. Time varies from realm to realm. We can leave this realm and find ourselves in a similar one, only separated by centuries. By this same process people sometimes believe they have discovered time travel. We escaped from Hameln in 1935, I believe. Five years ago. It is now the summer of 1940 and your country is at war. She appears to have conquered most of Europe."

The old newspapers gave no idea of what events had led to the current situation, but "brave little Germany" was now fighting alone against a dozen aggressive nations bent on taking back what little they had not already looted. According to the Nazi press, Germany for her part was merely demanding the land she needed for her peoples to expand—a region she was calling Greater Germany. A bastion against the Communist Goliath. Some European nations were already described as "provinces" of Germany while others were included in the German "family." France had reached a compromise, while Italy under Mussolini was an ally. Poland, Denmark, Belgium, Holland. All defeated. I was horrified. Hitler had come to power promising the German people peace. We had yearned for it. Honest, tolerant people had voted for anyone who would restore civil order and avert the threat of war. Adolf Hitler had now taken us into a worse war than any previous one. I wondered if his admirers were cheering him quite so enthusiastically now. For all our self-destructive Prussian rhetoric, we were fundamentally a peaceful people. What mad dream had Hitler invented to induce my fellow Germans to march again?

At last I slept. Immediately my head was filled with dreams. With violent battle and bizarre apparitions. I was experiencing everything my doppelgänger was experiencing. Only while awake could I keep him out of my mind, and even then it was difficult. I had no idea what he did, save that he had returned to Imrryr and from there gone underground. A scent of reptiles . . .

Awake again, I continued to read all I could. Most of what I read produced fresh questions. I could not believe how easily Hitler had come to power and why more people were not resisting, though the blanket of lies issued by the newspapers stopped many decent people from having a clear idea of how they could challenge the Nazi stranglehold. Otherwise, I had to piece together the picture for myself. It left many questions.

I learned most of the answers when we eventually found our way to Lobkowitz's apartment in Hensau, traveling at night for almost a week, scarcely daring the woodland trails, let alone the main roads. I was glad to sleep during daylight hours. It made my dreams a little easier. The newspapers, once read, were used to wrap around Ravenbrand. Our weapons seemed scarcely adequate to challenge the armaments of the Third Reich.

Everywhere we saw signs of a nation at war. Long trains carrying munitions, guns, soldiers. Convoys of trucks. Droning squadrons of bombers. Screaming fighters. Large movements of marching men. Sometimes we saw more sinister things. Cattle trucks full of wailing human beings. We had no idea at that time the scale of the murders Hitler practiced on his own people and the conquered citizens of Europe.

We traveled extremely cautiously, anxious not to draw the attention of even the most minor authority, but Oona risked stealing a dress from a clothesline. "The Gypsies will be blamed, I suppose."

Hensau, having no railway station and no main road, was relatively quiet. The usual Nazi flags flew everywhere and the SS had a barracks nearby, but the town was mostly free of military people. We could see why Lobkowitz had chosen it.

When we eventually stood before him, Oona in her rather flimsy stolen dress, we must have looked a wretched sight. We were half-starved. I was in rags. We bore incongruous weapons. I had not changed clothes for days and was desperately tired.

Lobkowitz laughed as he offered us drinks and told us to seat ourselves in his comfortable easy chairs. "I can get you out of Germany," he said. "Probably to Sweden. But that's about the limit of the help I can give you at present."

It emerged that he was running a kind of "underground railway" for those who had aroused Nazi displeasure. Most went to

Sweden, while others went through Spain. He regretted, he said, that he had no magical powers. No way of opening the moonbeam roads to those who sought freedom. "The best I can promise them is America or Britain," he said. "Even the British Empire can't stand against the Luftwaffe much longer. I have soldier friends. Another few months and Britain will seek an armistice. I suspect she will fall. And with the capitulation of the Empire, Germans need not fear American involvement. It's the triumph of evil, my dears."

He apologized for making such melodramatic statements. "But these are melodramatic times.

"The irony," he continued, "is that what you seek is already at Bek."

"But Bek is too heavily guarded for us to attack her," said Oona.

"What is it that we seek?" I asked wearily. "A staff? A cup? Isn't there another one that will do?"

"These are unique objects," Prince Lobkowitz said. "They take different forms. They have some sort of will, though it is not conscious in the same way as ours. You call one object the Holy Grail. Your family was entrusted to guard it. Wolfram von Eschenbach speaks of such a trust. Your father, half-mad, had not easily accepted this story. When he lost the Grail, he felt obliged to get it back and in so doing he killed himself."

"Killed himself? Then Gaynor's accusations were true! I had no idea—"

"Clearly the family wished to avoid scandal," Prince Lobkowitz continued. "They said he died in the subsequent fire, but the truth is, Count von Bek, your father was wracked by guilt—every kind of guilt—for your mother's death, his own failings, his inability to shoulder the family responsibilities. Indeed, as you know, he found it difficult to communicate with his own children. But he was neither a coward nor one to escape the inevitable. He did his best and he died in the attempt."

"Why should he place such importance on the Grail?" I asked.

"Such objects have great power in Teutonic mythology, too,

which is why Hitler and his disciples are so greedy to possess them. They believe that with the Grail and Charlemagne's sword in their hands, they will have the supernatural means, as well as the military means, of defeating Britain. Britain is all that stands in the way of the triumph of the German Empire. The cup is more important than the sword, in this case. The sword is an arm. It has no independent life. There should, in truth, be two swords on either side of the cup for the magic to work at its fullest. Or so I'm told. What Gaynor thinks he will achieve, I do not entirely know, but Hitler and his friends are convinced that something monumental will happen. I've heard a rumor about a ritual called Blood-in-the-Bowl. Sounds like a fairy story, eh? Virgins and magic swords."

"We must try to get the Grail back," I said. "That is what we are here to do."

Lobkowitz spoke softly, almost by way of confirmation. "Your father feared Bek would perish once the Grail left your family's safekeeping. He feared the entire family would perish. You, of course, are his last remaining son."

This was not something I needed to be reminded of. The waste of my brothers' lives in the Great War still made me despair. "Did my father start the fire which killed him?"

"No. The fire was a result of the demon who volunteered his assistance in fulfilling your family trust. A reasonable thought, I suppose, in the circumstances. But your father was at best an amateur sorcerer. The creature was not properly contained with the pentagram. Rather than defend the Grail, it stole it!"

"The demon was Arioch?"

"The 'demon' was our friend Klosterheim, then in the service of Miggea of Law. She was drooling crazy and feeling her power wane. Klosterheim served Satan until Satan proved insufficiently committed to the cause of evil and sought a reconciliation with God through the medium of your Bek ancestors. Through your namesake, as a matter of fact. Your ancestor was charged by Satan himself to find the Grail and keep it, until such time as God and Satan shall be reconciled."

"Fanciful old stories," I said. "They do not even have the authenticity of myth!"

"Stories our immediate ancestors chose to forget," said the Austrian quietly. "But you have more than one dark legend attached to your family name—even into recent times with the Mirenburg legend of Crimson Eyes."

"Another peasant fireside tale," I said. "The invention of the undereducated. You know that Uncle Bertie is now doing a perfectly respectable job in Washington."

"Actually, he's in Australia now. But I take your point. You must admit, my dear Count Ulric, that your family's history was never as uneventful as they pretended. More than one of your kinsmen or ancestors has reason to agree."

I shrugged. "If you will, Prince Lobkowitz. But that history has little to do with our current problems. We must find the Grail and the Sword but need your suggestions as to how we might get them back."

"Where else?" he said. "I have told you. Where the Grail has been for so many centuries. At Bek. That is why the place is so heavily fortified and guarded, why Klosterheim keeps permanent guard over the Grail chamber, as he calls it. You know it as your old armory."

That place had always possessed an atmosphere. I cursed myself. "We saw Klosterheim go to Bek. Are we too late? Has he removed the Grail?"

"I doubt he would wish to do that. I have it on the best authority that Hitler himself, together with Hess, Göring, Goebbels, Himmler and company, are all making plans to meet at Bek. They can hardly believe their luck, I'd guess. But they wish to ensure it! France has fallen and only Britain, already half-defeated, stands in their way. German planes have attacked British shipping, lured fighters into combat and weakened an already weak RAF. Before they invade by sea and land, they intend to destroy all main cities, especially London. They are preparing a vast aerial armada at this very moment. For all I know it is on its way. There is very little time. This meeting at Bek involves some ritual they believe will strengthen their hand even more and ensure that their invasion of Britain is completely successful."

I was disbelieving. "They are insane."

He nodded his head. "Oh, indeed. And something within them must understand that. But they have had total success so far. Perhaps they believe these spells are the reason for it. Clearly whatever supernatural aid they have called upon is not disappointing them. Yet it is unstable magic—in unstable hands. And it could result in the death of everything. Like Gaynor and the rest of their kind, their ignorance and disdain for reality will eventually destroy them. They relish the notion of Götterdämmerung. These people seek oblivion by any means. They are the worst kind of self-deceiving cowards and everything they build is a ramshackle sham. They have the taste of the worst Hollywood producers and the egos of the worst Hollywood actors. We have come to an ironic moment in history, I think, when actors and entertainers determine the fate of the real world. You can see how quickly the gap between action and affect widens . . . Of course they are expert illusionists, like Mussolini for instance, but illusion is all they offer—that and a vast amount of unearned power. The power to fake reality, the power to deceive the world and destroy it under the weight of so much falsification. The less the world responds to their lies and fancies, the more rigorously do they enforce them."

I began to realize that Prince Lobkowitz, for all his practicality, was a discursive conversationalist. At length I interrupted him. "What must I do when I have the Grail?"

"Very little," he said. "It is yours to defend, after all. And circumstances will change. Perhaps you'll take it back to its home in what the East Franconians called the Grail Fields. You know them by their corrupted name of the Grey Fees. Oh, yes, we've heard of them in Germany! There's a reference to them in Wolfram von Eschenbach, who cites Kyot de Provenzal. But your chances of getting to those *Graalfelden* again are also very slim."

I had the advantage, he said, of knowing Bek. The old armory, where the Grail was held, where I had received my first lessons from von Asch.

"Guarded presumably by these SS men," I said. "So there isn't much chance of my strolling in calling 'I'm home,' saying I've just dropped in to pop up to the armory, then tuck the Holy Grail under my jacket and walk out whistling."

I was surprised by my host's response.

"Well," he said with evident embarrassment, "I did have something like that in mind, yes."

# CHAPTER TWENTY

# Traditional Values

hich was how I came to be wearing the full uniform of a *Standartenführer*, a colonel in the SS, including near-regulation smoked glasses, sitting in the back of an open Mercedes staff car driven by a chauffeuse in the natty uniform of the NSDAP Women's Auxiliary (First Class) who, with her bow and arrows in the trunk, took the car out of its hidden garage into the dawn streets of Hensau and into some of the loveliest scenery in the whole of Germany—rolling, wooded hills and distant mountains, the pale gold of the sky, the sun a flash of scarlet on the horizon. I was filled with longing for those lost times, the years of my childhood when I had ridden alone across such scenery. The love of my land ran deep in my blood.

Somehow we had gone from that pre-1914 idyll to the present horror in a few short bloody years. And now here I was riding in a car far too large for the winding roads and wearing the uniform which stood for everything I had learned to loathe. Ravenbrand was now carried in a modified guncase and lay at my feet on the car's floor. I could not help reflecting on this irony. I found myself in a future which few could have predicted in 1917. Now, in 1940, I remembered all the warnings that had been given since 1920.

Years of antiwar films, songs, novels and plays—years of analysis and oracular pronouncements. Too many, perhaps? Had the predictions actually created the situation they hoped most to avert?

Was anarchy so terrible, compared to the deadly discipline of fascism? As much democracy and social justice had emerged from chaos as from tyranny. Who had been able to predict the total madness that would come upon our world in the name of "order"?

For a while we followed the main auto route to Hamburg. We saw how busy the roads, raillines and waterways had become. We traveled for a short while on an excellent new *Autobahn* with several lanes of traffic moving in both directions, but Oona soon found the back roads to Bek again. We were only fifty kilometers from my home when we turned a sharp bend in a wooded lane and Oona stamped quickly on the brake to stop us crashing into another car, quite as ostentatious as our own, swathed in Nazi flags and insignia. A thoroughly vulgar vehicle, I thought. I guessed it to belong to some swaggering local dignitary.

We began to move again but then a high-ranking officer in a brown SA uniform emerged from the other side of the car and flagged us down.

We had no option. We slowed to a stop this time. We exchanged the ritual salute, borrowed, I believe, from the film *Quo Vadis?*, supposedly how Romans greeted a friend. Once again, Hollywood had added a vulgar gloss to politics.

Noting my uniform and its rank, the SA man was subservient, apologetic. "Forgive me, *Herr Standartenführer*, this is, I regret, an emergency."

From out of the closed car now emerged an awkward, rather gangling figure in a typical comic-opera Nazi uniform favored by the higher ranks. To his credit, he seemed uncomfortable in it, pushing unfamiliar frogging about as he walked over to us, offering a jerky salute, which we returned. He was genuinely grateful. "Oh, God be thanked! You see, Captain Kirch! My instincts never let me down. You suggested no suitable car could come along this road and get us to Bek on time—and voilà! This angel suddenly materializes." His eyebrows appeared to be alive. His eyes, too, were very busy and he had an intense, crooked smile on his puffy, square face. If it had not been for his uniform, I might have taken him for a typical customer of the Bar Jenny in Berlin. He beamed at me. Raving mad but relatively benign.

"I am Deputy Führer Hess," he told me. "You will be well-remembered for this, Colonel."

I recalled that Rudolf Hess was one of Hitler's oldest henchmen. In accordance with the papers I carried, I let him know that I was Colonel Ulric von Minct and that I was at his service. It would be a privilege to offer him my car.

"An angel, an angel," he repeated as he climbed into the car and sat beside me. "It is the von Mincts, Colonel, who will save Germany." He hardly noticed the case containing the sword. He was too concerned with shouting urgent orders to his driver. "The flasks! The flasks! It would be a disaster if I did not have them!"

The SA man reached into the trunk of the car and carefully took out a large wicker basket which he transferred to our car. Hess was greatly relieved. "I am a vegan," he explained. "I have to travel everywhere with my own food. Alf—I mean our Führer—" He glanced up at me, like a small boy caught in some forbidden act. Clearly he had been admonished before for making reference to the Nazi leader by his old nickname. "The Führer is a vegetarian—but not strict enough, I fear, for me. He runs a very lax kitchen, from my point of view. So I have taken to carrying my own food when I travel."

The deputy Führer saluted his driver. "Wait with the car," he instructed. "We'll send help from the first town we reach. Or from Bek, if we find nothing else." He sat back in the car beside me, a signal for Oona to put the Mercedes into gear and continue the journey. He was a mass of tics and peculiar movements of his hands. "Von Minct, you say? You must be related to our great Paul von Minct, who has achieved so much for the Reich."

"His cousin," I said. I found it very hard to be afraid of this man.

Hess insisted on shaking my hand.

"A great honor, sir," I said.

"Oh"—he removed his elaborate cap—"I'm one of the old fighters, you know. Still one of the lads." He was reassuring me. Sentimentally he continued, "I was with Hitler in Munich. In Stadelheim and everywhere—he and I are brothers. I am the only one he truly trusts and confides in. It was always so. I am his spiritual adviser, in many ways. If it were not for me, Colonel von Minct, I doubt if any of you would have heard of the Grail story—or understand what it could do for us!"

Confidingly he leaned towards me. "Hitler, they say, knows the heart of Germany. But I know her soul. That is what I have studied."

As the huge Mercedes bowled along familiar country roads, I continued to speak with the man whom many believed the most powerful man in Germany after the great dictator himself. If Hitler were killed today, Hess would assume the leadership.

For the most part his conversation was as banal as that of most Nazis, but laced through with a mélange of supernatural beliefs and dietary ideas which marked him for a common lunatic. Because he understood me to have an affinity for the Grail and all the mysticism surrounding it, he was more forthcoming—about how he had read the Bek legends, how he had read books saying the Grail was the lost Holy Relic of the Teutonic Order. How the Bek sword was the lost sword of Roland, Champion of the Holy Roman Emperor, Charlemagne the Frank. The Franks and the Goths founded modern Europe, he said. The Norsemen were stern lawmakers, with no respect for the Old World's superstitions. Wherever their influence was felt, people became robust, masculine, vital, productive. Latin Christianity weakened them.

The destiny of the German nation, he told me, was to lift its brothers back to glory—to rid the world of all that wretchedly bad stock and replace it with a race of superbeings—superhealthy, superintelligent, superstrong, supereducated—the kind of breed which would populate the world with the best mankind could be, rather than the worst.

The more I listened to Hess, the more skeptical I became, the more convinced that he was a low-level lunatic with dull dreams and a psychological inability to consider any "truth" but that which he invented for himself.

However, as the man was so fundamentally amiable and clearly trusted me so completely, I had an opportunity to see what he knew of my father. Had he ever met old Count von Bek? I asked. The one who went mad and was burned alive. Killed himself, didn't he?

"Killed himself? Perhaps." Hess shuddered. "A terrible crime, suicide. Betrays us all. On a level with abortion, in my view. All life should be respected."

I had discovered quickly the trick of steering him gently back to the subject. "Count von Bek?"

"He lost the Grail, you see. He was entrusted with it. Father to child—son or daughter—down the centuries. 'Do you the Devil's work!' is their ancient motto. They were at the Crusades. The oldest blood in Germany—but tainted by decadence, madness, Latin marriages . . .

"Legend had it that the von Beks always protected the Grail, until such a time when Satan was reconciled with God. All stupid Christian nonsense, I know, and a corruption of our old, muscular Nordic myths. Those myths made us successful conquerors. It has always been our destiny to conquer. To bring order to the whole world. The myth still retains its power." His eyes were focused on me now, burning into me. "The power of myth is the power of life and death, as we know—for we have restored the power of the Nordic myth. And again we are successful conquerors. We shall challenge that other Nordic race, our natural allies, the British, until they turn with us against the evil East and defeat the tyranny of communism. Together, we shall bring civilization to the whole planet!"

A typical sample of his droning, pseudophilosophical nonsense. It explained why the Nazi chiefs in their lunacy placed such value on the Grail and the Sword. These things represented a *mystical* authority. Only with them in harness with their political power were they confident they had secured their victories. Triumph over the admired British Empire would be a kind of epiphany. An armistice achieved, together they would restore the purity of blood and myth to its proper place in the order of things.

"We only have to complete the destruction of their air force and they will call for a truce."

"I am impressed by your logic, sir."

"Logic has nothing to do with it, Colonel. Logic and the so-called Enlightenment are Judeo-Christian inventions, deeply suspect by all right-thinking Aryans. Those Nazis who cling to their pro-Christian beliefs are working for the Judaic-Bolshevik cultural conspiracy. The British understand this as well as we do. The best kind of Americans are also on our side . . ."

I think that in all my adventures I have only shown real courage and self-discipline once: when I restrained myself from throwing the glamorous deputy Führer out of my car.

"How," I asked, "did old von Bek lose possession of the Grail?"

"As you no doubt know, he was an amateur scientist. One of those prehistoric gentleman scholars. He knew of the family's trust, to guard the Grail until we, its true inheritors, should come to claim it. But he was curious. He wanted to examine the Grail's properties. Which meant that first he had to master the laws of magic. Of necromancy. His studies drove him mad, but he continued with his examination of the Grail, and in doing so, he summoned a certain renegade Captain of Hell . . ."

"Klosterheim?"

"Just so. Who in turn brought the help of another renegade. One of the company of Law. The immortal, extremely unstable Miggea. Duchess of the Higher Worlds." Hess grinned. He was in the know. He swelled, full of his own secrets. He twitched with supernatural intelligence. "Alf—our Führer—told me to find Gaynor, who was already an adept, and offer to blend our strength with his. Gaynor agreed and, rather later than he'd promised, brought the object of power back to Bek. With it we shall control history—the war against Britain is already won."

In spite of my direct experience of realities he had only heard of, I still found him hard to follow, exhausting in the way mad people often are. Therefore I was deeply relieved when the car began its final drive towards the gates of Bek. Because the deputy Führer was with us, our papers were never inspected. All I had to hope was that Gaynor did not recognize me. My hair was hidden under my military cap and I wore the dark glasses, which were an unofficial part of the uniform, to disguise my albinism.

Chatting easily with Hess I lifted the encased sword from the car. "For the ceremony," I told him. Hess was by far my best cover and I was determined to stick with him as long as I could. As I moved through my old home, however, it was difficult to restrain myself from exclaiming at what had been done to it.

I would rather Gaynor had destroyed it as he threatened. The house had been thoroughly violated. The place had been redecorated like a Fairbanks film set—all Nazi pomp and circumstance: gold-braided flags, Teutonic tapestries, Nordic plaques and heavy mirrors, freshly made stained glass in the old Gothic windows, one of which showed an idealized portrait of Hitler as a noble knight-errant and Göring as some sort of male Valkyrie. A *Rheinejungen* perhaps? Swastikas everywhere. It was as if Walt Disney, who so admired fascist discipline and had his own ideas for the ideal state, had been hired as Bek's interior designer. The Hitler gang's passion for the garish trappings of the operetta stage was demonstrated throughout. In so many ways Hitler was a typical Austrian.

I, of course, said none of this to Hess, who seemed rather impressed by the house, enjoying his reflected glory as every SS officer stopped to click his heels and give him the Nazi salute. I luckily stood in Hess's reflected glory and Oona in mine, and so we passed as if charmed through our enemy's defenses while the deputy Führer spoke warmly of King Arthur, Parsifal, Charlemagne and all the other Teutonic heroes of legend who had borne magic swords.

By the time we reached the armory, deep within the castle's oldest keep, I was beginning to wish Hess would return to his earlier topic of Nordic veganism. All in the repressed fear of my own imminent discovery and destruction!

The deputy Führer asked me to hold his canisters of food while he took a large key from his jacket pocket. "The Führer gave me the honor of holding his key," he said. "It is a privilege to be the first to enter and to greet him when he arrives!"

He inserted the key in the lock and turned it with some difficulty. I thought it wise of Hitler to have his friend go ahead of him like that. After all, the Führer could never be sure it was not an elaborate plot to end his life.

Thus, as members of Rudolf Hess's entourage, we passed into the high-ceilinged armory which had been spared redecoration and was lit by a high, circular window. A sunbeam pierced the dust and fell directly upon a kind of altar, square granite carved with the Celtic sun cross, which had recently been placed there.

Involuntarily, I moved towards this new object. How on earth had they carried such a weight of granite through our narrow corridors? I reached out to touch it. But Hess held me back. Clearly he thought I was eager for other reasons. "Not yet," he said.

As his eyes became used to the dim light, he looked around him in sudden puzzlement. "What's this—what are you men doing here before I ever crossed the threshold? Do you not realize who I am and why I should be here first?"

The shadowy group seemed unimpressed.

"This is blasphemy," said Hess. "Infamy. This is no place for ordinary soldiers. The magic is subtle. It requires subtle minds. Subtle hands."

Klosterheim, automatic in hand, came grinning into the sunlight. "I assure you, sir, we are nothing if not subtle. I will explain as soon as possible. But now, if you don't mind, Deputy Führer, I will continue to save your life—"

"Save my—?"

Klosterheim pointed his pistol at me. "This time my bullets *will* work," he said. "Good afternoon, Count Ulric. I had an idea you would be joining us here. You see! You're fulfilling your destiny whether you wish to or not."

Hess remained outraged. "You are making many mistakes, Captain. The Führer himself is involved with this project and will be arriving shortly. What will he think of a subordinate pointing a gun at his deputy and one of his top officers?"

"He will know what Prince Gaynor will tell him," said Klosterheim. He was careless of Hess's words. He hardly heard them. "Believe me, Deputy Führer Hess, we are acting entirely in the interests of the Third Reich. Ever since he was denounced as a traitor and his property confiscated, we have been expecting this madman to make an attempt on the Führer's life—"

"This is nonsense!" I began. "You know it is a lie!"

"But is the rest a lie, Count?" His voice grew softer, more intimate. "Do you think we expected you to give up pursuit? Wasn't it obvious that you would make some attempt to reach this place? All we had to do was wait for you to bring us the Black Sword. Which I note you have kindly done."

Hess was inclined to trust to rank. This was my only hope of buying time. As he looked to me for confirmation I shouted in my best Nazi-bark: "Captain Klosterheim, you are overstepping the mark. While we applaud your vigilance in protecting the Führer, we can assure you there is nothing in this room which offers him any danger."

"On the contrary," agreed Hess uncertainly. His eyes, never steady at the best of times, flickered from me to Klosterheim. He was impressed by Klosterheim's handpicked storm troopers. "But perhaps, given the circumstances, we should all step outside this room and settle any confusion?"

"Very well," said Klosterheim. "If you will lead the way, Count von Bek . . ." And he gestured with his Walther.

"Von Bek?" Hess was startled. He looked hard at me and began to think.

I had no more time. I pulled the protective fabric away from my sword. Ravenbrand was all that could save me now.

Klosterheim's gun cracked. Two distinct shots.

He had the sense to know when to stop me.

The sword was only half out of the case as I felt sharp pains in my left side and began to stumble backwards under the impact of the bullets. I struggled to stay on my feet. I wanted to vomit but could not. I fell heavily against the mysterious granite altar and slipped to the flagstones. I tried to get back to my feet. My dark glasses fell off. My cap was kicked away from my head revealing my white hair. I looked up. Klosterheim was standing with his legs straddled over my body, the smoking PPK .38 still in his right hand. I do not think I have ever seen such an expression of gloating satisfaction on a human face.

"God in Heaven!" I could hear Hess gasping. He peered down at me, his eyes widening. "Impossible! It is the Bek monster! The bloodless creature they were said to keep in their tower. Is it dead?"

"He's not dead. Not yet, Your Excellency." Klosterheim stepped back. "We'll save him for later. We have an experiment to perform. A demonstration the Führer has requested."

"The Führer," began Hess, "surely would have told me if . . ."

The pointed toe of a boot kicked me efficiently in the side of my head and I lost consciousness.

Dimly, as was constant with me now, I had been sensing what was happening to my alter ego. Suddenly my nostrils were filled with a pungent, reptilian stink and looking up I stared into the familiar eyes of a huge dragon. All the wisdom of the world flickered in those eyes.

I spoke to the dragon in a low, affectionate voice that had no real words to it, that was more music than language, and the dragon responded in the same tones. A thrumming purr came out of its monstrous throat and from its nostrils a few wisps of steam. I knew the creature's name and it remembered me. I had been a child and had changed a great deal. But the dragon remembered me, even though my body was covered in cuts and I was helplessly bound. I smiled. I began to speak a name. Then the pain in my side swept through me like a swift tide and I gasped, going down again into blackness that engulfed me like a blessing.

Had Prince Lobkowitz set this trap for me? Was he now in league with Klosterheim, Gaynor and the Nazi hyena pack?

And did Elric's fate, in his world, mirror my own? Was he, too, dying in the ruins of his old home?

I was aware of pain, rough hands, but could not bring myself out of sleep. I woke up to the smell of oily smoke. I opened my eyes, thinking at first that the armory was on fire. But the old flambeaux brackets had been utilized and a flaming brand guttered in every holder, casting huge shifting shadows.

I felt the tight cloth of a gag in my mouth, my hands were bound in front of me and my feet were free. I was relieved that most of my Nazi uniform had been stripped off me. I wore only a shirt and trousers. My feet were bare. I had been prepared for some kind of special treatment. I moved and agony flooded through me. I felt the wadding of a crude dressing on my wounds. My captors were not famous for administering pain relief to their victims.

At that moment they were not interested in me and I was able to watch what was happening. I saw Hitler, a rather short man in a heavy leather military coat, standing next to the plump, frowning Göring. Nearby, SS Commander Himmler, with the prissy severity of a depraved tax inspector, was talking to Klosterheim. The two men had a similar quality about them I couldn't immediately identify. Members of Hitler's crack SS guard stood at key points in the hall, their machine guns at the ready. They looked like robots from *Metropolis*.

Gaynor was nowhere to be seen. Hess was talking intensely to a rather bored-looking SS general whose attention was everywhere but on him. Oona was not here. It could mean that she had become alerted to the danger in time. Were her weapons still in the car? Could she at least get the Grail out of Hitler's clutches?

I knew suddenly that I was dying. I had no hope of recovering unless Oona could save me. Even unbound I could not reach my sword, which now lay on the altar like some kind of trophy. While the Nazis were careful not to touch it, they peered at it as if it were a dangerous dormant snake, which might rear up to strike at any moment.

I guessed the sword to be my only hope of life and that a slim one. I was not Elric of Melniboné, after all, but a mere human being caught up in natural and supernatural events far beyond his understanding. And about to die.

From the dampness of the heavy dressing against my side I

could tell that I was losing a great deal of blood. I could not tell if any vital organs were damaged, but it scarcely mattered. The Nazis were not about to send for a doctor. I could not imagine the nature of the "experiment" Klosterheim had in mind for me.

The group had the air of men waiting for something. Hitler, who seemed almost as twitchy as Hess, gave the impression of an impatient street vendor, forever on the lookout for trouble. He spoke in that affected German one associates with the Austrian lower middle class and even though he was the most powerful man in the world at that moment, there was a sense of weakness about him. I wondered if this were the banality of evil which my friend Father Cornelius, the Jesuit priest, used to talk about before he went to Africa.

I could hear very little of what was said and most of it sounded like nonsense. Hitler was laughing and slapping his leg with his gloves. The only thing I heard him say clearly was "The British will soon be begging for mercy. And we shall be generous, gentlemen. We will let them keep their institutions. They are ideal for our purposes. But first we must destroy London, eh?"

I was surprised that this was the object of their meeting. I had thought it to do with the "objects of power" Gaynor had brought with him from the Grey Fees.

The door opened and Gaynor stood there. He was dressed all in black, with a great black cloak over his armored body. He had the look of a knight from one of those interminable historical films the Nazis loved to watch. A copper swastika was emblazoned on his breastplate and another on his helmet. He looked like a demonic Siegfried. His hands were clasped around the hilt of the great ivory runesword. He stepped aside with a dramatic gesture as two of his men bundled in a struggling woman.

My heart sank. Our last hope gone. They had Oona.

She was no longer dressed in the Nazi uniform but wore some kind of heavy, oat-colored dress that engulfed her from head to toe. It, too, had a vaguely medieval appearance. Its collar and cuffs were decorated with red and black swastikas. Her wonderful white hair was contained by a filet of silver and her eyes blazed like dark garnets from the pale beauty of her face. She was helpless, bound hand and foot. Her face was expressionless, her mouth set. When she saw me a look of horror came into her furious eyes. Her mouth opened in a silent scream. Then closed more firmly than ever. Only her eyes moved.

I wanted to comfort her, but there was no comfort.

It was clear we were meant to die.

After greeting the others, Gaynor announced with some triumph: "Thus the game I planned reaches its conclusion. Both of these treacherous creatures have been brought to book. Both are guilty of numerous crimes against the Reich. Their fate will be a noble one, however. Nobler than they deserve. The Grail and the Black Sword are now back in our keeping. And we have the sacrifice we need to begin the final sorcery." With a flicker of mockery in his smile, he glanced at Oona. His disgusting appetite was about to be satisfied. "And strike our bargain with the Higher Worlds."

He intended to kill us both—and in pursuit of the Nazis' obscene, half-crazed supernatural nonsense.

The firelight reflected in the eager faces of Hitler and his comrades as they admired the struggling girl. Hitler turned to Göring and made some leering remark to which his lackey responded with a fat chuckle. Only Hess seemed ill at ease. I had the feeling he preferred fanciful daydreams to the actuality of what was evidently to be a bloody ritual.

Goebbels and Himmler, on either side of their Führer, both had tight, chilling smiles on their faces. Himmler's little round eyeglasses positively glinted with hellish glee.

With the sword in one hand, Gaynor reached down and grasped Oona by her moon-colored hair. He dragged her towards the altar. "The chemical and the spiritual marriage of opposites," he announced, like a showman taking the stage. "My Führer, gentlemen, I promised you I would return with the Grail and the Swords. Here is the white sword of Charlemagne—and there, unwittingly returned to its proper place by this wretched half-corpse"—he indicated me—"is the black sword of Hildebrand,

Theodoric's henchman. The sword called Son Slayer, with which he killed Hadubrand, his eldest child. The sword of good"—he lifted the ivory sword and pointed towards the altar—"and the sword of evil. Brought together, they will baptize the Grail with blood. Good and evil will mingle and become one. The blood will bring the Grail to life again and bestow its power upon us. Death will be banished. Our great bargain with Lord Arioch will be struck. We shall be immortal amongst immortals. All this King Clovis the Goth predicted upon his deathbed as he gave the Grail into the keeping of his steward, Dietrich von Bern, who in turn entrusted it to his brother-in-law Ermanerik, my ancestor. When the Grail is washed at last with innocent blood, virgin blood, the Nordic peoples will be united in a common bond and come together as one folk, to take their rightful place as rulers of the world."

Insane nonsense, a farrago of myths and folktales typical of the Nazi rationalizers and with scarcely any historical basis. But Hitler and his gang were entranced by the story. Their existence, after all, depended on myths and folktales. Their political platform might have been written by the Brothers Grimm. It was quite possible Gaynor had made up much of this ritual to impress them, for he had told me that Hitler was merely his means to a greater goal. If so, his strategy was proving effective. He was using their power to summon Arioch. Even the most gullible Nazis would not be able to absorb the actuality. Little comfort to me. Whether they were delusory or not, these ideas would not help me accept my coming fate—or avert Oona's bloody death!

Göring, grossly fat, uttered a nervous rumble of laughter. "We shall not rule the world, *Colonel* von Minct, until we defeat the Royal Air Force. We have the numbers. We have the ordnance. What we need now is the luck. A little magic would help."

"The luck has held. Because it is not mere luck, but the workings of destiny." This was Hitler muttering. "But there is no harm in ensuring our victory."

"It's always a help," said Göring dryly, "to have a god or two on your side. By this time next week, I assure you, Colonel, we'll be dining with the king at Buckingham Palace, with or without your supernatural aid."

Hitler seemed buoyed by his *Reichsmarschall's* confidence. "We shall be the first modern government to reinstitute the scientific use of the ancient laws of nature," he said. "What some insist on denigrating as 'magic.' It is our destiny to restore these marginalized disciplines and skills to the mainstream of German life."

"Exactly, my Führer!" Hess beamed, as if at an outstanding student. "The old science. The true science. The pre-Christian Teutonic science, untainted by any hint of southern decadence. A science which depends upon our beliefs and which can be manipulated by the power of the human will alone!"

All this I heard in the distance as my life began to ebb away from me.

"Nothing will convince me, Colonel von Minct," said Hitler with sudden coldness, as if taking charge of the situation, "until you demonstrate the power of the Grail. I need to know that you really have the Grail. If it is the actual Grail it will possess the power of which all legends speak."

"Of course, my Führer. The virgin blood shall bring the cup to life. Von Bek is dying even now. In a short while he will be thoroughly dead. With the Grail, I will restore him to life. So that you may kill him again at your pleasure."

Hitler waved this last away. A distasteful necessity. "We must know if it has the power to restore the dead to life. When this man is dead, we shall expose him to the Grail's influence. If it is the real thing, he will return to life. Immortal, perhaps. If its power can then be channeled to help our air fleet defeat the British, so much the better. But I will only believe that if its most famous property is displayed. And you have yet to produce the Grail, Colonel."

Gaynor laid the white sword beside the black sword, end to end, upon the stone altar.

"And the cup?" asked Göring, borrowing authority from his master.

"The Grail takes many forms," Gaynor told him. "It is not always a cup. Sometimes it is a staff."

Reichsmarschall Göring, in pale Luftwaffe blue and many trimmings, brandished his own elaborate mace of office. His was encrusted with precious stones and looked as if it had been made, with his uniform, by a theatrical costumier. "Like this one?"

"Very similar, Your Excellency."

For a few moments I lost consciousness. Bit by bit my spirit was leaving my body. I made every effort I could to hang on to life, in the hope I might find a way to help Oona. I knew I had only minutes left. I tried to speak, to demand that Gaynor spare Oona, to say that this ritual of virginal sacrifice was savage, bestial—but I would be talking to savage, bestial men, who embraced the monstrous cause. Death called to me. She seemed my only possible escape from all this horror. I never realized until then how easily one can come to long for death.

"You have still to produce the Grail, Colonel von Minct." Göring spoke precisely, mockingly. Plainly he thought this whole thing a nonsense. Yet neither he nor any other member of the hierarchy dare express skepticism to Hitler, who clearly wanted to believe. Hitler needed the confirmation of his own destiny. He had already presented himself as the new Frederick the Great, the new Barbarossa, the new Charlemagne, but his entire career had been based on threats, lies and manipulation. He no longer had any idea of his own reality, his own effect. But should these ancient objects of Teutonic power respond to him, it would prove that he was indeed the true mystical and practical savior of Germany. Something he did not always believe himself. All his actions were now determined by this need for affirmation.

Suddenly, as if he realized I was looking at him, Hitler turned his head. His eyes met mine for an instant. Staring, hypnotic eyes. Hideously weak. I had seen them in more than one obsessed lunatic. He dropped his gaze as if he were ashamed. In that moment I understood him to be a creature thoroughly out of its depth, fascinated by its own luck, its own rise from obscurity, its successful dalliance with oblivion.

I knew he could destroy the world.

Through a haze of death I saw them throw Oona onto the altar. Gaynor raised a sword in either hand.

The swords began to descend. She struggled, trying to fling herself off the granite block.

I remember thinking, as I lost consciousness again: Where is the Cup?

My mental turmoil was not made better by the knowledge that this scene, or a variant of it, was being played out on every plane of existence. A billion versions of myself, a billion versions of Oona, all dying horribly in violence at the same moment.

Dying so that a madman could destroy the multiverse.

# CHAPTER TWENTY-ONE

# Hidden Virtues

had not expected to return to consciousness. Dimly I was aware of other forces struggling within me, of some commotion at the altar. For a moment I had the delusion I stood in the doorway of the armory, the Black Sword in my hand. And I called Gaynor's name. A challenge.

"Gaynor! You would slay my daughter! So no doubt you understand how much you have angered me."

I forced my head up. Gradually I opened my eyes.

Ravenbrand was howling. She was giving off her weird black radiance. Red runes formed agitated geometries within her blade. She hovered over Oona and *refused* to carry out Gaynor's actions. The runeblade shook and writhed in his hand, trying to wrench itself free. Stormbringer lusted to kill, but Ravenbrand could not kill certain people. The idea of harming Oona was repulsive. Its semisentient constitution did not permit it to harm an innocent. In this it differed from Elric's Stormbringer, which more closely matched the attitudes of Melnibonéans.

Gaynor snarled. The light from the swords and torches painted the watching faces into Bosch grotesques. Those faces turned to look in astonishment at the man who stood in the ruined doorway—an identical black sword in his right hand, a sprawl of brown-shirted bodies behind him. The black blade ran with crimson. He wore torn armor and his own blood-soaked silks. He had the death heat in his wolf's eyes. He must have been through several battles single-handed, but Stormbringer was still in one bloody fist and his face betrayed the memory of a million deaths.

"Gaynor!" The voice was my own. "You run like a jackal and hide like a snake. Will you meet me here, in this holy place of power? Or will you scuttle as usual into the shadows?"

Slow footsteps, the weariness of centuries. My doppelgänger entered the armory. For all his exhaustion he radiated a power, a glamour, which the charismatic creatures of the Nazi elite could not begin to match. Here was a true demigod. Here was what they pretended to be. And he was all they claimed, because he alone had paid a price not one of them could even conceive of paying. Had faced such horror, stood his ground against such terror, that nothing could move him.

Almost nothing.

Only a threat to one whom, with all his complex and contradictory emotions, he had given his love. Love most Melnibonéans would never understand. With heavy, measured steps he made his way to the altar.

Gaynor attempted again to strike down with Ravenbrand at Oona's heart. The sword resisted him even more vigorously.

Gaynor screamed an oath, flung the screeching black sword at me, and seized the ivory blade in both hands. This time he would finish Oona.

The black blade did not reach its target. In fact it scarcely moved at all. It hovered in the air long enough for Oona to lift her bonds, cut through them, and scramble clear of Gaynor while making a grab at his belt. I was astonished at the blade's apparent sentience.

With a great deal of shouting and shuffling, Hitler and his people had already retreated behind their storm trooper guards. They trained a score of efficient modern machine guns at Elric as he made his way to the altar. He ignored all danger. He was oblivious to the Nazis, as one might be in a dream. There was a hard, savage grin on his handsome, alien features. Once certain that Oona was not in immediate danger, he turned his attention to Gaynor.

The ivory sword hummed and bucked as if it, too, would refuse to kill. I wondered if the swords were sentient or if something else checked them.

Gaynor displayed greater control over the so-called Charlemagne Sword. He stabbed again and again at the hobbled Oona, who had yet to cut her feet free. But the sword simply would not do what he wanted. Wild, mystical language began to pour from his twisted mouth as he summoned the aid of Chaos.

But no aid came.

He had not had time to fulfill his bargains.

Elric darted now, swift as a snake. His black blade firmly blocked the white.

"There is no pleasure in killing a coward," he said to Gaynor. "But I will do it as a duty if I must."

An arc of black and red. A crescent of silver. Elric's sword met the ivory blade. The two swords screamed in unison in every kind of anguish.

The Black Sword arced again. There was a dull, flat note as it met Gaynor's weapon. The ivory blade began to crack and flake like rotten wood, disintegrating in Gaynor's hand.

Gaynor cursed and discarded it. The thing had always been something of a forgery, with an unclear provenance. Jumping away from the altar, he sought to grab a weapon from the wall. But the weapons had been there years too long and had virtually rusted together. He screamed at the storm troopers to kill Elric, but the guards could not fire without hitting Gaynor or Klosterheim, who leveled his pistol at Elric. The demonic swordsman murmured a single, smiling word.

Ravenbrand plunged towards Satan's ex-servant. Klosterheim gasped. He understood all too clearly what his fate would be if she reached him. He shrieked in Latin. Few of us could understand him. Certainly not the sword, which barely missed him.

Klosterheim flung himself to the ground and Gaynor did the same. At once the machine guns began their mad cacophony, with bullets and spent shells bouncing everywhere in that huge, stone room.

Elric laughed his familiar wild laugh, dodging their fire as if charmed, then ducking behind the altar to be certain that his daughter had not been hit.

She smiled briefly to reassure him and then raced from her cover to where I lay against the wall. Gaynor's razor-sharp Nazi dagger was in her hand. Quickly she reached out, cutting my bonds.

Suddenly Ravenbrand settled herself in my fist, deflecting bullets as the guards turned their attention on me, still surrounding their precious leaders. Hitler and his gang backed hastily toward the ruined main door.

Power surged through me. I too was laughing. With fearless amusement I advanced on Klosterheim. Elric already engaged Gaynor. Oona had only Gaynor's dagger for a weapon, but she ducked behind the altar as the bullets ricocheted around us. They hit only one of the soldiers, causing a yelp of terror from the ranks of the Nazi elite.

Hitler had relied on his luck. But now the luck was with us.

They stumbled through the gap Elric had carved in the door. They tried to cover the ragged hole. They began to move heavy furniture into it. They could not know what we would do next. They gained time to make a plan.

I made to follow, but Elric held me back. He pointed.

Gaynor and Klosterheim remained at the far end of the hall.

"We still have the Grail," cried Gaynor. In his black armor, almost a parody of Elric's own, he looked like a massive, leathery bird prancing in rage as the firelight flared and faded and his shadows joined the dance. "And we still have aid coming from the Lords of the Higher Worlds. Be careful, my cousins. They'll not be happy if their ally on this plane is unable to bring them through."

Elric snorted. "You think I fear the disapproval of gods and demigods? I am Elric of Melniboné—and my race is the equal of the gods!"

But it was not the equal of Klosterheim's automatic which barked twice more and caught Elric entirely by surprise. "What's this?" Frowning, he fell backwards.

I leaped forward but Oona's dagger had already caught Klosterheim directly in his heart. He looked about to vomit, bending double and trying to pull the Nazi blade free.

Gaynor pushed his dying ally aside and made for the low oaken door which led to von Asch's abandoned quarters. Klosterheim did not move. He was evidently dead.

I was too weak to catch Gaynor. He was through the door and barring it after him as I reached it. I put my shoulder to it and felt a jolt of pain.

I looked down at my side, expecting to see more blood. Only a ragged scar remained. How much time had actually passed? Or was time disrupted as a result of Gaynor's selfish interference? Was the multiverse already beginning to disintegrate around us?

"Friends," I heard Elric gasp. "Up. We must go up . . ."

Oona tried to make a barrier in front of the ruined main door but the Nazis had done much of the work from their own side! We had no means of escape. By now Gaynor could be far ahead of us, taking the Grail back into the Grey Fees.

I continued pushing at the small door, but without success.

The miscellaneous furniture began to move in the main door. It looked like the Nazis had gathered their courage and were returning.

A crash came from the doorway. Hess stood there, waving his machine gunners forward. He was the only one of his kind with the guts to confront us. Now we had no chance at all of getting free.

I tried my shoulder against the other door, but I was still too weak. I called for Oona to help. She was supporting Elric. He was leaning on Gaynor's altar. Blood poured from his wounds and stained the dark granite.

Impatiently the Melnibonéan straightened himself and took hold of his sword, telling me to stand aside. "This is becoming my habitual method of opening doors," he said. Though full of bravado, his voice was feeble.

He gathered his strength and let the sword carry the blow as he brought it down upon the door, splitting the ancient oak in two. The pieces fell aside to admit us. We scrambled across it and up the stairs in Gaynor's wake. Behind us I heard Hess shouting hysterically to his men.

The tower had not been used for years. As we carried Elric through we discovered that many of von Asch's possessions were still where he had left them. Trunks, cupboards, chairs and tables were covered in deep dust. Books and maps were long neglected. He had taken his swords and some clothes, but little else. We could see from marks in the dust which way Gaynor had gone. While Elric lay in a collapsed state against the wall, Oona and I dragged heavy furniture out of the rooms to block the narrow staircase. Oona glanced quickly through the books and papers, found something she wanted and put it in her pocket. Carrying Elric, we continued upwards until a short corridor led us out onto a broad quadrangle surrounded by narrow battlements broken by chimneys.

Miraculously, Gaynor was still there. He had expected to find help or easy escape. But there was a sheer drop on all sides.

I flung myself after the dark figure I saw ahead of me. It dodged around a buttress, a chimney breast, but I kept it in sight. Then suddenly Gaynor had turned. He was in horrible pain. His whole body vibrated and shook with a wild silvery light. He was growing in size. But as he grew, he dissipated. Like ripples in a pool, each one a slightly larger representation of its predecessor, Gaynor grew bigger and bigger, pulsing and expanding like a great chord of music, high into the sky, into the fabric of the multiverse. He fragmented and became whole at the same time!

I stumbled on, still trying to lay hands on him. I reached him, tried to hold him. Something electric tingled in my fingers, I was blinded for a moment, and then Gaynor was gone. Silence.

"We have lost both Gaynors," I said. I shook with violent anger mixed with fear.

Elric gasped and shook his head. "All of them, for the moment. He has fled in a thousand directions, playing his most dangerous card. Fragmenting into a multitude of versions, each one a slightly larger scale. He dissipates his essence throughout the multiverse, so that we cannot follow. He is at his most unstable. His most dangerous. Perhaps his most powerful. He exists everywhere and nowhere. The risk is that he can be everyone and no one. He spreads his essence thinly. But one thing we do know of him—he has failed to keep his bargain with Arioch. He was attempting to bring the Duke of Hell into this realm.

"If Gaynor hasn't driven himself completely insane, he will do one of two things. He will seek to escape the Duke of Hell, which would be foolish and probably impossible. Or he will go to seek a compromise with him. Which means he must find a place of convergence. Bek denied him, he needs another place of convergence through which he can admit his patron. There cannot be many others in this world."

"Morn," said Oona. "It will be on Morn." She held up the paper she had taken.

"A place of convergence?" I asked. "What is that?"

"Where many possibilities come together," she said. "Where the moonbeam roads meet. I know this realm well. He will go to the Stones of Morn and attempt to gather all his many selves back into a single whole."

That was all she could tell me before there came a hammering from within the tower.

"How can we possibly follow him?" I asked.

"I have brought friends," murmured Elric. "Gaynor sought to use them for his own ends. But he lacks our blood. It is how I followed him from Melniboné. Swords call to swords. Wings to wings."

Hess and his men were breaking down the door.

I looked over the battlements. The drop would kill us. There was nowhere left to go. We had no choice but to take a stand. Elric stumbled back towards the tower dragging his sword with both hands. As the door came down he swung the sword. It took the three leading storm troopers by surprise. They went down at once and the blade shrieked its glee. Elric's breath hissed as he absorbed the blade's strength. The stolen energy was quickly restoring him.

Reluctantly I joined him and together we took another five or six men before they retreated into the tower and began shooting at us from a safer distance. The narrow passage made it impossible for them to see us or hit us and their ammunition was wasted.

Elric told us to keep the storm troopers diverted. He limped to the edge of the battlements and looked up into a night sky which boiled with dark cloud stained by an orange moon. He lifted the sword. It began to blaze again with black fire. Elric, in his ruined armor and torn silks, burned with the same flame as he lifted his skull-white face to the turbulent heavens and began the singing of a rune so ancient its words were the voice of the elements, the wind and the earth.

A few more shots from the tower. A cautious storm trooper emerged. I killed him.

Dark shapes roamed the sky now. Sinuous shapes slithered their way amongst the clouds.

Elric had drawn strength from his victims. He stood silhouetted against the battlements, sword in hand, screaming at the sky.

And the sky screamed back at him.

Like sudden thunder, there was a bang, and the sky began to bubble and crack. Forms emerged from the distance. Monstrous flying creatures. Reptiles with long, curling tails and necks, slender snouts and wide, leathery wings. I recognized them from my nightmares. The dragons of Melniboné, brought to my own realm by Elric's powerful sorcery. I knew Gaynor had hoped to recruit these dragons to his cause. I knew he had almost defeated Elric in the ruins of Imrryr. I knew he had found the hidden caves and sought to wake Elric's dragon kin. He had been successful. But he had not understood that the dragons would refuse to serve him. *Blood for blood; brother for brother.* They served only the royal blood of Melniboné. And that blood, by a trick of history, Oona and I shared with her father.

Two huge beasts circled the tower in the orange moonlight. Young Phoorn dragons, still with the black and white rings around their snouts and tails, still with feathery tips to their wings, they had not grown to the size of their elders, whose life spans were almost infinite, as dragons spent most of their time asleep.

Elric was weakened by his incantation, but his spirits were rising. "I prepared for this. But I had also expected to have the Grail with me when I summoned my brothers." Melnibonéans claimed direct kinship with the Phoorn dragons. In another age they had shared the same names, the same quarters, the same power. In ancient history, it was said dragons had ruled Melniboné as kings. Whatever the truth, Elric and his kind could drink dragon venom, which killed most other creatures. The venom was so powerful that it ignited in the air as soon as it spewed from the dragons' mouths. I knew all this, because Elric knew it.

I knew the language of the dragons. We greeted them affectionately as they landed their huge bodies delicately on the tower. They were steaming and shaking with the turbulence of their journey through the multiverse. They opened their huge red mouths, gasping in the thin air of this world. Their vast eyes turned to regard us. Expectant, benign, their monstrous claws gripped the stone battlements as they balanced there. The patterns of their scales, subtle and rich purples and scarlets, golds and dark greens, glistened in the moonlight. They were very similar in appearance, one distinguished by a blaze of white above its nose, the other with a blaze of black. Their great white teeth clashed when they closed their mouths, and on the edges of their lips, their venom constantly boiled. These were the beasts of the Siegfried legend, but far more intelligent and considerably more numerous. The Melnibonéans had made many studies of dragons, detailing all the various kinds, from the snubsnouted Erkanian, nicknamed the batwing, to these long-nosed hibernating Phoorn, whose relationship with us was oddly telepathic.

Holding his side, Elric approached the nearest dragon, speaking to her softly. Both dragons were already saddled with the pulsing Phoorn *skeffla'a*, a kind of membrane which bonded with the dragon above its shoulder blades, giving it the ability to travel between the realms. The *skeffla'a* was one of the strangest productions of Melnibonéan alchemical husbandry and one of the oldest.

Their names were simple, like most names given to them by men—Blacksnout and Whitesnout. Their names for themselves were long, complicated and utterly unpronounceable, detailing ancestry and where they had journeyed.

Elric turned to me. "The dragons will take us to Gaynor. You know how to ride?"

I knew. As I now knew most things connected with my doppelgänger.

"He's still in this world. Or at least certain aspects of him are. He could have exhausted himself and no longer have the power to travel the moonbeam roads. Whatever the reasons, the dragons can take us to him."

"To Morn," said Oona. "It must be Morn. Does he still have the Grail?"

"It's not something we'll know until we catch up with him . . ." Elric's voice trailed away as he was overcome with pain. Yet he seemed slightly stronger than a few minutes earlier. I asked him how badly he had been shot and he looked at me in surprise. "Klosterheim shot to kill. And I am not dead."

"I should also have died from Klosterheim's gun," I told him. "The wounds were very evident. I lost an enormous amount of blood. But the wound has now almost vanished!"

"The Grail," said Elric. "We've been exposed to the Grail and haven't known it. So it is either on Gaynor's person or hidden somewhere back there."

Hess's face emerged from the doorway. He ordered his men to stop shooting. His face bore an expression of sincerity, of urgency.

"I must talk to you," he said. "I must know what all this means. What kind of heroes are you? The heroes of Alfheim? Have we conjured our ancient legendary Teutonic world back in all its might and glory? Thor? Odin? Are you—?"

The dragons had impressed him.

"I regret, Your Excellency," I said, "that these are dragons of oriental origin. They are Levantine dragons. From the wrong side of the Mediterranean."

His eyes widened. "Impossible."

Oona helped Elric adjust his *skeffla'a* on Blacksnout's back. She climbed up behind him, signaling to me to take the other dragon, Whitesnout.

"Let me come with you!" Hess was pleadingly eager. "The Grail—I am not your enemy."

"Farewell, Your Excellency!" Elric sheathed Stormbringer and wrapped his hands around the dragon's reins. He seemed to regain his strength with every passing moment.

I climbed into the dragon saddle with all the familiarity of one born to the royal line. I was full of a wild, unhuman glee. Alien. Faery. Though I would have scoffed at such an idea a short while earlier, now I accepted everything. There is no greater joy than riding through the night on the back of a dragon.

The massive wings began to beat. Hess was driven back, as if by a hurricane. I saw him mouthing something, pleading with me. I almost felt sympathetic to him. Of all the Nazis, he seemed the least disgusting. Then I saw Göring and the storm troopers burst out onto the roof. The air was once again alive with popping bullets. They were no danger to us. We could have destroyed the tower and all within it by releasing a few drops of venom, but it did not occur to us. We were convinced Gaynor had the Grail and if we could catch him in time it would soon be ours.

The exhilaration of the flight was extraordinary! Elric led the way through the air on Blacksnout's back, while Whitesnout followed. I had no need to control my dragon, though I knew intuitively how to do so.

Every anxiety was left behind me on the ground as the mighty wings beat against the clouds, bearing us higher and higher, farther and farther west. Where? To Ireland? Surely not to England?

England was my country's enemy. What if I were captured, still in the vestiges of my SS uniform? It would be impossible to convince them of my true reasons for being there!

I had no choice. Blacksnout, with Elric and Oona, flew with

long, slow movements of her wings, gliding above the clouds ahead of me, sometimes casting a faint shadow. She flew steadily and Whitesnout, her junior by a year or two, let her lead. As the light grew stronger, the markings of the dragon's wings were clearer. They were like gigantic butterflies, with distinct patterns of red, black, orange and glowing viridian, far different from the green and yellow reptiles of picture books. The Phoorn dragons were creatures of extraordinary grace and beauty with a sense about them that they were wiser than men.

Whenever the clouds parted, I could see the patterned fields and nestling towns of rural Germany. They had known little of direct strife for more than a century and were secure in Hitler's assurances that no foreign bombers would be allowed to enter German airspace.

I wondered if Hitler would be able to keep his promises. My guess was that he would begin relying on magic as political and military means failed him. He seemed like a man riding a tiger, terrified of where it was taking him yet unable to jump clear because of the momentum at which he was moving.

Or a man riding a dragon? Did I think Hitler helplessly caught up in events because I myself was carried along by monumental realities?

Such speculation soon left my head as I relished the beauty of the skies. The smell of clear air. I was so enraptured that I hardly heard the first droning behind me. I looked back and down. I saw a carpet of airplanes, so thick, so close together, that they seemed at first to be one huge bird. The droning was the steady sound of their engines. They were moving a little faster than we were, but in exactly the same direction.

I could not see how any country, especially depleted, weary Britain, could stand against such a vast aerial armada. Nothing like it had been assembled in the world's history. The only equivalent sea force had been the Spanish fleet, massed to attack England during Elizabeth's reign. England had been saved that time by a trick of the weather. She could expect no such good fortune now.

I had seen whole civilizations destroyed since this adventure had begun. I knew that the impossible was all too possible, that peoples and architecture could disappear from the face of the earth as if they had never existed.

Was I, by some ghastly coincidence, about to see the last of England, the fall of the British Empire?

What I had so far seen was a squadron of Junkers 87s—the famous Stuka dive-bomber, which the Luftwaffe had traditionally used in their first attacks on other countries. But as we flew on, obscured by the cloud separating us from the air fleets below, I saw waves of Messerschmitt fighters, squadrons of Junkers and Heinkels, relentlessly moving towards an already battered Britain that could not possibly produce the numbers or quality of aircraft to combat such an invasion.

Was this why Gaynor was leading us to the west? So that we might witness the beginning of the end? The final battle whose winning would ensure the rule of the Lords of the Higher Worlds on earth? And would those same lords remain at peace? Or would they immediately begin to fall upon one another?

Were we on our way to Ragnarok?

The planes passed. A strange silence filled the sky.

As if the whole world were waiting.

And waiting.

In the distance we began to hear the steady, mechanical thunder of guns and bombs, the shriek of fighters and tracer bullets. Away to our east, we saw oily smoke rising from erupting orange flame, saw flares and exploding shells. Blacksnout banked in a long graceful turn into the morning sun and soon the sound of warfare was behind us. England could not last the day. The war against Europe was as good as won. Where would Hitler turn his attentions next? Russia?

I mourned England's passing with mixed feelings. Her arrogance, her casual power, her easy contempt for all other races and nations, had all been there to the end. These qualities were what had led her to underestimate Germany. But also her courage, her tenacity, her lazy good nature, her inventiveness, her coolness under fire, all these had been invested in her great warships, those fighting islands in miniature, each its own small nation. Those men of war had ruled the world and defeated Napoleon on sea, while together we had defeated him on land. A bloody, piratical nation she might be, ready to boast of her own coarseness and brutality. But her heroes had earned their power through their own determination, by risking their own lives and fortunes. And not a few of those great men had been great poets or historians. If she were decadent now, it was because she no longer possessed such men of integrity and breadth of vision.

This was her day of reckoning. The day to which all great imperial nations come eventually—Byzantium and Carthage, Jerusalem and Rome. Unable to conceive of their mortality, they know the double bitterness of defeat and slavery. Hitler had reintroduced slavery throughout his empire. The British, who had led the world in abolishing that dreadful practice, would again know the humiliation and deep misery of forced labor. Even as she set her national vices aside and called upon her virtues, the Last Post was sounding for her freedom and her glory. She would go to her defeat proving that virtue is stronger than vice, that courage is more prevalent than cowardice and that the two can exist together at a moment to which we can point years later as examples of the best, rather than the worst, that we can be. And show how virtue made us stronger and safer than any cynicism ever could. Why was that a lesson we had to learn over and over again?

Such philosophical meanderings while experiencing the physical exhilaration of riding on a dragon! What a typical thing for me to be doing! But I could not help grieving for that great country which so many Germans thought of as their natural partner, the best that they themselves could be.

Water now. Calm, blue sparkling water. Green hills. Yellow beaches. More water. Lazy sunlight, as if the world had never been anything but paradise. Little towns seemed to have grown from the earth itself. Rivers, woods, valleys. The distinctive domestic beauty of the English shires. What would become of all this once Germany crushed British air power and "Germanified" the world into a comic-opera version of its heritage? The bleak, black cities they all loathed, of course, were defending this tranquillity, this ideal, against the tyranny which, in the name of preserving it, would destroy their way of life forever.

So powerful were my feelings that I wished I was back facing the dangers of Mu Ooria. That would have been easier. Had Gaynor really destroyed that gentle race and left only a few survivors?

Over the sea again, gentle in a southerly breeze, to a tiny green spot looking scarcely more than a hillock, jutting out of the water and lapped by white-topped waves. The leading dragon banked again and circled the island, which was about half a mile across. I saw a Tudor house, a ruined abbey, a white peninsula, like a rat's tail, which served as a natural quay. No people were gathering to see us; nothing suggested the place had been occupied for a long time. The center of the island was topped by a grassy hill which bore a ragged granite crown of stones, marking it as the site of an ancient place of ritual. At one time, long ago, those stones had stood straight and formed a combined observatory, church and place of contemplative study.

And so we came to the Isle of Morn, to Marag's Mount, "whence all the pure virtue of the English race came so long ago," as their epic explorer poet Wheldrake put it. One of the great holy places of the West with a history even more ancient than that of Glastonbury or Tintagel. As the dragons landed gracefully upon Morn's pure white sandy beach, and the sea beat like a warning drum upon the rocks, I knew why Gaynor was here.

Morn was one of the great places of power which even the Nazis acknowledged, though its founders were Celts, not Saxons. The Isle of Morn, where all the old races of the world sent their scholars to exchange ideas and discuss the nature of existence, the differences and similarities of religions, in that Silver Age before the Teuton explosion. Before the violence and the conquest began.

To Morn had come bishops, rabbis and Muslim scholars, Buddhists, Hindus, Gnostics, philosophers and scientists, all to share their knowledge, At the abbey below the hill they had met regularly. An international university, a monument to good will. Then the Norsemen had come in their dragonships and it was over.

I climbed down from my dragon, scratching her neck under her scales, and thanking her for her courtesy. I removed the *skef-fla'a,* folded it and tucked it inside my shirt. Oona stumbled towards me, still finding her land legs in the soft, white sand. She pointed to the headland. There, at anchor, sat a German U-boat with two sentries standing guard on her low, water-washed decks.

A coincidence? The scouts for the invasion fleet? Or had Gaynor arranged for it to be here, to use it to escape, if need be? But why? He had not known we could follow him. It seemed an elaborate precaution to take on the mere chance of being found here.

Whatever the reason, the Nazi U-boat offered no immediate danger. I doubted they would have believed the reality anyway. Dragons rarely come ashore on small islands in the middle of the Irish Sea.

A word from Elric, and the great beasts were airborne again, arrowing to the upper regions of the air where they would wait out of sight.

Pausing only for a few moments, we struck inland through the cobbled streets of the deserted village, past the great Hall where Morn's independent Duke had ruled until 1918 and which was now boarded up, past a surviving farm or two which had no doubt been evacuated at the outbreak of this war, and up the winding lane which led to the top of the grassy hill and the ring of stones.

So far nothing was unusual about the place. Squabbling gulls cruised the waves and hovered in the air. Blackbirds sang in windswept trees, sparrows hunted in the overgrown hedgerows, and in the distance the surf drummed reassuring rhythms.

With some effort we climbed to the crest of the island where the granite standing stones leaned like old men, one against the other. Their circle was still complete.

We were approaching the stones, when I noticed a strange milky light flickering faintly from within. I hesitated. I had no stomach for further supernatural encounters. But Oona urged us on.

"I knew he would have to come here if we defeated him at Bek," she said. "He hopes to contact Arioch. But I think I'll have a surprise for him."

Oona led the way into the center of the stones. Beyond, the sea was very calm. Perfect weather for an invasion, I thought. I looked for the U-boat, but it wasn't visible from this point.

The translucent light washed around our feet and legs like surf. "Draw your swords, gentlemen," she said. "I will need their energy."

We obeyed her. This beautiful young girl and the confidence she radiated fascinated us. She held up her bow staff and then dipped it into the opalescent substance, drawing it up like paint and describing extraordinary geometric patterns in the air, linking one stone to another until they were crisscrossed with a cat's cradle of pearly, sparkling force.

At the same time Oona spoke. She murmured and sang, making spells. There was a sense of urgency about her movements and her voice.

Lights began to zigzag wildly until I was thoroughly confused and blinded. She took Ravenbrand from me and described a large oval with it. The oval undulated and formed a tunnel in the light. Walking along the tunnel of light towards us, I saw a figure.

Fromental!

The Frenchman strolled into the circle of stones as if looking for a good place for a picnic. To confirm this intention, he held in his hand a covered basket. He was completely unsurprised to see us and greeted us with a cheerful wave. Stepping into the stone circle, a crimson light surrounded him, wrapping around him like a bloody coat. It flared and was gone. The milky web also disappeared. A stink of something old and hot remained. I recognized the smell but did not know why.

"Am I in time?" he asked Oona.

"I hope so," she said. "Did you bring her?"

Fromental lifted the basket. "Here she is, Lady Oona. Shall I take her out?"

"Not yet. We have to be sure he is coming. He will get here somehow. As will Arioch. Gaynor expects to meet Arioch at the Stones of Morn. They have been here before."

"My Lord Arioch is with us now," said Elric quietly.

Elric's whole manner changed. He sensed his master's presence in the circle. He spoke rapidly, urgently.

"My Lord Arioch. Forgive us for this intrusion. Give us your good will, I beg, for the sake of our ancient covenants. I am Elric of Melniboné and our blood is bound to the same destiny."

A voice, sweet as childhood, spoke from the air. "You are my mortal offspring. You represent my interests in other realms, but not in this one. Why are you here, Elric?"

"I seek revenge upon an enemy, my lord. One who serves you. Who offered you this portal."

"One of my servants cannot be your enemy."

"One who serves two masters is nobody's friend," Elric replied.

The voice, whose warmth embraced and comforted like an old, loving relative, chuckled.

"Ah, bravest of my slaves, sweetest of my succulent children. Now I remember why I love thee."

My throat filled with bile. Being in the invisible creature's presence was almost physically unbearable. Even Oona seemed unwell. But Elric was if anything more relaxed than usual, even tranquil. "I am destined to serve thee, great Duke of Hell. The old pact is between my blood and thine. The one who dubs himself Knight of the Balance has already betrayed one Lord of the Higher World, and I know he would betray another."

"I cannot be betrayed. It is impossible. I trust nothing. I trust no one. I imprisoned Miggea for him. And this was to be my payment. This is a rich, delicious realm. There is much in it to relieve my boredom. Gaynor swore loyalty to me. He would not dare try my patience further."

"Gaynor's loyalty is to Law before Chaos." I heard myself

speak. My voice was a kind of echo in my own skull and sounded like Elric's. "And I assure you, Duke Arioch, I owe you no loyalty. It is not in my interest to allow you to enter my realm. Your forces already destroy too much. But I can offer you the means of claiming your payment from Gaynor."

Arioch was amused. I glimpsed the outline of a golden face, the most beautiful face in the multiverse, and I loved it. "Those are not my forces, little mortal. They are the forces of the Lady Miggea. They are the forces of Law who make war against your world."

"Gaynor wishes you to oppose them?"

"I have no interest in his wishes, only his actions. He merely offered me an opportunity. It is in my nature to oppose Law. "

"Then our interests are the same," I agreed. "But we cannot strike the same bargain with you that Gaynor struck."

"Gaynor promises me an entry into your realm. By means of his magic and his wisdom. You will not do the same for me?"

"No, master." Elric. "We do not have the means. The great object of power is lost to us."

"Gaynor will bring it here."

"Perhaps," said Elric. He spoke with respect but also with the firmness of one who regarded himself the equal of Gods. "Master, you have no rights in this realm."

"I have rights in all realms, little slave. Nonetheless, I grow tired of this game. I appear to be playing against my own self-interest. As soon as Gaynor brings the key, I and my armies will pass through to bring unbridled Chaos to a bored little world. Miggea's forces are without the guidance of a vital mind. We shall soon defeat them. Your fears are unnecessary."

"And if Gaynor does not bring the key, Your Excellency?" said Oona, gazing levelly up at the golden head.

"Then Gaynor is mine. Mine to eat. Mine to regurgitate whenever I choose. Mine to drink. Mine to piss. Mine to tickle. Mine to kiss. Mine to shit and mine to fart. Mine to take his heart. Mine to clothe with iron shoes. Mine to dance. Mine to bruise. Mine to use." The achingly beautiful lips smacked like a troll's in a fairy tale. I began to wonder if it were only Miggea of Law who grew senile amongst the Lords of the Higher Worlds. Could the whole race of gods have grown too old to have any clear idea of their desires or interests? Was the multiverse in the hands of such creatures? Was our own condition reflected in theirs?

Fromental, meanwhile, followed none of this. We spoke a language completely alien to him. He looked from Oona to me, eyebrows raised, asking a silent question.

Elric saw something and pointed. Without a thought, he folded both hands around Stormbringer's hilt.

Gaynor, still in his armor but looking somewhat the worse for wear, appeared on the white beach. Had the U-boat brought him to Morn? He clearly could not see anything within the stone circle and thus believed himself to be alone. He was swordless, apparently with no weapons. And he had no cup with him either.

We took a certain pleasure in watching Gaynor advance.

He paused before entering the circle. He peered in. We remained invisible to him. Ocher light filled the spaces between the stones.

"Master? Lord Arioch?"

Arioch's voice was a gentle invitation. "Enter."

Gaynor stepped through.

And found all his enemies awaiting him.

He turned in startled fury. He tried to step back out of the circle, but he was trapped.

"Have you brought me the key, little mortal?" Arioch spoke again with a delicacy suggesting he tasted each syllable before he released it into the air.

"I could not, sire." His attention was more on us than on the Lord of the Higher Worlds. "The thing has a mind of its own . . ."

"But it is your duty to control it."

"It cannot be controlled, my lord. It has a will, I swear, if not intelligence."

"But I told you all that, little mortal. And you assured me you had the means of gaining control. That is why I helped you. That is why I imprisoned Lady Miggea for you."

Elric laughed as Gaynor's confidence ebbed. "I came for more help," said our enemy almost pathetically. "A little more. But why? How . . . ? These are your enemies, my lord. They who would oppose you."

"Oh, I think they have shown me rather more respect, Prince Gaynor, than I have received from you. You seem to think it possible to lie to a Lord of the Higher Worlds. You seem to think I'm some bottle imp to give you as many wishes as you desire. I am no such thing! I am a Duke of Hell! I have ambitions which go far beyond your imaginings. And my patience is ended. How shall I punish you, little Prince?"

"I can bring you through, my lord, I swear. I just have to return to Bek. Mighty forces even now rise to dominate this realm. Hour by hour they gain more territory, more power. Only you, through me, can defeat them, my lord."

"I have no interest in saving this realm," said Arioch in regal astonishment. "I just wished to play with it for a while. Now my only pleasure, little Gaynor, will be to play with you."

Oona turned to Fromental and snatched the basket from his hands. She reached into it and lifted out its contents.

It appeared to be a miniature model. An intricate ivory cage made of thousands of tiny bones from which a tiny voice raged.

Miggea, still trapped, was furious.

"How did you do that?" I asked Oona in astonishment.

"It is not difficult. Scale is the only thing that varies from realm to realm. Each realm, as I explained to you, is on a slightly different scale, which is how we are able to navigate between them and why we are not immediately aware of their existence.

"I arranged for Lieutenant Fromental to bring her here. Miggea is very powerful, but quite thoroughly imprisoned. Given her own volition she would soon adjust her scale to the realm in which she finds herself. I do not have the power to release her. Only the one who imprisoned her can do that."

"You have brought another of these creatures to my world?" This seemed the height of irresponsibility to me. "To war against the one already here? To turn the whole planet into a battlefield?"

"You will see," said Oona. "But you must all leave the circle now. First, give me your sword."

Against all sense I handed her Ravenbrand. Then Elric, Fromental and I stepped outside the Stones of Morn.

The little we could see became a shadow play. The dark, lounging presence of Duke Arioch, the swift, elegant figure of Oona placing the cage of bone on the ground. Gaynor transfixed. Oona then touched the cage with the point of my sword. I heard Arioch's voice, faintly booming. "Well, my lady, it seems it is no longer in my interest to hold you captive."

A noise like splitting flint.

A terrible *crack*.

Something began to boil and writhe and grow within the circle. Something which cackled and squealed with idiot laughter and pushed against whatever force the stone circle held. Miggea, having escaped the cage, now sought to escape the circle.

The stones shook. They might have been dancing. Then they were still, straight, waiting. They looked to me as they must have looked when the first Druids newly erected them. Tall, white granite, flashing in the light from the sun.

Suddenly a figure of unstable fire stood before us, caught in the circle, writhing uncontrollably, screaming silently out at us. Gaynor's face was burning. His whole body was in flames. Burning with a million conflicts generated in his ungenerous heart. And there he was again, standing beside himself, still flaming, still screaming. He was begging us for something. Could it have been forgiveness? Or merely release? Another dancing, burning figure, and another, until they made a full circle within the circle.

From above, the shadowy golden face of Duke Arioch smiled and whistled as if watching a puppet show, and the senile, drooling, cackling creature that had once been one of Law's greatest aristocrats poked at Gaynor's twisting body, which changed shape and size, became many versions of itself, then one, then fragmented again. I heard his screams. They were like nothing else I had ever heard in all my life.

Arioch and Miggea tugged at him, breaking off pieces of his

many identities in their struggle. They played with him as cats
might play with a cricket. There was little animosity between
them. All their hatred was directed at Gaynor, stupid Gaynor, who
had thought he could play one of them off against the other.

He begged them to stop.

I was close to begging for the same thing! A thousand
Gaynors filled the circle. A thousand different kinds of pain.

Oona regarded this with quiet satisfaction, in much the same
way she might look upon a piece of domestic handiwork and con-
gratulate herself.

"He cannot bring himself back to his archetype," she said. "It
is the only way we survive. A sense of identity is all we have. At
this moment all Gaynor's many identities are in conflict. He is
being disseminated throughout the multiverse. The convergence
Gaynor sought to use for his own selfish ends has proved to be his
undoing."

"Too many!" Arioch swore. "You promised me the power of
Law. I already possess the power of Chaos. Where, fractured
Gaynor, is the Grail?"

The replies were various, multitudinous, horrifying. "She has
it!" was the only coherent phrase we heard.

Then Gaynor was gone.

Miggea was gone.

Arioch's voice was a satisfied, luscious whisper. "The Grail is
still there. At my point of entry, where he promised to bring me
through."

Monstrous lips smacked.

And then Arioch, too, disappeared.

Between them, he and Miggea tore Gaynor into a million psychic shreds.

A rustling, like an autumn wind, and sorcery was gone from
that realm. The old stones pushed their way up through ordinary
grass. A bright sun shone in the sky. The surf washing the white
beach was the loudest sound we had ever heard. I turned to
Fromental. "You struck this bargain with Oona when you met her
at Miggea's prison?"

"We did not know exactly what we would do with Miggea, but it was useful to have her in portable form." Fromental winked. "Now I must return to my friends. Tanelorn is saved, but they will want to know the rest of this story. I am sure we'll meet again, my friend."

"And the Off-Moo? Do you know their fate?"

"They have another city, that is all I know. On the far shore of the lake. They went there. Few were killed."

With the air of a man who had urgent business, he shook hands with me and walked back to the shore. A skiff with two seamen waited for him, offering him a salute as he got into the boat. I had made the wrong presumptions about the U-boat. Fromental had sent it ahead of him. He waved to us again and was then rowed quickly over to the U-boat. Perhaps I would never know how he managed to send a captured goddess to us by submarine!

As I watched the conning tower disappear below the waves, my attention returned to the depressing realities of my own realm. Where a conquering air fleet was ensuring that Adolf Hitler would soon control the world.

I reminded Elric that my work was unfinished. If the Grail was still at Bek, perhaps I could find a way of using it against the Nazis. At the very least it should ultimately be returned to Mu Ooria.

The dreamthief's daughter smiled at me, as if at an innocent. "What if the Grail always belonged at Bek?" she said. "What if it was lost and the Off-Moo were merely its temporary guardians? What if it decided to return home?"

I scarcely took this in as something else dawned on me. I looked urgently to Elric. "Klosterheim!" I cried. "Both of us survived his bullets because we were in the presence of the Grail and did not know it! The Grail works against dissipation. Gaynor could not have performed his magic with it on his person. The Grail's still there. But that means everyone who was in its presence survived. Which means Klosterheim could even now be in possession of the Grail."

Elric paused. I sensed that he was reluctant to stay in this dream. He wanted to rejoin Moonglum and continue his adventurings in the world he understood best. At last he said, "Klosterheim, too, has earned my vengeance. We'll go back to Bek." He paused, laying a long-fingered hand on my shoulder. For a moment he was a brother.

When we returned to the beach the dragons were already waiting for us, as if they knew we needed them. They were rattling their quills and skipping with impatience from one huge foot to the other. The sun flashed off their butterfly colors dazzling all around. They were young Phoorn, capable of flying halfway around the world without tiring. They yearned to be aloft again.

We unrolled our *skeffla'an* and saddled our dragons. Climbing onto their broad backs, we settled ourselves in the natural indentations which could, on a Phoorn, take up to three riders.

With a murmur from Elric, still the great dragonmaster, bright reptilian wings cracked and moved the heavy air, cracked again and took us into the afternoon sky with the steady beat of rowers across a lake. They increased speed with each mighty flap, tails lashing and curling to steer us through the rushing currents of the air. With necks stretched out and great eyes blazing, they scanned the cloud ahead. Ancient firedrakes.

We skimmed the sea, then swept gracefully upwards until we were flying east over the gentle wooded hills and dales again, back towards Germany.

This time Elric took a slightly different course, going farther south than I might have expected, perhaps to witness the devastation of the proud hub of Empire in defeat. He, too, understood the peculiar ambivalences of owing allegiance to a dying empire.

But now there was some extra purpose to Elric's flight as he led us down through the clouds and into the late afternoon light—to where an aerial dogfight was in progress. Two Spitfires wheeled and climbed as their guns blazed at an overwhelming pack of Stukas. The German planes had been deliberately fitted with screaming sirens to make them sound more deadly. The air filled with their dreadful Klaxons, but the Spitfires, with extraordinary lightness and maneuverability, gave back their best.

Elric was shouting as he urged his dragon down. I heard his voice faintly on the wind as I followed him. After the incredible exhilaration of our dive, Blacksnout turned her long head, narrowed her great yellow eyes, and snorted.

She snorted acid fire.

Fire struck first one Stuka and then another. Plane after plane went down in an instant as the dragon swept the squadron with her terrible breath. I saw looks of astonishment on the thankful faces of the Spitfire pilots as they banked upwards and flew as fast as they could into the cloud.

The few surviving Stukas turned to seek the relative safety of the high skies, but Elric ignored them. We flew on.

Ten minutes later we came upon a great sea of Junkers bombers. It struck me that their crews were my own countrymen. Some of them could be cousins or distant relatives. Ordinary, decent German boys caught up in the nonsense of militarism and the Nazi dream. Was it right to kill such people, in any cause? Were there no other alternatives?

Whitesnout followed her sister down the hidden air trails. Their tails cracked like gigantic whips, venom frothed and seethed in their mouths and nostrils. Our dragons fell upon their prey with all the playful joy of young tigers finding themselves in a herd of gazelle.

Guns fired at us, but not a single shot struck. The dragons' steely scales deflected anything that hit them. For the gunners it was impossible—they must have thought they were dreaming.

Down we went and all I saw were Nazi hooked crosses, a symbol which stood for every infamy, every dishonor, every cynical cruelty the world had ever known. It was those crosses I attacked. I did not care about the crews who flew under such banners. Who were not ashamed to fly under such banners.

Down I dived. Whitesnout's venom seared from her mouth, blown by red-hot air generated in one of her many stomachs. The flaming poison struck bomber after bomber, all still with their loads. They blew into fragments before our eyes.

Some of the planes tried to peel away. Some dropped their

bombs at random. But again the dragons circled. Again the planes were destroyed. The few that remained turned tail and raced back towards Germany. What story would they tell when they returned? What story would they dare tell? They had failed, however they explained it.

And thus we gave birth to a famous legend. A legend which took credit for the victory of the RAF over the Luftwaffe. The legend which many believed turned the course of the war and caused Hitler to lose all judgment and perhaps what was left of his sanity. A legend which proved as powerful, in the end, as the Nazi myth unleashed on the peoples of Europe. Ours was the legend of the Dragons of Wessex, which came to the aid of the English in their hour of need. A legend which elevated British morale as thoroughly as it crushed German. Even the story of the Angel of Mons from the first world war was not as potent in its time as the legend of the Dragons of Wessex. King Arthur, Guinevere and Sir Lancelot, it was said, all reappeared. Flying on the fabulous beasts of ancient days, they came to serve their nation in its hour of need. The story would eventually be suppressed, as Hess was to discover. The legend was so powerful that propaganda resources of both nations were devoted to promoting or denying it.

By the time we flew home to Germany, we had destroyed several squadrons of bombers and innumerable fighters. The Battle of Britain had turned significantly. From that moment on, Hitler acted with increased insanity as his predictions lost credibility. From that moment on, his famous luck wholly deserted him.

As the tireless dragon bore me back to Bek, I mourned. I endured the anguish of my own conscience. Though the cause had been right, I had still made war on my own people. I understood all the reasons why I should have done it, but I would never, for the rest of my life, be fully reconciled to this burden of guilt. If I survived and peace was restored, I knew I would meet some mothers whom I would not be able to look in the eye.

The joy of victory, the thrill of the flight, was tempered by a strange melancholy which has remained with me ever since.

By the time we reached Bek, the place was evidently deserted. There wasn't a guard in sight. Hitler and his people had left in disgust and everyone else had made haste to disassociate themselves with the place. There was nothing left to guard.

The place was oddly still as we landed on the battlements and cautiously made our way down into the old armory.

Scenes of mayhem were everywhere. Blood was everywhere. But no corpses. And no cup.

Where was the Grail? All the evidence indicated it was never removed from Bek. But did Klosterheim somehow take it?

Oona gestured to me to wait for her as she slipped away into the deserted castle.

I felt Elric's hand on my shoulder again, an affectionate brotherly gesture.

"We must find Klosterheim." I turned and started to make my way back up the stairs.

"No!" Elric was emphatic.

"What? It's my duty to follow him," I said.

"I'll follow Klosterheim," said Elric. "If I'm successful you'll never see him again. I'll return to Melniboné. These young dragons have done good work and must be rewarded."

"And Oona? Your daughter?"

"The dreamthief's daughter stays here." With a cold *crack* of his cloak he turned his back on me and strode for the steps leading from the chamber. I wanted to ask him to return. I had much to thank him for. But, of course, I had served him also. We had been of mutual help. I had saved him from eternal slumber and he had turned the tide of war. The Luftwaffe was crushed. By the courage of a few and with the help of a powerful legend.

Britain would gather strength. America would help her. Eventually the fascists would be ousted from power and democracy restored.

But before that moment came, the blood of millions would be spilled. It was hard to see who would win anything from that terrible conflict.

I looked helplessly around at our old armory. So much violence had taken place here. How would it ever feel like home to me again?

How much I'd lost since Gaynor's first visit to Bek! When he tried to get the Raven Sword from me in order to kill my doppelgänger's daughter! I had certainly lost a kind of innocence. I had also lost friends, servants. And a certain amount of self-respect.

What had I gained? Knowledge of other worlds? Wisdom? Guilt? A chance to turn the tide of history, to stop the spread of Nazi tyranny? Many yearned to be able to do that. Circumstances of blood and time had put me in a position to change the course of the war in favor of my country's enemy.

The guilt grew more intense as Allied bombing increased. Cologne. Dresden. Munich. All the beautiful old cities of our golden past gone into rubble and bitter memory. Just as we had blown the memory and pride of other nations to smithereens and defiled their dead. And all for what?

What if this pain, this pain of all the world, could be stopped? By the influence of one object? By the thing they called the Runestaff, the Grail, Finn's Cauldron—the object that created a field of serenity and balance all around it. Sustaining its own survival and the survival of the multiverse.

Where was it, this panacea for the grief of nations?

Where was it, but in our own hearts?

Our imaginings?

Our dreams?

Had all I experienced in Mu Ooria been a complex but unreal nightmare into which the dreamthief's daughter lured me? An illusion of magic, of the Grail, of unending life? Once I was in no doubt of the Grail's properties or of its power for good. But now I wondered if the thing actually *was* a power for good? Or was it self-sustaining and not interested in questions of human morality?

Was Gaynor right? Did the Grail demand the blood of innocents to be effective? Was that the final irony? No life without death?

Oona came through the ruined doorway, a shaft of sunlight behind her. She had found her bow and arrows where she had hidden them.

She looked at me and realized that Elric was gone.

She ran for the old staircase.

"Father!"

She disappeared up the steps before I could reach the door. I called after her, but she ignored me or did not hear.

I went up the stairs rapidly, but something made me slow when I reached the top of the tower and the narrow corridor which led to the roof. I moved reluctantly and looked out at the battlements where Elric held his daughter in a tender embrace.

Behind him the dragons muttered and stamped, anxious to be aloft again. But Elric was slow to leave. When he lifted his face those troubled eyes were weeping.

I watched him place a gentle kiss on his daughter's forehead. Then he strode over to the impatient Blacksnout and stood scratching the great beast under her scales. With a quick, graceful movement, he climbed into his saddle and called in his musical voice, called to his dragon sisters.

With a massive crash of wings the two great reptiles mounted the evening air. I watched their dark shapes circling against the great red disk of the setting sun.

They banked with slow grace into a dark shadow and were suddenly gone.

Oona turned, dry-eyed, her voice unnaturally low. "I can see him anytime I choose," she said. She held something in her hand. A small talisman.

"In his dreams?" I asked.

She stared at me for a moment.

Then I followed her inside.

# EPILOGUE

he rest of the story is a matter of public record. Neither Oona nor myself, of course, remained in Germany. Indeed, we were certain of arrest. And, if arrested, we had a clear idea of our likely fate. So Prince Lobkowitz helped us get to Sweden and from there to London. Having helped in the destruction of my own country's air fleet and begun the process of Hitler's defeat, I continued the war against the Nazis. I joined the BBC as a broadcaster for a while and worked as an interpreter with a Red Cross psychiatric unit when the Allies started moving into Germany and Austria. Even I, with my experience of Nazi brutality, could scarcely bear the scenes which every new day brought.

I saw little more of Lobkowitz, who was busy with the War Crimes people, and nothing of Bastable. Oona went to Washington when the United States entered the war and joined a special operations unit.

I saw Bek once more before the Russians took it over. The Red Army had billeted its officers there. Even they remarked on the sense of peace the old place had. I was bound to agree. Though its recent history had scarcely been tranquil, tranquillity is what that house radiated for a mile or more around it in the old Bek estates. I heard that the local authorities eventually turned Bek into a rest home for mental patients, and I was pleased.

When at last the Wall came down and I reclaimed my home, I allowed it to continue in its most recent function, asking only that I have a few rooms in the old part of the house, along with the armory and the tower. Here I study quietly in the sure knowledge that somewhere I will discover a clue to the Grail's current incarnation. That it lies at Bek, there is no doubt. Here all wounds seem eventually to heal. This is all we saved from the Nazis.

In May 1941 it became clear that the Luftwaffe was no longer capable of conquering Britain. Disturbed that Hitler was attacking the Soviet Union without first securing the alliance of her "natural brothers in arms," Rudolf Hess flew single-handed to Scotland. He parachuted out of his Messerschmitt and landed safely. He spent a few hours at Castle Auchy, the traditional home of the Clan McBegg, which had a bad reputation in those parts. He then set off to find the Marquess of Clydesdale, whom he wrongly believed to be a Nazi sympathizer. What Hess told the marquess and those sent to arrest him was that he had the secret of the Wessex Dragons who rose from their secret caverns under England's most beautiful downs to serve her in her hour of need. He claimed that he knew how to contact King Arthur, Sir Lancelot and Queen Guinevere, and that he also knew the whereabouts of the Holy Grail. He proposed that the Grail was the catalyst to reunite the Nordic peoples against the common Bolshevik/Asian threat. He asked several times to speak to Churchill, but published documents show that MI5 was of the firm opinion that Hess had completely lost his mind. All reports confirm this view. Churchill steadfastly refused to see him.

Hess was sentenced at Nuremberg as a war criminal and became the only surviving prisoner in Spandau prison. He allegedly hanged himself in his prison cell in Spandau in 1987. He was ninety-one. All that time he had been refused permission to publish and had given almost no interviews, though he insisted he had information of crucial intelligence to the authorities. There is a theory that he was murdered by the British Secret Service, who feared what he would tell the public when he was released.

Hess was to play no further part in my story. This would not be true of Elric, however. He is still in my soul. Still shares my mind. At night, when I do dream, I dream Elric's life as if it were my own. I have a sense that I live not only Elric's destiny, but the destiny of hundreds like us. I am never truly free of him. His story continues, and I continue to be a part of it, as does Oona, the dreamthief's daughter, who became my wife. We chose to have no natural children but adopted three girls and two boys. We intend to let our blood die out.

How the Grail was found and what happened to us is a story which, like that of Rudolf Hess, remains to be told.

Meanwhile, we are at rest here for the moment. Glad to enjoy some respite in the great struggle—that game in which we all have important parts to play. The never-ending game of life and death.